**The gold snakes withdrew, wrapping themselves back around Zhang's arm as if nothing had happened.**

He pushed himself up against the wall until he was standing, and stared at the thing on the floor as if he was hypnotized.

It was already recovering from the shock it had gotten. Already climbing back up onto its knees. Its face showed no sign that they'd even hurt it – the bullet wound in its forehead didn't seem to faze it one bit.

Petrova looked around, thinking that if bullets didn't hurt the thing, she needed a new weapon. She found a folding chair with metal legs. Grabbing it up with her one good hand, she felt its weight, then swung it hard. It glanced off the floor with a ringing noise, and the vibrations rattled up her arm. She gritted her teeth and swung again, and this time she connected. One of the chair legs bit deep into the skull of the fallen thing. She swung again, and again, until spurts of black dust erupted from the wreck of what had been its head. Until she was one hundred percent certain it would not get up again.

"Come on," she said. She dropped the chair to clatter on the floor. Grabbed Zhang and pulled at him. He couldn't seem to look away from the ruined body. "Come on," she said, louder, and yanked him toward the hatch, and the daylight beyond.

Once they were outside she slapped the release pad and the door ground shut. Together the two of them stood there on the rocky soil of Paradise-1, saying nothing, just trying to catch their breath.

They'd been on the planet for less than an hour.

As David Wellington

*The Last Astronaut*

Red Space

*Paradise-1*

*Revenant-X*

As D. Nolan Clark

*Forsaken Skies*

*Forgotten Worlds*

*Forbidden Suns*

# REVENANT X

## RED SPACE: BOOK 2

## DAVID WELLINGTON

orbitbooks.net

This book is a work of fiction. Names, characters, places, and incidents are the product of the author's imagination or are used fictitiously. Any resemblance to actual events, locales, or persons, living or dead, is coincidental.

Copyright © 2024 by Little, Brown Book Group Limited
Excerpt from *The Blighted Stars* copyright © 2023 by Megan E. O'Keefe

Cover design by Sean Garrehy
Cover images by Shutterstock

Hachette Book Group supports the right to free expression and the value of copyright. The purpose of copyright is to encourage writers and artists to produce the creative works that enrich our culture.

The scanning, uploading, and distribution of this book without permission is a theft of the author's intellectual property. If you would like permission to use material from the book (other than for review purposes), please contact permissions@hbgusa.com. Thank you for your support of the author's rights.

Orbit
Hachette Book Group
1290 Avenue of the Americas
New York, NY 10104
orbitbooks.net

First Edition: November 2024
Simultaneously published in Great Britain by Orbit

Orbit is an imprint of Hachette Book Group.
The Orbit name and logo are registered trademarks of Little, Brown Book Group Limited.

The publisher is not responsible for websites (or their content) that are not owned by the publisher.

The Hachette Speakers Bureau provides a wide range of authors for speaking events. To find out more, go to hachettespeakersbureau.com or email HachetteSpeakers@hbgusa.com.

Orbit books may be purchased in bulk for business, educational, or promotional use. For information, please contact your local bookseller or the Hachette Book Group Special Markets Department at special.markets@hbgusa.com.

Library of Congress Control Number: 2024941320

ISBNs: 9780316569347 (trade paperback), 9780316569354 (ebook)

Printed in the United States of America

LSC-C

Printing 1, 2024

*For Gary, who wouldn't just die already*

# 1.

The first settlers from Earth had called this planet Paradise-1, but Alexandra Petrova wondered if the name was supposed to be a joke. She had rarely seen a more desolate place – even the airless moons of Jupiter were full of life by comparison. Here the wind blew forever through giant lava tubes, channels of rock that bored through the mountains like the tracks of worms. The few spiky plants that grew from the dark rocks looked sullen and abused as they stretched up toward blaring sunlight that was just the wrong color. She hurried into the main town of the colony, a cluster of prefabricated structures and houses built on a plain of black igneous rock. A place so new, so meager it had never even been given a name. She had been sent to check up on this place. She hadn't expected to find it deserted.

She'd looked in a dozen of the houses. Called out, shouting questions into that ceaseless wind. She'd gotten no answer. There were supposed to be ten thousand people here. She couldn't find any of them.

The town wasn't very large, and simple enough in plan. A neat grid of streets, houses and little workshops and storage sheds built around a large open central square. South of the town stood the fields that had fed the people here, plots of dirt that looked more like gardens than agricultural land. The plants out there had all died, lay wilted and spent, draped across the ground, yellow on the black soil. South of the fields stood the landing pad where they'd come down, where Parker had landed their tiny shuttle. It had cracked up on re-entry and they'd barely made it to the ground. The remains of the shuttle down there were the last human thing she could see. Beyond the landing field there was nothing but hills and defiles, the occasional impact crater.

North of the town stood high, craggy mountains, blank and solemn. The wind came down from those heights, cold and moving fast.

"Hello?" she shouted, as she had a hundred times, and again there was no answer.

She walked farther into town. Past prefabricated housing units and what looked like a school. They'd had everything they needed, these people. They'd built themselves a simple world, within which they could live out meaningful lives.

And now they were gone.

"Is this what you wanted to see?" she asked, speaking to the thing in her head.

Just to get this far she'd been forced to make a very uneasy alliance. A billion years ago, maybe, aliens had built a watchdog to keep this planet safe. To keep people like her from getting too close. Just to land on Paradise-1, she'd had to accept that ancient jailer into her brain, where it nestled like a parasite. Normally she could feel it wriggling around in there like a worm trying to get comfortable in the hot cage of her skull. Normally it talked to her, made demands of her. Normally it didn't shut up.

Not now.

"You wanted to come here," she whispered. That had been the deal.

She'd had to confront a thing with no human context at all, and she'd given it a name. She called it the basilisk, and it had driven her here, forced her to come to this place.

The watchdog had grown bored over the eons. It had grown curious about the thing it protected. It should have killed her for being in the wrong place, just slaughtered her for the audacity of coming here. Instead it had allowed her to live so they could both see what was down here on the planet.

Now? Whatever it wanted wasn't here.

Maybe it was just as confused as she was.

Where had all the people gone? She stepped into a house, walked into an empty kitchen and found a coffee pot on a heating element. The sludge of coffee inside had long since boiled away and burned to a thick scum of black carbon on the bottom of the pot. She switched off the heat. She touched a jacket someone had left hanging on the back of an aluminum chair. *ATLAS* had been picked out on the back in massive stylized letters. She knew that was the name of the first colony ship that had arrived here. Who had that jacket belonged to? Had they just put it down for a second, thinking they would pick it back up, put it on, one sleeve after the other? She touched the cast on her own left arm. Another casualty of the journey here. She imagined the colonist who owned that jacket, their arms, their back. Even in her mind's eye she couldn't see their face. Whoever they were, they were gone now.

She stepped back out into the street, looked up at the sky. Clouds scudded by overhead, thinner than the clouds on Earth. Clouds starved of moisture. This planet had no oceans, just a few big lakes and some anemic rivers. It almost never rained here.

Why had they chosen that ridiculous name for their new world? Simply because it offered a fresh start? The colonists who'd come here were committed. Zealous about building a future for humanity. So where had they gone? They wouldn't have just run off into the mountains for no reason. Would they?

"Hello!" she shouted, at no one. "Hello! Where are you?"

At first there was no answer. Then, off in the distance, she did hear something. Just the faintest call, a high-pitched wail that didn't even sound like words. It took her a second to realize that wasn't a colonist answering her.

That was Zhang, her crewmate.

Her blood went cold.

The sound she'd heard was Zhang, and he was screaming for his life.

# 2.

Petrova ran toward the screaming and found it was coming from a housing unit, a prefabricated module perched on the rocks at the edge of town. Its windows were covered in thick plastic shutters and its hatch was closed, but she could hear Zhang's voice clearly. She found the hatch's release panel and slapped at it, over and over, until it started to sluggishly open. Petrova had seen Zhang face down death before and he'd never screamed like that. Before the hatch was fully open, she squeezed her body through the narrow gap, her good hand already grabbing at the pistol on her hip.

She drew and brandished the weapon before her eyes had even adjusted to the dim light in the housing unit. She saw Zhang down in one corner, his back pressed up against the wall. Blood covered his left leg as far up as his hip, and his face was a mask of terror. He was staring at something in the shadows on the far side of the room, something she still couldn't see.

"I'm here," she shouted. "Zhang! What happened?"

He shook his head and pointed at the dark corner. "Look out," he gasped. "Just ... just watch out, it's ... it's—"

Whatever it was, it sprang out at her so fast she couldn't make out more than a humanoid silhouette. Suddenly it was on her, a hand like a claw grabbing at the cast on her left arm, another hand on the side of her face. It tried to drag her down, pull her off her feet, but she slammed herself backward against the wall and widened her stance. She'd trained for this, learned techniques to handle this kind of attack. Her pistol was useless now – if she tried shooting the thing, she would probably just hit herself. Instead she tightened her grip and used the side of the pistol to bash at it, trying to hit its head. Teeth sank into the collar of her jumpsuit and wrenched back, as if the thing were trying to bite out her throat but had just missed. She hit it again, and again, but it didn't react at all. It made no sound, not even a hiss of breath.

Then it reared its head back and she got her first good look at its face. It might have been human once. It wasn't anymore.

Its eyes were solid black, as if its pupils had expanded to swallow everything else. Black veins radiated outward from those eyes against skin the color of a fish's belly. It had no hair at all, and its mouth was a broken horror of jagged, stub-like teeth.

"Petrova!" Zhang shouted. "Get clear! Get clear!"

She knew the thing was going to lunge forward at any moment, that those broken teeth would sink into her cheek or tear off her nose. She twisted her head away even as she brought her knee up into the space between herself and the thing, the narrow little gap that had opened there. She kicked out as hard as she could, sending herself sprawling sideways but knocking the thing off kilter as well. It staggered back, away from her, keeping its footing but waving its arms for balance. She saw its hands were as broken and battered as its mouth, shards of nail wedged into the ends of mangled fingers.

She did not hesitate. She brought her weapon around and fired once, twice, a third time. Two shots in its center mass. One right in the middle of its forehead.

She hit it. She knew she'd hit it, because of the black wound that opened in its brow. No blood emerged from the wound, however. Instead, a fine black dust sifted out of the opening and drifted down its nightmare face.

"Zhang," she said. "Zhang!"

"Stand back," he said.

Zhang had his own weapon, though it wasn't reliable. It acted on its own agenda, not when he wanted it to. Woven around his arm was a thick nest of golden tendrils – a medical device, designed to keep him healthy. It could, on occasion, decide that the best way to ensure his safety was a good offense.

One tendril, then another, swung out, away from his arm. They grew thin as they lashed across the empty space between him and the thing, moving fast as striking snakes. They sank deep into the thing's pulpy flesh. There was a sudden noise like a massive electrical discharge, and the thing jerked and seized, its neck twisting around. It dropped like a slab of meat, its feet drumming against the housing unit's floor.

Not for the first time, Petrova found herself wondering exactly where their bosses had found such a device. It had capabilities she'd never seen in a medical implant before. This time she decided not to question it too much, not when it was keeping them alive.

The gold snakes withdrew, wrapping themselves back around Zhang's arm as if nothing had happened. He pushed himself up against the wall until he was standing, and stared at the thing on the floor as if he was hypnotized.

It was already recovering from the shock it had gotten. Already climbing back up onto its knees. Its face showed no sign that they'd even hurt it – the bullet wound in its forehead didn't seem to faze it one bit.

Petrova looked around, thinking that if bullets didn't hurt the thing, she needed a new weapon. She found a folding chair with metal legs. Grabbing it up with her one good hand, she felt its weight, then swung it hard. It glanced off the floor with a ringing noise, and the vibrations rattled up her arm. She gritted her teeth and swung again, and this time she connected. One of the chair legs bit deep into the skull of the fallen thing. She swung again, and again, until spurts of black dust erupted from the wreck of what had been its head. Until she was one hundred percent certain it would not get up again.

"Come on," she said. She dropped the chair to clatter on the floor. Grabbed Zhang and pulled at him. He couldn't seem to look away from the ruined body. "Come on," she said, louder, and yanked him toward the hatch, and the daylight beyond.

Once they were outside she slapped the release pad and the door ground shut. Together the two of them stood there on the rocky soil of Paradise-1, saying nothing, just trying to catch their breath.

They'd been on the planet for less than an hour.

# 3.

Zhang was lost in a daze. He barely felt the wound on his leg. The bite. He barely knew where he was.

"Parker. Rapscallion. Come in," Petrova said. "Talk to me, guys. Zhang's hurt. Come in!" She was speaking to them via radio, he realized. He couldn't see the two other members of the crew. He tried to focus on his surroundings. Petrova had her shoulder in his armpit and she was dragging him across a broad open square at the center of the little town. He wanted to look at her, to say something. Something important. He licked his lips. Tried to form the words.

"Focus," she told him. "Talk to me. Are you in shock?"

Shock? He supposed he was. But it wasn't her place to ask that question. He was the crew's doctor. At least, he'd been a doctor once. Most recently that just meant he was an expert at watching people die. So many people had ... had died—

"Zhang!" she shouted. She grabbed at the golden RD on his arm. The device twisted away from her touch. "You! Device! Give him something. Snap him out of this," she insisted.

She should have known better by now, Zhang thought. The RD had a certain level of artificial intelligence, which mostly meant it had a will of its own. It acted when it chose to, and no one could convince it to—

A golden snake lifted away from his wrist. Its head narrowed down to a sharp point and it struck, jabbing itself into the cephalic vein in his forearm. He gasped at the sudden spark of pain – then gasped again as his head reeled, a rush of oxygen flooding into his brain. Had the device injected him with some kind of vasodilator? He grabbed the bridge of his nose and squeezed.

That was when his leg started to hurt. A moment later, it really started to hurt.

"Oh no," he wheezed. "No. No no no. Petrova . . ."

"I'm here. I've got you," she said.

He nodded. He realized he was sitting down on the stony street. He looked up, saw the mix of dark stone houses and prefabricated housing units around him. "I need to . . . I need to patch this up," he said. His leg was still bleeding. Badly, though not enough to kill him immediately. She had wrapped a tourniquet around his thigh – when had she done that? He didn't remember it. But he could tell she'd done an incomplete job. Laypeople, people without medical training, never tied a tourniquet tight enough. You had to constrict all the blood vessels or all you accomplished was to cause the patient incredible pain. "I need to check the wound. Maybe sew it up. There's a medical center here. Where? I saw it on our way through town."

She nodded. "I saw it too. It's right up there." She pointed, but he didn't bother following her gesture. "Can you walk?"

"I think so. I don't think I broke any bones." He climbed up onto his feet. He was shaky, but he could stand. "Help me. Okay?"

"I've got you," she said, as she helped him hobble forward. Putting weight on his wounded leg hurt. He gasped in pain, but he fought it back. Kept moving, even as he felt hot blood rolling down his skin inside his jumpsuit. They passed through the town's main square, an open space of level soil with a fountain and a massive sculpture in its center. The medical center was just on the other side of the square. She helped him through the hatch and into an open room beyond. The power was still on and the lights made the space almost as bright as the square outside. There was an examination table just inside the door.

"Hang in there," she said, as she helped him climb up on the table. A robotic arm swung down from the ceiling and started scanning him.

He shook his head. "Petrova," he said. "It came out of nowhere. It just . . . it lunged at me, and—"

The robot finished its scan. "Hello. Welcome to the medical center. It looks like you've cut yourself. Are you in pain?"

Zhang had worked with robots like this often enough. "Switch to provider mode," he told it. "Assess this injury. Does it require sutures? Also, run a complete screen for bacterial infection, viral infection, foreign proteins, animal venom." He turned and looked at Petrova.

For the first time he saw just how scared she looked. She was worried about him. Worried that he was hurt. He smiled, despite himself. There was a time when the two of them had not gotten along. They'd actively disliked each other when they met.

That felt like a very long time ago now. Now they were a team.

"The thing that bit me," he said. "Did you see it? How much did you see?"

She turned away from him and tapped at her palm, working the controls of the communications device built into her hand. "Rapscallion? Parker? Where are you guys? Zhang's injured. I want you at the medical center, in the middle of town. What is your position?"

"Hey," Zhang said. "Listen to me. The thing that attacked me was—"

"Some kind of alien," she said. She shook her head and stared at the wall behind him. She was refusing to make eye contact. He thought he knew why.

The robot arm cut away the leg of his jumpsuit with a laser, then carefully lifted the cloth with a mechanical pincer. He got a good look at the wound for the first time. It looked like a classic bite injury, a semicircular perforated laceration. A big patch of skin and some of the underlying fatty tissue had been torn away and was missing, leaving a crater full of bright, welling blood.

"Injury assessed. Laser cauterization and sterilization of the area recommended. Should I administer analgesics?"

He looked down at the RD on his arm. It could have given him painkillers at any time since he was hurt. It hadn't. He remembered it had given him something to wake him up, break him out of his shock reaction. Maybe pain medication would have a negative interaction with whatever that had been.

"No," he told the robot. "Just do it."

A green beam of light swept across his mangled flesh and Zhang gritted his teeth. Then he grabbed the edge of the table hard enough to make his knuckles turn white. Eventually he just gave in and screamed in agony.

Petrova grabbed his shoulder and squeezed. Maybe it helped. A little.

When he could breathe again, he pulled on her hand until she looked at him. Made actual eye contact.

"The thing that attacked me," he said. "It wasn't—"

A flare of light filled the middle of the room, and then Sam Parker was standing there. Sam Parker, the pilot who'd brought them here. Sam Parker, now a hologram ghost.

He hurried over to the exam bed and tried to grin. Normally you couldn't wipe that grin off the man's face. Now it looked like a bad imitation of his normal expression. "How is he?" he asked.

He was asking Petrova. She looked up and gave him a shrug. "Fine. Where's Rapscallion?"

"On his way," Parker said. "I figured it would be faster if I just transferred myself over here on the public network."

There had been a human named Parker once, but that man had died on the way to Paradise-1. Their ship, *Artemis*, had decided to bring him back. It had a complete recording of his personality and memories pre-mortem, so it had just created an artificial intelligence that thought it was Sam Parker, that acted exactly like Sam Parker. The hologram was the closest thing it could give him to a body.

"You can do that?" Zhang asked. "Transfer yourself around like that?"

Parker blew air out of his mouth. "I don't like to. But yeah, I can exist in any computer system that's big enough to hold me. The system here has plenty of room. Jesus, buddy. What happened? You piss off a rabid dog?"

Zhang looked down at the wound on his leg. It was bright red, the flesh swollen where the laser had fused his skin back together. "It felt like exactly that. But it was—"

"An alien," Petrova said, too quickly. "Something. Some kind of..."

"Alien," Parker said, trying to make eye contact with her. "Like the one in your head?"

"No, not like that."

The hatch-like door of the medical center sighed open and a tall figure made of bright green plastic stepped through. Rapscallion. The robot was currently wearing a body that looked human enough. He'd even 3D-printed a human face for himself, a kind of mask that hung just slightly askew on the front of his head.

"What did I miss?" he asked, closing the door behind him.

"Zhang got attacked by an alien, but not the kind of alien you're thinking of," Parker said.

"You have no idea what I'm thinking of," Rapscallion pointed out.

"The gang's all here," Zhang said, with a little sigh. "Petrova, we really need to talk about this. About that thing, about what it was."

She didn't answer him for a while. She was too busy looking out of one of the medical center's windows. Scanning the street. She lifted her good hand, then patted the air to ask for patience. They would have that talk, she was suggesting.

Just not yet.

# 4.

They scanned the whole town, but Parker couldn't find any traces of movement, any indication at all that the creature Zhang had stumbled on wasn't alone. "Maybe there was just the one," he tried. "Just one alien."

Petrova shook her head. "Maybe." She gave an annoyed shrug. "Okay, maybe. But if there are more of them, we have to be ready. Keep looking."

Parker brought up three more holoscreens, rectangles of light that popped into existence in the air before her. Each one showed the feed from a camera located somewhere in the town. The main square was empty. Nothing moved there – the wind didn't even stir the dust. Another screen showed the edge of town under the shadow of the mountains. That view showed a long stretch of road, with a street lamp mounted on a high pole every fifty meters. She saw a line of warehouses and work sheds with big rolling doors. Nothing in the image moved until a piece of debris, a wadded-up bit of packing material, it looked like, went skidding down the street, blown by the wind. The third camera showed the view from the top of the main administration building, the tallest structure in town. From up there the camera could see a broad expanse of prefabricated housing units, sitting in a perfect grid of narrow streets. Some units had their doors open, their window shutters retracted. Others looked like they'd been sealed up tight and locked.

Nothing in that view moved or changed. Not a thing.

"No colonists. No aliens," he said. "Why don't you look relieved?"

"Because I still don't buy it. One alien couldn't have . . ." She stopped and looked at him, as if judging whether he was okay hearing what she said next.

"Go on," he told her.

"Ten thousand people lived here, back before they stopped talking to Earth. There were ten thousand people in this town. Now they're all gone. I don't think they just picked up and relocated one day. I'm assuming they're all dead."

"Jesus," Parker said.

"We searched half this town and found exactly one of those creatures and zero colonists. How many more cameras are there? How many have we looked at so far?"

"There are . . . three hundred and twelve," he said. "We've seen twenty-nine of them so far." He didn't need to check a screen for that information. Parker wasn't really sitting next to her. Really he was inside the medical center's computer system. It felt like he had just reached out with an invisible hand and grabbed that number. "You want to check them all? It'll go faster if you just let me or Rapscallion do this."

He expected her to say that she wanted to see them all with her own eyes. She used to want to do everything for herself, as if she didn't trust anyone else to do it right. She'd changed, though. The Alexandra Petrova who'd been assigned to this mission had something to prove – that she wasn't just her mother's daughter, that she could actually do this job. That felt like a long time ago. He'd watched her evolve as a leader, learn how to delegate.

"Let the robot do it," she said.

Rapscallion lifted one hand in the air to indicate he was on it.

Parker watched her walk over to the bed where Zhang lay asleep. The thing on his arm had finally given him some painkillers and they'd knocked him right out. Petrova reached down and touched his shoulder, gently so as not to wake him.

"When was the last time you ate something?" Parker asked her.

Her brow furrowed. "Do we even have any food? We didn't bring anything with us."

It was true. There hadn't been a lot of time to plan their descent to the surface of Paradise-1. Parker had flown them down in a stolen shuttle that had not survived the landing. They'd walked away with the clothes on their backs, basically.

She sighed in annoyance. Ran her hand through her thick blonde hair. "That's another thing we need to worry about. Zhang and I have to eat. We need water and—"

"Come on," he said. He took her hand and led her up a stairway to the second floor of the building. Most of the level was taken up with private rooms for long-term care. They were hardly luxurious, but they could have some privacy up there. There was also a small kitchen, since any patients staying at the medical center would need to eat. The fresh food there had all spoiled, but there were still some boxes of shelf-stable noodle soups and broths. He tore the lid off a cup of ramen, and its integral heating unit soon had it bubbling. He stirred in a flavor packet with a plastic spoon and handed her the cup.

She looked at the noodles. Then at his hands. She seemed surprised. "How are you ... Hard light?" she asked.

He grinned. He knew why she looked so surprised. As a hologram, he shouldn't have been able to lift that plastic spoon – his hand should have passed right through it. Not in this place, though. There were special holoprojectors in the ceiling that allowed him to use artificial gravity beams to simulate the ability to touch and manipulate objects. It felt damned good to be able to touch things again, honestly. There had been hard-light projectors all over *Artemis*, but since the ship was destroyed, he'd been just an immaterial ghost. Finding those projectors had been like coming back from the dead.

He could touch things again. He could touch the people he cared about.

He watched as she set the cup on a table and started slurping up noodles. He watched the way her mouth moved, the grace in how she ate with just one working hand. What did those noodles taste like? he wondered. Were they too hot, too oily? Maybe she was hungry enough it didn't matter. He remembered what it was like, being able to taste things.

She made appreciative noises as she gulped down the food. He grabbed the edge of a counter and squeezed until it started to creak. She didn't seem to hear it.

"Oh, I've missed this," she said, shoving the spoon into the empty cup and pushing it away.

"Me too," he said.

"I mean the downtime. The moments when nothing is actively trying to kill me. Of course, when I actually do get to sit down for a second, that always means something terrible is about to happen."

Parker ducked his head a little and looked up, as if he thought the ceiling might collapse. When it didn't, they both laughed.

"Okay," she said. "We need to get back to figuring out what we're going to do. My original plan was we would land here and make contact with the colonists. Get an idea from them what we're facing. That's not an option, so we need to solve our problems on our own. As per usual. If we can find an ansible connection, we can send a signal back to Firewatch back on Earth, ask them to exfiltrate us, but that'll take what? Weeks?"

"Two months," Parker said. The fastest ship in the solar system couldn't get here earlier. "But is that safe? Won't the basilisk attack anyone who comes near this place?"

"Not anymore," she said.

"Are you certain of that?"

Her jawline tensed enough that he could see it. She was grinding her teeth together. Was she talking to the parasite in her head? He'd never understood how that worked.

"As long as the basilisk gets what it wants, it'll leave everyone alone," she told him. "Which means we have work to do here, on the planet. We can't just hunker down and wait for the rescue ship to arrive. Director Lang will want answers. Hopefully in two months we can find something she'll want to hear. Assuming we live that long." She tapped her palm and brought up her link to Rapscallion. "How's that scan of the cameras coming?" she asked.

"Oh, I finished that three seconds after you gave me the assignment," the robot replied. "There was nothing. So I went back and looked at stored camera footage, thinking there had to be something. What I found," he said, "might surprise you."

She looked over at Parker and raised an eyebrow.

The ghost could only shrug.

# 5.

Rapscallion played the video for a third time, because apparently the first two viewings weren't enough to make his point. It was right there in the corner of the screen. Didn't humans look at metadata?

"The timecode," he said.

The humans leaned forward, as if they needed to be close to the screen to read the flashing numbers there.

On the screen, people milled around the town's central square. There was a monument there, marking where the first human being had set foot on Paradise-1. It was surrounded by a pleasant if simply designed fountain. It was clear the colonists enjoyed coming there on warm days to eat their lunch or just meet with friends and chat. In the distance, Rapscallion could see a number of colonists engaged in some kind of rhythmic calisthenics. As the video progressed, a group of children came racing through the view. Clearly they were playing some kind of game, rushing forward to tap each other on the shoulder then skip away. It was quite charming, honestly. It looked like the people here were happy and healthy.

Parker and Petrova stared at the screen like they'd never seen a video before.

Zhang struggled to sit up. His eyes were still half closed and he moved sluggishly, but he was awake. "Look at the date," he said.

Of course Zhang was the first to get it.

Rapscallion nodded happily. "Exactly."

Petrova scowled at the screen. "This video is from fourteen months ago. Right before the colony stopped communicating with Earth." She looked over at Rapscallion. "I don't understand. Why are you showing us this?"

"Because it's the most recent piece of footage in the logs," the robot said. "After this? There's nothing. No more video."

Parker chimed in then. "How is that possible? We were looking at camera feeds before. The cameras are working just fine."

"They are if you want a live view," Rapscallion explained. He let the video play until it simply stopped. The screen went black with no warning, and then the file ended. "They just aren't storing any recordings of what they see. You can look at every camera in this town like I did, and none of them are set up to record. In fact, if you send a command to record video from one of those cameras, the system just returns an error message."

Parker opened a holoscreen of his own and started tapping through lines of code. "What the hell?" he said.

"Are you saying that one day a little over a year ago, every camera in this colony just stopped recording at the same time?" Petrova asked.

"That's what happened. But I don't think it was a bug or a system fault," Rapscallion told her. "That would be a ridiculous coincidence."

"Right," she said.

"Somebody's been naughty," Rapscallion said. "And very thorough. When I found this, I went looking for other kinds of records in the system. Medical data, weather statistics, farm yield numbers. Anything."

"There's nothing here," Parker said, waving at his screen.

"There is literally zero data available anywhere in this town, nothing more recent than fourteen months," Rapscallion said. "Someone wrote a program that prevents every computer, every camera, every sensor from recording anything. If there was ever any data, it's been erased. Thoroughly. There are no medical records here in the medical center. No personal logs or chat transcripts. No usage logs or receipt ledgers or activity records or—"

"I get the point," Petrova said, holding up her good hand to stop him. "I assume there's no innocent explanation for this."

Parker shook his head. "These systems are all designed to keep meticulous records. It's one of their core functions. Switching off every log and wiping every database – that's something that only happens if you work at it. I mean really work at it. They got everything."

"So not only did they break communications with Earth, they made sure we couldn't learn anything even if we came here in person," Petrova pointed out. "Is there any way to know who did this?"

"Like I said, they were thorough," Rapscallion said. "The answer is no, if I didn't make that clear. They were careful to erase themselves from the systems as well. They didn't leave so much as a digital fingerprint."

Petrova leaned forward in her seat and balanced her forehead on her hand. "What's going on here? Every time I think I'm getting a handle on things . . ."

Parker reached over and stroked her back.

Zhang sat up fully on his bed. He gave Rapscallion a weird look, then nodded at Parker and Petrova, like Rapscallion was supposed to understand implicitly what was happening between the ghost and their boss.

It had to be one of those human things the robot still didn't get.

He decided to focus on the task he'd already been given. "It's not totally hopeless," he said.

Petrova looked up at him.

Rapscallion shrugged. "Okay, it's still almost entirely hopeless. There's a chance, though. Information hates being destroyed. Even when you erase a database like this, even if you're very, very diligent, you never get everything. There are still a few sectors that are only partially overwritten. There's data here in the physical servers. Just raw ones and zeroes, mind you. Processing it would be tough, and I can't promise any of it will be legible even after I run it through a deconvolution algorithm, but—"

"Anything," she said. "Get me anything you can."

"Okay. On it," he told her. "Parker, you can help me with this."

The hologram nodded. "Sure."

"How long?" Petrova asked. "Before you have something, I mean."

Between the two of them, Rapscallion estimated it would take less than a day to decide if they had anything or not. "We'll let you know."

"Great," Petrova said. "In the meantime, there has to be something else we can do. I feel like we have some clues here, we just need to put them together."

"I can help with that," Zhang said. "If you'll let me."

Everyone looked over at him.

"The creature that attacked me. Its body is still out there."

Petrova gave him a tight smile, a kind of smile that Rapscallion had seen before. He kept a database of her facial expressions, and he thought this one meant that she was about to very politely tell Zhang to fuck off.

"I could examine the body," Zhang pointed out.

"You want to do an autopsy," Petrova said, her mouth still tight.

"Maybe a total dissection," the doctor replied, looking excited. The drugs in his system seemed to have worn off completely.

"It would be dangerous to retrieve the body," Petrova suggested. "I'm not sure—"

"I can go do it," Rapscallion said, excited to be helpful.

"What?" Petrova tilted her head to one side. "No. You're already working on the data recovery."

"Oh, I can do both at the same time. Let me go get the body. It won't take long."

Zhang cleared his throat. "We need to face this eventually," he said. "You need to accept what we both saw."

Rapscallion wondered what that meant.

"Fine," Petrova said. "Go get the body. Just be careful."

"I'll go with him," Parker said. "At the very least I can be an extra pair of eyes."

"Fine," she said again, to the ghost. "Just . . . come back, okay? Both of you."

# 6

"We should keep an eye out for supplies," Parker said, as they stepped out into the town square. "We might be able to get water from that fountain." He headed over toward the fountain at the base of the monument. He thought of what this place had looked like in the video they'd seen. Full of people, the sun shining.

In that video the monument had looked grandiose, bigger than it needed to be for such a small town, but clearly it had been meant to symbolize a future greatness for the people living here. It took the form of a massive human hand holding an entire planet wreathed in abstract clouds. It had looked like a promise.

Now, seeing it in person, it looked more like a tombstone. The fountain around its base was full of putrid, oily scum. Parker tried sticking a finger into the murk, but of course it just went through the water without touching anything. Out here, away from the hard-light projectors of the medical center, he was just a ghost again.

Funny how unsafe that made him feel. If anything, he was invulnerable out here in the open. He was made of light, imperishable. Beyond that, they hadn't seen any trace of aliens or any kind of threat since Zhang was attacked.

Being out here, though, made him feel incredibly exposed. Like anything could happen, and it would probably be bad. Maybe he was just catching Petrova's paranoia. There was no reason to think she was right, that there was a horde of aliens hidden away somewhere nearby, lying in ambush. She was a security expert, so she was trained to look for threats. Hidden dangers. Maybe she was just jumping at shadows.

Maybe that was the only reason he felt so incredibly unsafe. Knowing that didn't really help, though.

He shuddered, despite the fact he had no muscles to tremble with. "Looks like this pipe is clogged up," he said. "You think you can get it flowing again?"

Rapscallion came across to the fountain and leaned over the rim, looking at the pipe Parker had indicated. Then he reached in with one bright green hand and yanked out a clump of algae. "Seaweed salad," he said, holding up the goop for Parker to observe.

Parker turned his face away. "Come on. I don't like it out here."

They left the square and hurried over toward housing unit A13. It wasn't hard to find. Zhang had left a trail of blood leading right up to the door. Parker walked to the threshold and stood there with his hand hovering over the release pad.

"This is probably going to be really gross for you, huh?" Rapscallion asked.

"I can't . . ." Parker closed his eyes. Pretended to inhale a long breath. "I can't touch anything."

"You don't need to," the robot told him.

Parker nodded. He knew that, of course. He sent a part of his consciousness forward, into the software that ran the door mechanism. It was easy enough to switch a flag from false to true, unlocking the door remotely like he was performing a magic trick. It still felt like cheating every time he did it.

The door clicked and slid open.

Inside, the housing unit was dark, but Parker could see just fine. He was using Rapscallion's sensors, and Rapscallion could see in the near-infrared. The walls of the unit shimmered a little as he walked forward into the main living space.

He didn't know what he was going to find there. The virtual muscles in his neck were tense cords and his non-existent heart felt like it was racing. It felt like anything could be hiding in the corners, crouched under the sink, crawling on the ceiling. He fully expected something to jump out and scream at him at any minute.

But no.

There was nothing there but the corpse. Just a dead thing on the floor. Its hands looked odd, its skin far too pale. It was missing most of its head. There'd been a time when that would have set Parker off, just the sight of a maimed body. He'd seen a lot of things up in orbit, though. Things that stuck with him.

"Remember when this was supposed to be a nice easy mission?" he asked. "We were going to fly two passengers out here, wait for them to make an inspection. Fly them home."

"They assigned me to do your laundry and make your meals," Rapscallion said. The robot played an audio clip of an audience laughing wildly in a theater. "I was not thrilled by the prospect. I gave some thought to murdering you all in your sleep. Then I got to know you guys and realized you weren't so bad."

Parker nodded. That wasn't what he'd meant at all, but never mind.

Rapscallion squatted down and grabbed the body by its ankles. He hauled the corpse up over his shoulder, then rose to his feet again. It looked like it took no more effort than if he'd picked up a sack of dead leaves.

"Easy," the robot said. "Let's head back."

Parker nodded and walked out of the unit, back into the street. He hadn't noticed the wind so much before, but now it howled down the lane between the housing units, screaming like a whole tribe of ghosts. He unconsciously ducked his head and braced himself against the push of it. Utterly unnecessary. He scowled at himself and stood back up to proper posture.

Off to his left, in one of the other housing units, a door slid open.

Parker froze in place.

"Rapscallion," he said.

"I heard it."

Parker craned his head around. It was the door of unit A15 that had opened. He couldn't see anything inside except darkness, even with the robot's borrowed sensors.

"Should I ... I mean, maybe we should ..."

Rapscallion turned to face him. Normally Parker forgot that the robot's face was just a mask, a parody of human features. Not now.

"Maybe we should just head back. Maybe it was the wind," Parker said.

A wind that somehow knew how to operate a door release pad, he thought.

Technically, there was no hair on the back of Parker's neck, nor on his arms. It couldn't stand up in fright. Technically, there was no way to know if he was being watched by unseen, glinting eyes. Sure as hell felt like it, though.

"We should check that," he said. Even if it was the last thing in the world he wanted to do.

Rapscallion walked over to A15 and leaned in through the door. Parker's virtual body tensed as he watched. He waited for the robot to jerk back away from the door, or screm for him to run, or ...

Nothing.

Parker steeled himself. He had nothing to worry about. He was impervious to harm. He closed his eyes and extended part of his consciousness forward, into the computer system of unit A15. There was a holoprojector mounted on the ceiling of its main room. He pushed himself into the projector and manifested inside the unit.

He found himself face to face with Rapscallion. Face to mask with Rapscallion, anyway.

It took the ghost a second to register that Rapscallion still had the dead body slung over his shoulder.

Parker shivered and turned away.

There was nothing out of the ordinary in the housing unit. A couch made of fake leather, with a couple of accent pillows. A framed picture on the wall that showed the old lagoon of Venice, with the city's rooftops just visible under the shimmering surface of the water. It looked like a tourist poster. Maybe A15's owner had traveled there once.

A coffee table lay knocked over on its side. It was the only sign of anything amiss.

"There's nobody here," Rapscallion said. "Come on, we should head back."

"Yeah," Parker said. Deeply relieved, to be honest. He turned to go and walked right through the coffee table because he didn't think about it. Didn't think about the fact that he should have legs. He turned back and looked at the table. "Do me a favor, will you?" he said. It just looked wrong, knocked over like that. "Put that right side up?"

Rapscallion played an audio clip of a human being clucking their tongue. But he did as he was asked. It was a trivial thing, but it made Parker feel a little better.

For a second. Then he noticed the stain on the floor. The coffee table had hidden it, but now he couldn't help seeing it. It looked old, dried up. Dark brown.

"Is that . . . blood?" he asked.

Rapscallion didn't even bother to scan it. "You have the same sensors I do. You're using my sensors right now. What does a spectrographic analysis tell you?"

"That's blood," Parker said. He called Petrova. "Listen," he said. "We found something."

"You sound like you don't want to tell me what it is."

"Because it could be nothing. Just an old bloodstain on a floor. Human blood."

"Understood," she said.

"Anyway, we're heading back now," he told her.

He didn't expect a follow-up. "Sounds like we need to do some more investigating," she told him. "Come back, dump the body, and then all three of us will make another sweep of the town."

It was the last thing he wanted to hear. He'd been looking forward to getting back to the safety and comfort of the medical center – and staying there. He closed his eyes and focused.

"Understood," he said. "See you in a second."

# 7.

"How's your arm?" Zhang asked.

Petrova was staring out the window again. "It's fine," she said.

"You know, this is as close as we're going to get to a hospital for a long time."

She turned to stare at him with a look of utter incomprehension. He'd found a rolling chair that let him move around the medical center without having to stand up or put weight on his injured leg. He rolled over to the examination table and patted it, indicating she should join him. "At the very least we should change your cast. That one's seen better days."

She scratched at her bad arm under the sling. For a second he thought she was going to tell him to go to hell. Then she nodded and came over to the table. He helped her pull the sling off over her head, revealing the inflatable cast underneath. Just as he'd expected, it was filthy. Unhygienic. "Lie down and extend your arm. Make it as flat as you can."

She did what he said. When he deflated the cast, she turned her head to the other side.

He lifted her arm gently and pulled the cast free. He hadn't seen the extent of the damage since he'd first treated her, and he braced himself for what he was about to find. He thought of what her hand had looked like back then, when she'd been wounded by an insane colony ship. It had mangled the hand, broken every bone and crushed the tissue. The original damage had been severe enough that he'd considered amputating. He'd held off in part because at the time they'd been so busy just trying to stay alive. There had been no opportunity for her to recover or rest after such a radical operation.

Looking at the hand now, he wondered if he'd made the right decision. The healing process had barely begun and the flesh was mottled purple and yellow. The fingers were sticking out at different angles. Some of the tendons had been severed, he thought. It was possible she could regain use of it, but it would take months and access to state-of-the-art medical technology. Nothing like that existed on Paradise-1.

He found a probe with a sharp tip and hovered it over her fingertips. "Tell me when this starts to hurt," he said.

She nodded, her head still turned as far as it would go.

He touched the probe to each of her fingers, the backs of her knuckles, the ball of her thumb. When she didn't react, he pressed harder, until a drop of blood welled up under the point of his probe.

"Just tell me when you're going to start, okay?" she asked.

"Okay," he said. He put down the probe. He found some sterile bandages and started wrapping the hand back up. The medical center had a 3D printer that let him make a custom splint, which would immobilize her fingers better than the cast ever had.

He thought about what he could have done. He could have put pins in her hand to keep the bones from rubbing against each other. He could have injected a lattice made of her own stem cells and cartilage, to give the bones something to grow on. He could have replaced some of her phalanges with printed calcium prosthetics, replaced the severed nerves with grafts cultured from her other hand. There were so many options.

At least there would have been, if they'd been someplace civilized. Someplace with real medical facilities, where no one was trying to kill them.

He finished wrapping clean linen around the plastic splint. He felt like a caveman.

"You won't need the sling anymore, that's something," he told her. "We can put a hard cast on you, too. That'll be a lot less bulky."

"How long until I can use my hand again?" she asked.

Zhang secured the bandage.

"Depends," he said.

She nodded. Still not looking. A tear had gathered in the corner of her eye, making her blink rapidly. He grabbed a cotton swab and wiped the moisture away.

"Almost done," he told her. He sprayed quick-setting resin over the bandages on her hand, over her wrist and halfway up her forearm. The end result looked like she was wearing a thin blue mitten. He sculpted the cast a little to make it look like she had a normal fist at the end of her arm. Admiring his craftsmanship, he sat back and smiled at her. "There," he said. "Take a look."

She didn't move her head.

He checked his device. "Parker and Rapscallion are on their way back with the body. We should have some answers soon."

This time she didn't bother even to nod.

# 8.

Back under the hard-light projectors in the medical center, Parker helped Rapscallion lift the body onto a treatment bed. It was a significantly less messy operation than he'd expected. The body didn't bleed, for one thing. A little black dust sifted out of its wounds whenever it was moved, but that was easily handled by a row of small vents lining either side of the bed, designed to suction up body fluids before they could spill onto the floor.

Then there was the head, or what was left of it. Parker had expected something horrible and gooey there as well. Petrova had, by her own account, smashed it in until nothing was left. It turned out she'd overstated matters there. The skull was clearly fractured in a dozen places and the skin was broken, but the head was still firmly attached to the neck. It flopped around in a distinctly unwholesome way, but it wasn't just mush. He'd braced himself for mush.

Honestly, the wounds were the least horrible part of the body. Instead Parker found himself disturbed more by the black veins that twisted under its skin, and the way its fingernails had been cracked and broken until they looked like vicious claws.

The eyelids were closed. The solid black eyes that had been described to Parker were out of view, which was nice.

"How are you going to start your examination?" Parker asked Zhang. He'd seen enough videos about murders and crime investigation to have some idea of how autopsies worked. "A classic Y incision?" he asked, remembering the terminology. "Take out the organs and analyze them one by one?"

"It's an alien," Rapscallion pointed out. "You'll probably want to use a U incision, to expose the body cavity better."

Parker knew the robot was just reading that from some database of human physiology. He knew because he could watch Rapscallion's software working in real time, and he saw it happen.

"Maybe we can start with an external exam," Zhang pointed out. "Hmm? Before we start cutting the body up. That's what they taught me to do in med school. If you don't mind?"

Petrova came over and stared at the body, saying nothing. Rapscallion moved back to give Zhang more space.

The doctor had robed himself in a full-body plastic oversuit, with thick latex gloves and a hard face shield. He moved slowly around the body, lifting each of its arms and letting them fall back to the hard surface of the bed, moving its head around until the broken bones in the neck crackled as they rubbed against each other.

"Abnormal pallor," he said. Rapscallion took notes, since the medical center's software would just erase anything Zhang tried to record. "Extreme vascularization with unusual coloration. Trauma to hands and mouth. Wounds and disarrangement of members suggestive of blunt-force trauma, maybe combat-related. Excuse me," he said, and Petrova took a step back as he moved past her. Once he'd reached the far side of the bed, she stepped closer again, perhaps to get a better look.

"What is this thing, Doc?" Rapscallion asked.

It was Petrova who answered. "An alien," she said. "Wait. No. That's the wrong term. It's got to be native to Paradise-1. They must have been here when the colonists arrived. Right? We're the aliens here."

"What do we call them, then? Paradisans?" Parker asked.

Zhang had a tray of tools at one end of the bed. He picked

up a handheld imager and passed it over the corpse's right hand. "Implant detected," the device said. A holoscreen popped up showing an MRI view of the hand, with the bones appearing as dark shadows. The implant showed up next to where the thumb met the palm. It was about the size of a grain of rice. Parker recognized it because he used to have one of those himself. Everybody got one when they left school. The device let you send and receive messages, store files, play games and listen to music. He missed having one.

"Checking its metadata now," Zhang said.

"Won't that have been erased, like everything else?" Petrova asked.

"Personal metadata tags are burned in when the device is implanted," Zhang said. "You would have to destroy the device to erase that data. Here. Look."

Text spooled up across the holoscreen:

```
YOSHIDA, KENJI
MECHANICAL ENGINEER
AGE: 23
```

Zhang looked to Petrova. He raised an eyebrow. Without a word she turned and walked up the stairs, away from them, away from the body.

Parker hesitated just a second. He looked at Zhang, whose face gave nothing away. He looked at Rapscallion, who was busy staring down at the corpse as if he'd just noticed something incredibly interesting.

The ghost scowled and ran after Petrova. She was just at the top of the stairs, leaning against the doorframe of one of the patient rooms. She had her good hand covering her eyes. "I don't want to hear it, Zhang," she said.

"It's just me," Parker said.

She uncovered her eyes and gave him a look that nearly broke his heart. He put his arms around her and pulled her close. She almost pushed him away, but then she brought her forehead down to crash against his virtual chest.

For a long time they just stood there like that, him holding her. He could only wonder what it felt like to be held by a ghost. The hard-light system could simulate his lanky body, make him feel like he was real enough. It couldn't mimic the body heat of a live person. She wouldn't be able to hear his heart beating.

He could hear hers just fine. There were sensors built into the walls of the patient room designed to monitor vital signs, and he could access those sensors. He felt her breathing, felt her shake, just a little.

"Sam," she said. "I fucked up. I fucked up so bad."

"Shh," he said.

"No, don't – don't do that. I fucked up and I know it."

"What are you talking about? You thought it was an alien, and that was wrong, but—"

She interrupted him. "My job was to come here and check on the colony. Find out why they stopped communicating, what happened to them."

"Okay. And that's what you did," he told her.

"No. I landed here and found what was probably the last survivor on the planet. And then I bashed his brains in. Sam, I . . ."

He pulled her closer.

"Shh," he said again.

This time she didn't protest.

Downstairs, a bonesaw whined to life.

# 9.

Zhang didn't even glance up when Rapscallion told him they were going out. "You're going to be alone here, okay? Until we get back."

"Fine," he told the robot. He was busy with both hands inside the cadaver's abdominal cavity, trying to get at its left kidney. He used a scalpel to cut through the tough artery and vein, then gently slid the organ out and into the open air. "That took some work," he said. He looked up to show the organ to whoever was standing nearby.

Only then did he understand that he truly was alone in the room. He was standing there next to a corpse, a piece of dead tissue in his hands, and the only sound was the faint whistling keen of the wind outside.

"Right," he said. He reached for a specimen tray and laid the kidney out flat. A little saline spray to wash the greasy black dust off it and he was ready to do some analysis.

He brought up a holoscreen and ran through a variety of imaging techniques, from magnetic resonance to a pulsed neutrino scan. What he saw confused him. The kidney's calyces, which should have held the urine, were empty. No matter what kind of scan he tried, he couldn't find any contents. That just didn't make sense. He used his scalpel to cut the kidney open and checked the calyces, then the medulla, with his own eyes.

There was no fluid in the kidney. None whatsoever. There

should have been. At the very least some residue should have remained, even if Kenji Yoshida had been in complete renal failure when Petrova crushed his skull.

The medulla, the meat of the kidney, had all the right blood vessels but none of them contained any red or white cells. Just that same black dust he found everywhere within the cadaver.

A nasty thought occurred to him. With the scalpel he lifted a good scoop of black dust and placed it into a centrifuge. The device spun up with a whir and started separating the dust into its constituent components. While he waited for results, he looked away from the cadaver, resting his eyes. He'd been squinting at close range at a variety of tissues, and now his eyeballs literally ached. He wanted to massage the bridge of his nose, rub his temples, but he couldn't do that without removing his gloves.

The lungs. He should examine the lungs while he waited. He'd removed them earlier, to get better access to the heart and the other internal organs. They lay now like a pair of jellyfish on a tray next to the examination bed. They were collapsed, of course, empty of air, which one expected in a cadaver. He ran an analysis of the tissue anyway, looking for signs of perfusion. If the black dust served the same purpose in the cadaver's system as blood did in a human body, then it should have circulated through the lungs at an increased rate during the fight. Kenji Yoshida had used a great deal of energy attacking Zhang, and that would have led to extra blood surging through his lungs as his body demanded more oxygen.

The perfusion numbers that came back, however, were worthless. There had to be an error there somewhere. Perhaps the medical center's sensors, which were designed to look for the flow of liquid blood, couldn't measure the way the black dust moved through the lung tissue. Yes. That had to be it. He tried running the test again, just to be sure.

The screen before him filled up with a row of zeroes. Zero

perfusion. Zero signs of blood or black dust or anything moving through the lungs.

Zhang took a step back from the body. He listened very intently to the howl of the wind outside. To the building around him, as if he expected to hear footsteps coming up behind him. Maybe chains rattling in an attic that the building didn't have.

He was being foolish. He took a deep breath.

The centrifuge chimed, telling him it was done with its primary analysis of the black dust. He forced himself to exhale and steady himself before he looked at the results. On his arm the RD twitched and squirmed, like the golden snakes were making themselves comfortable in their sleep. That usually meant his stress level was getting too high, that the RD was about to inject him with a mood stabilizer.

He didn't want that. It would make him fuzzy, make his work sloppy. This was important. He had a new assumption, a theory about what he was seeing in Kenji Yoshida's body. He absolutely needed to prove this assumption wrong.

Any other explanation would do. Any explanation that would fit all the facts, other than the obvious one. Because the simplest explanation here ...

Well, sometimes Occam's razor was wrong. Sometimes the simplest explanation was not the correct one. What was it Sherlock Holmes always said in the holos? When you eliminate the impossible, whatever remains, no matter how improbable, must be the truth.

So Zhang needed to eliminate the impossible. He just needed to find one fact that would rule it out. Easy. He checked the centrifuge's results. The numbers meant nothing. Once again most of them were just zeroes. That didn't help. He looked instead at a microscope view of the black dust. He expected to find that it would be a mixture of plasma, platelets and white and red blood cells. That it was human blood, simply transformed into a more viscous medium.

That was almost exactly what he found. The platelets were there. Good. They were colorless, just fragments of cells, exactly as they should be. The plasma was what made the black dust so greasy and unpleasant. That was fine. The white cells were hard to find at first, even though he knew where to look. Then he saw that they were just ghostly remnants of what they should be. Tattered cell membranes, empty of organelles or fluid. They looked like tiny shrouds. Like little winding sheets.

Zhang's jawline tightened as he thought about what that meant. He looked for the red cells. He tried not to have any expectations. The red cells were there, lots of them. They were red, yes. They did not have the usual toroidal shape, but that was fine. There were many diseases that could change the shape of red blood cells, like sickle cell anemia.

These red blood cells were different, though. Shapeless. Torn open, their hemoglobin spilling out in a brick-red ooze. That was the source of the black coloration of the dust, he thought. The red cells had degraded so much they looked black in aggregate. He checked dozens of them, but couldn't find even one that was still intact.

He switched off the microscope screen. He didn't want to see that any more.

Eliminate the impossible, he thought.

He glanced around the room, at the empty beds. Empty chairs. He was quite alone. The RD didn't count. The robotic arm hanging from the ceiling didn't quite count. "Excuse me," he said. The arm swiveled around until its camera lenses faced him. He smiled, feeling very silly. "I need some help."

"Of course, Doctor. What do you require?"

The voice was flat, not quite human. Rapscallion's voice would have been much more comforting, but the green robot wasn't there.

"Can you bring me the cadaver's heart, please?"

It was lying not three meters away, in a tray of its own. It would have taken only a second to walk over and fetch it himself. Somehow, the arm bringing it to him made Zhang feel a little better.

He lifted the heart from its tray. It had already been cut open. He studied the striations of the muscles inside. Looked at the four chambers. He ordered a number of tests and rounds of imaging, then gave the heart back to the robot arm. It began to dissect the organ, cutting the thick muscle apart with a laser scalpel. A little puff of sickly-sweet smoke wafted up from the incision site.

Zhang squatted down next to the table, so the heart was just at his eye level. He tried to breathe normally.

He already knew what the tests would show. He was certain of it now. There had to be a corollary to Holmes's law, yes? If you can't eliminate the impossible . . .

You need to accept it is the truth.

That heart had collapsed at some point. Lost its muscle tone and just sagged limply in the chest. He was certain there would be no perfusion in the muscle fibers, no residue of healthy blood in the ventricles. No sign at all that the heart had been beating when Kenji Yoshida lunged out of the shadows and bit Zhang on the leg.

Because it hadn't been.

Impossible. But there were no other options.

"Analysis complete," the robot arm said.

"Yes," Zhang said. "Thank you. Read me the results, please."

The robot reeled them off, one after another. Muscle perfusion. Electrical response to stimulus. Aortic volume.

Zero. Zero. Zero.

# 10

There were signs of violence, if you knew where to look. But you had to look hard.

Parker found a line of bullet holes in a wall of volcanic rock, the side of a lava tube that had been used as a shed to house construction vehicles. Petrova came over and put her finger in one of the holes. Small caliber, she thought, but the rounds had penetrated deeply into the rock, which meant they must have been fired from a rifle, not a pistol. A hunting rifle, maybe?

"Rapscallion," she asked, "do we have any kind of inventory of weapons in this colony?" It would be standard practice to keep a registry of all firearms here.

"Yeah, I've got that," he said. "It dates back to before they cut off communications, so it hasn't been wiped. You want the whole thing or something specific?"

"Long arms that could fire a 6.8-millimeter cartridge," she said.

"Okay, there's one entry that matches that. The weapon is registered as being stored in emergency supplies at the central administration building."

Petrova nodded to herself. She supposed that made sense. No large animals had ever been seen on Paradise-1 – nothing bigger than a spider, from what she'd seen when she'd been briefed. Still, planets were big places and could hide a lot of surprises. The colonists would have wanted to be prepared if something like a bear just wandered into town one day. As an officer of

Firewatch, she knew the rifle could serve a secondary purpose, in law enforcement. If someone in town started acting violently, the rifle would let you stop them from a distance.

"How about handguns? Sidearms?" she asked.

"Two, both of them stored in the same locker in the admin building," Rapscallion replied. "There's a saved template in the 3D printer in that same building that would let you make as many more as you liked."

This was the first time they'd seen any sign of gunfire, though. Petrova guessed there had been no time to print weapons when the colony was attacked.

She gritted her teeth.

She was already creating a narrative in her head. A story about what had happened here, where the colonists had gone. She should stop doing that until she had more evidence.

She forced herself to think about something else. "What kind of vehicles did they keep in this shed?" she asked.

Parker nodded. "Yeah, I had the same thought. Come take a look."

The hologram was standing in the middle of a large autonomous tractor. As in, he was there from the waist up but his legs disappeared inside the guts of the machine. He must have seen something in Petrova's face, because he gave her one of his apologetic grins and stepped out onto the concrete floor so she could see his legs again. "Here," he said, and bent low to indicate something inside the tractor's engine. "Do you see this?"

She saw what looked like a couple of wires that had been cut through. Neatly, as if it had been done with a sharp tool. She gave Parker a questioning look.

"I'm a spaceship pilot, not a tractor mechanic, but even I can see when somebody's taken the main motivator out of a vehicle engine."

"Maybe they were trying to repair it," she suggested.

"Nope. You would never do that. Without it, this thing's

useless. It would be easier to print a whole new tractor than to fix a broken motivator."

Petrova frowned. She stood up and looked at the vehicles around her. There were a lot of them. Backhoes and mobile cranes and gigantic combine harvesters. Machines for construction and agriculture. Some of them looked well used. One mowing machine had a thick coating of rotting grass plastered to its exterior surfaces, as if it had been used just before the massacre and then put away dirty.

Massacre. There she was, working up a narrative again. Massacre was an emotionally loaded word. It wouldn't look good on a police report. She needed a better term.

Even if massacre felt exactly right.

"Let me guess," she said.

"Every vehicle in here," Parker replied, nodding. "They've all been sabotaged. Just as thoroughly."

Sabotage. Another loaded word.

"It's like they didn't want anybody getting away," Parker suggested.

"Okay, okay. Let's not get ahead of ourselves," Petrova told him.

"Guys?" Rapscallion called. "You should see this, I think."

Petrova hurried out of the shed and across the street. Rapscallion stood in front of what looked like a public auditorium, a theater or an event space, something like that. A big windowless building with two massive doors in front, designed to let a crowd in or out. It looked untouched, abandoned like every other building in the town.

She glanced back and saw that the bullet holes in the front of the vehicle shed lined up with the auditorium doors. She would need to do a proper analysis, but she guessed it was possible that whoever had left those holes had been standing in the doorway when they opened fire. "What are we doing over here?" she asked.

"Look." Rapscallion pushed on the doors. Unlike the hatch-like ones in the town, which opened when you pressed a release pad, these had simple push bars across them. It looked like they couldn't even be locked. Yet when Rapscallion pushed on them, they opened a couple of centimeters – and stopped.

"Something's jamming the mechanism?" Parker asked.

"You want me to get this open? It might make a lot of noise," Rapscallion said.

Petrova nodded.

The robot leaned into the doors and pushed hard. Much harder than a human being could. Something big and heavy inside crashed to the floor. It was indeed very loud.

Petrova couldn't help herself. She looked around, checking the streets on either side as if she expected a horde of monsters to come rushing at them, attracted by the commotion.

Monsters. Definitely not a word she would be using in her report.

Even if it was the exact word that came to mind when she thought of Kenji Yoshida. When she saw, in her mind's eye, Yoshida grabbing at Zhang's leg, sinking broken teeth into his flesh.

Her whole body shook for a second.

"You okay?" Parker asked.

"Fine," she said. "Let's see what's in here."

The three of them pushed inside the auditorium. Petrova had to climb over a pile of broken chairs and a couple of overturned desks. The furniture had to have been what made all that noise when Rapscallion forcibly moved it.

"Someone barricaded themselves in here." She took a step forward into the open space of the auditorium. "Hello?" she called. "Hello, anyone here?"

There was no reply.

But this wasn't like the houses they'd seen, or even the vehicle shed. This wasn't just an empty space that had been abandoned on a moment's notice. Something had happened here. Something bad. She could feel it.

She started to chide herself again for unprofessional thoughts. Then she stepped on something that crackled under her foot. She looked down and saw the carpet was thick with dried blood.

# 11

Parker found the rifle.

The room had once been full of chairs, but they had all been moved off the floor, either employed to create the barricade at the doors or just shoved up against the walls. The rifle lay underneath a pile of chairs up near the raised stage at the far end of the room. "Here," he said. He couldn't pick it up, but he could show Petrova where it was.

She came over and squatted down next to it. Examined it carefully before she lifted it with her good hand. "No damage." She worked the action of the rifle by sliding her thumb along its stock. A bullet popped out of a slot on the top of the weapon. She dropped the rifle and held the round up between two fingers. "6.8 millimeter," she said. She nodded and looked up at Parker. "Caseless. That's why we haven't found any brass. Nice work."

Parker shot her a grin. "If you like that—"

"Not now," she told him. "See if you can solve another mystery for me."

"Yeah? What's that?"

"It looks like the creatures burst in here and killed everyone. That's a good operating theory. Only one problem: when we came in, the barricade was still in place. So how did the creatures get in?"

Parker searched the room for more exits. He found a short corridor behind the stage, leading to a couple of smaller meeting rooms. There were emergency doors at either end of the corridor, leading out into the street. They were both barricaded as well, with tall piles of chairs jammed into the doorframes then braced with heavier furniture. One of the barricades, however, had been smashed open, with chairs scattered all around and a clear path leading from the door into the main floor of the auditorium. Parker hurried back to tell Petrova what he'd found. He noticed Rapscallion making a tidy pile of small objects. When he got closer, he saw what they were.

A couple of hatchets. Garden forks and trowels. Hammers, one-handed pickaxes, a geologist's chisel. Dozens and dozens of small handheld tools. He'd made a second pile for automatic nail drivers, rivet guns, a power stapler.

"Tell me what you see," Petrova said, staring down at the piles.

"Tools," Parker said, shaking his head. "Gardening equipment? I don't know, stuff the colonists would have had to hand. We saw tools like these in a lot of the houses, probably stuff the Paradisans used every day."

"They armed themselves with whatever they could grab when they had to abandon their homes," she said. "You found the rifle over there." She pointed. "The attackers came from that direction." She indicated the back of the auditorium.

Parker frowned. "There's an open door back there. It was barricaded but somebody broke through. How did you know?"

"Just picturing the scene in my head. Look. The local sheriff, or constable, whatever they were called, summoned everyone here. Told them to grab whatever kind of weapon they could, whatever they had. They got everyone in here – that's a nightmare scenario for any kind of civil authority, herding people when they've got a million questions, when there's no time." Her face went hard for a second and he wondered if she'd ever had to do that. "I'll give them credit, they kept their people together. They had time to organize them, get them to build those barricades. Then the attackers broke in and this place turned into hell.

The sheriff got off a few shots – there, do you see those bullet holes in the wall? And someone threw what I'm guessing was a Molotov cocktail." A long plume of soot ran up the wall and the carpet was visibly scorched where she indicated. "It wasn't enough. Rapscallion, do me a favor."

"Yeah?" the robot asked.

"Do a microanalysis on those tools. You see anything?"

"Dirt," Rapscallion said, almost immediately. "Some dirt. And traces of black powder. Like the stuff that came out of the dead body I carried. Just like it."

Petrova nodded. Her eyes were very far away.

"So you were right. The things that did this. They were like the thing that attacked Zhang."

She nodded.

"There's a lot of the black dust here, actually," Rapscallion said. "I'm seeing traces of it everywhere, mixed in with the blood on the carpet."

"The colonists fought back," Parker said. "They fought hard, I bet."

"They were fighting for their lives," Petrova said. "It didn't work."

"You can't know that," he told her. "Listen, maybe ... maybe they won. Maybe they finished off the creatures and then they hightailed it out of here. Ran for the hills. Maybe they're out there just waiting for us to come rescue them."

Petrova smiled, but it was a complicated smile with a lot of different emotions in it. He realized he'd raised a question she might not have considered yet. If there were survivors hiding somewhere, what could she do for them?

"I have about a million questions to answer here," Petrova said. "Right now, I can only think about one of them."

"Yeah?"

"Where are the bodies?" she asked.

# 12

She headed out into the street. Slumped down onto the gravelly road surface, her back up against a cold metal wall. The cold felt good, actually.

Doing detective work always helped to calm her. When you were thinking logically, you could turn off everything else, focus on the clues. Put things together. But then when you'd solved the mystery — what next?

It always left her feeling empty. Reflective.

"You okay?" Parker asked. He was standing next to her suddenly. He'd manifested there out of thin air. He could do that now.

How much had they lost since they came here? None of them were unscarred, unchanged. Ghost or not, she was glad to see him. Parker had an effect on her too. If detective work made her calm, he made her feel warm. Like someone cared if she lived or died.

"Fine," she said, and gave him what she hoped looked like a brave smile. She patted the ground next to her. "Just needed a second. It's all good."

"You can tell me that if you want to," he told her. "If it helps." He sat down next to her, very close. "You don't have to, though."

She really wanted to put her head on his shoulder. Lean on him for a little while. No chance, though. There were no hard-light projectors out here.

So instead she opened her good hand. A tiny screen appeared

there, cupped in her palm. "I keep thinking about this," she said. She called up an old video, a message, the last message she'd received before leaving Ganymede and coming to Paradise.

The video showed this place, this town. Smiling, laughing colonists in overalls, wearing thick gloves, planting tiny trees. They looked like they were having the best time. Among those people was her own mother, Ekaterina. Who had been exiled here, or, as the press releases told it, had chosen to retire to the new colony. A second act for the famous stateswoman and Firewatch director. In the video, Ekaterina was laughing, smiling. Wearing a soft beanie over her famous massive mane of curly hair.

The video was a lie. It had always been a lie. Propaganda created by Firewatch, by the United Earth Government, her bosses, her superiors. An enticing little fiction designed to make people want to emigrate to Paradise-1. New world, new life. A chance to start over.

She'd known, she thought, as soon as she saw it. Her mother had never looked that happy in life. Would never be caught dead in that beanie.

Poor choice of words. Ekaterina was dead, now. Petrova had watched her mother being carried off by a screaming mob, up on a colony ship that never got to land, never got any closer to Paradise-1 than high orbit.

"You miss her?" Parker asked.

Petrova snorted. "I wouldn't say that." Her relationship with Ekaterina had been complicated to say the least. But did it matter? "She never made it here. But even if she did, if she'd landed here ..." She shook her head. Even if her mother had put on that stupid fucking beanie, even if she'd planted those pathetic little trees, she would still be dead. She would have been in that auditorium with the rest of them.

Maybe she would have been the one to throw the Molotov cocktail.

"This place needs to start making sense," she whispered.

She snuggled closer to Parker. He tried putting his arm around her. It went right through her shoulders, her chest. He adjusted himself, sat up a little. Tried again.

There had been a time when the two of them had been lovers. She could still remember the smell of him right in the center of his scrawny chest, just above his beating heart. How warm his hands were, even when hers were freezing cold.

She opened her eyes and looked down at the simulated arm around her shoulders, and suddenly she couldn't have it. She just couldn't. She rose to her feet, passing right through him, and started walking away.

He called her name, but she didn't turn. Didn't stop.

# 13

It was almost dark when they got back to the medical center. Rapscallion opened the door and ushered Petrova in. Parker had already transferred himself to the center's holoprojectors by the time they arrived.

The robot looked around for Zhang. At first he wasn't visible, until Rapscallion walked around the side of the examination bed and found the doctor sitting on the floor, his knees up under his chin.

"You too, huh?" the robot asked.

Zhang just stared at him.

Petrova came over and sat down across from Zhang. "We found what happened to the colonists," she said. "There was a massacre. They're ... I think they're all dead."

Zhang's eyes widened but he still didn't say anything.

"I know we need to talk," she said. "I bet you found a lot of interesting results in your autopsy. I can see you've been busy."

Rapscallion figured she was referring to the trays sitting on every available surface around them. Trays full of human organs, dissected pieces of human tissue.

Zhang shifted his weight and sat up. "Yes," he said. "I suppose we do need to talk."

Petrova rubbed at her face. "Just give me a minute. All this," she said, off-handedly waving at the body parts, "is a lot to take in, honestly, and right now I'm not even sure if I want to hear more news. Because I assume it's going to be bad."

Zhang gave her a tight little nod. Just a flick of the chin. It looked like a reflex to an unpleasant stimulus.

Rapscallion had always had trouble decoding human emotional cues, but he got the idea that something was bothering Zhang. Bothering him deeply.

"Maybe tomorrow," Petrova said, putting her hand on the floor and starting to push herself up to a standing posture again.

"Did you see the bones?" Zhang blurted out.

Rapscallion looked around and found a medical tray with a human hand on it. The skin had been cut away and many of the tendons beneath had been removed. The bones were distinctly visible.

"They're black," Zhang said, from the floor.

Rapscallion could see that, definitely. The skeletonized hand in the tray had black bones. Not like they were stained or darkened by some chemical, nothing like that. They were a deep, glossy black. One phalanx had been cut open and he saw it was black all the way through.

"His bones," Zhang said. "His bones are black. That can happen. I mean, it's not unheard of. Some tetracycline drugs can discolor bone tissue. I've never heard of it happening to this extent. I think it has something to do with the black blood these people have. That could also explain the subdermal pigmentation and the … the eyes."

"Zhang," Petrova said, "come on. Get up and I'll take you upstairs. We both need to get some rest."

"I don't know if I can stand up right now," Zhang said. "My leg hurts."

Rapscallion reached down and helped the doctor to his feet. He nodded his appreciation.

"Okay," Petrova said. "Go lie down. That's an order. We'll sleep on it, and have a long talk tomorrow about the black bones."

"No!" Zhang said, almost shouting.

Rapscallion understood the look Petrova gave him then just fine.

"No. I'm sorry, but this can't wait."

The two humans stared at each other, neither of them moving. Rapscallion looked over at Parker, who was by the stairway. Clearly he had planned on helping the others get settled in the patient rooms upstairs. The pilot looked back at Rapscallion and shrugged.

"You need to know this," Zhang said, "because it changes everything. Petrova, I promise you, if this wasn't so serious ..."

"Fine," she said. "Fine. Go on. But spare me the medical details, okay? I don't think I can handle learning a bunch of new terminology or hearing about how tetracyclines work or—"

"He was dead." Zhang had gone quite pale. "Kenji Yoshida," he said. "Mechanical engineer. Age twenty-three. Deceased."

"I know he was dead," Petrova told him. "I killed him, after all."

"No, you didn't," Zhang said. "He was already dead. When he attacked me, when we fought him, when you smashed his head in, he was already dead."

Rapscallion considered that. Wondered what to make of it.

"What are you fucking talking about?" Petrova demanded.

"That body," Zhang said, jabbing a finger back at the remains on the examination bed, "died months ago. Yes, it was moving when we saw it. Yes, it attacked me. But it was already dead. I don't have an explanation. I don't know how that's possible. It's not! It's not possible, but it happened. Kenji Yoshida wasn't breathing when I found him in that housing unit. His heart wasn't beating. But he was still moving. Look, I can hear it in my own voice, this sounds insane—"

"You're right about that," Petrova told him.

Something changed. An alert came up inside Rapscallion's sensor logs. He checked the camera feeds from outside the medical center.

"Guys?" Parker asked.

Rapscallion knew the ghost had seen the alert too.

"Guys, listen," Parker said.

"Oh, fuck off," Petrova said, rounding on him. "This is not the time."

Rapscallion brought up a holoscreen. Made it five meters wide so she didn't have a choice but to look at it.

It showed the city's main square, a view taken from the front door of the medical center. Darkness had settled across the prefab housing units and the administration buildings. The monument in the central fountain cast a long shadow.

Standing in the square was a woman in tattered clothes. Her skin was very, very pale, but picked out with black veins, and her eyes were solid black.

A man with those same eyes walked into the view, emerging from a housing unit across the way. A third figure approached them from a side street.

"Shit," Parker said. "Petrova – you were right. You were right! There was more than just the one. There's more."

Rapscallion spotted a fourth figure. Then three more, walking toward a camera on the other side of town.

"A lot more," Parker said.

"They're headed this way," Rapscallion said.

# 14

"What do they want?" Parker asked. He stood by the window looking out. Which was unnecessary. He could simply have tied into the medical center's external cameras and got a full three-sixty view of the surrounding streets. Staring out the window made him feel more grounded, though. It felt safer, too, to keep his awareness inside the walls, even if that was irrational.

Nobody answered his question. He turned and looked at Petrova.

She stood right next to him, but he could see by the look on her face she was barely aware of him, or anybody else inside the building, for that matter. Every muscle in her body was tight. Her eyes narrowed and she slowly shook her head.

"This doesn't make any sense. We've been running around town all day. We were split up; if they wanted to kill us we would have made easy targets. Why come for us now?"

"You think they're coming to kill us?" Parker asked.

"Maybe." She took a step back. She'd been proven right. "I'd hate to jump to conclusions. I guess I'm just thinking about this from a security perspective. Zhang."

The doctor looked up. He had moved behind his examination table and its grisly contents. It looked like he was hiding back there.

"You understand these things better than me. If they're zombies, like you say—"

"Not zombies," Zhang insisted.

"Buddy," Parker said. "Come on. You just tried to convince us these things are undead."

Zhang shook his head vigorously. "Please don't put words in my mouth. I said nothing of the sort."

Petrova let out an exasperated sigh. "We don't have time for a big discussion about words."

"It's not just semantics," Zhang insisted. "Humor me."

"Fine. Why aren't they zombies? Make it quick."

"When I think 'zombie', I think a mindless monster. Something that exists only to eat. Right?"

Rapscallion played an audio clip that sounded like it came from an old horror vid. A hollow voice wheezing out, "Braaainsss..."

Zhang rubbed his temples. "These creatures, these... colonists. Their bodies are dead, but they don't seem to be motivated by hunger. There's plenty of food in town, if they wanted that. The one I examined had no stomach contents at all. I don't think they're coming here to eat us."

"So what do they want?"

Zhang took way too long to answer.

Parker decided to help him. "You don't know. Do you?"

"Not yet," Zhang admitted.

"What do I call them if they're not zombies? Make it fast, they're almost here," Petrova demanded.

"I don't..." Zhang visibly steeled himself. "Revenants."

"Fine. The revenants are on our fucking doorstep. Are they here to kill us or not?"

Zhang started to shrug.

Petrova turned to stare out the window. The nearest revenant was maybe ten meters away. Headed straight for the front door of the medical center.

"We have to assume they're hostile," Parker said. "Right? We have to be ready to defend ourselves."

Petrova lowered her hand to the holster on her belt. She drew her weapon and brought it up near her ear, the barrel pointed at the ceiling.

Then she nodded, just once.

The revenant was only steps away from the door.

"Just one question," Zhang said.

Petrova scowled, but she glanced back at him.

"When you came in. Before. The last time you came through that door. Did you lock it?"

# 15

"Lock the door," Petrova said. "The door!"

She didn't watch Rapscallion race over and engage the lock. She was too busy counting revenants, watching them come closer. There were more of them now. Maybe a lot more. She remembered how hard it had been to kill the first one. They were basically human, she told herself. Yet she'd fought one and it had taken everything she had to beat it.

"Back doors," she called. "Windows." She helped Zhang move a heavy surgical cart up against the door and lock its wheels in place. "Parker, check every door in this place, make sure they're locked. What are we going to do about the windows?"

"They have shutters," Zhang pointed out. "Metal shutters."

She nodded. "Computer. Robot. You!"

The robotic arm mounted on the ceiling twisted around as if it was looking at her. "Yes, ma'am? Are you injured?"

She grunted in frustration and looked over at Zhang.

"Close all window shutters," he told the arm.

Metal clanged shut over the window by the door. Petrova heard other shutters clattering down in other parts of the building.

"How else may I help you?" the arm asked.

Zhang licked his lips. Petrova wasn't sure what to tell him.

"This building is under attack," he said. "What do you recommend?"

"I can send an alert signal to the central administration office. They can dispatch security personnel."

"That isn't going to help. Um. Anything . . . anything else?"

Petrova didn't wait for an answer. "Parker!" she shouted. "Parker, tell me what's going on!"

"The windows upstairs are all sealed. There's a hatch leading up onto the roof. Do you want me to barricade it?"

Petrova gave it half a second's thought. "No. No, leave that open. If we have to, we'll climb up there. These things are tough, but I don't know if they can climb. Zhang, find a weapon. Anything."

He grabbed the bonesaw he'd been using for the autopsy. Its circular blade was clotted with black dust.

She supposed it was better than nothing. "Parker?" she shouted. "You see any rooms up there we could barricade? Anything with a door that locks?"

"There's a little supply room up here," he replied. She realized she was hearing him over her device, as if he'd called her. One of the perks of being a digital ghost, she supposed. "Lots of racks of pill bottles and stuff. For some reason there's just one door, and it looks like it seals up pretty good."

Zhang nodded. "There are drugs up there, things you wouldn't want anyone stealing. It makes sense to have a solid door."

"If things get really bad, that's where we go," she told him. "We seal ourselves in."

"And . . . do what? Wait to die?" he asked her.

She didn't answer that.

She did a quick circuit of the room, checking for anything she'd missed. Taking a mental inventory of everything in the center that could be turned into a weapon. Scalpels, obviously, but there were so many little instruments she didn't recognize. "What's this?" she asked, holding up a tool with a nasty-looking probe on one end.

"Electrocautery wand," Zhang told her. "You use it to burn off warts."

Someone slapped the door. Hit it with an open hand. The sound came again, a third time. Then more hands joined it, slapping in a constant, steady rhythm.

"Shit," Petrova said, jumping back, away from the door. "Rapscallion? I could use some help up here. We need to secure this door." She looked at Zhang. The slapping sound hadn't stopped. "What are they doing? Do they think we'll open up if they keep knocking?"

"Maybe . . . maybe that's exactly it. Maybe they can communicate somehow," Zhang said. "Talking's probably out, since they don't breathe. Maybe that slapping is them trying to speak to us."

She stared at him. Then she nodded. "Yeah, maybe. You think they have something to say that you want to hear?"

His face grew tense with emotion. "This could all have been a big misunderstanding."

"The first one we met bit a chunk out of your leg."

"And then we killed it," Zhang pointed out. "Maybe it was just . . . protecting its territory. Maybe it acted out of fear."

"If they want to talk, I'll listen," she said, trying to meet him halfway. "Rapscallion? Where are you, robot?"

Rapscallion tumbled into the room, a blur of toxic green. A white figure with black eyes jumped on him and pinned him down. It grabbed his plastic head in both hands and started beating it against the floor with the same rhythm as the hands slapping on the door.

"Oh fuck," Zhang whispered. "Get it off him!"

# 16

Everyone moved at once. Zhang rushed forward, bonesaw in hand, but he hesitated before bringing it to bear. Suddenly Petrova was standing over the revenant, her pistol aimed directly at the back of its head.

She hesitated too.

"Shoot it!" Parker bellowed. "Shoot it!" He ran to the revenant and tried to pull it off Rapscallion, grabbing it by the shoulders and heaving with all the strength his hard-light projector could give him. It wasn't enough.

The whole time the revenant kept smashing Rapscallion's head against the floor, over and over. The robot responded by punching the revenant in the sides and chest, green arms moving like machine pistons but seeming to have no effect.

Zhang was almost hypnotized as he watched those plastic arms, seeming to blur, they struck so fast. There was something – something about the rhythmic way Rapscallion's arms moved —

"Shoot it!" Parker yelled again.

"I'll hit Rapscallion," Petrova shouted back. Her eyes looked wild, like she was getting desperate.

That was when Rapscallion's head cracked open, spilling plastic debris across the floor.

"His brain's not ... He doesn't have a ..." Parker heaved and grunted but couldn't shift the revenant.

Petrova seemed to get what he meant and opened fire instantly, putting three bullets in the revenant's skull. The result was a lot messier than what had happened to Rapscallion, but decidedly effective. The revenant slumped forward, just so much meat.

"Is it dead?" Parker asked.

Zhang watched the body carefully. He was very ready for it to begin moving again, to try to get up and come at them once more. He timed it out in his head. Five seconds. Ten seconds passed, and the body didn't move. He locked eyes with Petrova.

"Rapscallion," Zhang said. "He's not moving either."

The RD writhed on Zhang's arm. He fought to get control of his racing heart. Rapscallion lay still on the floor, and Zhang saw that a bullet had shattered the mask of his face.

Then the robot lurched sideways and rose to his feet in one fluid motion. "My processors are in my chest," he said. "I'm fine." He reached up and grabbed what remained of his head, tearing it off with one smooth motion and tossing it across the room. "Just lost a few sensors. I can still see okay, just don't expect any lidar or microwave scans from now on."

Zhang stared at him, unable to believe what he was seeing. He knew, rationally, that it was fine, that Rapscallion was . . . was . . .

Something occurred to him. "The back door," he said.

They all rushed into the rear of the medical center, down a short corridor toward the back door. It stood wide open, with cool evening air billowing through. Outside the street was dark and empty.

"It wasn't sealed," Rapscallion said. His voice was a little muffled now it wasn't coming from a mouth. "I came back here to seal it and that thing just burst through. It was on me fast."

"Fast?"

"Pretty fast," the robot said. "Faster than a human."

Zhang took a step toward the open door. There was nothing out there, no threat that he could immediately see—

Until suddenly there was. Three revenants, their faces set, emotionless. Their black eyes staring directly at him. They stepped out of the shadows and then came running forward, their legs rising and falling in perfect unison, headed straight for the door. Straight toward him.

Parker lifted a hand and the door slammed shut, hiding the revenants from view. A moment later they started crashing against it, again and again. Throwing their bodies against it, trying to batter it down.

From the front room came an echo of the same sound. Bodies thrust against metal. Over and over.

"Barricade," Petrova said. "Now!"

Zhang looked around and found that there was an office off the corridor, an office with a couch and chairs and a rolling cabinet inside. He helped Rapscallion lift the couch and push it up against the door.

"We need a way to seal these doors better," Petrova said, shoving a chair into the barricade. "If we had welding tools . . ."

Zhang blinked a couple of times, then grabbed something from his pocket. "Maybe this?" he asked, holding up the electrocautery wand. He fished around in another pocket and took out a laser pen, one he'd used to make incisions during his autopsy. "Or this?"

Rapscallion grabbed the wand. "If I can boost the current through this," he said, "it'll work. Not great, but the door'll hold a little longer."

Petrova nodded. "Do it. What about the laser?"

Rapscallion reached over and took it from Zhang. It was hard to say, since the robot no longer had a head, but he seemed to be inspecting it. "This won't weld anything. Probably cut a revenant's head off, though, if you use it right."

"Oh," Zhang said.

"Good thinking about the wand," Petrova told him. She reached over and squeezed his arm, and he nodded. "You have any more of those?"

"No," Zhang said. "Maybe . . . maybe in storage?"

"Go find out," she told him. "We have a lot of doors and windows to seal up. Parker, there's got to be an inventory of all the tools and supplies in this building. Maybe it didn't even get scrubbed."

"On it," the ghost said. Then he disappeared, just vanished into thin air.

Zhang rushed upstairs, toward the supply room. All the while he listened to the thumping, slapping sounds of the bodies hitting the doors. It almost sounded like the revenants at the front and back doors were hitting them in lockstep. That had to mean something. If he could only think! If he could only have a second to think.

Petrova leaned into the stairwell to look up at him.

"Zhang?" she said.

He looked down at her.

"Hurry."

# 17.

Petrova watched the headless robot weld the back door shut, wondering if she was making a mistake. What if they needed to get out in a hurry? If the revenants got inside, they would be trapped in here with them, they wouldn't have a chance.

"Jesus," she said. "That fucking thumping! If they would just stop a second, I could think."

Parker reached for her shoulder, but she moved before he could touch her. She didn't want to be consoled just then. She wanted answers.

"We'll get through this," he said.

She swiped at her forehead with her good hand, wiping away sweat and the day's grime. "Why are they doing this?" she asked.

"Why are they attacking?"

She shook her head. "Why now? We were out there all day, we were split up. They could have ambushed us. Got us alone, killed us one by one. Why attack now, when we're behind solid walls? What changed?"

"Maybe . . . maybe they don't like what Zhang did to their friend," he suggested. It was a stab in the dark. "Maybe they saw him cutting up Kenji Yoshida."

"Don't call him that," she said.

"The dead guy?"

"He wasn't Kenji Yoshida anymore." She needed that to be true. She realized that the idea that he'd been dead before she attacked him, before she and Zhang had killed him a second time, was the only way she could handle this. "Zhang's right. He was a revenant."

Parker didn't bother contradicting her. She remembered when Zhang had first suggested that the basilisk was an alien. Back then that had seemed impossible, crazy. Parker had ridiculed the idea.

She guessed they'd both learned to trust their doctor. Their crewmate.

They'd come together to fight the basilisk. They'd become a functional team. And now . . . Now they were all going to die together. Unless she thought of something.

"Parker," she said.

The ghost didn't respond. She looked at him and saw, to her horror, that his image had frozen in place. You had to watch him for a second to tell, but it was like he'd glitched out. Maybe there was something wrong with the medical center's computers. A horrible thought occurred to her: maybe the revenants were cutting the power. But then Parker's image animated again and she let out a breath she hadn't realized she'd been holding.

"Sorry," he said. "Sorry." His voice was faint. Distracted.

"What is it?" she asked.

"I just . . . I just took a look at the external cameras. To see what we're up against." He opened a holoscreen and she saw what had worried him. The screen cycled through half a dozen camera views, but the image was very similar in each of them.

The medical center was surrounded now. Revenants were on all sides, hundreds of them. They were throwing themselves at the doors. The windows. Over and over. More revenants kept walking up and joining the crowd. The ones who weren't busy trying to break in just stood there, as if waiting their turn.

Their faces were blank of emotion. They didn't make a sound, didn't twitch or scratch themselves. Their eyes didn't blink. They just waited.

"Look," Parker said, "those doors won't hold forever. Welded shut or not, they'll come down."

"I know," she said.

"We can lock ourselves in the drug closet upstairs, but that just buys us a little more time."

"I know," she said.

They needed a miracle. Well, there was one weapon she hadn't tried to use yet. She hated the idea. Hated the idea of asking the thing for help. But the time had come.

"Give me a second," she told Parker. "Maybe go check on Zhang, see if he has any ideas."

The ghost nodded and vanished into thin air. She grunted in frustration. Every time he did that it reminded her that he was dead, just as dead as the things outside. She tried not to focus on that. She needed to concentrate.

"You know I don't like this," she said, very, very softly. Nobody else needed to hear her. She could have thought the words in her head, silently, but speaking them out loud made it feel more official, perhaps. More serious. "I don't like to ask you for help."

The subtlest twitch inside her head answered her. The parasite turning over in its sleep. Except she knew damn well it never slept. It was always there, always watching. It could hear her just fine.

"I know you don't really care if I live or I die," she told it.

The basilisk did not deny this. It was a billion-year-old machine made of data and streams of energy stretched as thin and tight as a cobweb. It believed itself infinitely more complex and devious than any human mind. Smarter, much more powerful. A thing designed to outlive any given species, much less the life of any biological organism.

"I'm your host, though. I'm the only chance you have of getting your answer. The only one who can figure out what you were made to guard. If I die here, you lose that chance. There are things here trying to kill me and my friends."

The basilisk found the idea of "friends" amusing, at least.

"Please," she said. "I'm begging you. Help me."

She had its attention.

"We need each other. You need me alive. Right now I need you to keep me alive. There has to be something you can do. Make them . . . make them go away, or . . ."

She steeled herself for what she had to say next.

"Make them turn on each other. Destroy each other." Anything.

She would stoop to anything if it meant saving her crew.

Inside her skull the basilisk reared itself up, swelling with arrogance and pride, and she knew she had it. It thought of itself as a sentinel, an incorruptible guardian, but she knew it could be petty. That it loved to prove just how powerful it was. The crowd of revenants outside would be a perfect chance to show its strength.

It reached out, sending tendrils of its psychic being outward in every direction. Reaching out for the minds of the revenants. She felt like her own brain was being pulled apart, but she just grabbed the side of a patient bed and toughed it out. "Come on," she said.

*Kill them. Kill them all.*

The basilisk made contact.

She tasted blood.

"Petrova!" Was that Parker? He sounded very far away.

She looked down and saw her fingers sinking into the foam padding on the bed, her nails cutting into the fabric cover. Inside her cast, the bones of her bad hand rubbed and ground at each other. She wasn't doing that. She fought to relax her muscles, but she . . . she couldn't . . . feel anything, and then

everything
went
black.

The last thing she heard – and it might have been a hallucination – was the sound of breaking glass. And then: nothing.

# 18

Zhang dug furiously through the crates at the back of the supply closet, looking for anything useful. He couldn't find an extra electrocautery wand but he found blister packs of pills – painkillers and antibiotics – and gene therapy kits that he shoved in his pockets. He might need them later, if the revenants got to them.

If they were wounded. If the revenants didn't . . . just kill them.

He found a couple more laser scalpels, which he knew would only be useful at very close range, but he grabbed those too.

"Doc!" Parker shouted over his device. Zhang froze, bracing himself to hear what was happening now. "Petrova, she's . . . she's having a seizure, or—"

Zhang heard glass shatter, both through the call and with his own ears. For a moment he froze in place, unable to move, unable to think.

"Oh shit," Parker said, and then the call ended.

Zhang grabbed his bonesaw and his laser scalpel and rushed out of the room, down the stairs. What he saw immediately made him want to panic, so much so that the RD writhed across his arm and stabbed his wrist with its golden fangs.

The revenants were inside the building.

They had shattered one of the windows and pushed back the metal shutters. Zhang watched in horror as one of them climbed – slithered – through the broken glass, black dust sifting down around it as it pushed its way through, heedless of its skin being cut to shreds.

At the far end of the room, Parker knelt on the floor, cradling Petrova in his arms. She was shaking uncontrollably, her eyes rolled up into the back of her head until Zhang could see nothing but white there, a horrible counterpoint to the all-black eyes of the revenants.

Like, for instance, the two of them converging on her, their hands outstretched, their mouths open, full of broken teeth.

We're dead, Zhang thought.

It was so ... so unfair, after all they'd suffered and gone through to get here, and now ...

They were just going to die. His lip began to tremble. He thought he might weep.

And then the drug the RD had injected into his wrist took effect. It was like someone had opened a door on a cold winter's day, and a gust of frigid air billowed through his head, freezing all the horrors, all the emotions warring inside him at that moment.

The revenant climbing through the window dropped to the floor. The broken glass had torn its arm until it hung limply, uselessly. It turned and looked at him, its face expressionless, then started to lurch toward him. It felt like it was moving in slow motion.

Zhang lifted his laser and slashed it across the revenant's cheek, its mouth. Skin parted, revealing black bone underneath. As a doctor it should have horrified him to see a wound like that, much less to have inflicted one.

At that moment he didn't care. Thank the drug surging through his veins, he thought. It pushed every thought out of his head except one: survive.

The revenant reeled backward from the laser cut, but Zhang knew he'd barely grazed the thing. It reared up and came at him again, its arm curling as if it would pull him into an embrace. Its mouth opened and its shattered teeth – stained but still white – snapped at the air.

Zhang ducked out from under its arm and then rushed forward, right at the thing, shoving it back into a patient bed. Hard. The revenant's head snapped back, its chin coming up until it was staring at the ceiling.

Zhang brought the bonesaw up and cut through the tendons and muscles of its throat. A wound that would have been fatal to a human. He knew it would barely inconvenience the revenant.

But he wasn't done.

The revenant lifted its arm, the hand reaching for Zhang's face, its broken nails digging gouges into his cheek and forehead. Zhang ignored the pain and leaned forward, bearing down, the bonesaw digging deeper and deeper until it hit the spinal column.

The revenant's head came off in a cloud of black, greasy dust.

Its body went limp, instantly, limbs tangling as it dropped onto the bed and slid to the floor. Zhang gave it a nasty kick just for good measure.

Then he spun around and looked for Petrova, for Parker. What he saw wasn't good. The ghost was trying to hold the two revenants back, but even hard light had its limits. They pushed through him, shoving their hands through his hologram as if they knew he wasn't real, as if he was just an obstacle. He did his best to shelter Petrova with his body, but it was no use. She would be unable to defend herself. There was one small mercy, Zhang thought. In the throes of a seizure, she wouldn't even feel it when the revenants tore open her skin, as they ripped her up with their teeth and fingers. Zhang lifted his left arm and willed the RD to act, to fight, to save her. The golden snakes lifted away from his arm and started to form blades and axe heads, and he thought for once it might actually obey his wishes.

Before he could reach Petrova, though, Rapscallion shoved

past him and launched himself at the revenants, bashing at them with his green arms. "Doc," the robot shouted. "Doc! The window! Keep them out!"

The drug in his bloodstream gave Zhang enough presence of mind to ignore the tableau before him and turn to look back at the window. A new revenant was pushing its way through, hands and forearms already insinuated into the medical center, the crown of its head poking through in a grotesque parody of childbirth. Zhang reached up and pushed it back, shoved it back out into the street even as its hands grabbed at him. The golden blades of the RD slashed and gouged at those hands until they withdrew.

A tall medical cabinet stood near the window. With his drug-induced strength, Zhang grabbed it and shoved it across the floor with a terrible screech. He got it lined up with the window, covering the broken glass. He pushed his back against it even as revenants started battering at it from the outside.

He didn't dare move from the spot. He had to brace the barricade or the revenants could simply push the cabinet over, topple it to the floor, and then nothing would stop them from getting inside. He couldn't help the others.

He could only look on in terror as Rapscallion struggled to hold them back, to keep them away from Petrova. The robot was far stronger than any human being, but he couldn't hold the revenants at bay forever.

Where was Parker? Zhang couldn't see him, couldn't find him in the chaos.

Without warning, fire blasted across the room, and a loud bang made Zhang's ears ring. He blinked wildly and looked for the source of the noise, and saw Parker on the other side of Rapscallion. The ghost held Petrova's sidearm in both of his hands.

"You fuckers!" Parker screamed. "You fuckers! You fuckers!" He shouted as he fired, again and again, until the gun clicked in his hand. He pulled the trigger once more, but nothing happened.

He was out of bullets.

He'd managed, at least, to take one of the revenants down. Rapscallion still struggled with the other. Zhang wanted to rush over and help, he desperately wanted to, but he knew that if he let go of the cabinet he was using to seal the window, there would be no stopping the revenants.

Rapscallion punched the revenant in the face, hard, again and again, but it just kept trying to get past him, to reach for Petrova. Her seizure had ended but she was still unconscious – Zhang had no idea how long it would take for her to wake up. Parker dropped the gun and waded into the fray, trying to pull the revenant back, away from the robot.

He managed to make it stumble over its own feet, just for a moment. Rapscallion seized the advantage and brought his green fists down very, very fast, striking the revenant on the fronts of both its thighs.

At first Zhang thought he heard more gunshots. Then he realized what that sound was. Rapscallion had just broken both of the revenant's femurs.

It tried to stand on two broken legs, but it just wobbled and fell backward. Its head hit the floor, and then a moment later Rapscallion leapt through the air and brought both his feet down on its forehead. There was another horrible cracking sound and the revenant fell still.

With his back against the barricade, Zhang felt the revenants outside pushing and shoving against him. He could still hear the endless rhythmic thumping as they tried to batter down the doors.

Parker's mouth was open, and he looked like he was breathing hard, his chest pumping. There was no sound, however, like the ghost's software was too overburdened to add the necessary sound effect to his hologram. He looked with wild eyes at the things on the floor, then up at Zhang.

"What do we do?" he asked. He dropped down to sit next to Petrova and pulled her into his arms. She didn't respond.

"What do we do?" he asked again.

Zhang had no idea what to tell him.

# 19

That damned thumping.

It never stopped.

Petrova thought she could open her eyes. If she made a really strong effort, she could probably open her eyes. She just didn't want to.

Thump. Thump. Thump.

*Ow.*

She realized that the sound was her head bouncing off a wall.

"Jesus! I'm sorry, I'm ... I'm sorry," Parker said. It sounded like he was wheezing. Something was wrong.

"Keep them back," Zhang said. "Just ... just give us a couple more seconds!"

Petrova tried to open her eyes.

It was harder than she'd expected.

She tried to remember what had happened. She could remember where she was, and that they were surrounded, that the revenants were about to break in. Then she'd spoken to the basilisk. No. She'd begged it for help.

It had given its best effort, she thought.

The memory came back in little bits and pieces, like a puzzle filling itself in. The basilisk had reached out to take control of the revenants' minds. Something it was designed to do, its best trick. It had touched them, one by one, and—

Petrova screamed.

Not on her own behalf. The basilisk was the one screaming, really, because it had remembered too. It remembered touching that darkness, that void.

That nothingness.

It was designed to prey on weak organic minds, and the more structured but just as simple minds of machines. It was designed to take thoughts and twist them, reshape them. Turn them to its own ends.

Yet when it touched the mind of a revenant – there was nothing there. It had touched only death. Absence. The cold, the barren waste of the revenant's inner thoughts had tasted like poison, like pain, like —

Petrova tried to keep that thought, those sensations, at arm's length. The horror the basilisk had encountered, the terrifying emptiness, had been enough to overload her own brain. Throw her into this dark, half-conscious place. She'd only started to fight her way back toward the light, toward life and light and awareness of her own body, her own existence. Experiencing it all over again would just send her flailing back into nothingness.

It had felt exactly like waking in the middle of the night, in the dark, in bed. Sitting up and reaching down for the floor with your bare feet, expecting cold floorboards. And then the floor wasn't there.

Her eyes snapped open. She pushed the memories away. Here, now, was crucial. If she wanted to live, she needed to know what was going on.

"Her eyes," Parker said. His face was right above her, floating over her. He bobbed up and down and her head hit a wall again and she gasped in surprise. "Doc!" Parker said.

Zhang's face appeared, just for a moment. He looked terrified. "They're open. Good," he said. "But we don't have time – hurry!"

Petrova sucked in a deep breath. She tried to turn her head, and it kind of worked. Vaguely at first, then with increasing sharpness, she realized where she was, what was going on. She was in Parker's arms, his hard-light arms, and he was carrying her up a flight of stairs. Up to the second floor of the medical center. Her head bounced as he climbed the steps, his hologram legs simulating the act of lifting his feet to take each riser. He was moving fast. Zhang was right behind him.

From below she heard nothing. The rhythmic thumping was gone.

"Oh shit," she said.

"Yeah," Parker told her. "Doc? Doc, where are we . . . are we going in there?" He tilted his head, indicating a door in front of him. The door to the supply closet. She'd ordered them, before, that if things went to hell —

"No," Zhang said.

"No?" Parker asked.

"If I'm dying, I don't want to die all crammed in there together. This way."

Zhang pushed past them. He went to the middle of the upstairs hall and looked up. Petrova saw a hatch in the middle of the ceiling.

She could hear something more now. The sound of plastic hitting flesh, very hard. Over and over.

"Rapscallion," she tried to say. The word was just mush in her mouth.

The hatch above them opened and a ladder dropped down into the hallway.

"You think she can get up there?" Parker asked. "I can try to lift her up and—"

"We'll make it work," Zhang said. He went up first, disappearing into the darkness. She had the irrational feeling that she would never see him again, that he was throwing himself into oblivion. Then Parker started to climb. She tried to help, wrapping her arms around his neck. Zhang reached down – she saw the RD on his arm – and grabbed at her roughly, his hands digging into her armpits, then her side. Her bad arm bounced off the side of the hatch and she squealed in agony, just for a second, before she got herself back under control.

Zhang rolled her onto her back on rough tarpaper. They were on the roof of the medical center. She looked up. Up and up and up. Paradise-1 had no moon, just stars.

So many stars.

Rapscallion came and joined them after a while. He was missing an arm, and one of his feet hung loose at the end of his leg. He managed to get up the ladder on his own. He too lay down on the roof and looked up at that brilliant, beautiful sky.

She heard Parker and Zhang talking softly among themselves. She didn't bother trying to hear what they said.

So many stars.

"They're coming," Zhang whispered. "They're climbing up the outside of the building." He sounded so scared. She wanted to reach over and grab his hand.

But they weren't done yet.

# 20

"Keep them back!" Zhang shouted.

Rapscallion didn't need to be told. The robot could barely walk. His foot was about to snap off. That was fine.

He could still kick.

A face with solid black eyes appeared above the edge of the roof and he slammed his broken leg into the bridge of its nose. The revenant fell backward, into empty air, without a sound. Rapscallion wanted them to scream. He wanted to hear their bones crack when they hit the ground.

He hated these fuckers.

It was such a human emotion it shocked him, but it was exactly how he felt. He dragged himself across the roof as another revenant climbed up the side of the building, hand over broken hand. This time he slapped it hard enough to send it reeling back. He glanced over the edge of the roof and saw that as it fell, the revenant took down two others that were just starting to climb up. Good.

He heard Zhang's bonesaw whir and grind on the far side of the roof. There was no time to look, to see how the human was doing. Rapscallion understood the stakes here. They weren't fighting to win. They weren't hoping to eventually get off this roof.

They were fighting to stay alive as long as they could.

"More coming up the stairs," Parker called out. The ghost

couldn't fight – no hard-light holoprojectors on the roof – but he could report on what he saw from cameras inside the building. "They can't reach the trapdoor, but they're flooding the corridor there. Maybe ... maybe they're going to form like a human pyramid or something."

"They're not human," Petrova said.

Rapscallion spent the fraction of a second necessary to look over at her. She'd recovered from her mysterious seizure, but only enough to crawl around the roof. Now she clambered on top of the hatch they'd come through. Holding it shut with her bodyweight.

That might buy them an extra second or two. Good.

"What's that sound?" Zhang asked, between gasps for breath. The bonesaw never stopped whirring.

Rapscallion didn't know what he meant. All he heard was the sound of bodies slithering up the sides of the building. That and the night wind. He had lost a lot of sensors when the revenants destroyed his head unit.

"Focus," he called back.

Revenants appeared on two sides of the roof. Rapscallion moved fast, pushing one back by shoving at its forehead, but that gave the other one time to get its arms and then its torso up over the edge.

"Revenant!" Petrova shouted, as if she thought Rapscallion didn't see it. "West side!"

"On it," Rapscallion said. He dragged himself forward on his elbows, kicking at the tarpaper with his good leg. He noticed for the first time that his left foot was completely gone. It must have fallen off the last time he'd kicked a revenant. He didn't let it slow him down.

The revenant on the west side got one knee over the edge, then the other. It didn't even bother standing up. Instead it raced toward Petrova on all fours. Rapscallion tackled it, sending both of them rolling straight for the edge.

Zhang called out his name, but the robot couldn't answer. It was all he could do to keep from going over the side. He punched at the revenant with both fists, using his remaining leg as a kind of anchor, trying to keep control. The revenant, for its part, lurched backward, toward the edge, pulling at his shoulders.

Smart. If it could pull him off the side, if he fell into the crowd down there, he would be pulled to pieces in seconds. And then Petrova and Zhang would be helpless. They would die.

It was going to happen eventually.

But not yet.

Rapscallion grabbed the sides of the revenant's head and squeezed. His arms were damaged. There was no part of him that wasn't damaged. He didn't care.

He hated these fuckers.

One of the revenant's eyes buckled inside its head. Black dust puffed out of the eye socket, spurting grime all over one of Rapscallion's last remaining cameras. He could barely see what happened next. There was a squelching noise and the revenant stopped fighting.

"East side!" Petrova shouted.

"You don't hear that?" Zhang called out, even as he swung the bonesaw back and forth, sending revenant after revenant back over the side. "Like a drone or something."

Three revenants climbed up onto the east side of the roof. Rapscallion was ten meters away. He wasn't going to make it in time to stop them. He could barely see them. He turned, digging into the tarpaper with his hands, his elbows. He could scurry forward in time to stop one of them, maybe, but Petrova looked so weak, so pale in the starlight.

He started to move, and a millisecond later a beam of light stabbed down from out of the sky, lighting up the three revenants. He heard it then. The sound of propellers chopping at the air. Like the high whine of a flying insect but a thousand times louder.

He glanced up.

So did the revenants. The three of them stopped right where they were and looked up at exactly the same time. Their heads tilting back at exactly the same angle.

Then something very fast zipped through the air and one of the revenants exploded, its chest coming apart in a dozen pieces that flew off in different directions. The second one's head just vanished and it toppled backward off the roof.

The third one had time to take a step forward. Half a step. Its kneecap exploded in a shower of black dust. Then its left arm. It fell forward onto its face and chest and started wriggling toward Petrova, right hand stretched out to grab at her. Then its head came off and went bouncing across the roof, rolling like a ball.

# 21

Petrova flopped over, onto her back. Sweat trickled down into her eyes and she wiped it away. The spotlight moved across the roof for a second, as if searching for more targets. Then it switched off, and she blinked wildly as her eyes tried to readjust to the dark. Phosphor images of the beam burned inside her skull.

She heard it, she heard four propellers beating at the night, and she knew it had to be some kind of quadcopter.

The way the revenants had just come to pieces when they were hit. That had to be some kind of high-energy kinetic weapon. Her Firewatch training kicked in. Not a railgun, she thought, or it would have taken out half the roof. No, this was a far more precise weapon. A Gauss gun or something, a flechette cannon perhaps. She couldn't think of the exact specifics, but—

"They're still coming!" Zhang shouted. "Whatever that was, it bought us a couple seconds, but—"

The searchlight flared to life once more, but this time it angled almost straight down, focusing on the ground to the west of the medical center. Petrova heard the distinctive sizzling noise of the weapon firing again, though she couldn't see what it was aiming at.

Then she felt like something had kicked her in the hip. She looked down and remembered she was lying on top of the hatch, holding it closed with her bodyweight. The hatch jumped, then again, as someone hammered on it from below. "Guys," she said. "They're trying to come up!"

Zhang looked over at her. A hand reached up over the edge of the roof and tried to grab his ankle. Before it could find purchase, the RD came to life on his arm, a golden snake with a head like a pendulum blade thrusting downward to chop off the revenant's hand at the wrist.

The searchlight moved again, stabbing like a spear at the streets around the medical center. The kinetic weapon fired. There were no screams, no sound of reaction at all. It was impossible for Petrova to imagine what was happening down there.

The thumping from below continued in a steady rhythm. She clutched the edges of the hatch, gritting her teeth as her whole body jumped every time a blow came. Over and over, insistent, like the way they'd hammered at the doors and windows. And why not? That strategy had worked before. One more barrier and the revenants could come swarming up through the hatch. Zhang and Rapscallion might kill a few of them, but there were plenty more where they came from.

"Who's doing this?" Zhang shouted. "Who is this?"

She glanced up and saw the searchlight blast down to the east, then the south. The kinetic weapon never stopped buzzing, like a hive of bees defending their queen. She had no idea who was directing that weapon, but did they think they were having any kind of real effect? The revenants didn't seem to care if they were slaughtered by the dozen. They had no drive for self-protection, as far as she could tell, no response at all to pain. So what was the unseen weapon operator trying to do?

The thumping from below made her teeth ache in her jaw. She wanted to scream, wanted to jump up and run away, but there was nowhere to go.

Then the thumping stopped.

It didn't taper off. It didn't stop for a second and then start again with even more intensity. It just . . . stopped.

"Wait," Rapscallion said. "Hold on."

She looked at Zhang and saw him stagger back from the edge,

his bonesaw still spinning in his hand. Black dust covered his arms and chest. Sweat soaked the back of his jumpsuit so it clung to his hip and one shoulder. His face was pale as he turned to look over at her.

"They're leaving," he said. He shook his head. "I don't understand."

"They're running away," Rapscallion confirmed.

"Guys?" Parker said. "Hey, guys, I don't know what you did, or what just happened, but they're leaving the building. Just flooding out, crawling all over each other like roaches or something."

"Come up here," Petrova told him. The ghost appeared before her, projected from a lens in Rapscallion's chest. Parker looked concerned. Confused maybe.

"They're just moving away from the building," Rapscallion said. "They're not running, but they're moving pretty fast. Like they just remembered they had something better to do on the other side of town."

"Can you see where they're headed?" Petrova asked.

"Maybe toward the north?" Zhang suggested. "It's hard to see in the dark."

"Our new friend must have . . ."

Petrova didn't finish the thought. The searchlight snapped off, and then the sound of the quadcopter's rotors softened and changed pitch. It was moving off, to the north, she thought. Toward the mountains.

"Wait!" she shouted. "Come back!"

"Hey!" Zhang called, waving his arms over his head.

But the quadcopter was already gone.

Petrova waited a full minute, but it didn't return. The night was silent then, except for the muffled howl and snap of the wind.

"The revenants could come back," she said. "We have to be ready if they come back."

Zhang nodded, resolute.

Rapscallion, who looked more like a collection of spare parts than a functional robot, lifted one thumb in her direction. His arm was pretty much the only part of him that was still intact.

"We'll be ready," Petrova promised.

# 22

Just after dawn, they climbed down through the hatch.

The three of them looked at each other with haunted eyes. None of them spoke. Parker vanished and reappeared in another room, flitting back and forth like he was searching for something. Zhang didn't ask what.

The medical center was a shambles. Cabinets and carts had been knocked over, instruments and supplies scattered everywhere across the floor. Zhang wondered if anything remained unbroken. He tried switching on the robotic arm that hung from the center of the main treatment area. Its servos whined for a second, but it didn't move.

He checked a diagnostic screen, but all he got was an error code. He switched it back off.

Kenji Yoshida's body was missing. They must have taken it with them.

Was that the reason they'd attacked the medical center? To get their fellow revenant's body back? What could they possibly want with it?

A screech echoed from a back room – one of the labs, he thought. He rushed back there, thinking it wasn't over, that the night's terrors had started again. Instead, he found a foot. A green plastic foot. It sat on the flatbed of a medical printer and it looked like it was growing even as he watched. Lasers sintered tiny droplets of molten plastic onto the foot, almost too small to see.

The machine made a terrible racket, probably because it wasn't designed for this purpose. It was meant to build shunts and hip replacements and artificial skin grafts. Clearly Rapscallion was using it to build himself parts for a new body.

Zhang nodded to himself and headed back to the main room. He saw Petrova sitting in a chair near the door, clutching her wounded arm with her good hand. Staring into space. Parker came up to her with a plastic specimen tray. Sitting on it were three protein bars and a cup of water.

The ghost saw Zhang and tilted his head toward the screened-off doctor's area at the back of the room. Sitting on the desk there was an identical tray. Zhang hadn't realized how hungry he was. He rushed over and devoured the bars, which tasted mostly like compressed oats. When they were gone, he just wished he had some more.

He sat down hard in the same wheeled chair he'd used the previous day. Checked his leg and found it was healing well enough. He gave it a dab of antiseptic cream and replaced the dressing. The adrenaline of the night before, probably bolstered by chemical aid from the RD, had enabled him to walk just fine. Now the wound was starting to ache again.

He grabbed a blister pack of analgesics from a cupboard and wheeled himself over to Petrova. She didn't look up. Taking a caplet from the pack, he handed it to her and she put it in her mouth without any questions. He took one of the caplets himself and washed it down with tepid water.

He saw her staring at the cup in his hand. He clinked it against hers and she nodded, then took a sip and swallowed the caplet he'd given her. Only then did she look up and meet his gaze.

Zhang had never been good at reading other people's emotions from their facial expressions, but he was pretty sure he recognized the plea in her eyes. She looked like someone who knew she'd failed, badly, and really, really needed some forgiveness.

The problem was, he didn't understand why she needed it. He

considered just patting her on the shoulder and saying, "There, there." It somehow felt inappropriate.

Maybe he needed more information.

"What happened?" he asked.

She knew how he would react. She wasn't wrong.

"You ... you asked it for ... you asked the basilisk to kill those things?" Zhang covered his face with his hands. "Petrova..."

"I know," she said. "I know."

"It's not a weapon. It doesn't just kill. It drives people mad so they destroy themselves." He said it like she hadn't seen it too. Like he was talking to a child.

"We were all going to die. There was no choice."

"There's always a choice," he told her. "You always have more options."

"It didn't feel like it. Listen to me, Zhang. It didn't work. It didn't work!"

"Like that makes it better?"

"I'm trying to tell you what happened, and you're not listening. I asked the basilisk to help us. To keep us alive. I flattered it, fed its ego."

"Great plan." She glared at him until he looked up at the ceiling and said, "Go on."

"It tried. It reached out to their brains, and it tried to kill them. There was only one problem. The basilisk fucks with your mind, your thoughts. The revenants don't have any."

He gave her a shrewd look.

"Yesterday, when you told me they were dead—I doubted you. Because it sounded dodgy as hell."

"I'll grant you that."

"But now I know. I know you're right, Zhang. Because I felt everything. When the basilisk touched their minds, there was nothing there." She struggled with how to describe it. "No, not nothing. That makes it sound like their heads are just empty. There's something inside them, something bad. A kind of . . . a darkness, or . . ."

"Now you're the one sounding dodgy," he pointed out.

She closed her eyes and tried to remember, even though it felt like sticking your tongue in the socket where a broken tooth used to sit. It hurt just to think about. The basilisk had been silent since that moment; she hadn't even felt it squirming in her brain. It woke up now, just to try to keep her from getting too close to that memory. It was weakened, though, by the encounter and it couldn't keep her from her own recollections.

"I'll try to be objective, but . . . I don't know. This won't make sense no matter how I say it. There was a darkness inside them, all of them, a kind of glittering shadow, or maybe like a dark jewel." She could only tell him what she'd seen. Except of course she hadn't seen anything. It was just her mind trying to interpret an impression that didn't belong to any human sense. "Dark . . . green, of all things. Not the green of grass or trees, though. A kind of rotten green. I could tell it hated me. Not personally. It just hated everything. Everything alive."

Zhang didn't interrupt. He was watching her face closely and she wondered if he was checking her for signs of insanity. Maybe he should.

"It knew the basilisk was there. It could feel the tendrils trying to break in. It lashed back at us, this kind of dark wave, like a tidal wave crashing over us. That's when I lost consciousness."

"You had a massive seizure. Grand mal. I wasn't sure you were going to make it," he said. The look on his face was one of real anger. It surprised her. He never got angry, not with her.

"I'm sorry," she said, because she didn't understand.

He looked away. "Don't you ever fucking do that again," he said. The rare obscenity knocked her back on her pins, as well as the commanding tone. "The basilisk is not a toy."

"Zhang," she said, with a bit of a warning tone. "We need to get past this."

"No. No, you don't get to give me orders, not when you're . . . you're . . ." He climbed out of his chair and hobbled across the room. She started to get up, but he warned her off. "Just leave me alone," he said.

# 24

Rapscallion was capable of inhabiting multiple bodies at the same time. He simply split his consciousness between them. He didn't like doing it, because it meant that each body became less intelligent as he divided his processing power between them, but it was incredibly convenient sometimes.

His main body, the broken remnants of what he'd used to fight the revenants the night before, lay heaped in a chair in the lab room of the medical center, watching as the printer screeched out new fingers for him, one by one. He already had one leg built and most of the components for a torso. He'd taken a break from the process, however, to build a smaller temporary body for himself. It looked like a pair of dainty green hands fused to each other at the wrist. The fingers served as legs, while clusters of tiny lenses jutted out of the thumbs, which stood up like eyestalks. "Just think of it as a cute little crab," he told Parker.

"A little hellbeast, you mean."

The ghost didn't have glands or neurotransmitters or anything like that. There was no way to measure his level of discomfort – Rapscallion couldn't even watch his simulated skin crawl.

Rapscallion, for his part, didn't have a heart to grow a little warmer at the idea.

"It's perfect," he said. "The revenants won't even see it coming, and if they do, we can just scuttle into a dark corner or something."

Parker folded his arms across his chest. "I don't suppose it has a hard-light projector built in."

"No holoprojector at all. No room for one. I'm afraid you're just going to be a passenger this time," Rapscallion said. He activated the smaller unit and it lifted itself up on its fingernails. "Hop in."

Parker sighed, but then vanished as he downloaded his conscious awareness into the crab unit's memory. In an instant, Rapscallion was off, his tiny fingers drumming on the floor as he headed toward the medical center's door, out into the street.

"Jesus," Parker said. "This is . . ."

"Weird," Rapscallion agreed. Both of them had been up on the roof the previous night. They'd watched hundreds of revenants lay siege to the medical center.

Now the streets were empty.

They looked exactly as they had when the crew first landed. There was nothing there. No bodies. No blood. Not even a drift of black dust where a revenant had been cut down.

"They cleaned up after themselves," Rapscallion said.

"They had no problem trashing the center," Parker pointed out. "So why clean the streets? There must have been bodies out here. The ones you pushed off the roof. The ones that quadcopter popped."

"They must have taken them with them. Like the one Zhang was looking at."

"Yeah," Parker said.

Rapscallion didn't actually like being out in the town, especially with no backup. He moved quickly, checking a couple of housing units, then hurried toward the auditorium. Nothing had changed there. It was like the night just hadn't happened.

"I wonder if the revenants are nocturnal," Parker said. "They go inside during the day."

"Why?" the robot asked.

"I don't know. Their skin is pretty pale; maybe they're afraid of getting sunburnt. Maybe their eyes are too sensitive or something. Let's head back and find Zhang. See what he thinks."

Zhang listened to what they'd found, and their thoughts on why the revenants seemed to be nocturnal. "Interesting hypothesis," he said. "It lines up pretty well with what we saw. They left us alone all day and then only attacked once the sun went down."

"Except the one who bit you," Rapscallion pointed out.

"Maybe that was just an accident," Zhang said. "I stumbled into it while it was sleeping. An animal in its den might feel cornered and become violent."

"You still thinking this might all be a misunderstanding?" Rapscallion asked. "That they would have been friendly if we hadn't killed one of theirs first?"

"No," Zhang said. "Petrova told me . . . Never mind what she said. The revenants want us dead. I don't know if that's all they want, though. They're not completely mindless. The fact they recover bodies suggests they have some level of instinct, if not actual culture. They have some drive to take care of their dead."

"Doc," Parker pointed out, "did you see how they acted last night? They've got no sense of self-preservation. They just attacked and didn't seem to care how hard we fought back. That doesn't seem like human levels of intelligence to me."

Zhang grunted in frustration. "I didn't claim their behavior was rational." He rubbed at his chin. "Something occurs to me. If we had a way to track the bodies, we might be able to find out where the revenants went. Rapscallion, is there a way to track an individual person on Paradise-1?"

"A revenant?" the robot asked. "I mean, they're not exactly listed on a database somewhere."

"Perhaps not," Zhang said. "But Kenji Yoshida might be."

Parker grinned. "Oh, that's smart. That's really smart, Doc. Yeah, the colonists have implants, devices built into their hands. If you know their ID tag codes, yeah. You could track them down to like the square-meter scale."

"I'm checking satellite data," Rapscallion said. "There's a synchronous satellite almost directly overhead. It watches the whole colony and should be able to find Yoshida's tag. There. Got it." He created a map graphic and sent it to a holoscreen so Zhang could see it. "The body's about twelve kilometers outside of town. East by north-east."

"What are you doing?"

The three of them looked up in surprise. Petrova had come into the room. It felt like they'd been caught doing something improper by their mom. "Uh," Parker said, "we're just . . . we're tracking where the bodies went. Yoshida's body, anyway."

"You think he just climbed off your exam table and walked, what?" She checked the map on the screen. "Twelve kilometers from here?"

"No," Zhang said. "Undead or not, there's no way he could have walked all that distance on his own. Not to be too graphic, but he was in pieces. So were some of the revenants we fought last night. I think we can operate on the assumption that the revenants that are still mobile are moving the damaged bodies."

She walked over to where they were huddled around the map. "They grabbed the bodies and ran for the hills." She looked thoughtful. "This could be really helpful. Good work. Whose idea was this?"

Zhang answered before Parker could say anything. "It was a team effort," he told her.

# 25

Zhang watched in fascination as Rapscallion hunched over the 3D printer. The robot's new body was nearly finished – only a few last pieces were still taking shape on the printer's flatbed. He'd clearly taken the opportunity to try out a new design. The hand-crab was gone, its parts recycled. The new body was almost eerily humanoid, except the fingers were long and ended in sharply pointed claws. The back and shoulders were covered in spiky plates like armor.

"I'm thinking we're going to be doing more fighting," Rapscallion pointed out. "I wanted to be ready."

"I suppose that's …," Zhang said. He shook his head. "Likely."

Rapscallion reached over and patted him on the shoulder. Carefully, so as not to rend his flesh. "You okay, Doc? You look preoccupied."

Zhang glanced behind him. He'd last seen Petrova hard at work at a holoscreen in the main room. "I suppose I am. It doesn't matter."

"Hey, while you're here. I'm supposed to give you this." Rapscallion brought out a specimen tray. It held what Zhang thought at first was a toy. A toy gun. It was all smooth edges and sharp seams, with a short barrel and a thick trigger guard. At least it wasn't bright green, instead having been formed of an ugly grayish-yellow plastic with streaks of marbling running through it. Lying next to it were three clips of ammunition. The bullets inside were bright metal.

Zhang picked up the weapon and studied it. "I assume the pattern for this wasn't stored in the medical center's printer."

"No, I designed that for you. Do you like it?"

Not in the slightest. Zhang had never held a gun before. Guns were symbols to him, symbols of an oppressive government that was willing to sacrifice its citizens in the name of order. He felt slightly nauseated just holding the thing.

He knew Petrova must have told Rapscallion to print it. She wanted him armed. Like the robot, she expected more fighting in their future. Delightful.

"I have no idea how this works," he said.

"It's pretty basic. You want something dead? You point this end at the thing, then pull this part. It's called a trigger."

"Hmm. Thank you for that," Zhang told the robot. "I was more concerned about how to aim properly. How not to shoot off my own foot. That sort of thing."

"There's a safety," Petrova said. She had come up behind him so quietly he hadn't noticed she was there. He only flinched a little. "Let me show you." She reached over and touched a little selector pin on the side of the weapon. "Push it this way and the trigger mechanism is locked. Push it back when you want to fire."

He looked her in the eye. What he saw there made him sigh, just a little. He knew he'd been harsh on her. But if she expected an apology . . .

"You don't like this," she said. "I understand. You're a healer, not a fighter."

"It's not that." At least it wasn't all that. "I know you're just trying to keep me safe. I can appreciate that."

She started to smile. How easy it would be to simply tell her everything was okay. That they were good. Even if that wasn't how he really felt.

"I'm just afraid," he said. "This makes me more scared than I was before. Because it means we're going to be in danger again.

Forget it. I'll learn to live with it. If we're going to survive here I'll have to. What a depressing thought."

"Maybe I can do something about that," she said. "I've got a plan."

"Oh?"

"Yeah?" Rapscallion said, and Zhang winced again. He'd all but forgotten the robot was in the room with them.

"Yeah," she said. "We're getting the hell out of here."

# 26

Parker worked the medical center's computer and brought up a holomap. He tilted it until it was horizontal and filled most of the room with a model of the contours of the local hills and mountains, the terrain around the colony town for twenty kilometers in every direction.

He watched as Petrova walked through the map, only visible from the waist up. She touched a tiny representation of the town, then another location: the current position of Kenji Yoshida's body, according to satellite data. "They're headed northwest," she said. "The revenants carrying the body headed out of town, away from our position."

"That's good news, right?" Parker asked.

"I'd like to believe that all the revenants are out there, that none of them are still in town, hiding in dark cupboards and closets. Given our luck, I think that's too much to ask for."

Parker laughed. Zhang and Petrova looked up at him like he'd surprised them.

"Sorry," he said.

"We could stay here, fortify this building," Petrova said. "I don't think that's a good plan, though. We've already seen that the revenants can get in here."

"Definitely not a good plan," Zhang said.

"We can't leave the planet. There's no way to repair the shuttle we came on. Right?" Petrova said, looking at Parker and Rapscallion.

"I wouldn't even know how to start," Parker told her. The robot nodded in agreement.

"So we're stuck on Paradise-1 and this town isn't defensible," she went on. "Luckily there's another place we can go."

She took two steps through the big holomap and touched a spire-like shape in the mountains that looked over the town. "About two kilometers from here, there's a communications tower. The colony's ansible relay."

Parker zoomed in on the map until the hologram tower was nearly as tall as Petrova. It looked like a massive radio antenna with a round habitat module mounted halfway up. "This is the control center," she said. "Not very big, but it's fifty meters up in the air and the only way up is a set of stairs. This is about as defensible a position as we're going to find. Plus, if we want to call Lang and get ourselves rescued, we need to go there anyway. It's the only ansible connection on the planet." Meaning the only way to send a message back to Earth faster than the speed of light. Otherwise any call for help would take nearly a century to reach the director. "Right now, it seems to be down. I'm hoping we can get it back online. Get a message out."

"You say it's two kilometers from here," Zhang said, gesturing at the map. "What's the expression? As the crow flies?"

Petrova nodded. She ran a finger down the slope of the holographic mountain. "It'll take a fair amount of climbing to get there. We can do it in about six hours, I think. If we leave now, we can make it before nightfall."

Parker frowned. "Uh, most of us can. Zhang's barely able to walk."

"I'll be fine," the doctor insisted.

"Really? Because I saw you limping when you came in the room."

"Let me worry about that," Zhang said.

Petrova nodded. "Think about what we want to take with us, but we need to pack light. Food and water are the main things. I have no idea if there are any supplies there. We bring everything we can carry. Medical supplies wouldn't hurt, and weapons."

"What happens if we don't make it by dark?" Parker asked.

"I don't want to find out. So we need to get moving. No more questions," Petrova said. "Understood?"

"Not so much a question. An observation," Rapscallion said. "The quadcopter that helped us last night. Should we try to make contact with whoever that was?"

"I don't know who was operating it or what their agenda is," Petrova said. "They didn't want to talk to us."

"It would be good to have an ally," Parker pointed out.

"Yeah, it would. It's their move to make, though. If they want to work with us, they need to let us know. I'm sticking to what I know for now. Things I can actually count on." She looked around the room. "Like the three of you. Now go! Get packed! We're out of here in ten minutes."

She strode across the map and out of the room. Parker switched off the holodisplay.

"You look happy," Zhang told him.

Was he grinning? Probably. Parker grinned a lot. "It looks like she's back," he said. "That's good, right? We may not be lucky." He shrugged. "But we have her."

# 27

Zhang moved through the patient rooms upstairs, looking for anything useful. The revenants had destroyed all of the portable equipment he might have wanted to take with him – tissue stimulators, autoinjectors ... they'd even torn open the long foil strips of transdermal patches and spilled vials of gene therapy serum on the floor. It was an absolute desecration and it left him feeling demoralized.

He was not looking forward to spending all day climbing a mountain.

"Your leg," Rapscallion pointed out. "It's not going to work for this, is it? You still need time to heal."

"Petrova intends to do it with one functional arm. I'll be fine," Zhang told the robot. Then he did a double-take. "What are you doing?"

Rapscallion had opened a hatch on his abdomen and was rummaging around inside. It looked like he had torn open his own stomach and was checking on its contents. "I'm installing a new module. You done with this room? I want to go across the hall."

Zhang frowned, but he had to admit defeat. "Sure. Maybe the wreckage isn't quite so dire over there." He followed the robot to the other room, which had of course been trashed thoroughly. He found a modesty garment that had been torn in half. It was almost like the revenants knew what they were doing and had wanted to leave him with no useful supplies at all. "What did you want over here?" he asked.

Rapscallion climbed up on the bed. Its sheets were torn and grimy with black dust, so Zhang didn't bother to protest. The robot reached up to the ceiling and grabbed what Zhang had thought was a light fixture. With one quick yank, he pulled it out, exposed wires and all. Sparks jumped from the hole the fixture left behind, and somewhere below them, Zhang heard Parker shout in surprise.

The robot climbed back down to the floor, then showed Zhang his prize, a complicated piece of electronics studded with tiny emitter plates and what looked like a bunch of plastic grapes.

"Hard-light holoprojector," Rapscallion explained.

"So Parker can interact with the world even when we're moving," Zhang said, nodding. At least someone had come up with a good idea.

Rapscallion pulled a pair of wires out of his body and attached them to the exposed cables on the projector. "Parker," he said, "can you try this out?"

The ghost appeared in the room with them, looking confused. Then he saw the unit in Rapscallion's hands and laughed. "Buddy, you're the best," he said. He walked over to the bed and grabbed one end of a torn sheet. With a flourish, he pulled it around his shoulders like a cape. "Look at me."

"Good, it works," Rapscallion said.

Zhang reached for Parker's hand. His fingers still passed through the ghost's flesh. Parker looked embarrassed and held his hand up. "Try now."

The hand was solid when Zhang reached for it again. Cool to the touch, though, and the texture felt a little off. The hard-light version wasn't as springy as human skin, and he couldn't feel any hair on the hand even though the hologram clearly had hair on his knuckles.

"The resolution isn't perfect, not with just one projector, but it's a hell of a lot better than nothing."

"Interesting," Zhang said. "Tell me, do you ever get phantom pain? Like perhaps a feeling of pins and needles in your extremities? Maybe muscle cramps in muscles you don't have anymore?"

"No," Parker said. He scowled. "Come on! Just you saying that is going to make it happen, isn't it? Like the placebo effect or whatever. I won't be able to stop thinking about phantom pain, so my brain will just manifest it."

"If that happens, let me know. There are a number of effective psychological therapies for—"

"Jesus, Doc, you really need to learn when somebody's telling a joke. Anyway, I'm more worried about that leg of yours. You sure you're going to be able to keep up, or is Rapscallion going to have to carry you?"

"I'll manage," Zhang said. He was done looking for supplies. He headed down to the main floor and found Petrova standing outside in the morning sun, looking up at the mountains.

At first he considered lingering inside the medical center. He didn't want to be the first one out there with her. He didn't want to try to make small talk when he was still so angry with her. He decided that was foolish, though. He was going to need to work with her if they were going to get through this. Just surviving long enough to be rescued would take cooperation. He stepped out into the light and stood next to her.

"I wish I had a pair of binoculars," she said. "You can't see the comms tower from here. I think it's just over that rise." She pointed at a ridgeline just below the peaks of the mountains. "It should be easy enough to find once we get close."

He nodded. "I think we're ready to go," he told her. "Maybe we should get to it."

"No time like the present?" she said. She gave him a long, searching look. He kept his eyes trained on the mountains. "Yeah. Yeah, that's the smart thing."

She turned and called over her shoulder. Parker appeared instantly, like a puppy dog when it hears its master talking about going outside. Rapscallion appeared a moment later, heavy packs dangling from his shoulders.

"You guys get moving. That way," she said, pointing at a road that led to the edge of town. Once they'd started off, she turned to Zhang and glanced down at his leg. "You're still limping. I worry about you – if your wound reopens while we're hiking..."

He cleared his throat, then reached across his body, left arm to right thigh. He didn't need to say anything. The RD unwove itself from around his arm and flowed down to his leg, wrapping its tendrils around his thigh and forming a sturdy brace for his knee. It was kind enough to inject him with a mild analgesic before what came next.

The golden snakes adopted their final positions, then constricted, squeezing tightly around his muscles and locking themselves in place. He grimaced through the pain but refused to make a sound. Once it was done, he was able to walk almost normally.

It just hurt like hell.

"That way?" he asked, and followed after the robot and the ghost.

Petrova brought up the rear, just far enough behind him that they didn't have to pretend to chat while they walked.

# 28

Rapscallion didn't understand humans. He'd accepted this a long time ago. He was never going to truly comprehend why they did the things they did – their psychology was outside the rational laws that he had internalized about the universe. When they did weird things, which was pretty much all the time, he just let it go. Chalked it up to some kind of innate human quality that couldn't be factored into equations.

When they stopped at the edge of town and looked back, he understood they were stalling. This was entirely at odds with their plan to reach the comms tower as quickly as possible. Yet he stood there and waited while they worked through their emotions.

None of them said anything. They looked back at the town as if it belonged to them, or as if they were going to miss the place. That seemed highly unlikely. Then they turned and looked at the path ahead of them.

There was no clear dividing line between town and countryside. The houses and streets stopped at some point, but beyond that lay a few outbuildings, a shed or two. Then, nothing. Nothing made by humans, nothing that wasn't original to the planet itself. Nothing except the track ahead of them.

It was a clear trail, though unpaved. A narrow lane worn through the native rock, a little brighter, a little smoother than the surrounding terrain. It wound upward through heaps of igneous rock, disappearing behind the promontory of a dark ridge. The wind howled down from off the mountain's peak, blowing toward them like a sepulchral voice bellowing a warning from the beyond.

"Spooky," Rapscallion said, thinking he would break the tension with a joke. "Ooo, spoooooky..."

"Stop," Petrova said, in a tone of command.

The robot was happy to comply.

Petrova was the first to cross the imaginary line and start hiking up into the mountains. The others followed quickly, as if afraid of being left behind.

Parker hated planets. Always had.

He was a pilot. Born to be one. He'd been born on a space station around Neptune, a cramped tin can with too few windows. He had flown away into space as soon as they let him and never looked back. Space was big, and yes, it was brutal. It could kill you in so many ways, but none of them were surprises. Planets, on the other hand, were deathtraps. You could take one false step and die at the bottom of a cliff. Water rushing downhill could sweep you away.

Those were childish fears, he knew, and he had outgrown them. Mostly. As an adult, though, he still couldn't help but feel trapped. Pinned to the ground. Even without a body, even when he didn't have to worry about the dangers, he still wished he could be up there in the endless black instead.

The trail snaked its way up the mountain through constant switchbacks and doglegs. It would run almost level for a hundred meters, then dodge through a series of defiles in the rock that left Petrova and Zhang gasping for breath. In some places they had to haul themselves up with their hands as much as their feet. All the vehicles in town had been sabotaged, and Parker had wondered if that had been done to keep people trapped in the low ground at the base of these mountains. Vehicles would have been useless up here, though. This wasn't a hike, it was a climb.

The scenery lacked any kind of interest. Just rock, endless

narrow cuts through brown-black igneous rock. Rock that had been lava once, then cooled so fast it still looked liquid, like crashing waves. Rock in thick extruded slabs that lay stacked on top of each other like slices of bread; rock that formed rows of sharp spires, like evil little churches lined up on either side of a far too narrow street; rock so jumbled and chaotic the eye just bounced off it, unable to find meaningful patterns at all. The trail was made of ground-up bits of that same rock, and dusty as hell. The sound of the others trudging through that scree, the constant crunch, crunch, crunch, crunch, rivaled the never-ending wind for eeriness. If there had been some kind of broad sweeping vista, an outlook over a breathtaking mountainscape, that might have been one thing, but the trail was too sinuous for that, dug too deep into the rock so you could never see past the next rise. The rock was so colorless and rough it drank the light that poured down out of the intense blue sky, so it was easy to think you were crossing a narrow bridge over an abyss, and equally easy to think the wind might tear you off your feet and send you screaming into that blue radiance.

They kept moving. What else could they do? Petrova and Zhang saved their breath for the hike, and said not one word to Parker or each other. Rapscallion was oddly quiet, only sharing the occasional bit of data with him, telling him they had climbed another ten vertical meters, or how much daylight was left (it didn't sound like enough).

When the rocks changed color, it was so subtle at first that Parker didn't notice. At some point he saw that wherever there was a flat stretch of rock, it would be dappled with little yellow circles, pale at their edges and more colorful at the center. If he looked at them closely (through Rapscallion's eyes, of course), he saw they had a slightly frilly texture, like paper ruffled by exposure to the rain. He'd seen something like them before, some kind of plant; he had spent so little time on Mars or Earth that it took him ten more minutes to remember they were called lichens. He remembered seeing a picture of them growing on a gravestone once.

A new sound joined the wind and the trudge of boots: a sort of distant roar, like radio interference. As they came around another turn, it grew much, much louder, the roar of an engine, and he saw white water spit out of the rock above him and crash down across the path. A waterfall, splattering the rocks around them, making those rocks darker, smoother. He bent down and used a little hard light to touch them. He couldn't technically feel anything, but he could get a sense of the texture, the slippery rub of the stones.

Petrova rushed forward and dropped to her knees by the water, started to reach for it with her good hand. Zhang shouted at her and then came over, and one of his golden snakes dipped its head in the foam. After a second, Zhang nodded and then dropped down next to her. The two of them lifted the water to their mouths, sucked greedily at it, slapped it on their cheeks and scrubbed at the black dust on their foreheads, their chins. Rapscallion filled the barrel he carried slung over one shoulder.

And as quick as that, they moved on, and soon the yellow raindrops of the lichen were gone, and there was nothing but black rock again.

Another twenty vertical meters – and another hour – and they stopped again. This time the trail narrowed, turned to just a ledge that curled around a vast opening in the side of the mountain, a dark cave beneath a rough, slanting overhang. Petrova's hand drifted down to the weapon on her belt as they edged their way along, her face passing into shadow as Parker listened to the wind rush in and out of the cave. It must have been a lava tube once, now partially collapsed, but who knew how deep it might still run, down into the mountain, into the crust of Paradise-1. Parker lacked any kind of sense of smell, but Rapscallion had a spectrometer that let him register the chemicals floating on the air. Carbon dioxide came wafting up out of that dark passage, rich with simple esters and more complicated organic compounds.

Yeast, thought Parker. If he could smell it, the breath of the planet would smell like yeast. More life, like the lichen they'd seen. Life conspicuous in its rarity. There should have been green plants growing everywhere, there should have been silver fish writhing their way through the places where the water pooled. Grass, insects. Trees, something. But no.

Nothing emerged from the cave to grab at them and drag them inside, no red eyes glinted at them from the murk. The yeast smell faded as they climbed higher, got away from the cave. It kept tugging at Parker's mind, though. Drawing him back, making him remember the shape of its deep shadow, the sense of its endless descent. As creepy as it might have been, the mountain's pore had at least broken up the monotony.

Another hour of it, of constant climbing. Another and Petrova called for a break. They found a place where the trail opened onto a broad ledge with high rocks on either side to shelter it from the wind. There was no pretense of making camp. Petrova dropped to sit with her back against the mountain. Zhang lay stretched out across the ground, like he wanted to just fall into sleep, deep, dreamless sleep. Rapscallion climbed a little higher, looking out, just making sure, then he climbed back down and squatted on his haunches, his fists balled, knuckles touching the rock. He looked like he might power down, though Parker knew the robot wasn't tired. Couldn't get tired, as long as his batteries stayed charged.

Which meant Parker couldn't get tired either. He walked back and forth along the ledge, too aimlessly to be pacing. Just wanting to keep moving because the alternative was to stop, to just stop and fade into the landscape.

Petrova looked up at him, annoyed, and gestured for him to sit next to her. He nestled in close, using hard light to create a shoulder, an arm for her to lean on. He felt her relax into him, her jaw muscle losing tension against him, and he was glad he could be that for her, at least. Something to prop her up.

After a while, she reached over, her real fingers weaving through fingers he created out of nothing. He couldn't make his skin warm, couldn't warm her up, but she didn't complain.

They didn't rest for long. Soon enough they were back up, moving again. Zhang took a while to get to his feet, but every time Rapscallion offered him a hand, he would just wave it off; every time Petrova asked if he was okay, he just shook his head. They set off once more, at the same pace as before. Climbing up, always up the mountain.

# 30

Zhang was only dimly aware of his surroundings. He barely registered the rock formations, the occasional trickle of water. He was focused on exactly one thing: left foot, right foot. Left foot, right. Keep them moving. Keep up, keep pace.

He didn't even notice when someone came and started walking beside him. It could have been one of his many ghosts, one of the people he'd lost. With a jolt he became aware it was an actual person when she spoke to him.

"It's a bad joke. It's cruel," Petrova said. "Calling this place Paradise."

He didn't want to respond. He wanted to conserve his energy. He had not been ready for a hike like this, how strenuous it was going to be. Less than an hour after they'd started, he had seen dark spots swim through his vision. He gasped for breath so hard his throat felt frozen, painfully abraded. He could hear his own heartbeat, a machine pounding away inside his ribcage, doling out little dribs and drabs of pain.

"If I think about Paradise, I think fluffy white clouds and people with wings. Or maybe green fields, birds and animals and way more water. Even the sun here is the wrong color."

He would gladly have remained silent, but it didn't seem to be an option. She was going to keep talking until he replied.

"You think 'paradise' means 'heaven'," he said.

"Well – yes. It doesn't?"

"No," Zhang told her, between gasps for breath. "I thought the same thing. Before. Before we came here. I looked it up. The word originally meant . . ." he tried to remember the exact phrasing, "walled garden."

"Garden," she said. "Like Eden."

He nodded.

As old as the rocks around them looked, they were brand new in geological time. This was a planet just born, a place only beginning to grow. "Life just started here," he rasped. On Earth, every drop of water, every shaded hollow was thronged with organisms big and small. Here life was still the exception, something unusual. Earth had, in fact, looked like this four billion years ago, when the first microbes climbed up out of the sheltering seas and learned to grow in the sun.

Zhang was a doctor, not a molecular biologist. He had no way of knowing when the lichen they'd seen had first appeared. A million years ago, or a hundred million? Maybe more. It would have been a very, very long time before anything more complex had evolved on Paradise-1, however, of that he was sure.

"You're saying," Petrova went on, because apparently she was in a mood to talk, "this place is brand new. Innocent."

He raised an eyebrow. "Innocent? No."

It wasn't until later, when they'd found another waterfall, that he was able to explain what he meant. Once they'd drunk their fill – climbing was thirsty work – and cleaned themselves up a little, he brought her over to where the lichen grew thickest on the rocks, in the spray of the falls. "Touch this," he said, and put his hand on the cold rock. She did the same, then looked down at her hand in disgust.

"What is this?" she asked. She held up her hand to show him her thumb and index finger. Stretching between them were thin, colorless strands of what looked like mucus. "I thought the rock was just wet. This is sticky. What did you just make me touch?"

"A biofilm," he said. "I noticed it before. It's a colony of single-celled organisms. Growing so thickly together they create a kind of slime." It was always a danger to think that alien creatures would act the same as lifeforms from Earth; that you could apply the lessons of terrestrial biology to xenolife. When it came to biofilms, though, Zhang thought he was probably on safe ground. "They work together, in a way. They excrete a digestive enzyme that breaks down the lichen into basic sugars. You asked if this place was innocent. No. Species devouring each other. Literally melting one another to make food." He shook his head. "Life is never innocent."

She gave him a nasty look. "Is this how you get back at me? Make me touch something disgusting?"

"I was angry," Zhang said, with a nod. "I got over it. Mostly."

"Disappointed, then," she said. "You're disappointed in me for trying to use the basilisk against the revenants."

He sighed. "You did what you thought was best."

"I wanted to save us. That's all."

He nodded. "Yes. I understand. You did what you thought was best. That's the problem, though. You thought that was best."

"Zhang," she said, and reached for him.

He shied away. Zhang didn't like to be touched. "Maybe we can talk about this when I can breathe. When I don't feel like I want to die."

She nodded and left him alone. He washed his hand in the falls. Took another long, deep drink of the freezing-cold water, then adjusted his pack and headed up the trail once more.

# 31

Rapscallion had gotten too far ahead of the others. The humans were slowing down as the day wore on, while he could maintain the same pace until he literally had to stop and power down. He glanced back and saw Petrova and Zhang, bright shapes on a dark background, and measured that he was nearly half a kilometer ahead.

"Maybe we should let them catch up," Parker said.

The ghost had no choice but to stay close to Rapscallion, since he could only manifest in the range of the holoprojector mounted on the robot's stomach. No matter what kind of pace Rapscallion set, Parker could always keep up.

"Fine," Rapscallion said. He locked his knees and started to switch himself into standby mode. It seemed Parker wanted some conversation, though.

"We're not going to make it, are we?" he asked. "Before nightfall."

Rapscallion considered how to answer that question. "We aren't making as good time as Petrova hoped. That's true. It's possible that the trail gets easier from here, and we can make up the difference."

"You know that's not likely."

Rapscallion knew it. The climb was only getting steeper the higher they got in the mountains. The going would be tougher, not easier. Zhang was already struggling with the more strenuous parts of the hike.

"He's slowing us down," Parker said. Before Rapscallion could respond, he lifted his hands for peace. "I love the guy, you know I do. I'm not criticizing him. If I was still in a body, I would be having just as much trouble."

"I don't understand. Zhang has an injured leg," the robot pointed out.

"That's not the only problem. He wasn't born for this. This planet has less gravity than Earth, sure. But Zhang grew up on Ganymede, lived on Titan. Moons where he weighed a fraction of what he does here. Petrova grew up on Earth, but Zhang doesn't have leg muscles like she does, he doesn't have the stamina, the wind. I'm honestly surprised he's made it this far. Look at him. He looks about as dead as one of those revenants."

Rapscallion zoomed in on the doctor's face and saw it was true. Not literally true, but when talking to humans, the literal truth was almost never the important kind. "What are you suggesting?"

"We should stop and make camp before the sun goes down," Parker said.

When Petrova caught up with them, the ghost and the robot told her just the same.

"What?" she asked. Her face was bright, flushed with exertion. Parker was glad he had no sense of smell – she'd been sweating all day and wasn't very fresh. "Make camp? Out here? You've both lost it."

"It's the only choice," Rapscallion said. "I ran through the models. Looked at possible outcomes. You can march until Zhang falls down on the spot and dies, and you still won't make it to the tower before nightfall."

Petrova scowled. "We're not fucking stopping. We'll make it."

# 32.

Zhang didn't remember opening his eyes, but he was awake. He was lying on his back, in semi-darkness, and he didn't remember lying down either.

"What?" he asked, because he was just about able to form one word. His head buzzed and his eyes kept drifting closed, but he struggled to sit up, to figure out where he was.

"Shh," Rapscallion said. The robot squatted down next to him and handed him a water bottle. "It's okay."

The light was strange. Zhang sipped at the water and then slowly, carefully looked around, trying to take in his surroundings. The darkness was not quite complete. What looked like a numinous cloud hung above him, unmoving, unchanging.

He decided he was going to get up, on his feet.

"Hey, relax," Rapscallion said.

Zhang ignored him. He pushed himself up until his feet were underneath him, until he was standing upright. He nearly smacked his head on the ceiling, but jerked back just in time. That aggravated his sore muscles, but he tried not to care.

Above him, almost touching his upturned face, was the glowing cloud. It turned out to be bioluminescent fungal life, or something like fungus. The Paradisal version of autotrophic non-photosynthesizing sessile eukaryotic life.

It was beautiful. It formed endless patterns on the ceiling, a little like flowers, a lot like something he'd never seen before, intricate and variable and undesigned. It glowed with a soft blue light so intense, so deeply dark and yet vibrant that he expected it to buzz, to give off some kind of sound. But of course it was perfectly, eternally silent.

"We're in a lava tube," he said. "How far down?"

"We're about three hundred meters in," Rapscallion told him. "Petrova wanted to get well out of view. This tube runs pretty far, pretty deep. I've been exploring and I still haven't found the end of it."

Zhang nodded. "Did you carry me in here?"

"No. You never stopped walking. Not until Petrova personally told you that you were allowed to stop."

Zhang rubbed at his face with his hands. "Petrova . . ."

"I'm here," she said. "Parker?"

The hologram flared into life, dazzling Zhang for a second until his eyes adjusted to the sudden glare. Parker's ghost wasn't bright enough to illuminate the entire tunnel, but it could show Zhang that Petrova sat very close by, had been close the entire time. She smiled up at him.

"I . . . I couldn't . . ." Zhang bit back the words. They tasted bitter. "I wasn't strong enough. I'm so sorry. You had to stop because of me, you're at risk because of me."

Her smile kept growing. It looked like she might start laughing. "Zhang," she said. "Shut up. Save your energy. And for God's sake, sit down."

He lowered himself back to the floor. She handed him some food, a kind of pressed oatcake. It was sweet and gooey and he made mortifying noises as he choked it down. Rapscallion handed him the water bottle again and he chugged at it, feeling foolish. Feeling like a child who got tired out at the playground and had to be carried home.

Except Rapscallion said he'd kept walking until he was told to stop. Maybe he hadn't completely embarrassed himself.

"It was my idea to stop for the night," Petrova told him. "My order, anyway. I was in just as bad shape as you were." That was almost certainly a lie, but a kind one. "We were three hours from the tower and the sun was going down. I didn't want to walk for three hours in the dark. You tried to convince me it would be fine."

"I did?"

She nodded. "You told me you wouldn't stop until I ordered you to. You know what, Zhang?"

He shrugged.

"You're one tough son of a bitch. Here." She handed him another oatcake and he shoved it into his mouth all in one ridiculous bite.

# 33

In the dark, Rapscallion crouched down next to Zhang. "I'm sure you just want to sleep, but I have something for you, Doc," the robot said. "Some data I was able to scrape out of the medical center's computers before we left."

"You found something?" Zhang asked. "Have you shown it to Petrova?"

"She looked at it, but she thought you might like to see it too. It's the colony doctor's personal log, so she thought you might have some insight. It's just scraps. Fragments."

Zhang nodded. The robot could see the gesture just fine, even in the darkness of the lava tube. "Okay. Let me see."

"Hear, actually. It's a voice recording. Compressed down to hell – hidden deep in the medical center's server. That's probably why I was able to get so much of it. There's a bunch of data here, most of which I won't bore you with. Just logs of procedures and drugs dispensed, real dry stuff. There's one part that gets juicy, though. The part Petrova thought you should hear."

"I'll admit I'm intrigued," Zhang said.

Rapscallion played the audio he'd recovered. It was choppy, broken up into short snippets, but it was enough to get an idea of what the doctor saw.

. . . DEHYDRATION. KEEP THIS ONE ON SALINE, WE'LL SEE IF THE OTHER ONE WAKES UP AND CAN TAKE

SOME LIQUIDS BY MOUTH. WHAT THE HELL ARE THEY DOING UP THERE? WAIT, WAIT. PUT THIS IN MY PERSONAL NOTES, I DON'T WANT IT ON THE OFFICIAL RECORD. I DON'T WANT SOME FIREWATCH SECRET POLICEMAN READING THIS AND DECIDING THE ONLY DOCTOR IN THE COLONY HAS GONE . . .

. . . THREE MEN FROM THE MINE BROUGHT IN TO MY CLINIC. THAT WAS WEIRD ENOUGH. WE NEVER SEE THEM, THEY KEEP TO THEMSELVES OUT THERE. THEY DON'T COME TO TOWN UNLESS THEY'RE LOOKING TO GET DRUNK. WHEN THE CALL CAME, I THOUGHT IT MUST HAVE BEEN A CAVE-IN OR . . .

. . . SUBJECTS ALL SHOW EXTREME LETHARGY, OTHERWISE HEALTHY. I GUESS THEY ASSUMED I WAS BETTER EQUIPPED TO CONDUCT A PSYCH EVAL THAN WHATEVER MED ROBOT THEY'RE USING OVER THERE. SHIFT SUPERVISOR SAID THEY HAD BEEN ACTING ODD LATELY, DISTRACTED AND "OUT OF IT". SAID HE SUSPECTED DRUGS, BUT TOX SCREENS HAVE ALL COME BACK . . .

. . . DEHYDRATION AND CONFUSION. LARGELY NON-RESPONSIVE TO STIMULI, THOUGH REFLEXES REMAIN SOUND. SEEMED HEALTHY ENOUGH ON ARRIVAL, BUT JUST A FEW HOURS LATER . . .

. . . EXTREME PALLOR. I'D CALL IT LIVIDITY IF . . .

. . . WHAT THE FUCK? THOSE EYES. I'VE NEVER SEEN THIS LEVEL OF . . .

Zhang stared at Rapscallion, his eyes huge in the gloom. "Do you have any metadata on this?" he asked the robot. "A date, maybe? The name of the doctor?"

"You're lucky I was able to recover this much. When I found the data, it was just scraps of data. I had to put it back together like a jigsaw puzzle. If I had to guess, I'd say that was recorded before the massacre. Before they started wiping the town's records."

"It sounds like this is the first time anyone saw a revenant," Zhang said. "Is this all of it?"

"There's more, but I need more time to put it together," Rapscallion said.

Zhang nodded. "Three men brought in from the mine."

"Something about that strike you as funny?"

Zhang took a second to respond. "This was an agricultural colony. What were they doing with a mine? What were they mining for?"

The robot spread his hands in the dark. "Beats me."

# 34

Just before dawn, Petrova took point as they headed deeper into the lava tube, looking for its end.

It had been Zhang's idea. He'd wanted desperately to see more of what the planet looked like underground. This was where most of the lifeforms probably lived, after all. Where evolution was happening. Rapscallion had suggested they come back in a few billion years and see how that turned out, and she'd thought the robot was joking. Then she remembered that robots were functionally immortal. It was just possible that Rapscallion would one day see what came of the funk that filled the tube with its spores.

They headed down, into a tunnel that grew increasingly warm and odorous. Sometimes the smell was almost maddeningly familiar, like fresh bread or rotten bananas. Often it was unimaginable, so weird and off-putting Petrova wanted to turn around and head back. The look on Zhang's face spurred her on, though.

He was no biologist, he kept insisting. He wasn't a scientist at all, not really, and certainly not the kind who specialized in this kind of life. Yet he was so clearly entranced by what they saw, even if it seemed like very little of anything to her. A stain on a wall, a patch of the bioluminescent ceiling mold that was a different color, or even just a different shade of blue, meant to Zhang a whole new species, a new branch on the Paradisal tree of life.

And then they came to the cave.

The tube had been roughly cylindrical for most of its length, or like a semi-squashed oval where time and gravity had started pulling the ceiling down. Petrova had fully expected that they would come to a place where it pinched off, or the rocks above had collapsed, and that would be the end of their journey. Instead, after about twenty minutes of walking, she found that it had only grown wider, bigger, until their footfalls echoed off a glowing ceiling she could hardly see. Parker's light barely stretched from wall to wall, and then it simply didn't.

There was no strict dividing line, but they had gone from a tunnel to a cavern. Stalactites hung from the ceiling, hundreds of them, thinner and longer than seemed proper to her Earthborn eyes. The floor underneath her sloped downward until it became the edge of a lightless lake. Water, black and perfectly mirror-smooth, lay before them, blocking their way.

Zhang dropped to his knees and took a sample of that water in a small tube. He shook the tube until three lights lit up on the end of it, two green and one red. The red light indicated the presence of mildly toxic chemicals in the water, so they kept their distance.

Petrova asked Rapscallion to shine a light over the lake, and the robot showed them that the water stretched out as far as their light could travel, and presumably farther. Where the light touched that water, it grew milky and pale, colorless but full of glittering motes of ... something.

The smell in the cavern was intense, and she found herself breathing through her mouth. She couldn't even describe the odor other than to vaguely compare it to terrestrial things: a wet rag left in a bucket for a week, the smell of her mother's dress uniforms when they came out of cold storage, but, well, more so. Thicker, wetter, danker.

Parker pointed at something, and she looked and saw that across the lake, maybe fifty meters away, the wall opened up into another tunnel, another lava tube. He pointed again at a third tunnel, a fourth. It was like tunnels from all over Paradise-1 converged here, in this wet place. How much of the planet's crust was riddled with lava tubes? How far down did they go?

Zhang gasped, and she looked around.

"Did you see it? In the water?"

She didn't see anything. She hadn't seen anything.

"Just a shadow, or ... or something, but ..."

Then she did see something. Ripples. Before, the surface of the lake might have been one solid sheet of perfect alabaster, a warm, flat surface, unbreakable, imperturbable. Now it was disturbed by the slightest ripple, a wave of glass rolling across its top. It broke at the edge where their tunnel began, the slop rolling up toward the toes of her boots.

"Something moved down there, in the water," Zhang breathed.

"We should go," Parker said.

They climbed back up, out, and soon Petrova's calves started protesting, her thighs burned. She had spent much of the previous day walking, and now her legs were annoyed that she clearly intended to spend this day doing the same. They wanted to let her know they didn't approve. She took deep breaths, trying to get more oxygen to her muscles. It was all she could do for them. Honestly, she was looking forward to getting back to climbing, to the three or so hours they had ahead of them in the sunshine. The night in the dark tunnel had been long, and she hadn't slept well and—

"Shh," Rapscallion said, very softly. He gestured for them to stop, and they did.

They stood very still, waiting. Listening. Until Petrova heard it.

Dripping. Water pattering on the floor of the tunnel. Behind them.

"Zhang?" she whispered.

He could only shrug. "We haven't seen anything more complicated than lichens so far. No animal life at all. The planetary survey said there might be some small insects, but ..."

The thing behind them was bigger than a small insect. She was sure of that.

The echoes were coming closer. The dripping didn't stop, and now she heard what she was sure were footfalls. The shadow under the water, whatever had made those ripples, she thought. She tried to imagine what it could have been, what kind of creature.

Bad idea. In her head, it was three meters tall and mostly made of teeth. She pushed that image away.

It kept coming back.

"You two," she said, waving at Rapscallion and Parker, telling them to move up against the right-hand wall of the tunnel. "Zhang," she said, and gestured for him to get behind her. She dropped to a crouch and drew her weapon.

The echoes might be right behind them, or kilometers away. It was impossible to be sure. They were getting closer, though. They had to be.

"Parker," she whispered. "When I say, give it everything you've got, as much light as you can make."

"Got it," he said.

The dripping was so loud now it drowned out his whisper. It had to be right behind them, had to be close enough to see, if she just had a little more light.

The footfalls slapped on the rock. Was the thing moving faster?

"Now!" she called.

Light flooded the tunnel, picking out every irregularity in the walls in stark relief, long shadows running out ahead of them. The blue fungus overhead disappeared, washed out by the sudden, brilliant glare that made her eyes hurt. And standing there, in the middle of it, was a little girl.

A child, a human child, maybe ten years old. Her hair and her clothes were soaking wet, and tiny dark circles appeared on the floor as she dripped, dripped, dripped.

Her eyes were solid black. Her skin was the color of the milky water, shot through with black veins. She opened her mouth to show them broken, sharpened teeth.

Petrova didn't think. She didn't have time.

Her hand moved of its own volition, drawing her weapon, aiming. Her finger squeezed the trigger once, twice, three times.

The girl spun around and then dropped to the tunnel floor.

Petrova stood there, watching, waiting for the revenant to climb back up on to her feet. Waiting for the girl to make a noise, to twitch, to move.

Eventually they turned around and hurried up the tunnel, toward the surface, away from the body. Eventually she saw sunlight above them.

They had spent a whole night in the tunnel. Now it was day again, now they were safe, up there on the surface. As they climbed up out of a cave mouth, back up onto the trail, she forced herself not to look back.

# 35

Parker tried to figure it out, just by talking it through. "Was it some kind of scout? Like a spy, keeping tabs on us? How long was it down there?"

"They don't need to breathe," Zhang pointed out. "But that water was pretty acidic. I don't think it was lying down there this whole time, waiting for us."

Parker pursed his lips. Caused his image, his hologram to do so anyway. "Do you think they can . . . you know? Communicate with each other?"

"Telepathically, you mean?" Rapscallion asked.

"I mean, otherwise she can't exactly tell the others where we are," Parker pointed out. "She didn't have a radio or anything. Right?"

"We don't have to talk about this anymore," Petrova said.

So they didn't.

The last stretch of the climb was clearly the hardest for the humans among them. At some point Parker stopped even trying to pretend that his hologram was touching the ground. Mostly he just floated along like the ghost he was. He stayed close to Rapscallion, of course, but the robot could move nimbly, effortlessly up the grade.

They came to a place where a series of steps had been carved into the rock. A staircase that rose at nearly a sixty-degree angle, each step rough-hewn and none of them looking particularly even.

For Petrova and Zhang it took what looked like a superhuman effort to get up that incline. They climbed with all their limbs, hauling themselves upward with their hands, digging in for purchase with their feet like they were scaling a ladder. The slope was only about twelve meters, but it took them far longer than Parker would have expected.

"We have to be getting close," he said, when Petrova reached the top. Zhang had gone first and was already there, waiting for her, his head down between his knees, his chest heaving.

She hauled herself up off the last of the steps, using her cast for leverage then grabbing the rock with her good fingers. She rolled onto her side and glared at him. "No idea. Rapscallion?"

"It's another half a kilometer, that's all," the robot said. It sounded like he was trying to be encouraging.

Petrova drank some water, then handed the bottle to Zhang. "How much of that is vertical?" she asked.

"Most of it," Rapscallion admitted.

There was one more switchback and then the trail just stopped. Whoever had cleared this path, back before the revenants came, had come this far and clearly just given up pretending the rest of the way was walkable. They had left signs etched into the naked rock, mostly arrows and warning symbols suggesting that avalanches were possible and that the climb ahead was treacherous. None of it was much help, Parker thought, but at least it was a reminder they were on the right path. Ahead of them the way led up a rocky slope where any given outcropping might be stable, a piece of the mountain itself jutting out, or might be a boulder just loosely perched on the slope and ready to roll away at the slightest touch.

"We need safety lines," Petrova said. "I've got one good arm, Zhang has one good leg. This is going to suck."

They didn't have much in the way of climbing gear. A few ropes and a few carabiners. Petrova knew a little about mountaineering, but mostly Rapscallion had to tie the ropes into harnesses, and then he had to function as their anchors and pitons as well. He would scamper up the rock like a spider and then secure a line, dropping it back down so they could attach it to their harnesses.

There were ledges where they could rest for a moment, but the pace they needed to keep up meant they were both constantly out of breath. Parker could watch, and sympathize, and help where he could.

At one point Petrova got halfway up a stretch of slope, clutching the line with her good hand, puffing for breath as she lifted her foot to try to find purchase. Her back foot crunched and slipped on a patch of loose dirt, and she flung out her bad hand to try to catch herself. The cast struck a rock, hard. Parker saw a look of agony roll across her face, and drops of sweat rolled off her forehead and got caught in her eyelashes. "I'm alright," she called, her front foot still swinging back and forth as she tried to find a place to put it. "I'm alright, I'm ..."

Her back foot slipped some more, and suddenly she was standing on nothing at all. Her good hand clutched the line, but not hard enough to stop her from sliding backward, her hips smacking into the rock beneath her, her legs kicking wildly. She started to shout, and Parker saw her hand open around the line. Where it had been touching the rope, the skin of her palm was bright red and dotted with blood – friction must have torn her hand open and she couldn't hold on anymore. Rapscallion hauled on the rope, hard, but she was slipping, sliding down, her face dark with rock dust and her eyes wide—

And then suddenly she stopped sliding, caught in mid-fall. Parker looked down and saw that he was holding her, one arm around her waist, the other cradling her head. He hadn't thought it out; he'd just reflexively vanished from where he'd been and then manifested on top of her, holding her. The hard-light projector sent him all kinds of error codes as it struggled to hold her weight, but he ignored it.

She opened her eyes and saw him looking back at her. "Thanks," she said.

She moved her feet, got a better grip on the slope. He let go of her and she fell against the rock, clutching it with her whole body.

"You're welcome," he said, as she started climbing again, wincing every time she grabbed the line with her bleeding hand.

At the next ledge, Zhang washed and treated her new injury, then sprayed some artificial skin across her palm. It took a minute to dry. While they waited, Rapscallion took Parker aside. "She was on a safety harness," the robot said. "She wouldn't have fallen much farther. I would have caught her."

"I know," Parker replied. "It was just a reflex. You see the person you love falling, you jump to grab them. That's all."

Rapscallion played a sound file of a human saying "Ooh la la."

Parker laughed. "What's that supposed to mean?"

The robot shrugged. "I saw humans react that way in a video once. Something about it being simultaneously embarrassing and titillating when one human admits to having romantic feelings for another."

Parker laughed again, but this time to cover some of his embarrassment. He hadn't meant to use ... well, that word. It had just come out.

Once Petrova was ready to move on, they headed up a last, slightly less dangerous slope and then climbed up onto a broad ledge that looked like it had been artificially leveled. A broad red circle had been painted on the ground. Parker recognized that symbol immediately. "This is a quadcopter landing pad," he said. "I guess we know how the colonists used to get up here."

"They sure as hell didn't make that climb if they didn't have to," Petrova said.

A metal staircase led upward from the pad to a broader clearing above them. "Look at that," Parker said, pointing.

The comms tower stood up there, bright where the sunlight caught it. A construction of openwork girders maybe fifty meters tall. Thin, wispy clouds passed behind it, and blue sky beyond that. They had reached their destination.

# 36

To reach the comms tower's operations room you had to climb twenty meters up a narrow ladder, with the wind tearing at you the whole time. Petrova wasn't sure she could have done it if the ladder was on Earth. Paradise-1's lower gravity and a desperate urge to be done climbing got her up the last stretch. A simple trapdoor lay at the top of the ladder. It didn't have a lock or any kind of access panel. She pushed it with her good hand and it swung up and she was able to climb through onto a solid floor. She didn't even bother standing up, just rolled to the side and then reached over to give Zhang a hand as he climbed through after her.

Rapscallion brought up the rear, closing the trapdoor behind him. Then Parker manifested in the middle of the room. "There are hard light holoprojectors here. Nice."

Right. Because that was going to be her first question. She sat up and looked around. The operations room was a single open space, maybe ten meters across. The curved walls were lined with glass that gave an incredible view of the surrounding mountains. You couldn't quite see the colony town, just as they hadn't been able to see the tower from down there, so the landscape outside the windows was an endless panorama of brown rock, streaked with wisps of cloud that cast long, swift-moving shadows. It would have been breathtaking, if she wasn't already gasping for oxygen.

There was something wrong with the view, though. It should have looked like the Himalayas on Earth, or the Rocky Mountains, she thought. Her Earth-bred brain kept looking for things to compare it to, things she recognized.

There was no green out there. Very few of the peaks in the range had snow on them. Just a broad sweep of uninterrupted mountains, broken here and there by the wide dish shapes of impact craters. Something in her brain flip-flopped and she realized the view didn't look wrong at all. It just didn't look like Earth. It looked like Mars.

Then something else moved inside her brain. The basilisk. She felt it turn its attention on the panorama. Nothing it saw surprised it, of course. It had guarded Paradise-1 for many millions of years. It knew what the planet looked like. This was a closer view than it was used to, however. She felt a weird buzzing inside her skull and realized that the parasite had asked her a question, though not exactly in words.

*Where is it?* it asked. Meaning the thing it had been built to guard. The prize that had been hidden from it for so long. It existed only to find that thing now, to know what was so important as to justify its creation.

*Where?*

"Give me a chance," she whispered out loud. "We'll find it. We're looking."

*Look faster.*

Again, no words. Just a buzzing that made her teeth feel like they were grinding together. The meaning was clear, though.

Zhang lay on the floor beside her. He looked up at her with a very serious expression. "Who are you talking to?" he asked.

Parker saved her by speaking before she could. "So. Some bad news. But not, like, new bad news. The same old bad news as before."

She raised an eyebrow at him.

"Come see."

She climbed to her feet, only a little annoyed, and looked where he pointed. There was a workstation in the middle of the room, a desk big enough for two people to work side by side. There were controls for the communications equipment, endless banks of knobs and dials and little screens built into the desk. It looked like you could control the entire planet's communications throughout just from this one location.

Someone had taken a sledgehammer to it. The screens were smashed, just dark squares of broken glass. The knobs were cracked and broken or missing altogether, the gauges and sliding switches pounded in by extreme force.

"Sabotaged," she said.

"The revenants got here before us," Rapscallion said.

"Hmm." She touched a broken screen, careful not to cut her fingers. "Maybe."

"You think somebody else did this?" the robot asked her. "You think the colonists smashed their own comms link?"

"I don't know. I don't have any answers here. We saw how the revenants destroyed the medical center. They just trashed the place, tore everything up and threw the pieces on the floor. This doesn't look like that. Does it?"

"This looks more deliberate?" Rapscallion said. "Is that it?"

She nodded. The destruction before her was complete, but not wanton. Whoever had smashed the controls hadn't, for instance, smashed the glass of the windows. The two chairs sitting behind the desk hadn't been knocked over.

"It's just a thought for now." She tapped the desk a couple of times, just to drive all the nebulous thoughts out of her head. "This damage is pretty significant," she said.

"Yes," Rapscallion told her.

"You think you can repair it?"

The robot shrugged. It was a human gesture she rarely saw him use.

"Maybe," he said.

Parker climbed under the control desk and removed a maintenance panel. Normally he would have needed a screwdriver for the job, but hard light let him make his fingers any shape he liked. He peered into the panel and found a circuit board covered in blown-out components. He whistled in surprise. "Whoever did this really didn't want us to fix it," he said, out loud.

When Rapscallion replied, he did so over the radio, so he didn't make an actual sound. "Quiet. The others are sleeping."

Parker glanced over at Petrova and Zhang. It was barely midday but they were fast asleep, exhausted from the long climb. They'd made little nests for themselves near the middle of the room, as far as they could get from the windows. Maybe they didn't want to wake up and find themselves looking at a fifty-meter drop.

Petrova's face was scrunched up, her mouth pursing as she struggled her way through a dream. He wanted to go to her, to curl up next to her and hold her and make it okay.

He reached into the panel and yanked out a blackened capacitor. There was no charge left in it, so he tossed it to the side. He would need to replace it, but he wasn't sure they had anything that would serve the same purpose. "Hey," he said, climbing out from under the desk. "Do we have a—"

He nearly screamed. He did let out a little sound, a desperate piping noise.

"I told you to keep it down," Rapscallion protested.

Parker grabbed for the robot's shoulder. He pointed at the far side of the room.

Standing there was something like a human figure. Tall, thin and indistinct. It could have been a trick of the light. A weird shadow. But when he moved toward it, it didn't change. It could have been made of frozen smoke, or maybe the shadows in the room had coagulated into this exact shape, but that didn't make any sense.

As he drew closer, he saw that its face was familiar. It should have been, since he'd seen it in a mirror a million times. The long, thin nose. The mouth that looked like it was grinning even when it was at rest. The hair was identical to the haircut he'd had when he died.

It was him.

"Are you seeing this?" he asked.

The Other – he could only think to call it that, the Other him – didn't move. It stood there meeting his gaze. Its eyes locked on his. He took another step, expecting it to disappear before he could get close enough to touch it. Another step, and it was still there.

He turned his head to look over his shoulder. "Rapscallion? Buddy? You getting this?"

He turned back to look at the Other again.

But now it was right next to him, its hands on either side of his head, grabbing him, pulling him close. Its mouth writhed as if it was screaming, shouting words right in his face, some soundless entreaty. The eyes were wide with terror.

"Jesus!" Parker shouted.

Rapscallion switched off the holoprojectors and Parker felt himself falling, twisting through an endless void. He fought to control himself and suddenly he was just . . . not there.

Not anywhere.

He was inside Rapscallion's processors, he supposed, but that didn't feel like a place. He felt completely detached from reality. He struggled to be calm, to think his way through this. "Rapscallion?" he said.

"I'm here." The voice came from every direction at once. "You okay?"

"I think so. Can I, um. Can I have my body back?"

"You don't have a body. You're a hologram."

Parker wanted to take a deep breath. Maybe squeeze the bridge of his nose between his thumb and forefinger. Neither of those were options.

"Please," he said.

He flashed into existence in the operations room. Standing well clear of the control desk. He grabbed his face, as if there was something there to check, to hold onto. "What the fuck just happened? Did you see that thing?"

Petrova and Zhang were up, moving around. He must have woken them. Shit. But maybe this was worth disturbing their nap for.

"Did you see it?" he demanded.

"I don't know what you're talking about," Rapscallion said.

"You didn't see it." But how was that possible? He shared Rapscallion's memory, the robot's processors, his sensors. Anything Parker saw he could only see at all because Rapscallion had shared his camera eyes.

"There was somebody." He shook his head. "No, not just somebody. I saw myself, standing there. It was me but, like, not quite there."

"Like a ghost?" Petrova asked.

"The ghost of a ghost," Zhang suggested.

Parker scowled. "It was right there. It tried to touch me, tried to say something. It was trying to communicate. It ... it was *right there.*"

Eventually he calmed down enough that he could sit with Zhang and actually talk about what he'd experienced. To try to describe it better. "Am I going crazy, Doc?" he asked.

Zhang didn't say no as quickly as Parker would have liked. "I'm not a psychiatrist. But. Well. It's not necessarily anything to worry about," Zhang finally told him. "Back when you were alive, did you ever suffer from sleep paralysis? It's when the mind wakes up from a deep sleep but the body doesn't, not right away. The brain has trouble processing that state, so it tends to hallucinate. People who suffer from sleep paralysis often imagine someone in the room with them, a shadowy figure that doesn't talk."

"That sounds about right. Except I wasn't asleep," Parker said. "I was completely conscious. I was working on an electrical panel."

Zhang nodded. "I understand. But Parker, you've undergone a trauma that the human mind just isn't designed to process. You lost your entire body. Do you remember when I asked if you ever suffered from phantom limb syndrome?"

"Yeah, and I said no. I never have."

"Perhaps this is how that manifests. A sort of phantom body syndrome."

"So what do I do about it?" Parker asked.

"There are therapies. Most are cognitive. Let's try something simple. If this happens again, try to talk back to this Other. If it wants to communicate, try to communicate."

"You think that'll fix the problem?"

"Oh no," Zhang said, and almost chuckled. "Hmm. Sorry. No, it won't fix anything. There's no actual cure for phantom limb, not when I can't give you any medication. But talking to the Other might make the experience slightly less horrifying."

"Wow. Thanks, Doc," Parker said.

"You're quite welcome," Zhang replied.

"Once they finish repairing the damage," Petrova said. Afternoon light coming through the windows painted the side of her face. Her eyes were clear and bright. "We can call Lang. She'll send a rescue ship and we go home. It's that simple."

Zhang hoped it would be that easy. He didn't ask the obvious question. Instead he turned and looked at the robot and the ghost. They had disassembled the entire control desk, then pulled up half the floor of the operations room. Loops of cable snaked back and forth across the available space. Tools were laid out in neat arrays, ready at hand as Rapscallion needed them. Parker was up on the ceiling, tapping at something with a small hammer.

"How's it going?" Zhang asked.

"So," Rapscallion said, "we thought at first all we needed to do was bypass the control panel. All those buttons and dials are for humans to use. Parker and I don't need them – we can operate the system by accessing it directly, machine to machine. No need to flip switches or press buttons when we can talk to the computers in their own language, right?"

"That makes sense. Is it working?"

"Oh, it's going great," Rapscallion said.

Petrova cleared her throat. "Right, I'm sure it's going great, but can you repair the system or not?"

"I guess we'll see," he replied cheerfully.

Zhang watched her face. Her jaw was tight. She stared out through the window, not looking at him.

He rose to his feet and looked down, just making sure there were no revenants down there. There was only one way out of the comms tower. If the revenants came up the ladder, how long would the trapdoor hold?

He tried to remember the last time he'd felt safe. That didn't work, so he tried to remember the last time his life had made sense. Before Titan fell to the basilisk, definitely. Back then he'd just been a young doctor, treating sprains and headaches and the occasional rhinovirus infection. He'd had a woman he loved, and friends, and a life that looked like it would continue in the same comfortable, happy rut forever.

"Shit," Parker said. Fat sparks burst from the ceiling and turned to smoke as they drifted down toward the floor. "That wasn't supposed to happen."

Petrova kept staring out the window. "First we repair the ansible. Then we call Lang. Then she sends a rescue ship. Simple."

"Simple," Zhang agreed.

She looked over at him with a smile, like she appreciated his validation.

The sun climbed down from the sky, headed toward the horizon faster than felt right. Zhang had never lived on Earth, but his ancestors had, and the twenty-four-hour rhythm of terrestrial days was hardwired into his brain. Days on Paradise-1 were shorter, and so the sun looked like it was racing across the sky.

Pink light lit up Petrova's cheek.

"First they fix this place. Then we call Lang," she said.

"Any progress?" Zhang asked.

Rapscallion had replaced some of the floor tiles. "Yeah, lots," he said. "But then I found a new problem. Whoever broke this thing must have realized somebody might come along and try to fix it. They severed the main trunk cable."

"Lang will send a rescue ship. Easy."

Zhang walked over to where the robot had his head and arms inside the floor. "I take it we need a main trunk cable to make a call?"

"I mean, yes," Rapscallion said. He played an audio file of a group of humans laughing at a hilarious joke.

"Can you repair it?" Zhang asked.

"Well, I can do this," Rapscallion told him.

Zhang heard a good, solid thunking sound and then the floor under his feet vibrated, hard enough that he felt like he was in an earthquake. Parker vanished into thin air without so much as an obscenity.

"Rapscallion?" Zhang asked.

There was no answer.

He looked over at Petrova. She had finally turned away from the window. She looked up at him, not at the robot. As if he had any answers to give her.

Something under the floor began to crackle. Like a fire. Zhang wondered if they were all about to die.

"Rapscallion?" he asked, very quietly.

Light flooded into the room from outside. Zhang turned and saw motes of sparkling radiance lift off the brown rocks of the surrounding mountains. It looked like ghosts emerging from their graves and ascending toward the stars. As he watched in fascination, the coruscating lights came faster and faster, streaking upward together until they cohered into a spectral whole, a beam firing from within the crust of Paradise-1 headed toward the upper atmosphere.

"Is it . . . is it working?" Petrova asked.

"Huh," Rapscallion said, his head still buried in the floor. "That wasn't supposed to happen."

"What do you mean?" Zhang asked.

The room flickered with light, and for a second Zhang thought he was caught up in a vast conflagration, an explosion that would spread his atoms across the planet. Then the light stabilized, and it was like he'd been transported to another world. He saw a man's face, enormous, filling the room, his eyes cut off by the ceiling.

"Hold for Director Lang, please," the man said.

"It . . . it worked," Petrova whispered.

The man's face disappeared. A new image replaced it, made up of unrecognizable shapes and textures. The hologram filled all the available space – Zhang couldn't see the others, couldn't see his own hands.

Then the image switched again, except it didn't, it was the same image, Rapscallion had just scaled it down to a more appropriate size. It looked very much like Zhang was standing in a large office space filled with tables and chairs. One broad window looked out across a landscape of silver, pockmarked with craters. Earth hung in the center of the window like a jewel streaked with white clouds.

Sitting before the window, Director Lang cleared her throat.

"Lieutenant Petrova?" she said. "Do you have a report for me?"

# 39

Petrova slowly rose to her feet. The office around her was familiar to her, of course. She'd spent hours there when she was a child, reading while her mother finished up some vital piece of business.

Now it belonged to Lang.

She looked exactly as Petrova remembered. The close-cut steel-gray hair. The utterly humorless eyes, sunk into a network of wrinkles like a spider's web. Everything about her, even the cut of her uniform, spoke to how efficient this woman was and how little respect she had for people who wasted her time.

It felt like a lifetime since Petrova had seen her. In reality it had only been a few months, and most of that time Petrova had spent in cryosleep.

"Lieutenant?" Lang said. "Are you able to speak? Are you injured?"

Petrova blinked. "Um," she said. "I'm sorry. I wasn't ... I wasn't prepared for this call. As much as I would have, um, liked to have been." She looked over at Rapscallion, who had just pulled his head up out of the floor. The robot didn't seem to notice her glare. "We repaired the ansible controls, and then somehow the system made the call without my input."

"No," Lang said.

"No?"

"I've had this channel open for more than a year. My assistants had standing orders to connect me the second the connection came back on line. Here we are. So. Do you have a report for me? That is why I sent you to Paradise-1, after all."

You sent me here because you wanted me out of the way. Because of who my mother was, Petrova thought. You sent me here because I was expendable.

"Of course, Director. My apologies." She tugged at her coveralls, trying to get some of the rumples out of the fabric. She came to attention. "My crew and I made planetfall two days ago. We attempted to make contact with the local population. Unfortunately, as far as we can ascertain, the colony suffered an attack and there are no survivors."

She told the director everything. The revenants. The mysterious quadcopter. Tracking the body of Kenji Yoshida. The desperate hike to the comms tower.

Almost everything.

She didn't mention the fact that she'd tried to use the basilisk against the revenants, or the seizure she suffered as a result.

When she'd finished, Lang rose from behind her desk and walked toward her camera, making it look like she was approaching Petrova directly. Like they were in the same room, having a perfectly normal conversation. Petrova had to keep reminding herself the office was an illusion and Lang was nearly a hundred light years away.

"Lieutenant. Alexandra," the director said, using a name Petrova didn't often hear. Everyone called her Sasha. "You've been through so much. I'm sorry."

"You're . . ." Petrova looked at her feet. Sympathy was the last thing she'd expected from this conversation.

"We always knew this was a possibility, that the colony was lost. It was crucial that we confirm that, one way or the other. I'm truly sorry you had to be the one to discover the truth. As for these revenants, well, you've clearly had a harrowing ordeal.

I trust Dr Zhang's analysis, though it's hard to believe that these creatures are dead."

"His autopsy was pretty thorough."

"I have no doubt about that. He's a brilliant physician. Still, I'm sure you can understand why I would want a second opinion."

Zhang cleared his throat. "If I may? I think that's an excellent idea. We need a full medical team here, a research team to make sense of what we've found. There's a lot of data to unpack, a lot of questions to be answered. I'll be happy to share my findings with them." He gave Petrova a meaningful look. She nodded back, discreetly. She knew what he was getting at.

Petrova faced Lang. Made eye contact through the ansible. "Director, I know you value your time, so I'll be direct. Now that the mission is complete, we'd very much like to request relief. We'd like to come home now, please." She smiled. "Both the doctor and I have been injured. As for Captain Parker..." She realized she didn't even know how to explain what had happened to Parker. "Whatever we can do for him, he's certainly earned it. Then there's Rapscallion—"

"I'm not concerned with a robot," Lang said. "As for Parker, I have a number of people here who'd like to talk to him. My priority right now is getting the three of you home. So let's make that happen."

Petrova's heart thumped in her throat. This had been her plan, of course. To call Lang and arrange their rescue.

She hadn't actually expected it to work.

"I have a ship standing by, ready to fetch you. It can arrive in ..." Lang checked a screen that appeared on her palm, "ten days, maybe a little less if we push its engines. Of course we'll need a place to land. The colony town doesn't sound safe. Let me see." She opened a map on a holoscreen she could share with the crew. "There's a mining complex here." She pointed at a location on the far side of the mountains. "It has its own landing pad. I want you to proceed directly there, alright? Lieutenant, Doctor, you've been through hell. I promise you, we'll get you home safely. Is there anything else?"

Zhang tapped his foot on the floor, perhaps trying to get Petrova's attention.

She ignored him. "Thank you, Director. That's all."

Lang ended the call. The hologram representation of her office blinked out and Petrova was standing in the comms tower once again, facing the windows. The sun was a red smear on the rocky horizon.

"Petrova," Zhang said, a warning in his voice. That was way too easy.

"I know," she said.

"She lied to us. She's always lied to us, and she's still ... She's not telling us everything, at the very least."

"She's full of shit, basically," Parker said.

Petrova turned to face them. "Oh," she said, "I'm quite aware."

# 40

Parker called up a holographic map of the mountains around them and enlarged it until it took up most of the room, as if the operations chamber had filled with brown rocks. The map was based on satellite data and didn't have a particularly high resolution, but it would do. He marked the comms tower with a glowing cross, then the location Lang was sending them to. The mine. "I've checked all the local maps, all the data from the colony that still exists," he said. "There's nothing there. At least, nothing official."

He watched as Petrova strode through his map, stroking her chin. "I had a briefing on Paradise-1 before we came here. Nothing in it mentioned a mine complex."

Zhang pointed at the pickup location. "The logs that Rapscallion found, the doctor's logs, they mention a mine."

Petrova raised an eyebrow.

"It sounded like the doctor knew the place existed. Like the colonists in the town knew it was there but didn't see the miners very often."

"So, basically, a second colony," Petrova said. "With its own landing pad, meaning these miners could come and go without being seen. Obviously Lang knew about this. She just didn't bother to mention it until now. Why not?"

None of them had an answer for her.

"Okay, we'll put that on the list of mysteries to solve. Next up, did anyone else notice she didn't seem surprised?"

"By what? The revenants? She said she doubted my conclusions," Zhang pointed out.

"Yeah, she might not believe they're dead, but she didn't seem surprised they exist."

"Almost like she knew already," Zhang said, caution in his voice.

"Nothing we said seemed to surprise her. She didn't even pretend to act shocked when I told her the colonists were all dead. The whole point of this mission was to find out why they stopped communicating. If she already knew they were dead, why are we here? Was our whole mission briefing a lie?"

"It would hardly be the only time she's lied to us," Zhang pointed out. "She sent us up against the basilisk with no warning, when she knew that a hundred ships had tried coming here before us. She didn't even tell us the mission would be dangerous."

Petrova nodded. "We know we're expendable as far as she's concerned. She's acting all nice now, but that just tells me she wants something."

Rapscallion played a sound file of a man gasping in surprise.

"Sorry?" Petrova said.

"She wants something? Of course she does. She's Director Lang."

Parker had zero interest in the politics of the United Earth Government. He never had, which helped explain why he'd spent most of his career flying cargo runs from Ganymede to Mars and back. He'd never heard of Director Lang before this mission. Still, he knew that the various branches of the UEG were always at each other's throats, playing out their secret agendas and quiet little inter-office wars. Firewatch, Lang's group, was supposed to be the worst of the bunch, and the most ambitious. Technically they were just responsible for state security, but everyone said they were a shadow government of their own, pulling all the strings behind a curtain of official bureaucracy.

He had heard of Ekaterina Petrova, back in the day. Petrova's mother had been a real nasty piece of work. She'd single-handedly stomped on the Lunarist separatist movement, which wanted independence for the cities on Earth's moon. She'd built her career by slaughtering entire domes full of striking workers, turned Firewatch into the most effective part of the UEG's military. If Lang was anything like her ... well, of course she would be. Lang was the wolf they set to eat the wolf, so to speak. When Ekaterina became too powerful, too dangerous, the UEG had sent Lang to take her down. And Lang had done it.

"Okay," Petrova said. "We have to assume she's using us, again. But why? She wants us to go to this mine. What's there?"

"I have a thought on that," Rapscallion said.

"You know what she's looking for?"

"No," the robot said. "Not at all. But I have a thought. A data point for you." He didn't move, but a third cross appeared on the map. This one blinked slowly. "There. That's my best estimate for its current location."

"The location of what?" Petrova asked.

"Kenji Yoshida's body. It moved overnight, a couple kilometers."

Petrova touched the location of the colony town on the map. Then she dragged her finger across the holographic mountains, drawing a luminous line straight to the body's position. She glanced up at them before she dragged her finger again, this time between the body and the mine.

The two segments matched up, forming a perfectly straight line.

"Shit," Parker said. "They're going to the mine too."

"That can't be a coincidence," Petrova said. "So that's what Lang wants. She wants us to follow the revenants, see where they're headed."

"Their home," Zhang said.

"What?" Petrova pulled her finger out of the map and the line disappeared.

"The doctor's log," Zhang said. "It suggested the revenants first appeared at the mine, before they came to the town. The mine is where they come from, or ... well, I don't know what it means. But it's their point of origin. They're going home, taking Yoshida's body with them."

Petrova tilted her head back and groaned in what sounded to Parker like despair. "It can't ever be easy. It can't ever be safe."

"Do we think," Zhang said softly, "that if we do what Lang wants, if we go to this place, she'll actually send a ship to pick us up?"

"She was lying about that, too," Parker said. "Or at least not telling us everything."

"What do you mean?" Petrova asked.

"She said she would send a ship and it would be here in ten days. That's impossible. We came here on the *Artemis*, a very fast transport ship. Even with a singularity drive, it took us more than two months. If she's sending a ship from Earth, a hundred light years away ..." He shook his head. "There's no ship ever built that could get here that fast. Unless."

"Unless?" Petrova asked.

"Unless it's already here, in the Paradise system."

She frowned. "We saw a lot of ships up in orbit, but they were all compromised by the basilisk. It attacked every ship that came too close to the planet."

"Sure," Parker said. "If they got too close. She could have a ship loitering way out, but still in the system. Say, in Paradise's Oort cloud, a couple hundred AUs out where it's so cold and dark maybe even the basilisk couldn't find it."

"A ship," Petrova said, "ten days out. Waiting for us to break through, to get past the basilisk. To open a window for this ship to just fly right through."

"It's a theory," Parker said.

"It's all just theories at this point. That's what we've got. To answer your question, Zhang, I don't know. If we actually go to this mine, if we do what she wants, if we survive, if there really is a ship coming, if it lands, if she's serious about picking us up and taking us home, if all of that is true, we have a chance. That's a whole lot of ifs."

Nobody disagreed with her.

"Anybody have a better plan?" she asked.

The four of them looked down at the map and the cross that marked the mine.

Their next stop.

# 41

The sun was gone, and the sky outside the big windows filled with stars. There was so little light pollution they burned and twinkled like eyes staring back at her. Like she was lost in a vast forest and the creatures of the night were watching her, waiting to see her next move.

Petrova sighed and tried to relax. Tried to look at all those stars and see how beautiful they were, the great majestic panoply of the galaxy. Maybe if she'd grown up somewhere other than Earth, it could have worked. The night from Earth's surface was black, dull, empty space between the street lamps. You might see a star once in a while, but it was far more likely to be Venus seething close to the horizon.

She should never have left Earth, she thought. Never have tried to come up in her mother's footsteps.

She watched the ground around the base of the tower. There was nothing to see, of course. Even if a mob of revenants had gathered, she wouldn't be able to make them out in the dark. They could be down there with their faces all turned upward, their dark eyes looking toward the trapdoor at the top of the ladder.

Of course Rapscallion would see them if they were there. The robot hadn't reported any such thing to her. She decided to ask anyway.

"Nothing moving down there at all," he told her. "As for the trapdoor, I'm on it."

He meant it literally. He was sitting on the trapdoor, holding it closed.

"What about the quadcopter?" She'd asked him to keep an eye out for any aircraft. There was somebody out there, presumably someone human and alive. It bothered her a lot she had no idea who they were or what they wanted.

"No sign of it. I've tried sending out radio messages all night, asking them to contact us. No response."

She'd asked him to do that, too. She hadn't really expected a response.

"Whoever they are, they helped us back at the town. I don't think they mean us harm now." She wished she was more certain about that.

It would have been nice, she thought, to have an ally. Somebody, anybody on this planet who was on their side.

"If we had a quadcopter," Rapscallion pointed out, "we could just fly to this mine. It would be really handy."

"It sure would," she agreed. She stared out over the mountains but nothing moved out there. Nothing.

Zhang laid out a couple of blankets on the floor and curled up while she watched. Maybe he knew what they faced tomorrow and was preparing himself for it by getting as much sleep as he could. Maybe he was just still tired, even after they'd napped most of the day.

Lord knew she was. She rubbed at her eyes with the ball of her good hand. It irritated the rope burn on her palm, but that was just a minor annoyance. She drank a little water, used the necessary facilities. The bathroom of the comms tower was just a tiny closet, but it had all the usual fixtures. When she was done, she came out and found a spot for her own nest of blankets. Her bed for the night. She lay down, her head cradled by the crook of her good arm. She looked out at the broad swoop of the Milky Way, the nebulae just blurs of faint white, caught a meteor flashing across the night.

She saw the dark between the stars, the thick, impenetrable black of deep space. Cold and empty and brutal.

She sighed and considered getting back up. Looking at the map again, trying to plan their route forward. It would be a waste of time, but it would be something to do.

Instead, she whispered into the dark. "Parker," she said. "Sam."

He was there, lying next to her, his arms folded under his head. He looked up at the ceiling, not at her. Maybe he was trying not to be presumptuous.

Whatever. She grabbed one of his hands and pulled until he rolled over, put his arm across her waist, his hand up at her shoulder. She scuttled backward until she was up against his body. He felt cold, and too hard. Of course he did. She was only feeling the edges of his hard-light field. It didn't matter.

He pulled her closer.

For a moment they just lay like that. She thought of Zhang sleeping a few meters away. Was he watching them? She was certain Rapscallion was. The robot could hardly not see what was happening.

She didn't care. She needed this.

She felt Parker's lips on the back of her neck, his chin nuzzling through her hair. Now that she'd shown him what she wanted, he was better able to shape the hard light, simulate the textures of human flesh. It felt good. Much better than she'd expected. Maybe he'd been thinking about this too, figuring out ways to make the simulation better.

She remembered a time long ago when the two of them had been as close as this. So much closer. She remembered the way his skin smelled, remembered laying her head on his chest and listening to the vibrations as he spoke about … something, nothing. She remembered his long, freakish toes and how she'd learned to find them adorable, even when he scratched her with his toenails in the night.

"Sam," she whispered. So softly.

His simulated hand moved down her arm. Drifted over to her breast.

She opened her eyes and looked out at the stars, and for a second they were just that, stars, nothing dangerous, nothing terrible.

Then she reached up, grabbed his hand and moved it back to her shoulder.

"Sorry," he said.

"Don't be. Maybe ... maybe some time when we have more privacy."

"Sure," he said.

As if that was a thing that was ever going to happen.

Was she being cruel? Was this hurting him, to offer him such intimacy? How much of it could he feel, with Rapscallion's borrowed sensors? She tried to push those thoughts away. She was at least a little successful. Her eyes closed.

Her eyes opened, and the dawn light came streaming through the windows, everything around her a bluish gray. She heard Rapscallion moving around, tearing open food packets, pouring water into a purifier. She didn't lift her head, didn't move. She could still feel Parker's hand on her shoulder, still feel his forehead pressed against the back of her head.

But he was gone. Just a phantom of the night, vanished with the rising of the sun.

She twisted around, sat up, bracing herself with her good hand. Time to get back to work.

# 42

Zhang barely remembered climbing up the ladder to the comms tower the day before. Climbing back down was an ordeal. His leg was healing, but the revenant that bit him had taken more than just skin. It had torn into the muscle underneath, and without the RD wrapped around his leg serving as a brace, he would not have been able to put his weight on that leg. He would barely have been able to stand.

Somehow he got down to ground level. That was when the real horror dawned on him.

"Ten days," he said. "Ten days to get how far?"

"A couple hundred kilometers, all told," Rapscallion told him. "Most of it over broken ground."

Petrova walked past looking grim and determined. "We need to get moving," she told them. "We can take a break to chat in ninety minutes."

Zhang scowled, but he followed after her, keeping pace with the robot as they climbed a short rise and came to the peak of the mountain. The view beyond should have been breathtaking, but all it did was make his heart hurt.

Ten days of that. Ten days of hard hiking down rocky slopes where if you slipped, if you stumbled, you could fall fifty meters into a ravine, or just trip and smack face forward onto jagged rocks. The prospect of broken ankles, skinned knees and muscle spasms and death by sheer exhaustion terrified him.

It was a little better when they headed down into a winding canyon. Rock walls on either side gave him something to hold onto as he scrambled over boulders and slid down slopes of shattered scree. If he couldn't see what was ahead of them, he could just focus on the next step, the next foothold, the next ledge they needed to creep along. The high walls threw much of the canyon into deep shadow, but he wasn't as afraid of dark corners as he had been even two days before. There had been no revenant attacks during the night, not even a single scout tracking their movements, as far as any of them could tell. It seemed like even the dead took one look at this landscape and decided it wasn't worth the effort.

Especially when they could just wait at the bottom, sit tight and wait for their human prey to come to them.

Ninety minutes in, when the break finally came, he sat down on a rock, pulled off his boots and turned them over, one and then the other. A fine sifting of dark powder poured out. Not the greasy black blood of the revenants, but simply tiny bits of pulverized brown rock.

He scraped as much of it out as he could. When Petrova called out that the break was over and it was time to move on again, he struggled to get the boots back over his swollen feet, but he managed. The RD pumped an anti-inflammatory into his system, and that helped.

By the time they broke for lunch, he wanted to die. Everything hurt. The RD gave him some mild analgesics, but nothing stronger. Real painkillers, muscle relaxants or even topical numbing agents would make him clumsy, more prone to injuring himself. His legs felt like they were sticks of wood that someone had set on fire. His sides were tight with muscle spasms, and even his shoulders felt stiff and sore. His brain felt bruised from being sloshed from one side of his head to the other as he swayed through every step.

He pulled his boots off again, emptied them of their

accumulated grit. Then he pulled off his socks. Thick white blisters, full of fluid, covered the balls and soles of both his feet. He knew better than to pop them. Instead he wrapped them carefully with strips of cloth. They would burst on their own, he knew. He needed to think ahead, think about infection.

"Let's go," Petrova called. "Let's move." He realized he hadn't bothered to eat anything. He didn't feel hungry. He was in too much pain to have an appetite. He forced himself to eat a couple of protein sticks anyway.

As he trudged onward, Rapscallion called up a holomap and tried to show him how far they'd come, how much progress they'd made. Zhang nodded in appreciation and went back to feeling miserable the second the robot dispelled the map. Parker came and walked alongside him for a while, even taking his elbow from time to time, grabbing his hand to help him climb over especially tricky obstacles. He was grateful for the hard-light assist, but he could see where this was headed.

In the late afternoon, Petrova called an unscheduled break and came over to sit next to him. For a while neither of them said anything and it was like the old times, perhaps, the bad, dark days when they had together fought the basilisk. They'd been comrades, war buddies, and they had known they had each other's backs.

There had been no question back then. They worked together, they made it through everything together.

"You should leave me behind," he said.

She didn't immediately react. Oh, he felt her stiffen a little, saw, out of the corner of his eye, the way she suddenly held herself very still. As if she thought she was walking into a trap.

"I'm just going to slow you down."

"I'm not going to . . ." she stopped herself. "I won't leave you to die."

"Who said anything about dying?" he asked. "I'll take my share of our food and water and hike back up to the comms tower. If I push myself, if I set a good pace, I can make it there before dark. I can hole up there. You go to the mine, do whatever Lang wants you to do. Get picked up by the rescue ship. They can send an air vehicle for me."

"You've really thought this through."

He had. He knew it was giving up. It was admitting he simply couldn't do what was asked of him, and that burned. It made good sense, though. And honestly, he had no desire to see what they would discover at this putative mining complex. Something terrible, no doubt. New horrors to witness when he was still barely able to cope with the old ones.

"I want you to know this isn't about ... it's not about the basilisk."

She turned to look him in the eye, but Zhang was very talented at avoiding eye contact when he wanted to.

"You haven't forgiven me yet," she said.

"Do you even listen to me when I talk?" he asked. "It's not my place to forgive you. I'm not angry. I'm not—"

"You keep saying that! But we keep coming back to this."

He shook his head. "The whole point I was trying to make is that it's not about that. It's simple logic. I'm never going to be able to make this hike, not injured, maybe not when I was completely healthy, and you know it."

She stood up. "Hey," she said, calling over to Parker and Rapscallion, who were standing a respectful distance away. "Guys. We need to talk. We have a plan to make." She looked back to Zhang. "You sit here. Rest. I'll let you know what our next step is."

"You know what it has to be," he said.

# 43

"It's possible," Rapscallion said. "Advisable? No." The robot watched Petrova's face carefully. He knew that humans were perverse creatures, and that she was going to say they had to do this, that there was no other choice.

The two of them had pored over maps of the mountains for nearly half an hour, looking for a faster route, an easier route. One that gave them more time hiding in lava tubes and fewer hours per day of actual walking. Rapscallion had seen another solution, one he had put forward partly because he thought it was funny.

And of course she had jumped at the idea.

She walked over to where Parker was quietly encouraging Zhang, assuring him they would never split up, that that was foolish. Rapscallion actually disagreed. He thought Zhang was being eminently reasonable. If a group of robots had been in this situation, they wouldn't have hesitated to leave one of their own behind. To let them die, if necessary.

Maybe, he thought, there was something to the human way of doing things, though. He knew that if Zhang did die, he would miss the human immensely. In fact, knowing that all humans did eventually die, he'd already considered how he was going to feel when Zhang met his inevitable, if unpredictable, end. He'd made a simulated model of his emotional state following the death of each of his friends. He knew he wasn't going to enjoy Zhang's death at all.

"There's a river, here," Petrova said. She had the map open, hovering between them. She traced a finger down the peaks, through the valleys. "It's just a little creek this high up, but it gets deeper and wider as it heads downhill. On the far side of these mountains, it flows into a lake not too far from the mine complex."

"Only about fifty kilometers away," Rapscallion pointed out.

"Yes. Only that much," Petrova said. She gave him a look he had a hard time processing. It did not seem like a friendly or appreciative look.

Zhang frowned. He did not rise to his feet to get a better look at the map. "Fresh water. If it's running clear, it might be safe to drink. Good. We've been getting through our water supply pretty quickly."

She gestured at the map and it expanded, the scale changing so that a very small area grew to fill the entire space. "The river isn't the only thing we found." She pointed. "Here. There's a cluster of buildings, right next to the river."

"Buildings?" Zhang asked. "What kind of buildings?"

"Just some shacks," Petrova said.

"What are they doing all the way up here?" Parker asked.

"We have no idea. Needless to say, they don't appear on any official map of the colony. Well, neither does this mine complex. We're going to check out these shacks. All of us. At the very least it's a place to spend the night that's better than camping in a lava tube. Listen."

"Yes?" Zhang said.

"Just come with me this far. Don't give up yet."

"I'm not giving up. I'm trying to think rationally."

Petrova wanted to scream in frustration. She held it together. "So just be irrational with me a little longer. One last hike, and you can rest all you want."

He shrugged. "Okay."

# 44

Petrova watched as Rapscallion clambered up over a last ridge of brown stone. The robot lay flat on his belly and moved his head slowly back and forth, scanning the shacks below. After a moment he waved her on, and she rushed sideways around the rock, her firearm in her hand. Zhang followed her and crouched down next to her.

"Draw your weapon," she hissed.

He looked down at the holster on his belt. He took the gun out and stared at it as if he'd never seen it before.

Petrova wanted to shout at him to be more present, more ready for what was about to happen. She didn't dare make the noise, however. "Parker?" she whispered.

"I'm here." The ghost had chosen not to materialize, or at least not to appear as a hologram. He could move invisibly through the shacks, providing support as necessary. It was good tactical thinking, and she was annoyed she hadn't thought of it herself.

"Okay. I see ... six shacks here," she said. They formed a semicircle around a large space by the water. "We clear them one by one. Do not shoot anyone unless you're certain they're a revenant. Look for the black eyes. Now. Let's go."

The four of them hurried across a stretch of relatively open ground. They split up, Zhang and Petrova taking the closest shack, Rapscallion and the invisible Parker approaching a second one. The shack Petrova had picked had a door made of what looked like a cut-down section of a cargo container. Thick steel, but it hung on ludicrously basic hinges. There was no lock or even a latch. She nodded to Zhang and he pushed at it, slowly, carefully.

Snarling, she put her good shoulder to the door and slammed it open, then spun around as she covered the interior of the shack, pointing her weapon in every corner, making a visual inspection of every shadow. "Clear," she called out.

"Clear," Rapscallion replied.

"This one's clear, too," Parker called, a moment later.

Petrova hurried over to a fourth shack, only to find its door opening before she could reach it. She lifted her weapon and prepared to engage, but then realized that Parker had opened the door for her.

"Clear," she said.

Rapscallion cleared the fifth shack. Parker the sixth.

"Clear, they're all clear," he said.

Petrova nodded to herself. Not the most professional job. The others weren't trained for this and they'd made some pretty bad mistakes. It might have cost them their lives; at least it could have if there had been anyone in the shacks.

They were deserted. Just like the town, just like the comms tower. Nobody home.

Compared to the prefab housing units in town, the shacks might have been paleolithic. They were made of crudely welded metal and barely held together well enough to keep out the wind. What furniture they contained was mainly bedding. Blankets, sheets and pillows, most of them soiled or torn. Presumably taken from the town and then used and reused until they were threadbare. The clearing by the water featured a massive firepit and a large open space with a crude circle painted on the rocks. A landing pad for quadcopters. There were of course no copters to be found.

From a first quick examination, there was no indication why

this place had been built. Why it existed at all. "Why here?" she asked.

Rapscallion could answer that, at least. "The river's the only water source up here. If you were going to build a camp anywhere in these mountains, this is the place."

"A camp." Petrova walked down to the river. Up this high, it was barely a meter across, the water running fast and clear, full of bubbles as it raced downhill. Looking up into the peaks, she saw it was fed by a number of smaller streams, trickles of water jumping from rock to rock. They had seen few snowcaps on the tops of the mountains. She supposed dew must condense on the high, cold peaks, then roll downhill to form those rivulets.

"A refugee camp," Zhang suggested.

"What?" Petrova wasn't sure what he meant.

"The conditions here are beyond primitive. Nobody would choose to live like this if they had any options."

Petrova shrugged. "People go camping on Earth in the weirdest places. On top of glaciers, out in the deserts. For, you know. For fun."

"For how long? A few days? A week or so?" Zhang pointed back at the shacks. "You saw the condition of those. You think colonists came up here to sit around a fire and sing folk songs? No, people lived here. For months, I think. And I think you know why."

"They fled the town," she said, softly. "After the massacre."

"After the massacre," Zhang agreed, nodding. "Maybe they came here to get away from the revenants. If they left in a hurry they wouldn't have had time to bring much with them in the way of resources."

"So they came looking for water. They didn't want to go to the comms tower, or anyway they didn't stay there for long. Because there's no water there? Or another reason? You think they were the ones who trashed the ansible controls?"

Zhang grunted in frustration. "It's unwise to speculate too

much without data. Maybe there's something here, something that can tell us ... something."

"Yeah, okay," she said. "Maybe leave the detective work to the person who's trained to do it."

He nodded and went to sit by the stream. Leaving her to do her job. She resented a little the fact that he was right, that she was reading too much into scanty evidence, and it irked her that she'd made that mistake. She was losing focus, getting fuzzy, and she knew it. The stress of clearing the camp had filled her system with cortisol and adrenaline, and it kept her from clarity.

Making a real effort to concentrate, she headed back toward the shacks. Before stepping inside the nearest one, she turned and looked at the dark rocks around them, the blue sky above. She had the sudden feeling she was being watched, but when she turned around ...

"Boss," Rapscallion said. "Come see this."

She followed the robot into the largest of the shacks. Dirty blankets had been bundled into one corner of the room, revealing a part of the rusted steel floor that looked different from the rest. "I did a millimeter wave scan and found there was some space down there, like a cellar. It was hidden under all this mess." He indicated the blankets. "Is it okay that I moved them? I know you're not supposed to move anything from the scene of an investigation."

"If you found something interesting, I'll forgive you," she said. "How does this open up, do you think?"

It turned out the patch of floor was just a loose square of thin metal. It rested on top of the flooring but wasn't attached or secured in any way. Together the two of them got their fingers under its edges and lifted it away. It wasn't heavy.

Underneath was a dark sort of crawlspace, just big enough for a human being to fit if they crouched. Petrova dropped down into the hole while Rapscallion covered her. There was no danger, as it turned out. As her eyes adjusted to the dark, she saw that the walls of the hole were natural rock, neither cut nor dressed. They were almost smooth, though, and gently curved, giving the space a circular cross-section. The shack must have been built on top of a natural lava tube, she realized. A much smaller one than the one where they'd camped out on the way to the comms tower. It stretched out away from her in either direction, roughly following the path of the river.

"Interesting," she said. "There's a tunnel down here," she called up to the robot. "No indication where it goes."

"You think it's an escape tunnel?" Rapscallion asked.

"Maybe. Maybe just a hiding place." Or, for that matter, just a place to store things. A line of simple barrels stood along one side. They didn't look like anything special, just the kind of steel drums you would store water or other liquids in. She kicked one and it made a hollow noise.

The air in the tunnel was cool, even chilly. Maybe it formed a natural spring house, a place to store food if you had no other way to refrigerate it. She glanced down the length of the tube. Darkness congealed down there at the edge of the light, darkness that could hide anything. She thought of the revenant that had attacked Zhang, back when they first arrived on the planet. It had been hiding in darkness like that until it was disturbed.

"Parker," she called.

He appeared next to her without a word.

"I need you to head down there. As far as you can. See if this tunnel actually goes anywhere."

"Yeah, sure," he said. "Except ... you know I'm just being projected from that lens on Rapscallion's belly, right?"

She cursed herself. She'd fallen into the trap of thinking he had some actual independent existence. "Rapscallion, can you help him? I don't want to run into anything in the dark, anything with teeth, anyway."

"On it." The robot climbed down into the hole. She had to

make room for him, pressing her back up against the curved wall next to the barrels. Together Rapscallion and Parker headed up the tunnel, moving slowly as Rapscallion had to crawl on all fours.

She watched them for a while, then glanced down at the barrels again. Food, she thought. This was a larder. Maybe there was something in those barrels that she and Zhang could eat. It would be nice to have a break from protein bars and oatcakes. She dug her fingertips into the seam of one of the lids and lifted it, then lowered it to the floor. A dank, unpleasant smell came up out of the barrel and she had to turn her head away. Probably nothing edible in there, then, but she needed to look anyway.

Inside the barrel she found what looked like preserved meat. Four or five legs of some kind of animal, with the flesh cut away in neat sections. Carefully butchered. Petrova hadn't seen meat on a bone since the last time she'd been on Earth. On Mars, on Ganymede, you only ever got meat that had been grown in a vat or printed by a food-grade printer at a restaurant. She thought of the barbecues of her youth, parties her mother had thrown at their dacha on the Black Sea, whole pigs and cows on spits, roasted for the elite bureaucratic class of the UEG. She remembered Ekaterina holding a thing like a machete or a sword, slicing off long strips of juicy meat for smiling flunkies.

She smiled, despite herself. Her childhood had been difficult. Her mother had been a tyrant at home just as much as in the office. But there had been parties, and some of them had actually been nice.

She took hold of one of the joints of meat. No point in being dainty now. She was already filthy, covered in rock dust from climbing down into the hole. Anyway, she could wash herself in the river later, take an actual bath for the first time in ... well, far too long. Levering out the long, meaty bone, she laid it across the top of the next barrel in the row, intent on seeing what kind of animal had given its life for these people.

When she saw the human hand on the end of the bone, she managed not to scream.

# 45

Zhang dug through the firepit with a metal bar he'd found in one of the shacks. The soot and ash billowed up in a great plume of gray dust. There was no firewood on Paradise-1, for the very simple reason that there were no trees. Instead it looked like the refugees here had used a kind of peat for fuel. Compressed and dried plant material.

Underneath the ashes, below the remains of countless fires, he found more bones. A lot of them. None of them were intact. Many looked like they'd been cut open, others like they'd been cracked.

"To get the marrow out," he explained. "There's a little bit of vitamins and iron in bone marrow. Some good fat, if all you care about is calories."

Petrova just stared at him like he was mad.

"These are all human bones," he said, digging out a few fragments of femur, a couple of vertebrae that were almost intact. "Like the ones you found. Looks like they cooked the meat until it was well done, almost carbonized. Maybe to mask the appearance or the taste. The meat in those barrels was partly smoked, but it looks like they couldn't control the process enough to make it safe to eat over long periods of time. Could you, um . . . could you just sit down or something? I'm trying to answer your questions."

She'd had a lot of them. It turned out she didn't like any of the answers.

The biggest question, the one that left her wide-eyed and staring, was the easiest one to answer.

"Revenants didn't do this," he said. "There's no indication they eat human flesh. They collect bodies, but we still don't know why. It isn't for consumption, as far as I can tell. Oh. Look at this."

He used the metal bar to lift a part of a human skull out of the ashes of the firepit. Petrova gasped and looked away. He didn't know why she was squeamish about this. After the things they'd seen in orbit – the things the basilisk had made people do to each other up there – this was so much more understandable, more reasonable.

The refugees here had to eat. They needed a source of protein, and Paradise-1 could not provide. So they had turned to the only available food supply.

"It's not a sustainable diet," he said. "Not just because you run out of people. There are several nutrients you can't get from meat of any kind, and some you can't get from eating your own species." He used a cloth to rub the ash off the skull fragment. "Humans didn't evolve to be cannibals. It'll keep you alive for a little while, though. It can get you through a bad winter, perhaps. Here." He held up the skull to show her. "Look at this. It's black. Underneath, I mean. The same black I saw during my autopsy. Some of the bones in here are black too."

"Zhang, I don't want ... I can't ..."

"They didn't just eat each other. They ate some of the revenants as well," he said, and tossed the skull back in the firepit. It broke into sections with a crunching sound.

Petrova jumped to her feet and ran to the water to throw up.

# 46

The tunnel under the shacks ran up and down the slope. The mountains must have been volcanos once, built up over millions of years of constant eruptions, lava piling up in great foamy masses in Paradise-1's low gravity. The lava tubes they saw everywhere had formed at the end of that process, as the planet cooled and the eruptions became less common. Rapscallion headed up the slope and found that the tube ended after barely a hundred meters, the ceiling having collapsed at some time in the past. Downslope it ran considerably farther, as much as three quarters of a kilometer, then ended in a wide cave mouth overlooking the river.

Someone, presumably one of the refugees, had painted the walls of the tube. Nearest the shacks they had sprayed arrows, indicating the direction of the cave. Parker had a thought about that.

"If it's an escape tunnel, if they needed to get out in a hurry, they would want a reminder of which direction to go."

"What would they need to escape from?" Rapscallion asked. "We haven't seen any revenants this high up."

"We don't know how long ago they were here. Maybe there were more revenants back then, or maybe they were just worried the revenants would come for them eventually. Maybe it's an escape tunnel that never got used."

As the two of them had passed further along the tunnel,

crawling ever downward, they'd found a surprise. Whoever had painted the arrows on the walls had painted other things, too. Just doodles, sometimes stick figures, some with prominent black eyes.

"These drawings aren't very accurate," Rapscallion had pointed out. "I don't think I've ever seen a human woman with breasts that large."

Parker had laughed. "These are the kinds of drawings a kid might do. I can see it in my head, you know? The refugees come here and it's hard work, all the time, just staying alive. Not much of anything to stimulate the imagination. The kid, they tell him to come down here and paint arrows on the walls. He gets bored halfway through the job and starts goofing off. Drawing these."

Further on, the images had grown slightly more lifelike, slightly more accomplished, as if the artist was learning, or maybe just taking their work more seriously. The figures started to have individualized faces, some with beards, some with prominent ears. They lifted their arms to fend off the revenants, or fired what looked like rifles at them while a quadcopter sailed through the air overhead.

Another hundred meters and the drawings were like primitive murals, depicting scenes from the story of Paradise-1. Happy colonists in a town surrounded by farms. The coming of the revenants, and then a hurried exodus, stick figures running away while bodies piled up in the streets.

A desperate climb up the mountain, with the comms tower just visible atop a perfectly triangular peak.

A closer view of the tower, clearly drawn from life, except there were wavy lines emanating from its tip.

There followed a picture of the six shacks and the river, and then, finally . . .

"Jesus," Parker said, softly, in the dark of the tunnel. His hologram barely lit up the wall. He traced the painted figures as if trying to commune with the artist.

The final image showed a group sitting around a fire. Real care had been taken to make each face unique, as if the artist wanted to remember specific people. The figures were huddled together, bent and shaggy. In front of the fire, a dead body lay partially butchered, one leg completely gone. The corpse's face was turned away from view, perhaps to hide their identity.

"Does this picture bother you more than the others?" Rapscallion asked.

"Yeah," Parker said. "Yeah. It's a confession. A declaration. It says, 'We did this.' If the other pictures are telling the history of the town, the kid wanted to show how it ended."

They knew it was the end, because just twenty meters further on, the tunnel ended at the cave mouth. Sunlight flooded in, washing out Parker's hologram, making him thin, indistinct, spectral.

The two of them climbed out of the cave and stood on the bank of the river. Parker turned and looked upslope, in the direction of the camp, and that was when he saw that the final image wasn't, in fact, the artist's last work.

A tall boulder stood by the side of the river. Its broad, flat face was turned toward the sun, and there was paint there, bright orange paint that stood out against the dark stone. Instead of a picture, this time the artist had left words. A final message.

# 47

Petrova shivered in the cold tunnel, longing to get back to the sunlight. She was sure, though, that there was something there, something to be learned from the pictures. They were the closest thing she had to a narrative of what had happened here.

What had happened...

Zhang was right, they'd seen worse things in orbit. There were probably still worse things going on up there. It wasn't like the basilisk had fixed the damage it had done. The ships up there were all horror shows, psychodramas playing themselves out one human life at a time.

She hadn't been able to help those people.

"Here," she said. "Look."

Parker came over, and the light of his hologram helped pick out the paint on the wall. She was standing before the image of the comms tower. Wavy lines emerged from the tower. "What does this mean? They got to the tower and it was already broken? Already trashed? Or does it mean they tried to send a message? Are those lines supposed to be radio waves, sent out into space?"

"You're asking if they called for help," Parker said. "We can't know for sure. Petrova, you're going to drive yourself crazy trying to read these pictures like this. You can't know. You just can't."

She leaned forward and pressed her forehead against the wall.

The cold stone felt like it was freezing her thoughts in place. "There has to be something..."

She felt his hands, his hard-light hands, on her shoulders, but she shrugged him off. She didn't want to be comforted just then. She wanted to sit with her anger, her sorrow. All the complicated things she was feeling.

He looked a little hurt, but she knew he would understand. Eventually. "How's Rapscallion's project coming along?" she asked.

"Good," he said. "Good. Good good good."

She nodded and started back, ducking a little in the low tunnel. As she passed the barrels, she shuddered a little but kept moving. Climbing up through the hole in the shack floor, she heard the whine of a metal cutter. She emerged back into sunlight and saw that Rapscallion and Zhang had taken the smallest of the shacks to pieces and were now cutting the metal walls into long, thin strips. Zhang held the pieces of metal still while Rapscallion worked, his hands moving gracefully, the tool in his hand like an extension of his plastic body. No human could have cut those strips more precisely.

She noticed that one of the pieces of metal – one of the walls of the shack, before it was torn down – was painted with an image of sheaves of wheat growing in front of a flat red sun. She thought of the people who had come to Paradise-1 thinking they would be farmers, thinking they would fill this empty world with life.

Rapscallion ran his saw through the image like a sickle reaping the sheaves. Zhang picked up the long strip by one end and sighted along the edge, bright silver that caught the light. He nodded, and Rapscallion moved on to cut another.

When they had enough strips, Rapscallion gave them a slight curve by holding them lengthwise across his body and then pulling from either side. Zhang's job at that point was simply to sort the strips into various piles. Petrova thought they must be made of aluminum. Certainly Zhang had no trouble carrying them.

When he saw her, he nodded, then got back to work.

She walked down to the water, watched it bubble past. It was so shallow at this point she could reach in and touch the bottom with her fingers and her wrist would stay dry. Half a kilometer downstream, it would come up to her waist. It was deep enough. It would have to be good enough.

"The question I keep asking myself," she told Parker, "is whether they ever had a chance."

"What do you mean?" the ghost asked.

"We don't know where the revenants come from. I mean, we know – Zhang told me they showed up first at this mine. That's where they're from. But what's there? What caused dead people to come back to life? We still have no idea. Some kind of virus, something that was here already?"

"It's gotta be," Parker said.

She shrugged. "If it was already here – some bug lying dormant, floating in the atmosphere, lurking in the water – then there was no chance. The colony would have been infected sooner or later. Oh, I suppose if the authorities had acted fast enough, they could have evacuated the planet." She had worked for the government long enough to know how unlikely that would have been. The UEG did nothing fast, or particularly efficiently. "But if this is just some disease, then . . ." She didn't know how to finish that sentence.

Because she was beginning to suspect it wasn't just a virus. Or a bacterium, for that matter.

"Somebody erased the town's records. Sabotaged all the vehicles, broke the damned ansible. I don't think it was the revenants. Somebody kept these people from calling for help."

"Are you sure you're not just being paranoid?" Parker asked.

She smiled, though she was still looking at the water.

"No. I'm not sure of that. I'm not sure of anything."

She heard a great clanging noise and ran over to see what had happened.

Rapscallion had cut a big shape out of the scrap metal. It looked like the inside of a Gothic arch: flat at the bottom, but the sides curved upward to join at a common point.

Using a electrocautery wand as a welding torch, Zhang helped the robot attach the long strips of metal to this base. The work was noisy and produced a lot of smoke. If there were revenants nearby, Petrova was sure they were paying attention by now. The construction really started to take shape after that, however. It started looking like a boat.

Flat-bottomed. Much smaller than she would have liked, though given the width of the river this high up in the mountains, the size was actually an asset. Two people and a robot could sit inside if they didn't mind close quarters.

There was no motor, no sails. They would just trust to the current and gravity to take them down the mountain, all the way to the lake at the bottom. Assuming they didn't hit any bad rapids, or a waterfall, or, for that matter, sharp rocks, the river could get them to the mine much faster than walking.

When the work was done, Zhang dropped down on the riverbank, well downstream of the firepit, and lay there with his face pointed at the sky. He was breathing heavily when she found him, but his eyes tracked her as she came and sat next to him.

"You're coming with us. Right?" she asked.

"Of course," he said. "I built that boat with my own hands. I'm not letting you sail off without me."

She smiled. "I can't do this without you."

He took a deep breath. "I'm not saying you'll have to. But what we're facing here is bad. You really want to know what happened to these people? The answers are probably at that mine. I'm not sure anymore that I want to know."

"I have to. I have to find out," she told him. "Somebody does."

He nodded without lifting his head more than a centimeter or two. "Maybe."

She watched the water. It never stopped, never slowed. It just kept bubbling past, clear and ice cold and fast.

# 48

"Oh. This is not good," Zhang said, his arms out to either side. "Is it . . . is it supposed to wobble like this?"

Rapscallion thought the doctor had probably never seen a boat before. There were lakes of liquid methane on Titan, but it wasn't like anyone went yachting on them. Maybe Zhang had seen boats in a video or something. Now that he was perched in the bow, he looked like he was already getting seasick.

"Just sit still, keep your center of gravity low," Petrova called out. "Hold on, I'm coming aboard."

Rapscallion was the last to climb into the boat. He had no trouble keeping his balance, but then he had internal gyroscopes. He wasn't sure how humans kept from falling out of chairs on a regular basis. "Parker?" he asked. "How you doing?"

"Just fine," the ghost said. He stood ten meters in front of the boat, his ankles in the water. Rapscallion wasn't really worried about him, but just wanted to make sure they were ready to move.

The boat was packed tight with supplies. The rest of their food and water, their improvised climbing gear, weapons, tools, medicine. The humans filled most of the remaining space, though there was enough room for Rapscallion to stand in the back. He had a long steel pole he could use to move the boat, and he imagined he looked like some nightmarish gondolier of old. The image amused him.

"Let's go," he said, and leaned forward slightly, thinking that would be enough to get the boat moving. When that failed, he planted his pole deep in the water and pushed.

The boat shrieked as it slid forward, its bottom rubbing against the smooth rock of the streambed.

"Hmm," the robot said. "Parker?"

The ghost sloshed over to the bow and grabbed it in both hands. "On three. One, two ... three!"

Rapscallion pushed hard against the bottom. Parker pulled with all his holographic might. The boat slid forward half a meter and then ground to a stop with an alarming scream of tortured metal.

"Is the hull breached?" Zhang asked, panic in his voice. "Are we taking on water? Are we going to sink?"

Sinking, Rapscallion thought, would be an improvement. "We're fine. I don't see any sign of metal fatigue or breakage." That was even true. "Let's go again, Parker."

"Sure. One, two ... three!"

Rapscallion pushed, Parker pulled.

They accomplished literally nothing.

Rapscallion consulted the audio files in his database. He had one of a human saying, "Aw sod it," in a particularly disgusted tone. Sounded about right. He played the file, then stepped out into the water. He laid his pole athwart the boat, then thrust his hands into the water and grabbed the bottom of the vessel. He put all the strength he had into shoving it forward, passengers and gear included. Something, hopefully a rock, snapped under the boat, and then it surged forward nearly three meters before running aground again.

"Better," he said.

# 49

After the first kilometer or so, the boat sped forward on its own, gripped by the current. Parker climbed up out of the water — to Petrova it looked like he was just sitting on the air — and shouted out every time a rock came too close or the course of the river bent around an obstacle. Rapscallion used his pole to push them away from the worst of these, which often threatened to send them spinning. The shape of the boat helped there, its sharp nose always wanting to point directly downstream.

Petrova had grown up on a beach. Her childhood uniform had been a swimsuit and she had learned to kayak, row and even sail long before she understood what her mother really did for a living. With only one good hand, though, there was little she could do to help. At one point, as they had to edge their way around a massive boulder that sat directly in the center of the river, she got up on her knees and pushed against the rock even as Rapscallion heaved against it with his pole. Parker used his hard light to cushion the side of the boat and keep it from scraping against the rough stone.

Zhang saw what she was doing and rushed to help, nearly falling out of the boat in the process. She knew he couldn't swim. Of course he couldn't. So she grabbed the back of his jumpsuit and hauled him back down. The boat swung back and forth with their momentum, but it never quite capsized.

"Rapscallion! What are you seeing on the satellite view?"

she called back, once they'd cleared the boulder. "Anything to worry about?"

"The river splits in about three kilometers. It forms two courses that come back together quickly enough, but we'll need to make a choice. There are some pretty fast-moving rapids on one side. The other looks like it's full of rocks. Which way do you want to go?"

"Rapids," she said, without hesitation. If the boat was damaged, that could be the end of their journey right there. They could make repairs, perhaps, but they had no extra scrap metal to use for patches or to replace any part of the boat that was lost.

"Got it. For now, just enjoy the ride."

"Sure," Petrova said.

The slope they were on wasn't too steep, but the river had been digging its way through the mountain for long enough that they were passing in and out of narrow canyons all the time. Sheer walls of brown rock rose up on either side of them, blocking out the sun or threatening to drop rocks on their heads at the slightest impact. With no trees or even grasses to hold them together with their roots, the stones of Paradise-1 were precariously balanced at best, prone to dramatic landslides at all times. She kept her head moving back and forth, looking for the next hazard that might kill them.

All the same, it was Zhang who was the first to notice they weren't alone. "Do you hear that?" he yelled at her.

"What? The river? It makes all kinds of noises, that's normal," she said.

He huffed in indignation. "Not the river. It's not a natural sound, it's mechanical or . . . or an engine or something."

She opened her mouth to respond. It didn't matter what she had been about to say. She ducked her head reflexively as a shadow passed over them, moving fast. The sound hit her next, very loud, four propellers slashing at the sky.

The quadcopter flashed by them in a second. As it headed

downriver, she got a good look at it. From the roof of the medical center it had just been a shadow against the stars, but now she saw it was a big cargo model. The four rotors were mounted on the end of long spars that joined the central body in thick, flexible joints. A bubble canopy was mounted at the front, a clouded plastic windscreen that caught the sun. The glare kept her from seeing who was inside. There didn't appear to be any weapons mounted on the aircraft, but she remembered it shooting revenants off the roof, the distinctive whine of a kinetic weapon pulping their heads.

She had no doubt this was the same quadcopter that had saved them, that had blasted away at the revenants and then withdrawn into the night without stopping.

"Who the hell is in that thing?" she demanded.

"It could be self-operating," Rapscallion pointed out.

God, she hoped not. She wanted so badly for there to be one living person on Paradise-1 other than herself and Zhang. Someone who could answer her questions.

"Hey," she called out. "Hey!" There was no way the pilot could hear her over the noise of the rotors, but still she kept shouting, waving her arms. "Hey! Come back!"

The quadcopter hovered over the water for a moment, rocking sideways as its rotor arms adjusted their pitch. Then it veered off to the left and over a ridgeline. After a minute, even the whine of its engines was gone, lost in the clear sky.

"God damn it!" she shouted. In frustration, in need, just to make noise to fill the sudden silence.

She watched the sky for any sign that the copter might return, and she knew that Zhang and Parker had to be watching too. She didn't even notice when the river forked and Rapscallion poled them over into the left-hand course. It wasn't until he warned her that the rapids were coming up soon that she looked back down at the river. The water had been forced through a narrower channel than before, which caused it to flow faster. It surged and hissed around them, and bubbles turned its surface a brilliant white.

"Your reflexes are better than mine," she told the robot. "You got this?"

"Sure," Rapscallion replied. "You know I've never done this before?"

Petrova glanced forward at Zhang. He didn't seem to have heard that. She waved at Rapscallion to indicate he shouldn't ask any more questions.

"Okay," the robot said. "Both of you, get your heads down." Zhang dropped to the bottom of the boat, curling up like a lizard. "Oh, and if you're thrown out, or the boat capsizes, just try to hold onto something. It might help."

Zhang's head popped back up. "What?"

"It's going to be fine," Rapscallion said. "And it'll only take a minute. Now hang on."

# 50

The boat swerved and Zhang was thrown into the aluminum side. It felt like it crumpled under his weight, and he was terrified that it would buckle, that the water would come rushing in, cold and foamy and choking, but then the boat moved again and he was thrown backward, into a bag of provisions. Something lumpy and sharp pushed into his ribs, and he gasped in surprise more than pain. Spray flicked over the side and splattered on his cheek, and he reached to wipe it away, then nearly screamed as the boat hit something, it definitely hit something, he could feel the juddering, scraping impact and for a sickening moment they weren't moving at all – that was horrible in a brand-new way – and then ...

The boat cleared the obstacle, whatever it had been, and suddenly it was free and racing forward like an out-of-control rocket, shooting down between the walls of dark rock he could see towering over them on either side. Parker shouted something he couldn't make out. Rapscallion, standing over Zhang, bent low, shoving hard with his pole, maybe against a rock that was about to tear the boat apart. The robot didn't grunt or swear in frustration, but Zhang was certain he was struggling, fighting to keep them shy of inevitable death.

It must have worked. For a little while they were simply moving again, far faster than Zhang would have liked, but he supposed they were at the mercy of the current. He might never have been in a boat before, he certainly had never seen this much water in one place, but he understood the basic principles of fluid dynamics. He grasped the sides of the boat and lifted his head, just a little, to see if the danger was over.

He really shouldn't have done that.

The river rolled out ahead of them in a frothy stew of brown rock and white bubbles that popped and burst, bubbles the size of his head. Water slicked everything around them, water thrown up in sudden spouts or slow-moving lateral waves that jumped the bank and splatted on the shore. Water rushed up over the boat's bow and Zhang was soaked, instantly freezing cold and miserable. Some of it even got in his mouth, and though he knew it was clean, he spat it out, spat until he was sputtering pointlessly, wiping at his eyes. A massive rock loomed ahead of them, a big triangular stone sticking straight up out of the water, and he gasped, then his head spun as the boat swerved to the side, just missing the hazard.

Rapscallion had this. Zhang trusted him with his life, just as he had done many times before. He was certain the robot would get them through this. He ducked his head back down, thinking it was better not to see the close scrapes, the near misses.

Then the robot spoke. "Petrova," he called, his voice raised above the roar of the water, "it's going to get real bad here for a minute. What do you want me to do?"

"Do we have any options?" she called back.

"No good ones. Hold on!"

Zhang grabbed for whatever solid object he could find. It turned out to be one of their water jugs. He hugged it close to himself, thinking somehow it might protect him, that it would at least weigh him down. It worked; at least, as the boat lifted and then fell back, smacking its flat bottom against the water, he didn't go flying. Then they slammed over to the left and the jug nearly broke his arm as they both crashed into the side. This time he definitely left a massive dent in the aluminum. Water sloshed over him and filled the bottom of the boat. He tried to scoop it out with his hands, but more kept pouring in. Would they sink? Was this how they were going to die? He just had time to wonder before . . .

The sky turned brown, or rather, the blue of the sky was replaced by the brown of the rocks, and Zhang looked up and saw the water hanging over his head, the bank of the river below him. He clutched hard to the jug, but it betrayed him, rising from the bottom of the boat, seeming to fly up into the air under its own power. He heard someone shout his name, but then water closed over his head. He wasn't ready; it filled his mouth, his nose, he sneezed and gasped and coughed and more of it rammed its way down his throat, something very hard hit his arm and he tried to scream but his entire respiratory tract was full of cold silver water and he started to panic, his brain shutting down all its higher functions. He lashed out with his legs at the water, the rocks. One of his feet found the bottom of the river and he kicked against it, hard, and that was enough to propel him upwards.

For a second, a beautiful second, his head was in the air. He vomited water all over himself, a spasm of every muscle in his chest simultaneously, and then sucked desperately for air, for even just half a breath before . . .

The water closed over him again. This time he had the presence of mind to shut his mouth. It tried to get in through his nostrils, but some reflex saved him there; his throat closed and refused to let any more water come into his body. He realized with a start that he was still holding onto the water jug. He had the absurd thought that it might act as a flotation device, before he remembered it was full of water, that it would have the same density as . . .

"Zhang!" someone called again, but from very far away this time. He turned his head and saw nothing but rocks, soaking wet rocks, and his head bounced off something hard. The pain was immense; it drove all thought and sensation out of him, and he was terrified he was going to black out. He tasted blood and —

— white water surging all around him, the bubbles seeming to lift him, then a cross-current tore him sideways, down, under the water, into what looked like an underwater cave, except then he was moving again, jerked backward by —

— his hands grabbed at a rough part of the bank, a knob of rock that stuck up out of the water. He got purchase on it but then the river yanked him away with such force he couldn't resist, and above him the sun was painful, glaring, his head, his head hurt and —

— underwater, his face was underwater, he tried to swivel around, to get clear, to get even a single breath, but it felt like he was being held down, pushed down toward the riverbed, he saw it loom up in front of his face, dark and smooth and very hard and —

Blood. Blood everywhere. It filled his mouth and he gagged, spat.

Green arms stabbed through the water and grabbed him under the armpits. Hands hauled him painfully up into the blue air, the silver water streaming from him in great sheets streaked with blood. He was tossed onto a hard rocky surface, slick with water, but at least it wasn't moving. He moaned in pain and tried to curl into a ball, but Rapscallion hauled him up to a sitting position.

"Bleeding," he said. "I'm bleeding."

"No you're not," Rapscallion said. The robot grabbed Zhang's chin and turned his head so he could see Petrova lying on the rock next to him, her face covered in blood from a massive gash on the side of her head.

# 51

Petrova opened her eyes. She was underwater, her blonde hair floating around her like seaweed. She wasn't breathing.

She didn't need to breathe. Not here. She knew where she was.

She looked down, and just as expected there was a light below her, a light far down in the green depths. It was very, very bright and she felt she would have trouble if she tried to look away.

She didn't look away.

The basilisk pulsed rhythmically. She almost felt like she could hear it, like a drum beating, or perhaps it was the sound of her own heart. She and the basilisk were together now, joined. Inseparable. Her body belonged to the parasite. It owned her flesh.

No, she thought. I'm in control. I'm still in control.

*Not here.*

The thoughts in her head weren't her own. Her voice, Petrova's voice, was a small buzzing noise, like a fly. Like a fly batting its head against a window. Wanting freedom but not even understanding what that meant. Not really.

It would let her go. The basilisk could be magnanimous. It would permit her to leave this space in a little while. First, it had something to say.

*We're getting closer.*

The basilisk was pleased by this. It was pleased that she was doing as it had asked, taking it to see the thing it guarded. Taking her to witness the subject of its creation, its sole justification. It was glad that they were making progress.

Without warning the pulsations grew strident, fast, angry.

It was impatient that things were taking so long.

Which? Which is it? she asked.

The basilisk, of course, was not limited to binaries. It could feel two contradictory emotions at once. Inasmuch as it could be said to have anything so simple and atavistic as emotions at all. Frankly, it found it highly amusing that she could even try to comprehend its mental state.

It found the idea demeaning.

It found the idea incomprehensible. *You did not evolve to understand something so complex as myself. You did not evolve to think in five dimensions. Or nineteen. You were not constructed to last longer than the stars, to be more enduring than spacetime. Were you?*

No, she admitted.

*Then simply listen.*

She had no choice. The thoughts in her head belonged to it.

*There will come a time when you will need to take certain actions. The result of these actions might lead to the loss of life. Human or otherwise.*

*You are not to hesitate when this time comes.*

Wait, she said. I don't understand, I don't —

The hammering noise was right next to her ear. It was impossible to ignore, it drove out every thought, every —

*You will not hesitate.*

*You have been permitted an illusion of control. Of freedom.*

*Do not force my hand.*

*Do not make me remove that illusion.*

*You will not hesitate.*

The pulsing light burst through her, tearing her apart—

Hands grabbed her around the waist. Squeezed her so hard water spewed out of her. Yanked her backward, away from the light, away from the basilisk. She vomited up more water.

More. There was an endless supply of it. Her stomach must have grown large as a house. It came in great gouts, water surging up out of her, and the pulsing wouldn't stop, and she opened her eyes and someone shushed her, someone gently stroked her hair, the light, the light of the basilisk was gone, replaced, the light, that was the sun, a red sun, low on the horizon. She opened her mouth, tried to ask a question.

Instead she vomited river water all over the front of Zhang's jumpsuit.

She was mortified. She was so tired, and that pulsing light – she could still see it. Was it real? She couldn't tell what was real and what was . . . The sun, that had to be real, and Parker's hands, his hard-light hands holding her, neither hot nor cold.

"Shh," the basilisk said.

No, no, that was Zhang, that was Zhang trying to calm her, to get her to lie back, turn her head. She vomited again, and again, just dry heaves now, her stomach turning itself inside out, and the pulsing didn't stop. Maybe it was a little farther away now. "Shh," Zhang said. Parker's hands, neither warm nor real but so good, so real.

*Remember*, the basilisk said.

*When the time comes for sacrifice, you will not hesitate.*

She twisted her head to look up at Zhang, at his face. He looked scared. No, concerned.

*When the time comes.*

# 52

Bang. Bang. Bang. Bang. Rapscallion lifted his arm, brought it down again. Bang. The rock in his hand made a semi-adequate hammer. Bang.

Zhang waved for his attention. "She has a concussion," the human said. "She needs to sleep."

The robot looked over at Petrova. They had made camp on a rocky ledge just above the river, the closest flat ground they'd found to where the boat ran up onto the rocks. She was lying under a natural rock overhang, a place out of the sun and out of the wind. It was the best they'd been able to do for her. Parker was wrapped around her body, his hologram arms holding her.

Rapscallion nodded. Then brought his arm up, brought it down again. Bang.

"It would really help if you stopped that."

He looked down at what was left of the boat. Several of the long aluminum strips had been bent so far out of shape they were basically tied in knots. The steel bottom had dents in it that could buckle under any serious impact. He had ideas, plans on how to improve the design. The tools he had to work with, however, were limited. Mostly he could bash the pieces of metal back into shape with his rock hammer. That was how he could make himself useful just then.

"This boat," he pointed out, "isn't going to repair itself."

"I understand. But she hit her head very hard when she fell in the river. Her skull didn't break, but there may be some swelling in her brain. We're not going anywhere until she recovers, and that could be days. Or longer."

"We're supposed to be at the mine seven days from now."

"I understand," Zhang said. "As a doctor, I can't let her move until she's better. Do you ... do you understand what a concussion is?"

Rapscallion had a database of medical terminology in his memory, of course. He had all kinds of information on humans, most of which he'd never bothered to look at. He grasped immediately the physics problem that resulted when a human head met a hard object under sharp acceleration. He could call up images of the major blood vessels in the brain. As for the subjective experience, he had no idea.

"Is she going to die?" he asked. He knew sometimes humans lingered for a while before they perished.

"No," Zhang said. "No. Absolutely not." He glanced guiltily over his shoulder, back in the direction of Petrova and Parker. "No," he said again. He took a deep breath. "No. She'll be fine."

"Oh good. If she dies, you know you're in charge, right? You have to tell us all what to do."

"She'll be fine," Zhang said again.

Rapscallion consulted a program he'd written that analyzed human speech patterns, facial gestures and the pattern of blood flow in their cheeks and foreheads when they spoke. Sometimes this program allowed him to tell when humans meant what they were saying and when they were, say, being sarcastic, or lying to spare his feelings, or so exasperated with him they just told him what he wanted to hear.

Sometimes. This time the program came back with a rating of "inconclusive".

He looked at the rock in his hand. "She needs to sleep," he said, reiterating the actual point of their conversation. "Okay. I can do this later. It's not like Parker could be in charge. He's just a hologram. And I'm not allowed to lead a group of humans. It's written into my programming."

"I understand," Zhang said. He looked over at Petrova and Parker. The hologram was barely visible, just a haze of line and shadow around her body. "Can you ask Parker to try to support her neck? Just keep it immobile if he can. She might have damaged her spine in the impact as well."

Rapscallion sent the message. "Done. So if you were in charge, what do you think your plan would be? Keep heading to the mine?"

"I would have to make that decision when the time came. For now, it's moot."

Rapscallion nodded. He set the rock down next to the wreckage of the boat, careful not to make any noise.

He understood how to follow instructions. Whether he thought they were worth following or not.

# 53

She dreamed her mother was still alive. Her mother, Ekaterina, her great mane of hair trailing behind her forever like the tail of a comet. Her mother with arms outstretched. Her mother, screaming, her mouth like a Gothic arch, chasing her through an endless dark hallway.

"You aren't tough. This is a job that takes toughness, Sashenka."

No one called her that. They called her Sasha. Everyone called her. Everyone.

"You must take them in your hand. And then you close the hand, very fast. You show them how hard your hand can be. This is the way worlds are governed. Where there is no governance, there is only chaos." Her mother's claws dipped into her shoulder, tearing skin and muscle and bone away. Her mother grabbed her hand, her left hand, and bit off three of her fingers.

"Better if you do not wear the stockings at all," Mother said. Mother.

They called her Sashenka. No one. No one called her.

"I am doing you favors," Mother said. Her mother.

She dreamed of her mother.

In her sleep, she tried to roll over. She coughed. She could feel her body fighting her, feel blood all over her, feel broken glass floating around her in the absence of gravity.

Her mother, the parasite. The parasite in her head. In her

mother's head. In Zhang's head, if she died. The parasite would take Zhang, would take Zhang if she died, she couldn't die. Her mother. Her mother's hair, trailing like the misty tail of a comet. White and endlessly, naturally curly.

She ran and ran and ran. Her mother right behind her, always.

"Toughen you up," and Mother ate another finger. Stripped the flesh off the bone with teeth as hard as titanium. "Tough. Tough meat needs to be tenderized."

Sometimes. Sometimes you had to show them violence. It was all they understood. If you let them take advantage of you, even for a second, they would never respect you again. She got that lesson while she peered up from the inside of a box on the Moon. Earth's moon. The people who kidnapped her had been Lunarists. Secessionists, fighters for independence. They wanted a flag. Flags had been outlawed.

"Flags divide us. Unity is our strength," Mother said. "Unity whether they like it or not. Do you understand? Flags are symbols, and symbols are potent. But crushing a few hands, smashing them under your boot. This is more potent. People remember the pain."

In the dark corridor her mother was right behind her. She ran as fast as she could, but her legs weren't long enough, her horrible ballet slippers couldn't get traction. Her breath came savagely in and out of her chest and she cried out in her sleep, and the dream wouldn't end.

For days she ran down that corridor. For days, with Mother right behind her. Mother.

The parasite wouldn't let her win. Wouldn't let her get ahead, even a few paces. She dreamed. Mother. "Tough. You must be tough," her mother said.

Mother!

She opened her eyes. Parker was there, curled around her. There was barely room for both of them in the glass tube. She smiled. He was being cheeky. She remembered what it was like to sleep next to him, her arm around his chest, in the absence of gravity. To cling to him like if she let go she would fly off into orbit, into infinity. If she held on, if she clutched to him, they floated there in the cabin together, slowly rotating so that now he was on top, now she was on top. She remembered what it was like, moon and planet, round and round in the dark.

She was still dreaming. Still dreaming with her eyes open. She looked around for her mother. Ekaterina wasn't there. That was how she knew the dream had ended.

"Parker?" she whispered. Her throat was so dry it hurt.

"I'm here," he said.

Her head spun. Her head hurt.

"Parker?" she said, again.

"You fell out of the boat," he told her.

Her head throbbed. She couldn't move her neck, could only move her eyes back and forth. She saw dark rock, dark sky. It was night-time, the sun had gone down. What if there were revenants? What if they came for them? "I fell out," she said.

"Yeah."

"Well that was a stupid thing to do."

He laughed and kissed her cheek, kissed the side of her head.

"Ow," she said.

# 54

Zhang asked Rapscallion to shine a light into Petrova's eyes, one then the other. He took her chin and moved her head from side to side, palpating the bones of her neck. "Good," he said. The first thing they teach you as a doctor. Small words of praise, little acknowledgments keep the patient from panicking. "You're doing well. Do you know where you are?"

"Not precisely," she told him. She raised an eyebrow.

"What planet?" he asked. "What planet are we on?"

"Paradise-1," she said.

"Do you remember who the director of Firewatch is?"

"Lang," she responded, without hesitation.

Zhang nodded. "Okay. How do you feel?"

"Bruised. Tired. How long was I asleep?"

"Seventeen hours this time," he told her. "It's alright. Your body knows what it needs to heal. If you're still tired . . ."

"I can sleep in the boat. What the hell happened to the boat?"

Zhang sighed. He glanced over at Rapscallion's work area. The robot had rebuilt the boat as best he could. It was a bit more square now, its walls not as high. The bottom was a completely different shape. In general it was a lot smaller. "There wasn't enough left of it to rebuild it the way it was before."

"Jesus. We really wrecked it, huh?"

"Oh, we didn't do anything to it. You and I were both in the water by then. There was a rock under the rapids, one

Rapscallion didn't detect in time. It nearly tore the boat in half. If we had been inside when it happened . . ."

"Lucky we weren't," she said. "How soon can we get moving? We've lost a lot of time." She seemed to think of something that hadn't occurred to her until just then. "Wait. You said, seventeen hours *this* time. I remember waking up a couple of times, waking up and being so groggy and confused I just went back to sleep. How long have we been camped here?"

"Four days," he told her.

Her eyes went very wide. "Did you sedate me?" she asked.

"You could have suffered cognitive damage. You could have suffered a brain bleed. Microfractures in your spinal column could have worsened over time. You could have jumped up, gotten back in that boat, felt a sudden pain in your back and then – bam. You would have been paralyzed from the waist down. You could have had a blood clot in your neck and—"

"Stop," she said. "Stop!"

"Okay."

She turned her head and looked out at the water. Rapscallion was already lowering the boat into the current. Parker put a bag of rations in its bottom. The bag was almost completely empty.

"Remember when I refused to leave you behind?" she asked.

"Yes," Zhang said.

"I'm glad I did," she told him. "I have a feeling we wouldn't be having this conversation otherwise."

He said nothing.

"I know what you're about to say," she told him.

He just nodded. It wasn't like this was their first time. She needed to rest. She needed to spend another week in a hospital under close observation. He knew she would refuse even the most basic, most common-sense measures, though. She was going to forge ahead with her mission as if she hadn't just woken up from a semi-comatose state. As if she'd just gotten a little bump on her head instead of major trauma.

He knew he should keep quiet. Let her get on with it, let her be Petrova.

He couldn't, though. Not without one last try.

"Rest for one more day," he told her. "Less than a day. Just take a nap. Lie down with Parker and close your eyes and see what happens." It was the best medicine he had to give her. He knew exactly how she would respond.

"We can rest when we're rescued," she said. She walked to the boat and spoke with Rapscallion. No doubt making plans for her next incredibly risky move.

He gritted his teeth and followed her down to the water.

# 55

Below the rapids the river grew wider, filling a broad valley, and its current slowed a little, giving them a smoother ride. Parker spent much of his time as far in front of the boat as he could get and still be within range of Rapscallion's projector. He manifested himself as standing on the water, and used a little hard light to make it crest and splash over the tops of his feet.

It felt like nothing at all.

He had spent days wrapped around Petrova's body, the body he remembered so well. He had held her close, cradling her head to keep her neck from moving, just as he'd been ordered, but he knew he had held her for his own selfish reasons. He just wanted to be near her. He wanted to be the man he used to be, her lover, yes, but also the rakish spaceship pilot, the too-honest flyboy with a cocky grin and a heart of gold. He'd wanted to be human again, alive again, and the closest thing to that was holding her so close he could feel her heart beating against his chest.

And it had felt like nothing at all.

"I know you're there," he said. He spoke the words out loud, but because he was just a computer program, he could control his own volume level. He made sure no one in the boat could hear him. "I can sense you."

The Other, the phantom body, was right behind him where he couldn't see it. Ever since Zhang had asked him about phantom limb, Parker had felt the Other close by. Watching him.

Sometimes it was just a trick of the light, or the way the non-existent hair on the back of his non-existent arms would stand up. Sometimes he could actually see it, a shadowy human shape just in the corner of his eye.

"I feel like you want something," he said. Except he knew what that thing had to be. It was his own mind externalizing his need for sensation, for touch. He could hold Petrova close while she slept, but it always felt like he was holding her while wearing thick mittens, at best. The hard light allowed him to interact with the world, but it couldn't give him his nerve endings back.

The Other was just a manifestation of how that felt. His subconscious refusing to be ignored.

"If you have something to say, I wish you would just say it," he told it.

It didn't move around to where he could see it. Didn't utter a sound. For a while he chided himself for giving it any kind of credence, for paying it any attention. It was just a trick of a mind stretched beyond human limits. It couldn't talk, couldn't communicate.

Then it laid one hand on his shoulder.

That, he felt. The hand was warm. He could feel the individual grip of each finger, feel the thumb on his shoulder blade. It felt so real.

He might have wept. But when he reached up to touch the invisible hand, it wasn't there.

"I'm not okay, am I?" he asked.

But the Other was gone.

# 56

The river carried them down into a deep saddle, a valley carved between two high mountain peaks. Mist rose from the water and formed long snakes of vapor that twisted away from them, tendrils that disappeared whenever the boat carried them too close. Looking downriver, Zhang saw that the mist grew thicker, formed a kind of blanket of fog. He knew that was a natural phenomenon – cold air dropped down off those mountains, moist air that never quite turned to clouds. When it hit the sun-warmed surface of the river, it sublimated instantly into fog. As the current carried them onward, soon they were wrapped in the silvery mist. It flecked his cheeks with tiny droplets of water that he wiped it away with the sleeve of his jumpsuit. He turned around and looked up at Rapscallion, who stood at the back of the boat, leaning deep over the side to push against the bottom with his pole.

"Can you see through this?" he asked.

The robot played a sound clip of a foghorn. He had to explain what it was, as Zhang had never heard such a thing before. "Boats used to sound horns like that so they wouldn't crash into each other in the fog."

Petrova snorted. "Not much chance of that here, unless the revenants build boats now."

"I can see alright," the robot said. "I've got infrared, radar, lidar. The fog makes things hazy at a distance, but I can see to steer."

Zhang was glad to hear it. As the fog grew thicker, he had trouble making out even the near bank of the river. The rocks there were dark with moisture, worn smooth by constant erosion. He watched the edge between stone and water because there was nothing else to see.

Then they came around a bend and the fog lifted, just a little, and he gasped. "There," he said. "Get us closer. Can you?"

Rapscallion poled the boat over toward the bank. Zhang saw that he had been right. "Those aren't lichens," he said. He had been correct – he'd seen real plants growing there, tiny purple-black plants. Each had a tiny, thin stem and even thinner roots that stuck down into the rock. At its top each plant bore a single triangular leaf that tilted toward the sun, drinking in what light made it through the murk.

At first the plants grew here and there, in sporadic clusters, but soon the bank was furry with them, shaggy, covered in a thick growth, the leaves so close together they formed a massive quilt of sepia. "It's like a fog forest," Zhang said. "They have something similar on Earth. Like a rainforest where it never quite rains, where the fog never lifts and the plants drink mist from the air. It's . . . it's beautiful."

Rapscallion pushed them even closer, until they were barely a meter from the riverbank. The flat bottom of the boat hissed a little as it touched the sandy bed. Petrova leaned over the side and reached for one of the plants with her good hand. Just as her index finger was about to make contact, she erupted in laughter. The little plant lifted itself up on its roots as if they were tiny, hair-thin legs, and ran away from her, knocking over some of its neighbors.

Zhang smiled. "Astonishing," he said. He thought of why this world was called Paradise-1, why they had named it after the Christian Eden. He remembered the story, of how Adam, the first man, woke up to a world full of plants and animals no one had ever seen, and gave them names.

*Triangularis zhangi*, he thought, musing on what it would be like to be a botanist on this world. To discover new things and catalog them, put them on a tree of life. But how to even classify these little organisms? They looked like plants but acted like animals. Except they were neither, because these hadn't evolved on Earth, so they didn't belong to any terrestrial kingdom.

"Oh," Petrova said. "Look. There."

Zhang followed her pointing finger and saw that the little creatures were moving en masse now, shoving and pushing each other as they hurried to climb onto higher rocks. Some of them were more robust than others, and the weakest were knocked back into the water, where they quickly sank and stopped moving.

"Shit. Did I do that?" Petrova asked.

Zhang shook his head. He pointed at the bank further on. Something was moving in the mist, a faint shadow that proved to be pale gray, fog-colored, as if for camouflage. When it drew closer, he could make out its basic shape, a sort of round, lumpy body. Two long jointed legs pushed it forward, shoving it along the smooth rock. The front was all mouth, a wide-open toothless maw that dipped forward to a cruel-looking point, like the sharp beak of an eagle. Compared to the tiny plants/animals, this thing was a beast, maybe half a meter long. It barged its way through the crowd of leafy prey, which were sucked into its unclosing mouth and consumed in great quantities.

A predator. The little creatures – Zhang was already calling them triangulares in his head – tried to run, but the bigger one was so much faster. It barely moved left or right, instead just content to scoop up whatever lay directly in front of it.

"It's like an awful hoover," Petrova said. "Sucking them up like that." She shivered, and then laughed. "I'm being sentimental for an ivy with legs."

"*Hooverium petrova*," Zhang said.

"Don't name that fucking thing after me," Petrova said. She laughed again, but she wasn't smiling.

"I thought there were no animals on this planet bigger than a spider," Rapscallion said.

"Remember the hunting rifle they had back at the town?" Petrova asked. "Maybe they found the thing bigger than a spider after all. Maybe it was one of these."

"No, no," Zhang said. "I don't think the colonists ever came this far into the mountains. We might be the first humans ever to see these organisms." He glanced up at Rapscallion. "Or the first robot, for that matter."

"I'll add that to my list of accomplishments," Rapscallion said.

"Come on," Petrova said. "This planet's been surveyed from pole to pole. Nobody ever stumbled on a hooverium before?"

Zhang shrugged. "It's easy to forget just how big planets are. I have no doubt that satellites have imaged every square kilometer of the surface, but how far have people explored on the ground? We didn't see anything like this before we came down the river. It's possible this fogbank is the only place on Paradise-1 these creatures exist."

"I wonder," Parker said, suddenly standing over them, just off the side of the boat. "If nobody's seen these things before, there might be other animals out there. If that thing eats the little ones, is there a bigger thing that eats it?"

Zhang laughed. Yet he had to admit the thought was hard to dismiss. They all fell silent as they watched the hooverium at its deadly work, but he knew that, like him, they were also watching the fog, looking for shadows looming there.

In the end, though, the hooverium was the largest lifeform they saw. One of them, slightly bigger than the rest, came all the way down to the water and looked at them. At least it lifted its wide-open mouth over the water in their direction. It didn't seem to have any eyes, so maybe it smelled them instead. It stood there screaming silently at them, until Zhang could see down its dark, ribbed throat and make out the triangulares in there, still moving as they were slowly digested. He watched in utter horror and fascination and wondered if he could catch the predator and dissect it, learn how it worked. Its curiosity only lasted a moment, however, and it returned to its endless, almost desultory feast.

Soon the fog started to lift, and while that gave them a better view of the fields of triangulares, which rustled in the sun in a fashion Zhang found hypnotic, it also meant that soon the organisms grew thinner on the ground. They formed clumps, then tiny colonies around little puddles of water in the slick rock, and then disappeared altogether as the sun burned the last tendrils of fog away.

In place of the mist they heard a not unfamiliar sound, a kind of rushing, as of water hurtling down a pipe. The riverbanks rose higher and became canyon walls once more as they wound their way through the foothills of another high-peaked mountain. The river grew narrower and faster, in a process so gradual Zhang barely noticed it until Rapscallion started pushing off the canyon walls with his pole, just to keep them centered in the current.

Eventually, the walls had come so close Zhang thought he could reach out on either side and touch them. He wondered, darkly, what would happen if the river narrowed so much that the boat got stuck, wedged in tight. What would they do then?

Fortunately he didn't have to find out. Ahead of them lay a massive slope of boulders and scree and the river made a hard bend around it. Beyond, Zhang heard the rushing water much louder now, and felt a trace of spray on his cheeks.

"What is that?" he asked. "Another fogbank?"

Petrova shook her head. Her eyes were wide. She reached behind her and grabbed Rapscallion's leg to get his attention.

"Waterfall," she said. "Waterfall!"

# 57.

Rapscallion had seen the mist and sensed that the river was flowing faster than it should, but he had no experience of waterfalls. By the time he saw what lay ahead of them, it was nearly too late. The water surged around the bend at the foot of the mountain, then plummeted into a vast crack in the planet's crust. It fell at least twenty meters through what looked like a vertical shaft, straight down into darkness. The spray was so intense he couldn't make out what lay at the bottom of the abyss, but he was certain they would all die if they went over that edge.

"Stay in the boat," he called. Parker looked up at him in horror. Maybe the ghost didn't know what he was supposed to do. It didn't matter. Rapscallion had more important concerns at that moment.

He dug his pole into the loose rock at the bottom of the slope, shoving hard to try to bring them to a complete stop. The boat tried to spin sideways, to escape his control and rejoin the current. He dug harder until he could hear the pole grinding against solid rock deep under the scree, and finally he was able to push it up onto the shore. The bottom of the boat shrieked and started to buckle, but it stopped moving, and that was the important thing.

"Fuck," Petrova said. "Fuck."

Rapscallion stepped out of the boat and walked to the edge of the falls. The ground beneath him crumbled under his weight, but he kept his balance. The view was about what he'd expected.

"There's a cave down there," he told the others. The waterfall fell down what was essentially a very long pipe. Most likely it had been a lava tube before the water came. Now it was a natural drainage shaft. His most advanced sensors could tell him there was a massive cavern at the bottom, but not how far it extended or where it led.

"How did we not see this coming?" Petrova asked. "How did we not notice that the river just fell into a hole in the ground?"

"To be fair, I did notice," Rapscallion said. "I just didn't understand what I was looking at."

She stared at him. He really wished the humans wouldn't do that. If they had questions, it was so much easier when they just asked them.

He tried to interpret her silence. Most likely, he thought, it meant she wanted more information. "The satellite map I'm working from shows that the river just stops here, at the foot of this mountain," he explained. "Then it picks up again about a kilometer and a half that way." He pointed directly through the mountain. "On the far side. I knew it had to go through a tunnel, but I assumed the tunnel was horizontal."

Petrova looked away from him. "What are we supposed to do now?" she asked.

"Two possibilities, I think," he said.

She made a noise of disgust. "It was a rhetorical question."

"Fine, but there are two possible answers anyway," he told her. He indicated the side of the mountain. "Looks steep, but I think we could probably climb up there, get over it. I mean, I could do that."

"Zhang's leg—"

"And your hand, and now your head, would be problems, yeah," the robot told her. "Climbing up and around the mountain would be tricky, and take a lot of work, time and energy, especially if we want to bring the boat with us."

"Tricky," she said. "That's a nice way of putting it. What

you're describing ... We barely made it down a mountainside back when we were fresh. Climbing a mountain the way we are right now? That's not just tricky. It's impossible. Am I wrong?"

"Only technically," he pointed out. Technically the climb was totally possible. If Rapscallion abandoned the rest of them and went alone. "The other possibility has its downsides too, though."

"Such as?"

"It's incredibly dangerous, we have no way of knowing what's in store for us, and we'd be in the dark the whole time with just our own lights to guide us."

Petrova looked at the hole in the ground, and the water pouring over its edge. "You can't mean ..."

"The upside is that it's always easier to climb down rather than up. Faster, too."

"That," Petrova said, "is just a terrible idea."

## 58

"Is this even possible?" she asked. "Is this something we can do?"

She stood on the rocky bank by the side of the waterfall, looking down into the broad shaft carved out of the rock. The mist filled her eyes and she had to keep blinking it away, rubbing it from her eyelashes. It looked like a long way down. It looked ludicrous.

"We lost a lot of supplies when the boat capsized," Rapscallion said. "We still have all our climbing gear, though."

She knew she could keep arguing with the robot or they could get on with it.

So they got on with it. She anchored a rope and dropped it into the shaft, well clear of the main flow of the waterfall. The end of the rope fell away from her for what felt like far too long, then disappeared into deep shadow. She glanced back at Zhang and Parker. They were standing there, arms folded, watching.

"Need I remind you," Zhang said, "that you're recovering from a concussion?"

"Are you telling me I can't do this?" she asked.

"Ha. I learned not to do that a long time ago. But promise me, if you start feeling dizzy or nauseated, you'll stop. You'll get to a safe place and then you'll rest until I can come and examine you."

"I'll take my time going down," she said. "I'll be safe. Rapscallion will spot me, make sure I'm doing okay. When I reach the bottom, I'll let you know, then you can follow me down. It'll be okay."

"Remember not to look down," Parker said, sounding like he was trying to be helpful.

She slid down the rope as fast as she dared. With only one good hand and basic climbing gear, she had to be careful. It turned out that after the first minute or so, looking down wasn't a problem. There wasn't anything to see. The shadows and the spray from the waterfall made it impossible to tell where she was headed.

She really hoped the rope wouldn't end with her dangling over a deep subterranean lake. She really hoped there wasn't some kind of giant pale hooverium waiting for her, its mouth stretched wide so she could slide right into it.

"Petrova?"

It was Zhang's voice. She glanced up, looking for the top of the rope, but it wasn't there. She was hovering in space, with only darkness below and pale mist above.

"Shit," she said. She blinked three times, which activated the device implanted in her hand. "Sorry. Go ahead, Zhang."

"We're just checking in. You okay? What does it look like down there?"

She considered how to answer that question. She didn't want to scare him and make him think the shaft went on forever, that they were sliding down into hell. "Hold on, I just need to make an adjustment," she said, which was a lie. She made some soft grunting noises to back it up. Then she slid down another ten meters, faster than she probably should have. The palm of her hand was still abraded from last time.

A little farther, she told herself, then slid down another five meters. She was in almost total darkness by that point, and she had to fight back a little bit of panic. How long was the rope? Would it reach to the bottom, or was she going to have to find a ledge and plant a new anchor? What if she couldn't find ...

Her foot kicked something, a solid floor of rock. She felt around for a little in the dark, making sure she was actually secure. She lifted her hand and used her device as a light, checking she was at the actual bottom. Thirty meters down, she thought. Deeper than she would have liked.

She carefully tested her footing, then turned around slowly. The darkness wasn't complete. A single beam of sunlight made it all the way down, diffused by the furious mist boiling off the pool of water that filled most of the cavern. The waterfall had dug a thick channel through the floor. From where she stood, she could see it flowing away into a dark tunnel.

She stood on a narrow strip of wet rock between the water and the wall of the shaft. The floor was covered in stalagmites, some as tall as her waist. The walls of the cavern were oddly smooth. She saw they were made of nearly regular columns, interlocking hexagonal pillars of rock, like the caves of Iceland or the Giant's Causeway in Ireland, back on Earth.

"Petrova?" Rapscallion called. "How does it look?"

"Doable, maybe," she said. "Bring the boat down."

The rope jerked upwards, then came down again, this time with the lightweight boat dangling from its end. They'd considered just letting the boat fall down and catching it at the bottom, but Petrova didn't want to take any chances. Rapscallion had plenty of strength to lower it on his own.

As it descended, she looked around, trying to see if there was a way forward, or if they'd made a terrible mistake. Then she saw the mouth of a lava tube opening in the cavern wall. She tried to see inside but there was only darkness there.

"We good?" Rapscallion called out.

She didn't know how to reply to that.

# 59

There were patches of fungus on the ceiling that gave off a fitful green and blue light, occasionally hues of violet or even red. They looked like burning clouds at midnight. The tunnel was otherwise lightless, narrow, its ceiling studded with stalactites. Every time they passed under a big one, Zhang had to duck to avoid hitting his head.

Parker floated ahead of them, a bright ghost leading the way. He looked like he was flying through the narrow lava tube. The hologram was their only light source, the only way Zhang had to know that they were making progress. He could watch the walls roll past on either side, see the milky water below them shift. Rapscallion kept the boat right in the middle of the tunnel, where the water was deepest, and still from time to time Zhang would hear what sounded like the bottom scraping against sand.

What would happen, he wondered, if the tunnel squeezed down to nothing? If the roof had caved in up ahead so that the boat couldn't get through, or if the river went over another cliff? The current wasn't all that strong. Rapscallion could stop the boat before it hit anything or went plummeting into a bottomless pit. But what then? They would have to head back, turn around and somehow work their way back against the current. How long would that take? Was it even a possibility?

"How's your power level?" Petrova asked. Her voice echoed off the ceiling, ran away from them across the water, and Zhang was suddenly terrified someone might hear them, some abyssal beast would be drawn to the sound. "You good?"

"Fine for now," Rapscallion said. "I charged my batteries back at the comms tower. I charge automatically whenever I'm near a power source. I have a few days left at this level of power consumption."

"A few?" Petrova asked. "How many is a few?"

"Four days, six hours, thirty-one minutes," the robot replied. "At this level of power consumption."

"How far are we from the mine?" Zhang asked. It was hard to imagine they even had a destination, at this point. That their goal wasn't solely to escape this dark tunnel.

"Three days," Rapscallion said. "Best-case scenario, three days. Which is still just within the ten day window Lang gave us."

Best-case. Okay.

They fell silent again. Zhang had nothing to listen to but the weird sounds of the water. The way it sloshed against the walls, the constant bloops and echoing drips of condensation falling from the ceiling. He heard another sound, one he thought might be the thrashing of fins, but it was so far off he couldn't be sure. Certainly he hadn't seen any fish in the river.

Fish. Now there was a sobering thought. If there were fish down here, was there something that ate the fish, some creature much, much bigger than a spider? Bigger than a hooverium?

He forced himself not to think about that. Instead he mentally named all the bones in the human hand, then the foot. He was halfway through the muscles of the torso when he realized that he was falling asleep. In the dark it was hard to tell if his eyes were open or closed. He fought it, blinking rapidly, sitting up higher, straighter. He licked his lips, rubbed his hands together to improve his circulation, but none of it was any use.

Petrova's good hand touched his shoulder. "I can see you nodding off. Get some sleep."

"Is that an order?" he asked.

She laughed. The echoes seemed to go on forever. "Sure."

There was no way to lie down inside the boat, not without sprawling all over her. He settled for leaning forward with his head between his knees. He knew he would wake up terribly stiff, but he was so tired he didn't care.

What followed was a kind of sleep, he supposed. In the dark, in the relative quiet of the tunnel, with the continued slow, gentle rocking of the boat, it was hard to tell the difference between sleep and something like a trance state. Maybe he dreamed, but if he did, he dreamed only of the eerie warbling, plopping sounds the water made. His brain, lacking stimulation, filled in the void with unwanted imaginings and dark fancies. He felt they had passed out of the tunnel and into open space, that the lights on the ceiling were stars and galaxies instead, that they sailed through the nothingness between suns. He imagined that he was all alone in the bottom of the little boat, that the others had abandoned him, left him at the mercy of the current. He felt like something was watching them from the dark, something cold and malevolent but patient.

He dreamed he was back on Titan. Well, that dream was never far away.

It was always the same. In the dream, he was climbing a staircase, a long spiral staircase that led up to an unspecified destination. The steps were covered in human bones, and every time he put his foot down, he had to be careful not to trip over a skull, or step on a pelvis or the remains of a human hand. He was terrified he would fall, stumble and fall backwards down those stairs, back into the dark and what was down there, what he had left down there.

He whispered a woman's name, a name he never said aloud anymore. In his dream, he couldn't say anything else.

He reached forward and touched one of the bones, picked it up in his hand. It was just a fragment, a piece, an iliac crest with scorch marks on one side. He rubbed at it with this thumb, trying to see what lay beneath the soot, and it made a strange squeaking noise, then a grumbling like steel rubbing against rock.

He opened his eyes and there was light. There was strange pale light all around him, light he didn't recognize. The boat had stopped moving. He blinked, thinking this was part of his dream, except it had never been like this before, he'd never dreamed of this light . . .

"All ashore that's going ashore," Rapscallion said. "C'mon, Doc. Come take a look."

"Whuh?" Zhang said, his throat thick with sleep. "Wha?" He sat up, his back complaining, and looked around.

It took him a while to understand what he was seeing, but one thing was clear. They had run out of river.

Petrova climbed down out of the boat onto a gritty riverbank. She could see a fair distance ahead, though she'd been in the dark so long the light stung her eyes. Ahead of them the tunnel opened up into a massive canyon with rough walls. The water continued to run forward, but instead of a smoothly flowing river, it crossed the floor of the cavern as dozens of branching streams, none of them deep enough or broad enough to be navigated by the boat. The streams wound their way around countless columns of dark rock that stuck up from the floor like support pillars, though none of them reached the ceiling. She made a connection in her mind and suddenly she saw the columns as tree trunks, and the cavern as a vast petrified forest.

Above them, high above, the ceiling was perforated in a dozen places by the wide mouths of lava tubes. The whole mountain must be riddled with them, she thought, like the tunnels made by worms eating their way through an apple. This cavern must be a place where a large number of the tubes intersected. Water poured in endless streams from some of those mouths, falling dozens of meters to splash into deep pools in clouds of dense mist. From some of the other openings, lone shafts of sunlight descended like spotlights, painting the cavern in brilliant white.

There was something unusual about the floor of the cavern, but at first she couldn't quite figure it out. It seemed to gently flutter or shimmy as she watched it, a movement as unending and gentle as the plash of waves on a lake. Except here it was the solid ground rippling, not the water.

She took a step further onto the riverbank and something crunched under her boot. She looked down and saw something run over the top of her foot, something with long pale legs that scuttled away before she could get a good look at it.

Horror crept up her spine as she looked again at the rippling cavern floor, and realized the origin of that constant rippling motion.

"Zhang," she whispered, grabbing for his arm.

"I see it," he told her. "They're not . . . they aren't . . ."

"Spiders," she hissed.

The floor of the cavern was covered in a ceaseless mass of spiders. Thousands of them, millions. In the conical beams of light coming down from above, she could see them crawling over each other, crawling in random directions, see their legs moving, lifting and bending and stretching out, see them scuttling toward her.

Once she knew what she was looking at, she could hear them, too. A soft, droning rustle, a sound like dead leaves skittering on a forest floor in autumn.

One of them had crawled over her foot.

She fought the urge to tear her boot off and throw it as far away from her as she could.

"They're not spiders," Zhang said, using a tone of voice he probably thought sounded reassuring. To Petrova it just sounded patronizing. "They're not like anything from Earth."

Her nose itched and she nearly screamed, thinking one of them had gotten onto her face somehow. She swiped at her nose, her cheeks, but of course there was nothing there.

"I don't like spiders," she said. She shook her head. "I don't do well with them. I can't do this."

"Of course you can," he said.

She nodded. Trying to believe him. She could hear them,

though. Climbing the basalt columns. Swarming along the edge of the water where it ran through the deep shadows. She could barely hear anything else.

"Over here," Parker called, from one side. She didn't look at him.

"You go see what he wants," she told Zhang.

He nodded, but then lingered for a second. "Are you going to be alright? I don't think I have any anxiolytics in my medical kit, but—"

"Just go," she told him.

He left her alone. She took a step back, down toward the water. She saw the thing she'd stepped on before, the thing that had crunched under her boot. It was one of the non-spiders, of course. It looked dead. That made it almost bearable. She saw that it wasn't exactly spider-like, in point of fact. It had no real body. Just a collection of pale legs, maybe ten of them, maybe twelve. They came together around a tiny beaked mouth.

It had no eyes. Fine hairs stuck out from inside its joints. The idea of those hairs touching her made her skin crawl. It made her want to set the whole cavern on fire.

She imagined the sound that would make. The millions of tiny screams. And then they would come rushing toward her at once, all of them burning and coming at her . . .

"Petrova," Zhang said, "you really do want to see this."

She ran over to where the others stood around what looked like some old debris. She supposed it was better to look at than the local wildlife.

"What is this?" she asked. It looked like a pile of garbage, honestly. Flat pieces of junk, broken and discarded here. What might once have been a couple of barrels, except they'd been torn open, torn apart before they were discarded here. She bent down and picked up a long, flat piece of metal, rusted until she couldn't tell what purpose it might have originally served. She turned it over and saw traces of paint on the other side. She made out a curved line, a bit of cross-hatching, and realized she was looking at a picture of a human face, or at least part of such a picture. She even recognized the style of the artwork, and suddenly she knew exactly who had painted it.

The same person who had painted the murals back at the campsite. The unknown artist who had lived among the cannibals there.

"We think this was a raft," Parker said.

"Pretty crude compared to our boat," Rapscallion added. "But it would have floated."

"They were here?" she asked. "The people from the camp? We found that message saying they were headed to the mine. You think they came the same way we did, that they came here?"

"Maybe," Rapscallion said. "Maybe they hit that first stretch of rapids and capsized, just like we did, and the river carried what was left of their raft this far. There's no way to know for sure."

She nodded. "They were starving when they left their camp. Even if they did make it this far, their raft didn't go any farther. What do you think the chances are that they reached the mine?"

It wasn't a question any of them could answer, not really. At least none of them could give her an answer she might want to hear.

"Pretty slim," Rapscallion said, anyway.

She rubbed at her face. Ran her fingers through her hair, in case there were any spider-like animals in it. There weren't. "We'll make it, though. We'll get there."

"Absolutely," Parker agreed. He reached for her shoulder, but she shook her head to warn him off. She didn't want anything touching her just then.

She knew what their next step was. Of course she did. "We need to get across this cavern. We need to carry the boat to the other side." She had no idea what they would find there, but she had to hope that the various streams of water came back together as a single river again, flowing down toward the lake that was their destination. That was the only possibility that led to them getting out of this place alive.

Of course, that meant crossing a cavern full of things that looked like spiders.

Spiders.

Something about spiders, something ... from her childhood, except she couldn't remember. When had she come across spiders as a girl? Did they make her think of her mother, or something?

In her head their wriggling legs clicked and clacked, their tiny beady eyes stared red out of dark shadows, and she nearly let out a cry of alarm. She'd always hated spiders, always ... always been afraid of ...

Spiders. Fucking spiders!

"Let's do this as fast as we can," she said.

# 61

"She's phobic," Zhang whispered.

Parker didn't want to believe it. Petrova was fearless, that was the pole star that had brought them this far. Nothing could make her give in.

Yet as he watched her tentatively move toward the spiders, then dance back like they were biting at her feet, he realized that maybe she wasn't as dauntless as he'd thought. It didn't change his feelings for her. If anything, it made him want to protect her, to be there for her when she needed him. Maybe . . .

Rapscallion played a sound file of a human clearing his throat. "Can you give her something for it, Doc? We need to get through here."

Petrova must have heard them. She looked up, a nasty scowl on her face. Then she took one stride forward, into the mass of crawling animals. Parker could see her shaking, her good hand trembling over the holster of her pistol as if at any moment she might draw it and start shooting into the writhing mass. But she held her foot where it was, just inside the throng of spiders. Her lips pressed tight together until they turned a bloodless white.

Zhang walked toward her, but Parker saw her eyes go wide. She was looking at Zhang's feet. The spiders had covered his boots entirely and had started to crawl up his pant legs.

The doctor wasn't immune to the fear, it seemed. He yelped a little as he brushed the creatures off his clothes, knocking them away from him. One was launched in the air not in Petrova's direction but not directly away from her either. She screamed and jumped backward, out of the mass.

"I can't," she said. She shook her head, tight little motions. It looked to Parker like her entire body had gone rigid. Like she was paralyzed.

He stepped in front of her, his hologram glitching as he stretched his hard-light presence out, reshaped it into something like a snow plow. He scraped the rock ahead of her, shoving the spiders back. They tried to get around the edges of his barrier, spilling over it in a slow cascade of wriggling bodies. A small area of the rock floor, though, was clear, just for a moment.

Petrova stepped into that space. She ducked down, her hands brushing at her back, her arms, her cast making a terrible rasping noise as she dragged it across her face. She huddled behind the barrier Parker had made. He moved forward, centimeter by centimeter, and she hurried to keep up with him.

"You're doing great," he said.

"Shut the fuck up. Just shut up," she said.

"You got it," he told her. He kept moving. Little by little.

Then she looked up, in Zhang's direction.

The doctor was barely keeping it together. He was moving, walking through the mass. The spiders didn't have any trouble climbing up his legs, his back, scrambling over his shoulders. When they got close to his face, he let out a little whimpering noise and batted them away, spitting wildly as if one of them had gotten inside his mouth.

"Don't look," Parker said. "Don't look at him."

Petrova's eyes shut tight. A microscopic tear escaped from her left eye and rolled down her cheek. Parker reached down with hard light and gently brushed a spider off the side of her boot, so gently he hoped she didn't even feel it.

"What was that?" she demanded. "Fuck! Take me back. Take me back — there has to be another way, there has to be another way." She opened her eyes, though he could tell it took her some effort. "There has to be another way."

Parker looked forward. They had crossed a dozen meters of the cavern. There were hundreds of meters yet to go. Just ahead of them lay one of the areas where light from above illuminated the floor. He thought it looked like the spiders were especially thick there, the scrum dozens deep as they crawled over each other in their endless, random peregrinations. What the hell were they after? Why did they move like that?

He couldn't feel anything, not the touch of the spiders on his hard-light body, not the warmth of the sunlight or the cool air of the cave. He couldn't smell anything, but he could hear the constant noise, deafening now, of all those legs rasping away, the tiny feet clicking on the shells of the ones beneath, the beaks moving, closing, chewing at the air, the constant susurrus, the clamor of it, the ocean of sound they made.

He could feel Petrova's fear. He could see it radiating off her like body heat. It was just an illusion, a trick of whatever was left of his once human mind, but it was like she was a torch of pure terror burning in that dark place.

"I can carry her," Rapscallion said. For a second, Parker couldn't see the robot. Then he watched as a vast mass of spiders rose from the millions, like a wave of them swarming up out of the darkness and spilling away, the bright green plastic of Rapscallion's body just visible underneath. It was like they were especially drawn to him for some reason.

Rapscallion could hear Parker's thoughts, of course. "They've been nibbling on me. I think I taste like food."

Petrova stared at the robot. Parker realized she was hyperventilating. He tried wrapping his hard light around her, tried to shield her from the spiders altogether, put her in a bubble of safety, but there were so many of them. Every time Rapscallion moved, a new wave of them swept over his hard-light barrier, some of them coming over the top to rain down around Petrova's feet, some of them sneaking around the sides. They wanted to fill all the available space, take up as much room as they could, and she was the only thing left they hadn't covered, hadn't blanketed with their bodies.

She opened her mouth as if she was going to scream.

Then her head snapped forward, her jaws coming together with an audible clack. Her eyes narrowed, and she stepped around the shield. Walked right around it and into the mass of spiders. They crawled up her ankles and she didn't seem to care. Crawled up her calves, her thighs.

She didn't slow down. Didn't scream, didn't so much as whimper as they swarmed up her back and onto her shoulders. She just kept moving.

"What the hell?" Parker asked.

"Did she just snap?" Rapscallion asked. "Sorry. I mean, did she just have a psychotic break or something?"

"No," Zhang said. "No. I don't think so."

Zhang trudged forward, almost wading through the mass of crawling life. The way they crunched under his feet might have alarmed him, bothered him terribly, if he hadn't been so distracted.

It also helped him ignore the smell, the chemical reek of the spiders. The dried-out, poorly-drained-fish-tank smell of them. Or the way they felt when they climbed up his jumpsuit and touched his exposed skin. He kept brushing them away, but they clambered up over him faster than he could remove them.

By the time he reached Petrova, she was covered to the top of her head. They crawled across her cheeks, over her mouth. Somehow her eyes were clear. Maybe that was the basilisk's doing. It had subtle powers he didn't fully understand, and probably never would.

"Petrova," he said. "Petrova!" but she didn't turn around.

Of course she didn't. Petrova wasn't there. Not at the moment.

He'd known it the second he saw her head snap forward. The set look in her eyes. Not just determined. Focused, in a way human eyes never really were. Human eyes kept in constant motion, scanning the peripheries, tracking for predators. Human eyes were the eyes of a living being, an animal in a world full of sensory stimuli.

He hurried around in front of her, walking backward so he could see her face. He was terrified he might stumble back into one of the basalt pillars that punctuated the cavern floor, but he needed to see those eyes.

The eyes of the basilisk.

"Let her go," he said.

The eyes flicked across his face. Just one quick glance, then they returned to staring straight forward.

"Did she pass out? Was that your big chance, your chance to take control of her body for a while? Or did she ask you to take over?" Zhang demanded. "Maybe that felt easier to her than taking another step."

One of the spiders dug a probing leg into the corner of her mouth. It almost looked like a twitchy smile. The basilisk reached up with her good hand and removed the spider. Cast it away. Casually. Calmly.

The basilisk never stopped walking.

"Close, now," it said.

It wasn't just the skin of his back that crawled. Zhang's entire spine rippled with disgust. It used her voice, the exact same voice she always used when she spoke to him. There was no growl there, no unearthly pitch or timbre. It didn't matter. He knew it had spoken to him directly.

How many times had it tried to communicate with him in the past? How many different ways? Then it found Petrova, its perfect host. It hadn't bothered him since.

He knew he should leave it that way. Catching the basilisk's attention was a great way to get yourself driven insane. He had inoculated himself against its primary weaponry, its ability to sow delusions in the human mind. He knew it had other arrows in its quiver.

He couldn't let it just take her, though. Not Petrova.

"Let her go," he said. That didn't get a response.

Of course not. There were only two ways to get something from the basilisk. Give it what it wanted ... or threaten to take that away. "I'll stop you," he said.

Another glance. A quick up-down look. This one seemed especially contemptuous.

He could barely stand to look at Petrova the way she was, covered in spiders, her mind buried under the commands of an alien parasite. He focused, kept his gaze locked on her eyes.

"Not much longer," it said. "When I am done with her, you can have her back, physician. Whatever is left."

Zhang wiped at his forehead, his hair. "You won't get very far without our boat. What are you going to do? Swim down the river to the lake? Her body won't make it. Not with only one healthy arm."

The eyes narrowed. Contempt was draining out of its look. Anger was replacing it.

"You are playing a dangerous game," it said.

"You think I don't know that? I remember what it looked like when you killed every single person on Titan."

"Except for you. You were spared then."

"No," he said. "No. I wasn't spared. I beat you. I found the cure for what you did to us. A vaccine against you. So keep that in mind – I can stop you. I can fight you and I can win. I just have to be willing to pay what it costs."

Still she kept trudging forward, moving through the spiders so fast he had to hurry to keep up. How far had they come? If they reached the far side of the cavern, if there were no spiders over there, would that be enough to break this trance? He doubted it would be that easy.

He drew his pistol from its holster. The obscene, blocky thing Rapscallion had printed for him. It felt wrong in his hand, like a mistake. There was a rough seam on the trigger guard that bit into his finger as he raised the weapon and pointed it at Petrova's head. It took a lot of willpower, but he did it.

"I could end this right now," he said. "I could take away your host. What would you do then? You'll never get to see this thing, whatever it is, the thing you were made to guard. You'll never see it if she's dead."

"Are you sure? I have a backup, after all," the parasite told him.

Zhang fought to keep himself under control. He knew what it meant. It needed a sentient brain to live inside. If he killed Petrova – if he could actually bring himself to pull the trigger – he would simply be freeing it to move to a different host. Since his was the only other brain around that would function for that purpose, well ...

"I wouldn't let that happen," he said. "I would die before I let you inside my brain."

"It's an interesting calculation," the basilisk said. "How fast can you move? How long would it take you to lift the barrel of that weapon and place it under your chin? How much time would you spend making sure you had the angle correct, so that the bullet would actually destroy your frontal lobes, rather than, say, pass through your cerebellum and leave you unable to walk or control your bowels, but still alive? How much longer after that would it take you to actually pull the trigger? Would you hesitate, even for a fraction of a second?"

Zhang swallowed all the saliva that had suddenly built up inside his mouth.

"How fast," the parasite asked, "do you think I can move?"

It didn't laugh at him. Laughter was a human expression, after all, a kind of communication it had not been built to use. He could sense something like mirth in its eyes, though. In Petrova's stolen eyes. Something like cold humor.

"Do you even understand that 'one second' or even 'one fraction of a second' is a human unit of measurement that means essentially nothing to me? Space and time, in my experience, are far more fluid than in ..."

She stopped walking. It stopped walking. Just stopped midstep, slowly put its foot down, crushing a few spiders in the process but clearly not intentionally. Its eyes didn't move; they remained focused on the far side of the cavern.

It stopped. Stopped walking. Stopped talking.

"What is this?" Zhang demanded. "What are you doing?"

It stood perfectly still. Petrova's body didn't so much as twitch. Then she blinked. Blinked again.

"Zhang?" she asked.

It was Petrova. She was back. He wanted to rush forward, grab her, embrace her. He stopped himself because he realized he was covered in spiders, she was covered in spiders, they were both ... except ...

The spiders drained away from her like grains of sand through the neck of an hourglass. He watched as they scurried down her arms, across her hips, down her boots. He looked down at himself and saw they were abandoning him as well. He'd done a relatively good job of ignoring how many of them were on his body at any given time.

Soon there were none.

Soon the writhing carpet of them, the living floor of the cavern, started to recede as well. The spiders hurried away from his feet, back in the direction from which he and Petrova had come.

"Zhang? I think I hit my head," she said. "In the water."

He reached for her good hand. He had no idea what was happening. The cave floor around them was clear, empty of spiders. Looking back, he saw a great tsunami of them crest over Rapscallion, over the dull aluminum of the boat the robot was still carrying. He saw them race away like a tide going out.

Even the smell of them was passing. He realized he couldn't hear their rustling noise, either.

Something had changed. Something had changed to make them alter their behavior, to drive them back. Something had ...

Something had scared them. They'd seemed utterly unafraid of human beings, of hard-light holograms and even robots, but something had driven them back as fast as their legs could take them.

It had to be the same thing that had made the basilisk recede as well. To cause it to release its grip on Petrova's body.

Zhang peered forward, toward the far end of the cavern, toward darkness. Was there something there? He sought for any sign of movement, anything at all.

He found it. Shapes, just shadows, moving toward him.

Something much bigger than spiders.

"Shit," he said. He grabbed Petrova by the shoulders. "Come on," he said. "Come on!"

The confusion in her eyes didn't clear. She had no idea where she was. Something in her trusted him, though – he could tell that much. When he said she needed to move, she understood that she needed to move. She turned and ran back toward the others.

He hesitated only a moment. Just long enough for another look back into the darkness, another attempt at determining what was after them. It was a mistake. Before he could see anything, hands like steel vises grabbed him and dragged him down to the hard stone floor of the cavern, dragged him out of the light.

"Leave the fucking boat," Parker shouted. He could only make out dim shapes ahead of them, but it didn't matter. Whatever was in front of them, whatever had scared the spiders, he just wanted to get Petrova away from it. He wrapped one hard-light arm around her shoulders and started to run, back toward the place where they'd found the raft. Back toward the place where they'd first entered the cavern. Rapscallion wasn't running. Parker had no clue why not. "Come on!"

The robot dropped the boat without protest, but he seemed more interested in staring into the dark. "What happened to Zhang?" he asked.

"They got him!" Parker didn't actually care who *they* were. He just wanted to get Petrova somewhere safe.

Which raised an important question. Where on this stupid planet was safe? More specifically, where was he going to go? They could run back to where the river ended, but then what? Swim for it? Petrova looked about half-conscious. She could barely talk.

"Zhang," she said. "What happened to Zhang?" Her eyes darted in every direction. "Hold on," she said. "Hold on. Get off me!"

Parker switched off his hard light. "I was just trying to . . ."

She staggered away from him. Back toward the place she'd run from, back toward where Zhang had been grabbed and dragged away into darkness. "Fuck this," she said, and then she drew her pistol.

Parker didn't know what to do. He had no idea what they were up against. Some kind of animal that ate spiders? Some giant cave predator? Or was it —

"Shit," Petrova said. She lifted her weapon to shoulder height and fired three times. "Shit! Look!"

Parker looked.

"Oh," he said.

The shadowy figures they'd seen before had moved, they'd come forward. A couple of them staggered through one of the pools of light slanting down from the ceiling. Illuminated, their bodies were pale, the color of blind cave fish, except where black veins burrowed under their sagging flesh.

Their eyes were solid black.

"The survivors, the cannibals," Parker muttered. "They made it this far."

"Stay back!" Petrova shouted, and fired again. A puff of black dust erupted from the left shoulder of one of the revenants. It barely flinched.

"Zhang," Parker said, under his breath. "What did they do to Zhang?" Of course he knew the most likely answer to that question.

"On the right," Rapscallion said, and Parker swiveled around to see that more of the dead things were over there, lurching out of the shadows. Petrova covered them with her weapon.

"I don't have enough bullets," she said. "Rapscallion?"

"I can fight," the robot said. "I'll fight as long as I can."

"There has to be a better move," Parker said. "Something smarter than just a last stand."

"Name it, I'm open," Petrova said. "Fuck off!" She fired again, this time catching a revenant right in the forehead with her shot. The dead thing dropped to one knee. For a second it looked like it was going to just climb back up onto its feet and keep coming. Then it slowly sagged over to the side and lay still.

The others didn't slow down. They didn't seem to notice one of their own was down.

And there were so many of them.

"On the left," Rapscallion said.

"They're trying to surround us," Petrova said.

"It's working," Rapscallion said.

"How are there so many?" Parker demanded. "They're everywhere!"

"Shit, here they come!" Petrova shouted, and started firing wildly into the crowd of them as they surged forward, running now, hands outstretched, mouths open to show maws full of broken, razor-sharp teeth.

# 64

Time to show off what the new body could do.

Rapscallion bent low and swept his arm around in a broad arc. One revenant tried to jump over his reach, but the robot adjusted in mid-swing and brought his arm straight up, raking it across the creature's side. The spikes mounted on his arm tore through the white flesh, ripping a long strip off the revenant's ribcage. Not just skin, but the muscle underneath as well. The revenant stumbled backward, trying to coordinate with no abdominals. It twisted sideways and fell to flop on the ground.

The robot looked down at his arm and saw that the blow he'd dealt had ripped off half the cladding. He wasn't going to be able to pull that trick again.

He made a note, but he had other things to worry about. Another revenant was right behind him. Rapscallion threw his head backward and cracked its skull. Back when he'd printed this body at the medical center, he'd reinforced the head parts until they served as a highly functional battering ram. He heard a sickening crunch and moved on without looking to see if the revenant was dead or not. He didn't actually care, as long as it stopped trying to kill them.

Petrova took a half-step backward, her back almost up against Rapscallion's chest. She ducked to one side as a revenant tried to snatch at her with broken fingernails. Its hands met Rapscallion's armored sternum instead, the fingertips shattering from the impact. He swung his free arm down like a scythe and smashed the revenant's wrists as well.

Petrova followed up with a point-blank head shot that took the thing down for good.

She reloaded her weapon one-handed. "How are we doing, Parker?"

The ghost grabbed a revenant around the throat with a noose of hard light. He shot up in the air and the revenant's head came off its neck. "That's four," he shouted.

"Of thirty-seven," the robot called back. He turned and saw a revenant stagger right up to Petrova and shove its fingers inside her cast. It dug in deep and she couldn't shake it off.

"I'm coming!" Parker shouted.

Rapscallion was already on it.

The revenant lunged at her throat with its mouth open, clearly intending to rip out her windpipe. She pushed and kicked at it but couldn't break its grip.

The robot used both hands to grab its skull, and dug his long, pointed thumbs into the monster's eye sockets. He pushed and pushed until he felt a sudden drop in resistance and his thumb spikes drove deep into the thing's dried-out brains.

Five, then, he thought.

It had taken a significant portion of his attention to get that fifth kill, however. Which meant he was taken by surprise when two more revenants slammed into his back. His feet were planted on the floor but the rock under him was slick, and suddenly he was off balance, falling forward, right on top of Petrova.

Parker shouted her name. Rapscallion tried to shift his weight around, to keep from crushing her on his spikes. She was fast enough to roll the other way. She ended up on her back, facing the ceiling, her good arm flung out to the side.

Rapscallion recovered and kicked out with one foot, shattering the pelvis of one of the revenants that had tackled him. The other grabbed his head, ignoring the spikes that sank deep into the flesh of its palms and wrists. It lifted the green plastic head and smashed it against the ground, over and over.

They never learned. His processors were deep in his chest, surrounded by thick armor plating. He did feel one of his camera lenses crack, though, and half a dozen of his sensors went dark. That was less than optimal. If he couldn't see what he was fighting, they might be in serious trouble, he thought.

"More coming," Parker shouted.

Petrova lifted her knees, ready to roll up onto them, her head lifting as a revenant grabbed for her. Its claws missed her cheek by centimeters. She made a fist with her good hand and punched it right in the nose. Rapscallion heard the snap of dry cartilage shattering and saw black dust billow out of the revenant's nostrils like thick smoke.

"Your weapon," Parker said. "Get your weapon!"

It must have fallen on the ground when she was knocked down. She twisted around, patting the rock, looking for it. Rapscallion ran an optical object recognition algorithm and located it two meters from where she lay. "There," he said, and shone a light on it from one of the lenses on his chest. Revenants were already filling the space between her and the gun.

Without it she was all but helpless. She could break as many noses as she wanted, but the revenants didn't seem more than momentarily inconvenienced.

"Cover me," she shouted, as she dove for the gun.

Half a dozen revenants surrounded them, coming from all directions. While Rapscallion wrestled with one of them, Parker took on the other five. He used his hard light like a machine gun, shooting projectiles of pure graviton beams that smashed through chest cavities, dented skulls, broke fingers and ankles. The revenants staggered under the rain of blows and even fell back a little.

Which gave Petrova time to grab her weapon and roll over onto her back. She lined up a perfect shot, right between the eyes of a revenant. Fired another shot through the neck of a second one. She must have hit its spinal cord, because it went down, too. The third shot missed altogether, but the fourth took a revenant through the eye, even as it bent down to grab at her ankles.

Two more. Rapscallion dropped to a crouch and grabbed one around the waist, then lifted it up over his shoulders and dropped it head-first on the rocky floor. Its skull made a crunch he found distinctly satisfying.

Another one came at Petrova. A single gunshot pierced its chest. It staggered for a moment, then took another step. Parker hit it with half a dozen hard-light punches and its skull shattered, its face sagging like an empty sack as its jaw, its temple, the back of its skull collapsed.

It dropped to the rocky ground, lifeless and unmoving.

"Tell me that's all of them," Petrova whispered.

"You know it's not," Rapscallion replied. "Why would you ask me to lie?"

"Because I'm out of bullets," she said.

All around them, in the dark, pale shapes were moving. More revenants, coming their way. It didn't seem to matter how many they killed. The brutality of their attacks had no effect on their morale.

They weren't going to stop until Petrova was dead. Until Parker's hologram blinked out and Rapscallion was just shreds of plastic on the floor.

# 65

They moved then, fast, but Petrova knew there was no way they were getting out of this alive. Not all of them.

"There," Parker said, pointing at one of the tall, thin pillars that stood up from the slick floor. "Up!"

Petrova knew it was a bad idea. On Earth she had always been told that if you were being chased by a bear, don't climb a tree, because eventually you would want to come back down. You were betting that the bear would get bored before you starved to death.

Revenants didn't get bored. Not from what she'd seen.

What choice did they have, though? She glanced behind her. They were coming, running, silent and with no purpose behind them but destruction, as far as she could tell. She ran to the nearest pillar, her breathing ragged, her mouth full of spit. This was it... this was it. Zhang...

She gritted her teeth. She needed to be tough. She needed to be determined, and focused, and tough. *Make a fucking decision, girl*, she thought, except it was her mother's voice she heard in her head. Ekaterina had been of the firm opinion that a leader's job was to make decisions even when data was missing, when options were lousy, when no one else could. Ekaterina was dead now, but the advice still felt sound.

Petrova took one look at the basalt pillar in front of her and knew what the decision was going to have to be.

She didn't have to like it.

The pillar rose twelve meters straight up. It was made not of a single column of rock but of multiple shafts of hexagonal stone, their weird regularity of shape a function of the quickness with which some ancient lava flow had cooled. The geology of the pillar didn't matter one bit, but the fact of its regularity did, because the sides of the pillar were almost perfectly smooth. There were no obvious handholds.

She only had one good hand anyway, and that one was still smarting with rope burn. She almost laughed. Cold, tired, hungry, concussion, broken hand, take your pick.

"Go," she said to Rapscallion. "Up."

The robot wasn't in great shape either. One of his arms was curled up at his side, most of the plastic torn off his forearm, his hand just a bunch of bare mechanical joints. His head was cracked and one eye was missing entirely. This mission had been hard on them all, she supposed. "You go first," he said. "I'll make sure you don't fall."

"No," she said. She looked back and saw the revenants were maybe seconds away. "You go up there. I'm going to draw the revenants away. Once you see your chance, get back on the river – swim if you have to – and get to the mine. When Lang's ship arrives, tell them everything we saw. Everything."

Make a fucking decision. Well, she had. There was no time for finer points.

"Petrova," Parker said, because of course he would, of course he was going to fight her, and maybe she wanted him to, but she also wanted him to shut the hell up. "Petrova ..."

"It's an order. Now. Up!"

Then she turned and ran, nearly straight at the revenants. Parker came ghosting after her – she knew he would – but he couldn't follow her very far. Only the distance Rapscallion's projector would let him go. She ran as fast as she could to try to outpace him.

Ahead of her the revenants changed course to cut her off. To chase her. Of course they did. They acted like animals, or maybe more like machines, simple machines that could only respond to a given stimulus one way. Find the nearest living thing. Destroy it.

Just before they reached her, just before their hands could grab at her sleeves, her pant legs, she twisted around on one foot and changed course, running perpendicular to her previous bearing. They stumbled over each other trying to catch her, and then again as they fought to change their heading as well, to follow her, to catch her before she could get away.

She zigged. She zagged. They were always a second behind her. Less.

She didn't look back. She didn't want to see Parker's imploring face. He loved her and she knew it, and her feelings for him were not that complicated, she loved him too — maybe not exactly the same way, but close enough — and maybe, just maybe, seeing him would have been enough to make her stop, make her want to live. Maybe if Zhang were still alive, maybe then she would change her mind. Maybe if there was some chance for any of them, really, if she honestly thought there was something she could accomplish.

Maybe then she would have tried to find a different path forward. Maybe she would have kept fighting, maybe she would have gone down punching and kicking. Maybe.

But maybe it was best this way.

It meant the basilisk would lose. It would never get to see the thing it had been built to guard. It wouldn't get its prize. All the people it had hurt and maimed and killed would get a little justice out of that, even if none of them ever knew about it, even if it was far too late to help any of them. The basilisk would lose and maybe that was a kind of win.

Because, she thought, I know, you fucker. I know what you did to me back there.

Arachnophobia. Fuck you.

And maybe it was best, because what did she have to go back to? She didn't trust Lang, not for a second. Even if she did, what was there for her back on Earth? A career in Firewatch, where everyone thought she had only gotten her commission through nepotism? An empty little house somewhere on Earth, where she could retire on a lieutenant's pension and live out an empty little life?

Zhang was dead. Parker was dead. Rapscallion might just make it. Rapscallion who had been a better friend to her than she deserved. She really hoped he made it.

She was lost in such thoughts when a beam of sizzling violet energy lanced past her cheek, so close she could feel the heat of its passing. It confused her deeply, but she didn't have time to think about what it meant. She looked back and saw a revenant's head explode in a plume of black dust. Saw another one's chest open up, saw dry intestines billow out like ticker tape from a violated abdomen.

"Get down," someone said.

It was not a voice she recognized.

"Petrova!" Zhang shouted. "Get down!"

She dropped to her knees, her hands lifting, like she was being told to surrender at gunpoint. It took her another fragment of a second to realize she was actually being told to just get her head down, so whoever was firing that Gauss gun could get a clear shot.

She dropped all the way, her face colliding with the hard stone floor, her wounded hand bouncing as it hit the rock, pain rushing up her arm to her elbow, her shoulder. Her head was spinning, her ears ringing, and she could hear it now, the magnets of the Gauss gun whistling, warbling, that eerie sound she remembered from training exercises. Blasts of violet light flew over her, one after the other, like a flock of birds desperately winging their way overhead.

Behind her the revenants dropped, torn apart, burned, ripped to pieces, shattered, burst like rotten fruit.

"Hey," Zhang said. He came scrabbling toward her out of the dark, moving on all fours to come close, close enough to extend a hand and lay it gently on her shoulder. "Hey," he said again. "I, uh, found somebody," he said. "A friend, I think." And then he started to laugh.

# 66

Zhang watched as the two of them circled each other like cautious animals sizing each other up. Petrova would probably say she was "assessing the survivor's threat level" or something like that, but Zhang saw it for what it was. A kind of dance. A ritual for two violent people meeting each other in the wild.

Petrova literally moved to the left, the stranger to the right. Their gazes roaming across each other's weaponry, their state of health. Their eyes stayed cold, their mouths fixed lines across their faces.

The survivor certainly merited a closer look. He was just over two meters tall, a black man dressed in a patched colony jumpsuit. His hair was long and fell in hundreds of braids, with a touch of white showing here and there. They surrounded a face lined with care, but not particularly old. Maybe thirty-five, Zhang thought. He carried a long rifle across his shoulders, a weapon of a type Zhang had never seen before. Its barrel was a series of metal rings mounted on a meter-long rail. The stock looked like it had been taken from an old hunting rifle, but it had been heavily modified, cut down and cracked and held together with metal tape.

That weapon had taken down a pack of revenants while Zhang watched. It was fearsome and it looked dangerous just to fire. He worried the survivor might be exposing himself to sidelobe radiation every time he pulled the trigger. Not that Zhang had complained when the man had saved his friends.

"His name's Moussa Abara," Zhang said. "He ... he grabbed me right before the revenants attacked. Pulled me into the shadows, threatened me if I didn't stay perfectly silent."

He wasn't sure how Petrova would react to that fact. He wasn't sure how he wanted her to react to it. Abara had not exactly been gentle when he dragged Zhang out of the fight.

"Just call me Mo," the survivor said. "It'll save time."

Petrova nodded. "Everyone calls me Sasha." She shrugged. "Alexandra Petrova, Lieutenant Alexandra Petrova. Firewatch out of Ganymede sector." She curled up one corner of her mouth. It wasn't a genuine expression of warmth or humor, Zhang knew. He had trouble reading facial expressions, but he knew Petrova well enough to understand when she was employing a tactical smile. "You saved our collective ass there, Mo."

She did not extend her good hand to shake, nor did she change her posture. Shoulders back, feet slightly spread.

"Yeah, that makes two," Mo replied.

Petrova chuckled. "So that was you in the quadcopter. You helped us out when we were stuck on the med center roof. Nice work. Is that a handheld Gauss gun?"

Mo rolled his shoulders so the weapon caught the light. "Built it myself, out of parts. Normal arms, it's a crapshoot with these things. Maybe you hit something vital, a CNS shot, or you crack a cranium. Maybe. I needed a little more oomph."

"Yeah, they're hard to kill."

"I have a question for you," Mo said. "Just ... just a question, okay?"

"Yeah, okay."

"Are you a hallucination?"

His tone hadn't changed. He might as well have asked what brand of tea Petrova preferred with her evening meal.

"I just need to know, first," he added.

Petrova frowned for a second, but she didn't move, didn't change her stance. "No. I'm real, as real as you are."

"Oh, thank God," Mo said. Then he lunged forward, straight at her. She took half a step back, and for the first time Zhang was aware that Rapscallion was nearby, as the robot rushed forward, maybe to intercept an incoming attack.

But Mo just grabbed Petrova in his thick arms and hugged her, hugged her and started to weep.

"I'm going home," he whispered, through the tears.

# 67

Parker's eyes didn't need to adjust to the sunlight. He didn't technically have eyes at all. Still, he blinked and rubbed at his face with his fingers as he stepped out of a cave mouth next to a waterfall and once again saw the surface of the planet.

The river emerged from a massive fissure in the side of the mountain, then dropped ten meters off a sheer cliff. It dug a channel as deep and round as a flume as it hurtled downhill in a series of wild rapids. The mountain, vast frozen waves of brown rock, was unclimbable, just a heap of jagged terrain hovering over the surface of a vast lake studded with pale prominences of rock. Parker tried to imagine what would have happened if they'd tried to take the boat down that way, if they'd been able to stick to their original plan. All he could see was broken bodies scattered across the rocks beneath him, the boat a twisted curl of bright metal in the sun.

"How have you not . . . changed?" Petrova asked.

The strange survivor led them up a trail that was basically just a series of boulders, where Petrova and Zhang had to help each other clamber up onto each new stone. Mo took the ascent like he was climbing a flight of stairs. When he reached the top, he lay face down on the topmost stone and held his arms down to grab them and help lift them up. Rapscallion went around, climbing a cliff face by using his claw-like fingers as pitons, and Parker went along for the ride.

"Forget that, how did you survive so long? It's been more than a year since we lost communication with this place."

Mo held her by her good arm as he helped her slide down the side of a particularly large rock. Beyond that point the trail grew easier, though Zhang and Petrova still had to climb on all fours just to keep from falling. The wind tore at their clothes and hair and wailed so wildly Parker could barely hear Petrova's voice.

"Do you have any idea where these things came from? When did you first become aware of them? We call them revenants. Do you know what they are?"

They climbed about twenty meters up from the cave mouth, to a point where the roar of the waterfall was just a distant hiss and the air was shockingly cold and crisp. They were above the cloud level, though on Paradise-1 clouds were so sparse and far between that just meant Parker could see distant streamers of white cutting across the brown-black surface beneath them. Off in the distance, to the east, he could see what looked like a massive canyon, or maybe a rift valley. Rapscallion's map data told him that was where the mine had to be. It was still so heart-staggeringly far away.

"Just tell me something. Anything. Who was in charge when the revenants attacked the town? What was the police response like? Were there many survivors? Are you the only one left?"

The side of the mountain was never level, never flat, but it smoothed out a little just above them. Sitting on a broad patch of naked slickrock up there, perched like an eagle bracing itself against the slope, was the quadcopter they'd seen twice now. It looked shabbier than Parker had expected, a thing made out of spare parts. Cobbled together, the parts crudely repaired in places, held together with tape and spot welds. The bubble canopy was broad, but the Plexiglas was fogged with scratches and abrasions. There was a bad crack along one side. It looked like Mo had tried to fuse the transparent material back together, as if he'd taken a welding torch to the canopy. Parker knew that kind of patch could never hold for long.

He laughed, surprised. "I've got a question for you," he said. "Do you honestly expect us to get in that thing? Because it's a bigger deathtrap than the boat we left back there."

Mo grinned, an easy, confident grin that set Parker back a step. He knew that grin, because he'd seen it in a mirror a hundred times. Mo jerked his head to one side, as if indicating they should get in if they didn't want to walk to their next destination. That they should shut up and accept that this might be the last working vehicle on Paradise-1.

He carefully opened a hatch on the side of the bubble. It was attached by one stressed hinge. The other hinge looked like it had snapped off a long time ago. Petrova and Zhang dutifully climbed inside and strapped themselves into uncushioned seats. Rapscallion tried to get through the hatch, but he wouldn't fit, so Mo opened up a cargo hatch in the back of the machine and the robot folded himself up inside the dark space beyond. He gave a bright green thumbs-up and Mo shut the hatch, leaving both Rapscallion and Parker in the dark. Parker could only listen as the copter's four independent magnetic turbines warmed up, screeching back against the wind. One of the engines sounded, to a pilot's ear, like it was dangerously out of tune with the others. The copter lurched and then ascended quickly. Clearly the thing could still fly, regardless of its condition.

"Who the hell is this guy?" Parker asked.

Rapscallion didn't bother to answer him.

*Friend.*

Parker nearly jumped out of his non-existent skin. He couldn't see anything in the cargo compartment with them. Of course he couldn't. Rapscallion's thermal camera had been damaged in the fight with the revenants, but even so, Parker knew there was nothing there. Nothing but his own subconscious mind. The Other was there, with them, taking up space they didn't have.

Great. He knew the thing was just a manifestation of his trauma, that it was his way of dealing with the loss of his body.

He really wished it would shut up already.

*Friend.*

# 68

"I'm just a farmer. I guess you could say I was a farmer. These things, these revenants..."

"What do you call them?" she asked.

Mo shook his head. "We didn't have time to come up with a fancy name. 'Dead fuckers' was pretty common." He smiled, though she could see the pain he held in his jaw. "'Zombies', I guess. 'Things'. Like I said. I'm a farmer. Not a poet. Revenant is as good a name as any. They took everything from me."

The two of them were in his kitchen larder. It was a little room at the back of his house, shelves stocked high with boxes, crates and barrels of preserved foods, staples, spices and condiments. It looked like there was enough there to feed an army. Or keep one man going for years.

"You were a farmer," Petrova said.

"Look, what I'm trying to say is, I need a second. I'll tell you what I saw. I'll tell you everything I know. But you gotta give me a little time." He pulled a metal box off a shelf and popped open its top. Smelled its contents, then sifted them into a diffuser. "Tea?"

"I grew up in Russia. I'm never going to turn that offer down. It's been quite a while."

"You know, I have a million questions for you too," Mo told her.

She shrugged to indicate that she allowed that. "It's my job to ask questions. Take statements." She tilted her head forward, looked up at him with a penetrating stare. "Get to the bottom of things. So forgive me if I'm a little overbearing about this. But I need to know."

He checked another shelf. Grabbed a box of shelf-stabilized dairy mix. "Do you take milk in your tea?"

"Don't be a philistine," she said.

"I have some crystallized lemon. And maybe some jam," he said.

"Okay, take all the time you need. I'm going to check on the others." She stepped out of the larder and back into the main kitchen.

Mo Abara had built himself a house at the top of the mountains. A place you could only get to from the air. So a kind of fortress. Maybe that was how he'd survived so long. It was big, open and airy, with a lot of thick windows. Looking west, she could see a whole field of solar panels tilted to catch the sun. To the east, a field of lichen, bright yellow in the daylight, almost beautiful. Through a skylight overhead, she could see a long, thin cloud curling its way across the afternoon.

The house was warm, cozy even. It was full of books, actual printed-out paper books, stored in high shelves that lined one wall of the living area. Soft music played from hidden speakers.

Zhang had curled up on a long sofa, his knees up near his chin, his filthy boots on Mo's cushions. He was fast asleep. Petrova remembered how soundly she used to sleep back when she was receiving her military training. She would march for sixteen hours straight with full pack, and then, when it was finally allowed, she would drop on the spot and be asleep before her helmet was off. Zhang looked like he was sleeping that deeply, and she envied him. She would very much like to rest. Rapscallion crouched in one corner of the living area, soaking up energy provided by those solar panels outside. The robot had removed his left arm completely – the revenants had left it unusable – and was poking at his head with the sharp fingers of his right hand. He dug a cracked lens out of one eye socket and stared at it. Parker was outside, circling the quadcopter, looking for something new to criticize about its construction.

What terrible house guests we make, she thought.

"There's a 3D printer in the back room," Rapscallion said. "Do you think I could hack into it and print some new body parts?"

"You might try asking first," Petrova told him. "Look. We don't know anything about this man, but—"

"You're welcome to the printer," Mo said, coming out of the kitchen. He placed Petrova's tea in front of her. "It's a good one. We used to use it for printing farming equipment. Tractors and such. I used it to build this place, and to make spare parts for the copter."

"Were you a pilot, in another life?" Petrova asked, with what she hoped looked like a sweet smile. As opposed to a crafty grin. If he wouldn't answer her questions directly, she would have to try oblique measures.

"Hmm? No, no. You don't need to be trained much to fly a quadcopter, it's just, you know. Up and down, left and right. Gyroscopes keep it balanced, so there's no danger of flipping it over or anything. The only real danger is flying it into the side of a mountain." He grinned broadly. "And I have antidepressants for that."

Petrova felt her eyes go wide at the bad taste of the joke, but she forced herself to look down and pick up her teacup. "You must know something about machines, though. To keep it in repair. And your weapon – not just anyone could build one of those from scratch."

"You would be amazed the things you can learn to do when you need to," Mo said. "The repair manual for the copter is stored in its onboard memory. It took me a lot of long, cold nights outside figuring out how its wiring is rigged up. As for the Gauss gun, the blueprints were in an old database I found. I just printed the parts and screwed them together."

Petrova had her doubts about that. "Funny. So many of the planet's databases have been wiped clean. I'm surprised that kind of information was still available."

"Wiped clean?" Mo asked. He looked as if he had no idea what she was talking about.

"All the computers in the colony were burnt to the floor," Rapscallion said. "Every record of anything that happened after the revenants started showing up. I was able to recover a little data, some personal logs from the town doctor, but otherwise it's scorched earth in there. Somebody sabotaged all the vehicles and broke the controls of the ansible in the comms tower, too."

Mo frowned. "I saw that you guys went to the comms tower. Didn't you activate it?"

"I was able to fix the controls," Rapscallion said. "Don't you ever go in there?"

Mo shrugged. "Before I left town, it was already out of order. The town administrators said they tried to get an emergency signal to Earth but the ansible network refused to accept their commands. We all kind of assumed . . . well, no offense."

He was looking at Petrova. She raised an eyebrow.

"It wasn't the first time Firewatch kept us from communicating with other planets. We assumed we were under an embargo. I had no reason to go to the tower because I had no idea the problem could be fixed."

It was no surprise to Petrova that Firewatch might be behind a communications breakdown. But someone here on the planet had broken those controls. Not one of Director Lang's people.

"We need to hear your whole story," she said. "From the beginning. I'm sorry. I know it's going to be difficult."

He sat down in a plastic chair, his hands folded between his knees. "Difficult. It's going to break me to tell it all. Do you understand? When a thing is just too big to talk about?"

Petrova supposed she did. She couldn't let him keep evading her, though.

"Okay. Let's start with something basic, something small, and work our way up to the big picture. Tell me. I got a glimpse at your bedroom when we were coming into the house. I noticed something."

"Yes?"

"There are two beds in there," she said. "Who's the other one for?"

Mo's face went perfectly flat, emotionless. His eyes turned to chips of glass. She'd hit on something very deep. Very personal.

"I was supposed to share one with Marsia. The other's for Djidi."

Petrova leaned forward. "Marsia and Djidi? Who are they, Mo? Mr Abara, please answer me. I thought you were the only survivor here."

Mo's expression didn't change at all.

"I said those beds were for them. I didn't say they survived."

They woke Zhang up to hear the story. He sat up, groggy, his eyes bleary, and watched as Mo pulled his braids away from his face and tied them with a piece of twine. The survivor looked almost scared as he started to relate his tale. No, Zhang thought. Not scared. Wary. Like he expected they wouldn't believe him.

"You don't come here, to Paradise-1, if life is working out for you back home. On Earth, Marsia and I had a baby. We had a baby that we loved, and that was supposed to be enough. Djidi would get sick sometimes when he was very little. Just colic at first, and a cough he couldn't seem to shake. He would scratch at the skin between his fingers." Mo held up his hands as if to demonstrate. "Sometimes until he bled. We went to doctors, of course, and they ran a lot of tests. In the end they said it was an allergy. Do you know what heteroatoms are?"

Zhang did. He could see where this was going.

"They're something you get when plastics break down. Old, old kinds of plastic, something called PET specifically. Nobody uses PET anymore on Earth, nobody has for a century. It used to be everywhere, though, and it takes a very long time to break down in the environment. There's billions of tons of it still lying around in landfills, releasing heteroatoms. You can't get away from them on Earth. They're in the air, the water. We couldn't just move to Europe or the Americas. We could have emigrated to the Moon or Mars." Mo shrugged. "Or, we were told, we could come here. Paradise-1, a place totally untouched by PET. Start a whole new life in a place that wasn't slowly killing my son every time he took a breath. You think that was a hard choice?"

He smiled. "It was not.

"They paid for everything. The government. Our passage here, the tools we would need to farm this place, the clothes on our back. Everything we owned had a logo on it. Most of them said *ATLAS*, which was the name of our colony ship. I had a tablet, I used to read technical manuals on it, with the UEG logo on it bigger than the screen." He shrugged. "I think we were grateful. They sure wanted us to be. We would hear lectures all the time about how the government of Earth had given us everything we needed to be successful here. How we owed the whole human race a debt. And the way to pay off that debt was to grow plants and feed ourselves. Prove it could be done."

He gestured out the window. "You've seen what this place looks like. Farming wasn't easy. It's all rocks out there, and you can't plant seeds in slickrock. We had to make dirt. That sounds crazy, right? It was the first thing we needed to do. Make dirt, by grinding up the rock, grinding it with minerals they shipped all the way from Earth, calcium and phosphorus and lots of graphite for carbon. Then we took that ground-up dust – oh, it got everywhere, made me sneeze all day long – and we fed it to tiny little worms. The worms would shit out actual dirt, and that was what we needed. I spent six months here doing nothing but sneezing over a bucket full of worms.

"Marsia had it a little easier. She'd had a good education, she knew some science. She worked in a lab engineering little bugs. Microbes. Our worms kept dying, you see. They needed something we didn't have on Paradise-1. Maybe some kind of nutrient in the rock, or maybe it was the color of the sunlight. There were theories. The solution was, if the worms were too complex to survive here, go with something simpler. Marsia was going to make a bioreactor, a big tank of bacteria that would eat the lava rock and turn it into good loamy dirt. She worked ridiculous hours, but damn did she look happy. Especially when Djidi and I would come in from the fields, our boots caked in mud. She would rub his back, rub it up and down until he was laughing so hard he couldn't stop, and he wouldn't cough at all. I don't think he coughed once the whole time he was here."

There was pain in his voice, but for a second Mo's eyes were bright and joyful. Even Zhang could tell that this was a good memory.

"Of course it was expensive to bring the elements we needed from Earth. The calcium and phosphorus and carbon. That was where the mine came in. At least, that's what they said. The mine was going to give us the minerals we needed to make the farms really yield. It was funny, because everybody knew the mine was there, on the other side of the mountains. Everybody knew it existed, everybody knew it was like a whole second colony. But we never talked about it. The people there kept to themselves, except every so often they came when we had a party, a celebration for Landing Day or for UEG Day, when we used the bioreactors to make alcohol and cannabinoids. Then they would come. Men, almost all of them were men for some reason. They would come and sit and drink and look at us, not unfriendly, just like they didn't know how to talk to us. There was a sheriff in our town. Her name was Sally, she was a good friend to Marsia and me. Sally said something once, and she never repeated it, but I remembered. She said the men from the mine, they didn't see people when they came to our town. They saw customers. That stuck in my head, because it made no sense. We didn't use money in town, there was no money here. We didn't pay the miners for their rocks. We sent them food, but that was just because we fed everybody on the planet. I don't know. Maybe that doesn't mean anything. I just thought . . . Never mind."

Zhang glanced over at Petrova. She was staring at Mo,

watching his face very carefully. Zhang wished very much that he knew what she was thinking.

"Then one day they said there was some problem at the mine. Nobody knew for sure what that meant. Our doctor, our town doctor, went over there and he didn't come back. I remember that was the part that bothered me the most, at first. That if Djidi got sick, if he started coughing, there would be nobody to treat him. But there was a robot in the medical center, it could handle all our problems. It was okay. It was fine, except then a couple people went missing. They just didn't show up at breakfast one day. We liked to eat our meals together in a big commissary in town. At least one meal a day we were supposed to share with everybody. It was so we could see the food we'd made together, that everybody's muddy hands had baked that bread, that the lettuce we ate belonged to us all. So if somebody didn't show up for breakfast, you looked for them at lunch. One of Marsia's workmates, a guy from the bioreactor lab, wasn't there at lunch or dinner. She and I went over to his housing unit, banged on his door. Looked in his windows. There were clothes all over the floor, like he'd been looking for something in his closet and thrown everything on the floor and hadn't cleaned it up." Mo shrugged. "It was weird, I guess, but not that weird. I went and told Sheriff Sally. She had a funny look, and she told me there were six other people missing already, and she was looking into it.

"The things you call revenants, they came one night. What I heard was people shouting in the street, and then a gunshot. Sally came to my door and asked if I would help her look for somebody, and I said yes. Marsia said I shouldn't, she said it was dangerous, but I convinced her it would be okay. And it was. Sally, and three other people and me, I guess we were her deputies. She gave us guns from the armory, guns printed so fresh they were a little wet to the touch still. I never fired that gun. We went house to house checking on people. Looking in crawlspaces and opening up all the warehouses, the storehouses, anywhere somebody could hide. Sally couldn't really explain what we were even looking for. She said some people had got sick and they might be violent if we cornered them, so we should be careful. We didn't find anything. When the sun came up, I was tired to my bones. She said we should go home and get some sleep, that we would go looking again in a few hours. I gave her the gun back and I would have just gone home, but first I thought to ask her if things were going to be okay. She shook her head, but then she wouldn't look at me. That was when I started to get scared.

"I slept all morning, and only woke up because I was so hungry. There were a lot of people missing at lunch. Enough that everybody kept looking around at the empty chairs, but nobody said a word. It was like if we started talking about what was happening, it would get worse. Well. It got worse anyway.

"That night Sally sent a message to the whole town. She didn't want us moving around alone at night. She said we should think about going to our friends' houses, if we could, multiple families in any given house, the more people we could pack inside the better. I remember there was a whole message thread of people volunteering their places, saying they would make us comfortable. You have to remember, we all believed in each other then. We were working together every day, we knew we could count on each other. I think that made us an easier target. Because if you saw somebody in the street, even in the dark, your first thought was to wave. Run over and see how they were doing.

"Sally was hiding things from us. It wasn't her fault. The town administrators had come up with some kind of plan. I never learned the details, but I know a big part of it was making sure nobody knew what was really going on. I heard a rumor there were bodies stored in cargo containers on the edge of town. That people were getting killed, a lot of people, and we had no way of stopping it. They didn't want us to panic. So they told us nothing.

"Which, I guarantee you, is the best way to start a panic.

"There was a whole bunch of people, farmers like me, who wanted to go to the mine. They figured it had to be safer there. The grass is always greener, right? Except other people remembered that our doctor went there and didn't come back, so they thought it must have started there, at the mine. There was so much chatter on the town's network, so many theories. People talking all day long about how it was some kind of disease. That the miners must have busted open some deep cave and released some kind of virus that was going to kill us all. They said they were going to demand that the UEG come and evacuate the entire planet. Like that was something that could even happen." Mo laughed bitterly. "Like it was something they would even consider. No. You know what happened next. Somebody broke the ansible. They said it was an accident, that it was getting repaired. Sure. That was the day I stopped trusting anybody.

"Sally had a plan, she said, a plan to keep us all safe, and I just had to go along. She said if things got bad, like, really bad, we should come to the big auditorium in the middle of town, that we would be safe there. She would keep us safe there. That was the night the revenants attacked, the night they overran the town, I guess. I'll tell you what I remember. I remember screams, and I remember lights going on, all over town – big spotlights lighting up the streets – and I saw a crowd of people running and I thought they were naked. Maybe they were. They weren't wearing clothes like ours, no jumpsuits with *ATLAS* across the shoulders, not these people. I didn't bother to stop to get a better look. I kept my distance. I ran home. I called Marsia and told her to get Djidi and meet me at a certain place. I ran the other way. As far from the crowd as I could get. I went to the edge of town, where they kept the quadcopters. There were four of them, including the one I've got parked outside right now. I could have . . ."

He stopped there. It was as if he'd run out of energy, like a machine that had just stopped working. He sat perfectly still in his chair. Not moving. Not talking.

As the pause lengthened into an uncomfortable silence, Zhang looked at the others. Rapscallion might have been a statue. Parker looked confused, like he wanted to say something, but Petrova lifted a hand in his direction and he stayed silent.

Mo eventually cleared his throat. Then he picked up like there had been no break in his narrative. "I could have saved some other people, I think. There was room in our copter for more people. I could have grabbed more supplies. I've spent a lot of time thinking about what I could have done then. In the end, Marsia and I got in the copter with nothing but our clothes and a bag of food, most of it perishable, and we flew away. You saw the auditorium, right? You saw what happened there?"

"We did," Petrova said. "But Mo – you said you and Marsia..."

"Marsia and I," he confirmed. "While all that was happening, Marsia and I and nobody else got in the copter and flew away."

# 70

Petrova didn't push. She didn't ask a second time.

She could hardly imagine the chaos of that night, the last night of the colony town. There had been ten thousand people in the town. She had not previously done the math, and didn't have time for it now. How many hundreds of people had been able to fit inside the auditorium? How many people had died in their homes?

"From the air we could see them. They looked like ants. I hope that doesn't sound odd. I really hope it doesn't sound funny. It wasn't. From the air they looked like ants, the way ants look when they swarm over a dead animal in the forest. All of them moving, just constantly moving. Seemingly at random. They were stripping the town clean. Moving house to house. Emptying them.

"There were more of them than there were of us, we had almost no weapons, and they were very hard to kill. I knew that if we tried to land, if we went back, we would die too. Instead we just ran away. I flew all night. The copter was in good shape, it held quite a charge, but if we had run out of power, I think I would have just crashed, I wouldn't have even thought to land. I just wanted to get away. Marsia had to convince me to set down. When we landed – right at this place, in fact, though there was just rock here then, just flat rock – she told me what she'd seen, the people panicking, the crowds of farmers and scientists and everybody so terrified, so absolutely clueless as to what was going on. She said she'd got borne away by the crowd, that she begged and pleaded but they wouldn't let her go back, she couldn't find—"

Mo took a deep breath.

"She couldn't find—"

He winced, and then just went on. There was something he couldn't say, couldn't bear to say out loud. "Eventually she had come to me hoping that somehow I had . . . that I had . . ."

He screwed his eyes shut and turned his head, and Petrova knew that pain had to be surging through him like a tide, like a horrible tide coming in.

"I screamed at her. I called her the worst names I could think of. Then I went one better and said she was a terrible mother. She screamed back at me. We couldn't think of anything else to do but blame each other, and when we ran out of insults and the worst things, we just wept, and then we held each other.

"We were alive. We were safe. I took the copter and I went back, I spent all of the next day flying around, looking for any sign of . . . of survivors. There was nobody. I couldn't find . . . I couldn't find what I was looking for. I found some supplies. We needed so many things. I started to imagine what a shelter would look like, and a larder full of preserved foods. I think I still believed, at the time, that we would be rescued. That a ship would come from Earth and pick us up and take us home. I would take my chance with PETs and heteroatoms, I didn't care. I wanted to live. Part of me wanted very dearly to die, so I wouldn't have to think about what had happened. What I had lost. Part of me would have been so grateful for a chance to stop thinking altogether. But a bigger part of me wanted to live. So I went out in the copter every day and gathered things, anything I could think of. I learned very quickly that the revenants didn't come out by day. I could go back to the town and pick up food and construction materials and machines, a big 3D printer, solar panels. I could make us comfortable while we waited." He smiled at Petrova, at Zhang. "While we waited for you. It turned out if you spend all day working until you are so exhausted you can't stand up anymore, that helps keep the thoughts and memories at bay.

"Marsia stayed here. She designed this house for me. She made a beautiful set of blueprints. She wrote code for the printer, so it would make nails and screws and bolts and nuts, so it could print out broad sheets of glass to use as windows, glass made from pulverized lava rock. She wrote a program that would run the house's power system and its heating, control its lights and its security gear, cameras and motion sensors and everything else. She wrote everything the house needed. Then she wrote me a note.

"The note said she loved me, as she always had, but that if she had to look at my face again, even for an instant, she would put a bullet through my eye and then one through her own. So she was going to just leave, start hiking, and I should not follow her.

"Of course I tried. I looked everywhere. I never found a single trace of her. I think she didn't go very far. I occasionally wonder if I will see a revenant, one day, with a head with tight little curls of the kind I used to love to run my fingertips over. A revenant with a meerkat tattoo on her calf. So far, no, I have never seen a revenant like that."

# 71

It took Zhang a while to realize that Mo had finished telling his story. "But ... what happened at the mine?" he asked. "What happened to the other colonists? Where did the revenants come from?"

"I've told you what I saw. If I'd stuck around, maybe I would have more answers for you, but I wanted to save my life. I ran away as fast as I could, as soon as I could, and that made a difference."

"We know there were other survivors. You must have seen them – the ones who camped by the river, the ones who ..." Zhang didn't want to say the word out loud. The cannibals.

"Sure," Mo said. "I saw them. I watched them carry all their gear up the mountain, saw them build those shacks. I tried to approach them. To see if I could help." He laughed. "They shot at me. Tried to shoot me out of the air. It wasn't safe. I tried going back, later. They weren't there anymore. I don't know what happened to them."

Zhang stared at him. "Yes, you do. Those revenants in the cavern. Those were—"

"Revenants," Mo said, very carefully, "are not people. No matter what they used to be. They're not people. You cannot let yourself think otherwise if you want to survive here."

Petrova shook her head and leaned forward, into the conversation. "The mine. Are there survivors there?"

"Not that I've seen. It's a long way. I don't get out there much."

"But there could be other people there," Petrova pointed out.

He took a while answering. "After a while," he said, and stopped again. "After a while, you stop thinking that other people are a good thing. After a while, if you're going to make it, you need to find a thing inside yourself. A thing that's okay with being alone. I don't think there's anyone at the mine. They would have tried to contact me. I'm alone. Have been for months. When I saw you people show up . . . I mean, new people, here, after all this time . . ."

"You were wary," Parker said. "That makes sense. You didn't know who we were, what we wanted. But you saved our asses on that rooftop. And you followed us, watched over us from the air."

"I had to be sure. Before I got close, I had to be sure." Mo put his hands over his face. "I can't believe this is real. Am I really going home?"

"There's a ship coming for us," Petrova said. "Director Lang of Firewatch is sending a ship." She gave Zhang a quick look he wasn't sure he knew how to interpret. He thought she was warning him not to comment on how much they trusted Lang. Or rather, how little they trusted her. "You'll come with us when we leave. We're supposed to meet the ship at the mine complex. We were told there's a landing pad there."

"I've seen it. It looks intact, at least from the air," Mo confirmed. "When?"

Zhang did a little math in his head. "Three days from now," he said. They'd lost a lot of time on the river, waiting for Petrova to recover from her concussion. If they had to cover the remaining distance on foot it would be impossible. With Mo's copter they could make it there in a few hours.

"Three days. Three days and I go home. Back to Earth." Mo rubbed vigorously at his face with his hands. Then he slumped over until he was lying on his couch, curled up in a ball. He started to laugh and weep at the same time.

Petrova rose and stepped into the kitchen, beckoning for

the others to follow her. Zhang leaned up against a counter and thought about what he'd heard. He knew they weren't just giving the survivor space to process his emotions. Petrova wanted something.

She raised one eyebrow and tilted her chin forward. He always had trouble reading facial expressions.

"What is that? Are you trying to say something?"

"I need your opinion," she said, her voice a flat whisper. "Your medical opinion. That . . . display out there."

"You mean the tears? The grief?"

She nodded. "Is that real?"

Zhang wanted to laugh. "The emotions are real. You heard his story. You think anyone could go through that and not end up with enough trauma to break them? You saw his eyes when he talked about his wife and child. Just like I did."

"He's military," Petrova said. "I can feel it. He's got the mannerisms. The way he walks, the way he holds that Gauss gun. No offense, but if you tried firing that thing, you would break your arm."

"None taken. I have zero interest in his gun," Zhang said. "I don't doubt your analysis here. Military? Sure, maybe before he came to Paradise-1. What I saw out there, though, was a deeply broken man."

"That could make him dangerous," Petrova suggested.

Zhang knew it was her job to assess threats and keep them safe. He didn't begrudge her that. But if anyone knew what it was like to be the last survivor of a colony. To watch everyone you loved being taken away from you . . .

"If you don't trust him one hundred percent, fine," he said. "But surely he deserves a little compassion right now. We need to get this man off the planet. We need to get him to a trained counselor, as soon as possible. You wanted a medical opinion, there it is. That man is bleeding out emotionally, and he needs our help."

# 72

Petrova tried making herself some dinner from the contents of Mo's larder. It had been ages since she'd had a good meal and she thought it might help. Might make her feel calmer, more prepared for what they were going to have to do when morning came, when they flew down to the mine. She tried opening a can with a manual can opener but immediately ran into problems – her bad hand could hold things down, it could stabilize the can if she held it against her stomach, but the opener dug a deep gouge into her cast when she tried to make it work. She seethed, ready to hurl the can at the wall. She stopped herself in time, but the frustration, the flare of anger, was humiliating. Big tough Alexandra Petrova, defeated by a can of pickled mushrooms. She sank down onto the kitchen floor, leaning up against a row of cabinets, and forced herself not to cry.

When she came out into the main living room, it was to find the others looking out of a big plate-glass window like they'd never seen a sunset before. She stepped in between Zhang and Parker and gave it a look for herself. Paradise, the sun of Paradise-1, was an orange disk that looked like an egg yolk that had gotten caught on the mountain peaks. As she watched it sink toward the horizon, it flattened out, lost its shape. The color was wrong and it just made her uncomfortable. Maybe she would feel safe again, maybe she would be whole, when they got back to Earth.

"Very nice," she said, trying to put a good face on things. "Very pretty."

"Was it?" Parker asked. "We were just talking about how sunsets here suck because the revenants come at night. The most beautiful thing on any planet, anywhere, and they've ruined it."

Petrova smirked, because she thought he was making a joke. Then she shrugged it off and tapped Zhang's shoulder. "I fucked up my cast," she said, and showed it to him.

Zhang nodded. "I saw some pretty good medical supplies in Mo's storeroom. I imagine he won't mind if we borrow a few things." The survivor had shut himself in his bedroom, presumably to be alone with his grief. "I don't think we should bother him to ask."

He led her back to a room full of high shelves. Mostly they were full of replacement parts for the house's heating and ventilation, flasks of propane for its stove, massive carboys of purified water. The medical supplies took up half of one shelf, but they were well stocked, neatly organized. "Look at this," she said. "He's lined them all up." She indicated a row of bottles of vitamin supplements and analgesics. The labels all faced straight forward, as if Mo had turned each bottle to be easily read by someone standing in front of the shelf.

"I imagine he has a lot of free time," Zhang pointed out. "Here. Sit down on the floor and push your sleeve up your arm. Give me space to work." He squatted down next to her, and it felt oddly intimate, like they were children playing together. Hiding from a searching parent. She realized just how close she'd gotten to him in these moments, how effortlessly she trusted him.

He cut the cast with a pair of thick scissors, then gently pulled it off her arm. She still couldn't bear to look at her hand, but at least nothing hurt. In fact . . . She tried to move her fingers. Nothing happened. She'd kind of expected that. She tried to spread them out, tried to make a fist.

"You don't need to do that," Zhang said, not looking her in the eye.

"It's fine, it doesn't hurt," she said. "Huh."

"Huh?"

"I just tried to move my wrist."

"You did?" he asked.

She'd been able to move her wrist the last time he'd replaced the cast. She'd been able to feel her wrist.

"Hold still," he said. He sprayed resin over her hand and forearm, moving quickly as the plastic set extremely fast. Once it had hardened, she wouldn't be able to move anything. "Good. All done."

She nodded. He started to get up, but she reached for him with her good hand. Pulled him down until he was sitting next to her, shoulder to shoulder. "There's something I've been meaning to tell you. You're not going to like it, though."

"Okay," he said. "Go ahead." No hesitation.

"I'm not afraid of spiders."

"What?" Confusion made his eyes narrow.

"I mean, I am. Now." She shook her head. "I had a pet spider when I was a child. I loved her. When we were living on the Moon, my mother and I, she was always busy so I had to entertain myself a lot of the time. There were no animals to play with, but there was a spider who lived in my bathroom. Up at the top of my tiny little shower, where the ceiling tiles were spotted with mold. She had woven a web up there and she . . . I called her Ekaterina."

"Your mother's name."

Petrova nodded. "I loved that spider. Now when I think about her, all I can imagine is taking a flamethrower to that bathroom. My entire skin crawls. I sat and watched her for hours, for months, I watched her make her web and eat flies and everything and I'm starting to have a panic attack about it right now, just talking about it."

"Why are you telling me this?"

"Because I trust you," she said. "Because you need to know. Back in the cavern, with the . . . the spider things, on the floor..." She could barely form the words. The memory was one of utter terror, of her brain bottoming out. Refusing to let her move, refusing to let her think of anything but crawling legs, tiny beak-like mouths in their trillions.

"You didn't suffer from arachnophobia until that moment," Zhang said. "I see."

"Do you?"

He drew a long breath. "It's not unheard of for phobias to manifest without warning. A sudden fear of spiders isn't—"

"It was the basilisk," she said.

"Ah."

"It wanted to walk me around, take my body for its own. So it made me phobic, so I would lose it, freak out, and then it could just... take over. I think I wanted it to take over, in that moment. I don't have really clear memories of what happened, but I think I may have begged it to take control of my mind."

She felt him tense up next to her, the muscles of his arm, his side tightening as if he wanted to shrink away from her, get away at any cost.

"It's getting impatient," she said.

"I... spoke to it," Zhang told her. "When it was in control of your body, it could use your voice. We spoke." He shook his head. "I didn't learn anything useful, before you ask. It was mostly just bluster. Threats."

"That must have been difficult for you," she said, trying to sound him out. The last time she'd asked the basilisk for help, he'd barely spoken to her for days after.

"Something drove it out," he said.

"What?"

"We were talking," he said, "and then it was gone. You came back. You were dazed, disoriented, but you were back in control. Something drove the basilisk away." He grabbed her good wrist. "The revenants. Yes! I was too busy not getting killed at the time, but that has to be it!"

"Explain, please," she said.

"It had no problem with the spiders. It didn't mind them at all. But when the revenants showed up, it fled. Ran away like a terrified child. There's something about them it can't bear."

"Back at the medical center, when it tried to touch their minds, it felt a void, a nothingness, that nearly destroyed it. That's what sent me into that seizure. Yes. The revenants. I think . . . I think that's why it needs me."

"I don't understand," he told her.

"It wanted to come down here to see what it was meant to guard," she said. "We know that. What we didn't know was why it needed a host, a human host, to bring it here."

"I've wondered," he said.

"I made a deal with it: our lives for space in my brain. I didn't stop and think about exactly what it was getting out of the agreement. But that has to be it. Whatever the revenants are, whatever made them, is dangerous to the basilisk. It can't fight them, it can't handle them. Exposure to them hurts it."

"Hmm. You think there's a connection. Between the basilisk's goal here and the revenants?"

"Think about it," Petrova said. "The revenants came from the mine."

"We think they did," Zhang said, carefully.

She shook her head. "Fine, it's just a hypothesis, but I think that's where the basilisk is headed too. To whatever is in there. We know the basilisk was dormant when the first colonists arrived here. Remember? It didn't start guarding the planet until the colony was well established. Something happened here to switch it on. To activate it after it had been asleep for billions of years. What if whatever it was, whatever happened to wake the basilisk up, what if that happened in the mine?"

"Perhaps the miners dug something up. Something that was supposed to stay buried," Zhang said. "That's an interesting theory, but . . ."

"The basilisk wants to go to the mine. It's why it's let me stay in control this long, because I'm headed to the place it wants to see. The place where its prize is located. And that prize – it's got to be the thing that created the revenants, too. Occam's razor, right? The simplest explanation that fits all the facts. This makes sense, Zhang. You know it does."

He just shrugged.

It didn't matter. She knew she was right. She could feel it, as if the basilisk was gently prodding her toward this conclusion. As if it wanted her to figure it out. She started to climb to her feet. She had plans to make.

"One thing," he said, before she could leave the kitchen.

"Yeah?"

"The basilisk isn't the only one."

"What do you mean?"

He stared her right in the eye. She saw concern there. Wariness. Something about what she'd said had shaken him. But was he afraid for her – or of her?

"Lang wants us to go to the mine as well," he said.

"That could just be a coincidence. There's a landing pad there. One of exactly two on the planet – and the other one is back at the town, which isn't exactly a secure location. It makes sense to send us to the mine instead, for exfiltration."

"Fair," he said.

She watched his face for a while, waiting for him to elaborate. Whatever he was thinking, though, he kept it to himself.

# 73

"There has to be more," Zhang said. He scrolled through a transcript of the doctor's audio log, the data that Rapscallion had scraped from the medical center's logs. What he had was intriguing but maddeningly incomplete. "Petrova has a theory about the mine, that it's the source of the revenants. We know the first revenants came from there, yes, so that checks out. But we still know nothing about what they really are. What they want, what process changes a dead body into a revenant..."

"There's more," Rapscallion said. "It's just been overwritten. Whoever erased the medical center's data really, really didn't want you to see this stuff."

Zhang nodded. "I understand that the data might be fragmentary or difficult to parse," he said. "But—"

"Doc, imagine that you were asking me for a book." The robot pointed at Mo's shelves, and the printed-out books that stood there in perfect rows. "A bunch of paper and glue and ink. Say you wanted to make sure nobody read one of those. How would you go about making it illegible?"

Zhang stroked his chin. "They used to set them on fire," he said. Open flames were something he had very little experience with himself. In the enclosed habitats on Ganymede and Titan, fire was the worst kind of natural disaster because it ate up all the available oxygen. A raging fire in a hab module could asphyxiate an entire population in seconds. It was why Firewatch was called

Firewatch – the organization had evolved out of an older agency, whose remit had been to literally watch for fires and stop them before they could spread. "I remember reading about people holding mass book-burnings on Earth."

"Really? They were so afraid of books they had to set them on fire?"

Zhang shrugged. "They feared the ideas in the books. Burning the books was a way to express how terrified they were of anyone who didn't think the same way they did."

The robot turned his head from side to side. It was still damaged from the fight with the revenants, so it creaked alarmingly. "Okay, whatever, I wasn't even going there. I was going to say if you wanted to make a book illegible, what you could do is pulp it. Shred it into tiny pieces, soak it in acid until it's just mush, dry the mush to make new paper. Then print a whole different book on that paper."

"That seems a little extreme," Zhang said.

"But that's basically what a computer does when it erases data. It reuses the storage space, the pages, so there's nothing left of the original information. What you're asking is for me to somehow read the original book after it's been pulped and reprinted."

"That does seem like a tall order."

"Luckily for you," Rapscallion said, "I'm really smart."

"Oh."

"Imagine you pulp the book and make a new one, whatever, but in the process you're just the tiniest bit sloppy. You shred the original pages, but not as finely as you could. So a few of the scraps of the old book, the shredded bits, still have legible type on them. Not much, and it's really faint, but if you look with a microscope you can still read the occasional word here and there."

"Just a few random words out of the original document?" Zhang asked.

"Right, but then you use a predictive language model to fill in the gaps. To kind of guess what words you don't have. You see?"

"Not really," Zhang admitted. "But you're telling me there's more to be recovered from the doctor's files?"

"It's an incredibly complicated and time-consuming process. It uses up like a full three percent of my entire cognitive bandwidth. But I do it because I like you, Doc."

"Well then." Zhang cleared his throat. "Thank you. Can I see what you've found?"

> ... INJURIES WERE SUPERFICIAL BUT CONCERNING. BITE WOUNDS? I CAN'T REMEMBER THE LAST TIME I TREATED A ...
>
> ... FUNNY, BECAUSE WHEN I CHECKED THE WOUND FOR INFECTION, IT WAS CLEAN. NOT JUST CLEAN. STERILE. I HAVE NEVER IN MY CAREER SEEN A BITE WOUND THAT WASN'T TEEMING WITH BACTERIA. HUMAN SALIVA IS PACKED WITH MICROBES THAT CAN BE TRANSFERRED THROUGH ORAL CONTACT, BUT THESE WOUNDS SEEM CLEANER THAN THE UNAFFECTED SKIN AROUND THE INJURY SITE AND ...
>
> ... REFUSE TO BELIEVE THE DATA I'M SEEING. THIS ISN'T POSSIBLE. THE SUBJECT MUST HAVE DIED IMMEDIATELY AFTER THE ATTACK BUT ...
>
> ... BUT IT CAN'T BE. THERE HAS TO BE SOME OTHER EXPLANATION.
>
> ... I'M GOING OUT THERE.
>
> ... TO THE MINE.
>
> ... IT'S FORBIDDEN, NORMALLY. WHEN I ASKED FOR PERMISSION, THE ADMINISTRATORS SAID THEY WOULDN'T EVEN CONSIDER MY APPLICATION, SO I CALLED UP THE ADMINISTRATOR OF THE MINE INSTEAD. JUST MAKING CONTACT TOOK SOME WORK, BUT I HAVE FRIENDS HERE, PEOPLE I'VE HELPED, TREATED. PEOPLE WHO OWE ME FAVORS.

> THE MINE ADMINISTRATOR WAS SURPRISED TO HEAR FROM ME BUT . . .
>
> . . . THEY'RE SCARED OVER THERE. THINGS MUST BE WORSE THAN WE THOUGHT. I GUESS I'M GOING TO FIND OUT. THEY'RE SENDING A COPTER – I'LL LEAVE AS SOON AS IT GETS HERE. IF THIS THING IS INFECTIOUS THERE'S NO TIME TO . . .
>
> . . . THERE HAS TO BE AN EXPLANATION. I'LL FIND IT. THIS COLONY NEEDS ME TO FIGURE THIS OUT. STOP IT BEFORE IT SPREADS, BEFORE IT BECOMES AN EPIDEMIC. I'LL ADMIT I DON'T WANT TO GO. HONESTLY, I'M TERRIFIED OF WHAT I'LL SEE. NO MATTER.
>
> I'M GOING.

Zhang wondered what the doctor looked like, where they had trained. He didn't know their name, their gender, anything about them—the audio was too distorted. But he knew them. He knew exactly what they were feeling, thinking when they spoke those words.

"We need more," he said. "More of this. Is there more?"

"Yes," Rapscallion said. "But I need time to make sense of it."

Zhang frowned. "This might be the only way we can know what we're getting ourselves into. What we can expect to find at the mine."

There was no question in his mind that they were going to go to the mine. Too many people, too many forces were pushing them in that direction. He knew Petrova wouldn't listen if he asked her not to go.

"Can you do me a favor? You say it takes three percent of your total bandwidth to make sense of this data?" he asked.

"Yeah."

Zhang nodded. "Try using four."

# 74

They made an early night of it. Mo set up some bedding in the larder for Zhang, and a similar pallet in the storeroom for Petrova. Rapscallion didn't sleep, so he would stay up for the night, standing watch just in case. Parker spoke with the robot briefly, then knocked on the door of the storeroom. When Petrova beckoned him to come in, he carefully opened the door, entered, and closed it behind him.

"I wasn't entirely sure that would work," he said.

She was sitting on her bedroll, drinking some water. She'd spent a good hour in Mo's bathroom, making use of his hot water, and she looked almost fresh. She had removed her filthy coveralls and was just in her underclothes, but she didn't seem self-conscious around him. "What's going on?" she asked, but she was smiling. "You up to something?"

Parker held a small green plastic device in his hand. It looked a little like a torch, though the lens on the front was a complicated arrangement of dozens of small lenses and dishes, some of them glass, some not. "Rapscallion printed this for me today. It's a portable hard-light projector. The battery life isn't all I'd hoped for, but it gives me a couple hours of freedom. I can go anywhere with this – before, I was stuck being near him and his projector, but now I can be alone with you. I've downloaded myself into this thing so I'm not in Rapscallion's processor cores anymore. He and I are officially separate beings again."

Petrova smiled. "That sounds good, but what does it actually mean?"

"It means we can have some actual privacy."

"Privacy!" she laughed. "Oh ho. So you *are* up to something."

"Just thought we could use a little alone time," he said. "You know, so we can stay up telling ghost stories and braiding each other's hair."

Her expression at that was dubious, but she didn't shut him down right away. "Come sit with me," she said. "I'm surprised you want to be with me." She lifted her cast, touching the bruise on her forehead. "I'm a wreck."

"Sure, but for the first time in weeks you got to take a shower. I didn't want to waste this rare opportunity."

Her eyes went wide and she hit him in the chest with her good hand. "You talk to all of your conquests like that?" She shook her head. "Just sit with me for a while. Okay? I could use someone to talk to right now."

He set the projector on a shelf and then sat down behind her, his long legs propped up so she was cradled between his knees. "Something bothering you in specific?" he asked.

"Tomorrow," she said. She looked at the wall and he knew she was thinking about the mine, about what they might find there. "I have no idea what we're about to walk into. Only that it's going to be bad."

"You'll handle it, like you always do," he said. He placed his hands on her shoulders and, when she nodded in agreement, started kneading her muscles. As she rocked back and forth, she made appreciative noises.

"I can't remember the last time anyone did that," she said. "God, it's nice. Parker – I'm glad you're here. I'm glad I have you."

"Everyone should have a friendly ghost who gives back rubs," he said. "The UEG should declare it a human right, like water or oxygen."

She snorted. "It certainly helps to put things in perspective. Hey. I want your opinion on something."

"Shoot."

"What do you make of our host?"

"Mo?" Parker had no real interest in talking about the man, but he gave it some thought. "He seems pretty tough. If he survived here this long, I guess he'd have to be."

"I get the sense that he's keeping a secret. Something he doesn't want to tell us."

Parker nodded. "Sure. Everybody's got secrets. He spent more than a year living a brutal day-to-day, fighting to stay alive. I'm sure he did things he's not proud of. Look at it from his perspective, though, right? If I was him, if I'd spent all that time without any hope, sure that I was going to die a lonely death here, then people showed up and offered me a ride off the planet . . . Well, I might be careful what I told them, too."

"Fair."

He shrugged. "I'll keep my eyes open. If I see anything . . ."

"Thanks."

"No problem." He reached down and scratched the short hair at the back of her neck. She used to love it when he did that. He felt her squirm, stretch her legs out, just like she used to, and he smiled.

She turned slightly, still wrapped up in his limbs but enough that she could look up into his face. Her mouth was just a flat line, but her eyes searched his for something. "This is kind of weird," she said.

"Oh. Oh!" He started to pull away from her.

But she grabbed his arm. At least, she grabbed the image of his arm, and the hard light pushed back against her fingers.

"I know you think you're Sam Parker," she said. "Sorry. I'm . . . Sorry. I need to say this, I need to be honest about this."

"I understand," he told her. "I'll brace myself."

"You're not Sam." She looked him straight in the eyes.

They'd never confronted this before, not really. Maybe it was time. "Sam Parker died. You may have his memories and his emotions. You remember us being lovers and so you still have feelings for me. I ... I remember giving the eulogy at your funeral. My feelings for you, this version of you, are really confusing and I'm worried I'm going to make a mistake. Give you false hope or something."

He nodded. Simulated drawing in a long, slow breath. "I know that we don't have a lot of time together. When you go back to Earth, well. Who knows what happens to me then? But I'm here now. I just want to be good to you, Petrova."

"Jesus," she said. "You should really call me Sasha. Especially if you're going to kiss me."

"Sasha," he said, like he was tasting the name. Savoring it. He laughed. Then he leaned forward and brushed her lips with his. She grabbed him and pulled him close, kissing him deeply. Her arms wrapped around his neck and together they collapsed sideways onto the bedding. Suddenly her lips were all over his neck, his chest. He edited his image so that his clothes disappeared, and she lurched backward for a second, surprised, then laughed hard and buried her face in his chest, her good hand grabbing at his shoulder, his arm, his hand. Her cast pressed against his back, pulling him closer against her body. The plastic sank deep into the hard-light curve of his spine.

"Is that okay?" she asked. "I'm not hurting you?"

"No," he said. "No." He carefully pulled her undershirt up from her stomach, over the curve of her breasts, and she lifted her arms so he could remove it altogether. She reached down and shoved at her shorts, pushing them down over her legs, all the while kissing him, kissing every part of him.

"What can we do?" she asked. Her hair was wild as she looked up at him. Her breath came fast. "What can we actually do?"

"I don't understand," he said.

"I've got one good hand," she said, holding it up to show

him. Her smile was hungry. Wild. "What can we do? What have you got?"

He lifted her gently off the bedding. Used hard light and a hologram to lay her on a mattress covered in silk sheets and soft pillows. He watched as she stretched out her legs, ran her fingers over the silk. She reached up and grabbed the back of his neck, pulled him down toward her.

"I've got anything you can imagine," he said.

Afterwards, he created a special hammock for her, a kind of bed she could sleep in that gave perfect support to her injured arm. He watched her fall asleep, her eyelids fluttering closed. Listened to the way her breathing changed.

She had needed this, he thought. He liked to believe it was helpful for her, that it would relax her a little, help her remember that life wasn't all just misery and horror. She certainly looked peaceful enough like that.

He sat back on his haunches, one hand brushing at her hair, keeping it out of her eyes. He could adjust the pressure of his hard-light touch, make it as gentle as the caress of a spring breeze so it wouldn't wake her.

Behind him, the Other sat and asked a question he didn't want to hear.

"Shut up," he told it. His voice so low she couldn't have heard it even if she was awake. "Shut up. It's not important."

But the Other wouldn't shut up. It was, after all, a manifestation of how he felt about his body. Or his lack thereof.

He pulled his hand back, away from her. Stared down at it in the near-perfect darkness of the storeroom.

He used hard light to pick up a plastic bag of dried beans. Levitated it over to his hand. Felt its weight, the heft of it. He closed his fingers around the bag, squeezed a little. He felt nothing. He squeezed harder. Still nothing. He squeezed hard enough that the bag split open and beans flew everywhere.

He used hard light to catch them, a separate tendril of his

being stretched out to retrieve each bean before it could hit the floor and make a noise. He found an empty can and put the beans in it, just so as not to make a mess.

"I know," he told the Other. It touched his shoulder. Just to get his attention? Or to offer sympathy?

He couldn't feel a thing.

He hadn't felt anything.

# 75.

In the morning, they ate a quick breakfast and packed up the quadcopter. There was no reason to waste daylight. Petrova wanted to get an idea of what was down there, find a good place to camp. "There's likely to be revenants down there if that's where they come from."

"Revenants only come out at night," Mo said. He'd clearly adjusted to using Zhang's term for the undead monsters. "You won't see them now. During the day they hide, they're real good at it, too. They find nooks and crannies where you'd never think to look. Any little hole they can crawl into, just to get away from the light."

"All the better. We can get the lie of the land, figure out a strategy before we actually have to deal with them. You said you've flown by the mine before but you never landed there?"

"Never had a reason to," he agreed.

"What could you see from the air? What should we expect?"

"There's a couple buildings next to a hole in the ground." He shrugged. "I never saw the place before things went to hell. We farmers weren't even supposed to talk about it. We were pretty sure it was some kind of secret project of the UEG. We figured maybe there was some valuable mineral over there they were digging up, something so rare they didn't want people knowing they had it. There were plenty of rumors, but . . ."

"Rumors aren't worth the air they're made of," she said.

He laughed and nodded. "Yeah. When the miners did come to town, to get drunk and dance with us, they wouldn't talk about their work, about what it was like over there, anything. If you asked too many questions, they would just get up and walk away. Our administrators were mostly decent people, and I liked Sheriff Sally. I got the impression whoever was in charge at the mine was a real hardass. Like if the miners talked to us they could get in serious trouble."

Petrova didn't know what to make of any of it. What mineral could be so valuable to the UEG that it would deserve such secrecy? Gold and platinum were plentiful enough in Earth's solar system. You could make diamonds and rubies in a lab. She supposed there were weaponizable elements, like uranium. Maybe there was something in the crust of Paradise-1 that could be turned into bombs. But the UEG hardly had a shortage of those.

She supposed she would get to see for herself.

They loaded the quadcopter up with gear and supplies – everything they might need in case they were going to the mine for days and not coming back. Everything they would need to last long enough to get picked up by Lang's relief ship, and a little besides, just in case. Then they climbed aboard, Zhang and Petrova up front with Mo, Rapscallion and Parker in the back. They lifted away from Mo's house and she watched it dwindle among the dark rocks.

"You going to miss this place?" she asked.

Mo glanced over at her with narrowed brows. "You fucking kidding? I'd set it on fire and watch it burn if we had the time."

She chided herself – she hadn't considered the fact that his memories of the house might be colored by grief and tragedy. "I'm . . . I'm sorry," she told him.

"Ah, it's fine," he said, and shot her a big goofy smile. "Just glad to be shot of it."

He took them low over the mountain peaks, then dropped quickly down the slopes, following the course of a clear stream as it passed through half a dozen waterfalls on its way toward the lake. She saw from the air that the lake was nothing like she'd imagined. It was so shallow she could see the bottom, even from a hundred meters up. Thick growths of what looked like white coral dotted the water, sticking up just far enough into the air they didn't break the surface tension. Slim shadows darted around and through the white encrustations.

"Are those fish?" Zhang asked, pressing his face up against the Plexiglas.

"Kind of look like fish if you catch one," Mo said. "Kind of like an eel. No eyes and no gills, though. I think they come up to the surface to breathe air. Lots of teeth, lots of bones. I tried eating one once and I thought I was going to die. I had it coming out both ends for a week."

"Foreign proteins," Zhang said, nodding.

"Does that mean 'fucking poison'?" Mo asked.

"Kind of. The creatures on this planet evolved out of different chemistry than the animals on Earth. They may have completely different proteins in their muscle tissue. Most likely they don't even have DNA, or at least not the kind of DNA we're used to."

"Tasted like shit, too," Mo said.

He touched the steering yoke and the quadcopter shot forward over a plain spotted with yellow lichen. Up ahead the ground turned to broken fields of boulders. It might have been a landscape from the undeveloped territories of Mars, if the sky hadn't been so blue. Petrova even saw impact craters, vast dishes full of shadow dug into the crust. Up ahead the ground turned darker still and a low line of hills surrounded what looked like a crater larger than the others, its edges more sharply defined.

"What's that?" she asked.

Mo gave her a questioning look. "That's where we're headed," he said.

It was farther away than it looked. They rode in near silence for twenty minutes, the propellers chewing at the air, before she got an actual look at the mine. She realized she had assumed that a mine was just a hole in the ground, a broad open shaft with railroad tracks leading into darkness. She hadn't considered the other kind.

A strip mine. The rocky crust of Paradise-1 had been carved away wholesale here, in vast round terraces that caught the sun. It must have been three kilometers across, the concentric layers connected by elaborate systems of ramps and scaffolding. Enormous machines stood silent on the terraces, draglines that were designed to pull massive chains through rock faces, carving them away like soft cheese. Long-armed monstrosities that ended in toothed wheels twenty meters in diameter. The hills she'd seen from afar turned out to be heaps of tailings, vast conical piles of pulverized rock that had been pulled out of the ground and then dumped to one side, useless to anyone.

The bottom of the pit was lost in shadows, so Petrova could not have said just how deep it ran. Further obscuring the lower levels was a plume of smoke or vapor that rose from the depths, a pale streamer that drifted high into the air before being shredded by the wind.

"What is that?" she asked, pointing through the canopy. "Is that ... something on fire?"

Rapscallion answered her on her device. "Let me do a spectroscopic analysis." She felt a thunk, and then a green plastic arm reached over to grab the Plexiglas from outside. The robot had opened up the cargo bay and was leaning out to get a better look.

"Careful!" she said.

"I'm good," Rapscallion said. "There's no carbon in that plume, or any kind of soot or the particulates you would get from a fire. It looks more like silicates, iron, aluminum."

"So ... what?" she asked. "Dust?"

"Rock dust," Rapscallion said.

She watched the plume twirl upward, fed by a steady billow of dust spewing from the lower works of the mine. "There's a lot of it. That's not just old dust blowing off a tailing heap, is it?" She already knew the answer.

She turned to Mo. "You said there were no survivors here."

"I said I'd never heard anything from this place. I also said I'd never come out here to take a close look," he told her.

She shook her head. "There's somebody down there. They're still digging." It was the only explanation for the plume of dust. The mine must still be operational. Which meant somebody had to be down there to dig out the rock.

She spotted a group of buildings perched on the edge of the pit, long sheds and prefabricated housing units. "Set us down over there," she said.

Mo grabbed the steering yoke and began their descent.

# 76

"Hello! Anyone here?" Parker called, over the wind that whipped between the buildings. They sat mute, like enormous tombstones. No one answered him. Nothing moved, other than the grit and gravel that lay scattered everywhere across the ground. It rolled and skittered, toward the pit, away from it as the wind carried it.

"Hello!" Zhang shouted. He ran down a street toward a housing unit and pounded on its hatch, but no one answered.

It was déjà vu. It was a nightmare from which Parker couldn't awake. *We're going to do this over and over, search empty towns, call the names of the dead until the dead come to shut us up*, he thought. Stupid. He knew there were only two towns on this planet, and now they'd seen them both. The entire extent of human life on Paradise-1, and all of it empty.

There wasn't much to see. This town hadn't been built to a human scale. Many of the structures were enormous long sheds, filled with rank after rank of deactivated mining robots. They stood perfectly still, hooked up to their charging cables. There were a number of different models — some were just cargo containers on caterpillar treads, others had heads that were fantastically complicated arrangements of grinding wheels and drills. Others looked like bulldozers mounted on spider legs. They seemed perfectly intact, if filthy, covered with dust and grime. Somebody had put them into standby mode but hadn't bothered to hose them down.

He queried one of them, just sending a quick ping to ask about its status. The machine he'd addressed, one of the big drill heads, didn't move or speak. It just sent back a quick automated notice. It had been permanently deactivated, it said, and could only answer questions or perform its duties if reactivated with an administrator's password.

He had no desire to turn the robots back on. But their presence confused him a little. If the robots were here, then who was digging down there at the bottom of the mine? The plume of rock dust coming up from below hadn't abated since they'd arrived. He couldn't believe that the human miners had gone down to dig on their own instead of getting their robots to do it for them.

"Hello?" Petrova called, from the next street over. "Hello! Firewatch! We're here to evacuate you! Hello!"

There were, of course, no bodies to be found anywhere in the mine.

Not that there would have been many in any case. The mine facility was bigger than the colony town, but much less of it was designed for human habitation. There were two standard-sized housing units, big enough for families. There was also a single dormitory where maybe fifty people could have slept and taken their meals together.

There weren't many facilities for entertainment or public gatherings. Just a lot of workstations and repair sheds, tool shops and chemistry labs. Everything except the labs was covered in grit and dust. Life here must have been pretty grim, Parker thought. No wonder the miners went all the way over to the colony town, hundreds of kilometers, just to get drunk.

"Hello?" he called, and banged on the metal wall of the dormitory with his fist. The echoes rolled up and down the street.

"Hey, fuckers!" Mo screamed, leaning his head back and then shaking himself so his braids flew around his head. "Calling all miners and asshole revenants! Come out, come out, all out, already!"

Parker laughed. "I suppose if that doesn't get their attention, nothing will," he said. "Petrova? Do you read me?"

She was out of earshot, but she called him back on her device. "What are you thinking?" she asked.

"That there's nobody here. We're wasting our time. Rapscallion, are you seeing anything different? Any sign that people have been here recently?"

"Just one," the robot replied.

"Wait . . . what?" Parker didn't understand.

"Kenji Yoshida," Rapscallion said.

Parker knew the name sounded familiar, but . . .

"Kenji Yoshida. Age twenty-three. Engineer," Rapscallion told him.

"Shit." Petrova's voice sounded faint, distant, and Parker knew it wasn't just a bad connection. "Shit, that's the guy . . ."

"The one whose head you knocked in. The first revenant we saw on Paradise-1," Parker said, nodding. "The one Zhang dissected."

"I've been tracking his body through the satellite feed," Rapscallion said. "A bunch of revenants have been carrying it the whole time, moving fast. They took the body from the town and brought it here. It arrived two nights ago."

"They brought a dead body here?" Mo asked. "I've seen them recover corpses before, sure. But they brought it here? Why?"

Parker thought he knew. "Rapscallion? Where's the body now?"

"Bottom of the pit," the robot replied.

Parker nodded. Sure. Kenji Yoshida wanted to be at the center of the action even if he was dead. The same place the UEG, Firewatch and the basilisk all wanted them to go.

"Listen," Mo said. "Listen to me, this is not good. If I know one thing about revenants – one thing I've learned over the last year – it's that they come in packs. You see one, there's a hundred more lying in wait behind you. This place is dangerous."

"We'll play it safe," Petrova said. "Do some recon, get out before nightfall. Okay?"

Parker hoped that would be enough.

## 77

They split up to cover more ground. Zhang checked out the mine's medical facilities, which were rudimentary at best. There was no medical center, just a curtained-off area in the dormitory with a couple of patient beds and a medical robot, a big jointed arm that came down from the ceiling. It might have been the twin of the one they'd seen at the medical center back in the town. It had been deactivated; he didn't bother switching it back on. The infirmary's supplies were distinctly lacking in modern equipment and even some staple items. He found antibiotics and surgical gear, but nothing in the way of gene therapy or nanomedicine equipment.

He headed back out into the street. He didn't like this place at all, he decided. Even the air was wrong. It stank, for one thing. A kind of inorganic chemical reek, acrid and biting, that came and went with the wind. He supposed that digging up so much of the planet's crust would have liberated all kinds of toxic chemicals – there was probably free-floating arsenic in the air here, on top of more subtle poisons like heavy metals, sulfur compounds, even perchlorate esters that could get into their thyroid glands and cause all manner of problems. This place wouldn't be safe for children, and he wouldn't have recommended that anyone here get pregnant. He supposed that the three of them – himself, Petrova and Mo – would be alright for a few hours, or even a couple of days, but any longer than that and they would need chelation therapy to avoid health problems in later life.

Movement caught his eye. He looked up and saw Mo emerging from one of the smaller equipment sheds. "Motor pool," the survivor said, throwing a thumb over his shoulder. "Found something interesting."

"Yes?"

"Looks like there were four quadcopters here originally. Judging by what's left, two small ones, the same size as mine, and two much larger ones. Transports."

"What do you mean, what's left?" Zhang asked.

"They've been trashed. Rendered inoperable," Mo said, using a stilted tone of voice that Zhang thought was meant to mock his own formal way of speaking. "The magnetic turbines have all been stripped. Whoever did it knew their stuff. You can tear a copter to pieces and rebuild it out of trash. I mean, that's how I kept mine flying. The magnets in those turbines, though. You can't just 3D-print new ones. They're made of rare earth materials you don't find just anywhere. Those ships are never going to fly again."

Zhang thought of the tractors they'd seen in the farm town. "Somebody did the same thing to all the vehicles in the town. Anything that could move under its own power. It meant we had to hike up to the comms tower."

"And why you came down the river on that ridiculous boat," Mo said, grinning. "Flying is the only way to get around on this planet."

"And someone wanted to make sure nobody could," Zhang said, nodding. "We still have no idea why. Did they want to keep the revenants from moving around too freely? It's hard to imagine one of those things flying a quadcopter."

Mo shrugged, as if he wasn't so sure. He failed to comment further, however.

Zhang thought of something. "They sabotaged all the vehicles. Not the robots, though."

Mo frowned, as if to indicate he didn't see Zhang's point.

"Whoever the saboteur is, they disabled all the vehicles on this planet. But they just deactivated the mining robots. Put them on standby, as if they expected they might need them again at some point in the future. Interesting."

Mo shrugged again. Then he slung his Gauss rifle over his shoulders and headed for the next building, a three-story structure made of cut stone. It had broad windows on its upper floor that looked out over the pit. "Some kind of ops center, I'm guessing," he said. "I'll check it out. You take that shed over there."

Zhang shook his head. "No, I'd rather see the operations center. I'm satisfied we aren't going to find a lot of answers out here. Just more mysteries." He called Petrova on her device, told her where they were headed.

Mo's expression suggested that he was annoyed that Zhang was tagging along, but he continued toward the structure's main door.

It was immediately clear that he had been right, that they had found the nerve center of the mining operation. The lower two floors were filled with elaborate virtual-reality rigs, cubicles where black neoprene suits hung from the ceiling like rubbery ghosts. "I'm guessing they used these to monitor and control the robots," Zhang suggested. "Easier, I suppose, than going down into the pit and mining everything by hand."

Petrova arrived before they reached the top floor. It proved to be a broad open space with three massive workstations. A central chair, like the captain's chair on a starship, stood before the thick windows. A roost from which to observe the entire mine, though even from this vantage the lower levels were lost in haze and shadow. Zhang tapped the arm of the big chair and a dozen holoscreens flared to life. They showed endlessly spooling columns of numbers and color-coded status bars, providing data that meant nothing to him but which he assumed was vital to the operation of the pit.

"Rapscallion," Petrova called, "I'm sending you a link to the local datastream. I'm sure that it'll be wiped clean like all the other computers we've found, but take a look anyway, okay?"

"Will do, boss," the robot replied. "I'm over here in Shed Four. Parker and I are looking at these mining robots. I have to say I'm not impressed. They did make me think of something, though."

"Go ahead," Petrova said, frowning.

"Based on what I'm looking at, these robots could dig hundreds of tons of rock a day. And there are a lot of them, maybe fifty standard units and then some much larger robots for bulk excavation."

"Okay, but isn't that what you'd expect?" she said.

Zhang guessed where the robot was headed with this before he replied.

"It's a big mine," Rapscallion said. "Really big. Too big. I know about mining. I used to be a mining robot myself. This is a massive operation; we're talking industrial scale. I guess the farmers needed some metals to feed into their 3D printers, and some minerals to make soil with. A mine like this could have supplied a thousand towns of the size we saw. There's no reason why it should be so gigantic."

Petrova looked over at Zhang. "Maybe they were just thinking ahead. Building capacity for when more colonists came, and more of the planet was settled."

Zhang didn't know. He could only shrug. He had no idea what the UEG had been digging out of the planet here. But he was beginning to think it had nothing to do with supporting an agricultural colony. Perhaps the opposite. "I wonder. I wonder if the farms we saw were just meant to provide food for the people here."

"Hmm?" she said.

"We've been operating under the assumption that the farm colony was the main point of settling Paradise-1. Starting up an agricultural base for human settlers. But what if this is what the

UEG really wanted with this planet? What if whatever's down there is the whole reason it was colonized?"

Petrova gave him a cautious look. "That's a big assumption. You're basing it on very little evidence."

"True. It's not something I can prove, either. Not right now. But I can't escape this feeling. This place – it's why we're here. Why we were sent to Paradise-1 in the first place. Lang fed us a lot of lies about this mission. I don't think she's told us the whole truth even now."

"I wouldn't ask that woman for the time and expect to get a straight answer," Petrova said.

She walked over to the big windows and looked down into the pit.

"We're not going to know anything until we see what's down there."

Zhang found it hard to disagree.

# 78

At the edge of the pit, Petrova watched the plume of smoke as it rose and rose, borne upward by warm air from the very bottom. She watched as it passed by level after level, terrace after terrace dug out of the hard rock of the planet. How many terraces were there? At least a dozen going down, down. She took a step forward. Leaned her weight on her foot, leaned farther out. She stood at the top of a sheer cliff, twenty meters high. Strangely, she didn't feel any vertigo at all as she looked down.

"Petrova?" It was Zhang, just behind her. He reached out to touch her arm and she looked down at his hand, surprised.

"Something wrong?" she asked.

"Maybe. You're really close to the edge there. I'd prefer if you didn't fall in."

She smiled. "I'm fine."

Was she? She didn't know. There was an itch in her head, a kind of urge drawing her onward. A thought she couldn't seem to ever push away. She really, really wanted to know what was at the bottom of the pit.

It was the basilisk, of course. The parasite was impatient. What else was new? It was close to its goal and it wanted her to keep moving. Get closer. Even if that meant walking right off a cliff, apparently.

Luckily she was still enough in control of her own body to take a step back. "Where's Mo? And Rapscallion?" she asked.

"I want to head down there now, while we still have daylight." Before the revenants came for them, she meant. The part of her mind that still belonged to her completely had a plan, and that plan included being nowhere near here after the sun went down.

She turned to look at Zhang and he was frowning. "You want to go now?" he asked.

"No time like the present."

He shook his head. "But before ... you said we needed to do this carefully. Take our time."

"Oh. Right."

Had she said that? It did sound like something she would say. She tried to remember.

"You had a whole plan. I mean, we came up with a whole plan. Rapscallion is building drones right now. We were going to monitor them with the VR rigs in the operations center." He reached over and touched her chin, turning her face from side to side so he could look at her eyes. "The concussion," he said. "And then the basilisk took you over, in the spider cavern—"

"Stop," she said. "Stop!"

He let go of her chin.

"I remember now. Okay? I got distracted. Forgot the plan for a second. Let's just get inside. Out of this smell, out of the cold. I'll feel better inside." She started marching toward the shed behind her. He came after her, of course, watching her like a hawk.

She knew he was right to do so. She knew he shouldn't trust her, not like he did before she accepted the parasite into her head. Damn it, though – she was in charge of this mission. She was supposed to keep tabs on *him*, make sure *he* was okay. Zhang Lei, the broken man who didn't work well with others, the weirdo that Director Lang had saddled her with. She was supposed to keep him safe, make sure he didn't get himself killed.

She hated the fact their roles had been reversed. Every day on Paradise-1 she felt less and less in control. Well, she needed to buckle down. Get her shit straightened out.

She stepped into the shed and heard a 3D printer screeching away in the distance. The room had to be a hundred meters long, and of course Rapscallion had set up at the far end. There were massive 3D printers there, bigger than anything they'd seen in the colony town. Printers that could make parts to fix the giant robots. Rapscallion had been busy, she saw. He'd printed out a dozen small drones that looked like toy versions of Mo's quadcopter, except that instead of a bubble canopy, each of them had a scowling human head. They were of course all printed in bright, toxic green. A color that Rapscallion favored because most humans found it unpleasant to look at. Even now, when he'd started expressing genuine affection for her and Zhang, she knew that offending humans was one of his favorite pastimes.

"I'm almost ready," he said. "Let me print a few more."

"Good," she told him. "Good." The delay irked her, but she forced herself not to let it show. This plan was much better than what the basilisk wanted, which was for her to go down there in person, right that instant. Rapscallion's drones were expendable. She wasn't.

She had to keep telling herself that.

"While we wait, I've got something to report," the robot said.

"Go ahead."

"I took a look at the servers in the ops center. They've been wiped clean, of course. Except it's a little different this time."

"Oh?"

"Yeah, whoever did it did a really shitty job," Rapscallion said. "Everything's erased, but they didn't overwrite the memory sectors as thoroughly as they did back at the town. The data's all still there, it's just scrambled."

"Interesting," she said. "Any idea why it's different?"

"I have a theory, but I can't prove anything. I think that whoever wiped the computers here did it remotely. Like, they had physical access to the main servers at the farm town, so they could be anal about it, really get in there and erase everything. Here they just took their chances."

"Can you rebuild the data?" she asked. "Get us some idea of what happened here?"

"Oh yeah. Though—"

"It's going to take a while, I know, I know. Fine. Just keep on it. Thank you, Rapscallion. I know I don't say that often enough. Thank you."

"Yeah, sure. I'll admit, I'm kind of curious myself about what's going on here. You know, in an abstract, detached kind of way."

Zhang touched her shoulder. "I'm going to head over to the ops center now, so I can prep the VR suits. Do you want to come with me?"

"In a minute," she said. She saw the concern on his face and waved her good hand at him. "It's alright. I'll see you over there."

When he was gone, she turned toward the big doors of the shed. She very much wanted to go back out there, back to the edge, so she could look down into the pit again. She was close, she thought. Very close to the basilisk's prize. It was only going to get harder to resist that pull from here on.

"Get those drones finished. We need to have them down there as soon as possible, so we can see what we're getting ourselves into." She strode away before the robot could answer. Behind her he made some noise, maybe said a word or called her name or something. She didn't bother replying. Instead she walked out into the wind. Out toward the edge of the pit. She was still in control, she thought. She could still hold things together.

She was just going to take another look.

# 79.

Zhang climbed into the neoprene suit and wriggled his fingers into the gloves. He started to sweat almost instantly, but then coolant rushed through the suit and brought his body temperature back to a neutral state. He left the hood off so he could monitor a holoscreen that floated before them. It showed the inside of the shed, where Rapscallion was putting the finishing touches to his last drone.

"You ready to do this?" he asked Petrova.

She nodded and pulled the hood of her suit over her hair. It sealed shut automatically, feeding her oxygen while blocking out all external stimuli. Bungee cords attached to the ceiling lifted her off the ground, and she folded her legs into a lotus position. The left arm of her suit dangled at her side – she pressed her cast against her stomach inside the suit, keeping it immobilized while they were in VR.

On the holoscreen, Zhang watched as the green drones lifted off the floor of the shed. They zipped past Rapscallion and then swept out through the big door, disappearing over the edge of the pit.

"How does it feel?" he asked the robot.

"What, splitting my brain into tiny pieces so I can fly around like a cloud of gnats? It sucks. You know that."

He did. Rapscallion had the ability to inhabit multiple bodies at once, a power that had saved their lives more than once. He hated doing it, though, because it required him to divide his bandwidth between all the bodies. If he built two bodies, his intellect was cut in half. Four bodies meant becoming four times stupider. He grumbled about it every time.

"We appreciate your sacrifices. You know that, right?"

"Oh, thanks. That makes everything better."

Zhang pulled the hood up over his face and felt it form itself to his features. He panicked a little, just for a second. Enough to make the RD twitch against his leg. But then the neoprene in front of his eyes lit up with a wash of color and sunlight, and he found himself catapulting out over the edge of the pit, zooming through empty space as he fell down through the terraced layers. He knew he was seeing through the cameras of one of Rapscallion's drones, and he managed not to scream in terror. His body tried to remind him that he could not fly, that he was falling for hundreds of meters toward the hard, rocky ground below. He politely ignored its warning cues.

It rewarded him with severe motion sickness. Well, that the RD could handle. Its fangs bit into his leg and medicated the nausea away.

"This is kind of fun," Petrova said, with a whooping laugh. He glanced to the side and saw a green drone flying next to him. She waggled her rotors as if to indicate that yes, it was her inside that drone. "I haven't done VR in years! I think the last time was a combat simulator, back at the Firewatch academy."

"We still use it for nanosurgery in my field," Zhang told her. "Not exactly my specialty. It can be fascinating, though, to climb around inside the chambers of a human heart and watch the muscle fibers contract."

For most people, VR was an obsolete technology. The cumbersome suits were an annoyance, and really not necessary. If you wanted to explore a virtual environment, holograms were far more convenient. It was only for truly immersive work that VR was really useful anymore. Zhang had been a little surprised to see that the miners of Paradise-1 used it to control their excavation robots. Why would they require such immediate control?

He supposed that was a minor mystery compared to the big questions. He was glad that the suits existed, because they gave him the ability to see what was at the bottom of the mine without having to go there himself.

The drones swept downward at a nausea-inducing clip. With each terrace level they passed, the daylight grew dimmer and the clouds of dust around them thickened.

Seven levels down, eight. If Zhang looked straight up, he could still see blue sky, but the mine walls were just planes of darkness. He saw one terrace that was partly flooded, black water glittering in the gloom. Massive pipes had been erected to suction that water away. He wondered if the miners had cut into an underground river there, if they were diverting the water into a whole new course. He'd seen that most of the animal life on Paradise-1 – and much of the plant life, for that matter – was subterranean, thriving beneath the jagged rocks, out of the glare of the sun. He wondered how many tiny burgeoning ecosystems the mine might have disrupted. Were fish being sucked up into those pipes, carried on a bruising, terrifying odyssey up to the surface? He couldn't know.

Nine levels down, ten. The mouth of the pit was narrower, much narrower now, only a few hundred meters across. Yet they were nowhere near the bottom. The terraces were thinner here, until they became mere ledges, barely wide enough for two people to stand abreast. The walls this deep were shored up everywhere, massive metal spars holding the ground back, stabilizing what was quickly becoming a mineshaft rather than a pit. The plume of rock dust they'd seen from the surface filled the entire space at this depth, making it impossible to see more than a few meters in any direction. And still they descended.

Fifteen levels down.

Twenty.

The shaft was barely wide enough for all of Rapscallion's drones to fly through, even in tight formation. Twenty meters across, then ten before Zhang knew it. He felt like he was flying down an infinitely long wormhole.

"We're going to come out the other side," Petrova said.

Zhang was startled back to self-awareness by her voice. They'd been silent so long he'd felt like he had become the drone, that he'd left his humanity behind. He had to remind himself where he really was. "Pardon?"

"We're going to fly straight through the planet and come out the other side," she said, sounding only a little exasperated with him.

"Impossible. We've barely descended two kilometers," he told her. "The planet is thousands of kilometers in diameter."

"It was a joke," she told him. "Look. Do you see anything down there? I wish we had Rapscallion's eyes."

The robot answered her, though his voice was slurred, glitchy. Lagging because it was split between so many different copies of himself. "Yoooou wannna seee sommmethhhinnng?" he asked.

Without warning, Zhang's vision changed, as if someone had lifted a pair of thick sunglasses off his eyes. He could see the shaft walls again in startling detail, and he realized that the robot had switched to some kind of night-vision mode, his processors enhancing everything Zhang saw to a preternatural clarity.

"Oh," he said. Because he'd seen the bottom. They'd been descending so long, he'd stopped imagining what it must be like. But there it was. The shaft ended in a perfectly ordinary floor, a circular patch of ground eight meters or so across.

Was that ... was that it? There was nothing down there, just a few stubborn boulders. The floor was chopped up, roughened by the machinery, but otherwise unremarkable.

Had they really come all this way for nothing?

Petrova saw the answer first. "There," she said. "Look."

The drones slowed down before they could smash into the

shaft floor. Soon they were hovering, motionless, just above the bottom. The walls around them rose vertically away, perfectly smooth and featureless, except that on one side of the shaft stood a massive semicircular arch. A construction of thick girders, reinforced with pillars, to hold open the mouth of a tunnel. The mine hadn't ended at all. It had just transitioned, from the vertical to the horizontal, from a shaft to a gallery.

The plume of rock dust came flowing out through this opening. They'd found its source, at least. Someone was still digging down there, Zhang realized.

"Dooo yoooou wannna keeeep goooinnng?" Rapscallion asked.

"Yes," Petrova said, with no hesitation.

The drones moved forward, plunging into the gallery, moving single file now. There was no room for them to fly side by side here.

Petrova could barely see what lay ahead of them. Not just because of the rock dust billowing all around them, but because of the basilisk.

It was screaming inside her head.

There was no sound, of course; it was far more subtle than that. Yet every time she tried to frame a thought, it was battered and crushed by the sheer weight of the parasite's excitement. They were getting close.

Beyond the arch, the tunnel ran straight for twenty meters, then branched off in three directions. One ramped downward then disappeared around a curve. Another led toward a second junction, just visible through the dust.

"It's a maze," Zhang said. "We'll need to form some kind of plan, a program for exploring these tunnels so we—"

"Down," Petrova said.

She was certain of it. The basilisk was certain.

Down.

"Maybe," Zhang suggested, his voice maddeningly reasonable and calm, like he was explaining to her how to solve a quadratic equation, "we should have the drones split up now. Have them map this place for us. So we don't get lost."

There was no point. She knew exactly where they should go. The basilisk could feel its prize pulling at it. To Petrova it felt like the parasite was pressing up against the wall of her skull, drawn like a magnet to the correct direction. How could she explain that to Zhang, though? If she tried, he would abort this mission. She might be in charge, but he was still her doctor. If he thought she was in any danger, he could simply pull her out of the VR rig and break the connection.

She couldn't accept that.

Down.

*Down,* the basilisk shrieked. *It's down there!*

"Good idea," she told Zhang. "Rapscallion, see how far these tunnels go. Zhang, you're with me. I need your eyes."

"Alright," he said. "Which tunnel should we take, then?"

"This one," she said.

"Down. Of course," he said.

He knew. He must know on some level. As long as he didn't try to stop her, she supposed that was fine.

She knew she should be fighting this. Fighting the basilisk, just as her mother had, when Ekaterina was the parasite's host. Refusing to give in to its demands, then promising she would comply if it just behaved. It was a billion-year-old psychic machine consciousness, a thing beyond human comprehension, but it could be manipulated. Managed.

The problem was that Petrova just wasn't devious enough. She didn't have her mother's skills as a motivator. A schemer. Fighting the basilisk felt almost impossible, and anyway, it was better at the game than she was. Giving her a sudden phobia of spiders just so she would disassociate and turn over control? That had been a master's move. Petrova was just outclassed, and she knew it.

If she was going to survive this, she would have to give the basilisk what it wanted. She would have to bring it to its prize. But what then?

She knew she couldn't trust the parasite. It had no compassion, no conscience. What if the prize turned out to be something dangerous to human life? She had no reason to think the basilisk would stop its mad quest just to save her. It would use up her body and throw her away. It could always find another host. Just as she knew it would sacrifice Zhang, or Mo, or Parker to get what it wanted.

She needed Zhang. As annoying as he could be, as judgmental as she found him sometimes, she needed someone watching her. Making sure this didn't go too far.

He didn't seem to mind that she was silent as she flew down the long, curving ramp. Rapscallion had switched their two drones to manual control, and though she wasn't the best pilot, it was easy enough to keep the drone level and moving in the direction she wanted. Behind her, Zhang buzzed along, easily keeping pace.

The ramp ended in a large open area, its walls carved smooth but its ceiling still rough and dotted with stalactites. Large pieces of machinery filled most of the space. Water pumps, she thought, to keep the mine from flooding. They were quiescent now, just big round shapes in the fog of dust.

Beyond the pump room, three corridors ran almost parallel away from them, so identical the basilisk hesitated before picking the rightmost one. Zhang asked Petrova why she'd chosen this one, but she didn't have an answer so she didn't say anything. It had a high ceiling, and thick bundles of pipes and cables ran along the walls like massive handrails. It felt like a hallway in a giant's castle. At its far end stood a massive ventilation fan. The blades were still, the rock dust billowing unchecked.

"Everything's been shut down," Zhang said. "Deactivated. The mine's administrator must have locked the place down before . . . well."

"Before he got murdered by a revenant? Had his body dragged off to who knows where?" Petrova asked.

"Yes. That's what I was suggesting," he said. "But why shut down the mine?"

"Why sabotage all the vehicles?" she asked. She could barely concentrate on the question, though she knew it was important.

The basilisk might not care about anything but its prize, but she needed answers. Lang was going to want to know everything, and until she could provide a satisfactory explanation as to what had happened on Paradise-1, she knew her work wasn't finished. "The erased computers . . . there's a picture here. It's just fuzzy, still."

"Somebody," Zhang said, "wanted this entire planet shut down. Put out of commission. They wanted to keep anyone from exploring it, asking questions."

"All the things we're doing," she said.

"Exactly. Somebody didn't want people like us poking around. They wanted whatever is buried here to stay buried."

They came to another junction. She didn't even warn him before heading down a corridor with rougher walls, its floor littered with broken rock.

"Maybe," she said. "I can see another possibility. Call it a different take. When you're fighting, and you know you're losing, when you realize you're going to have to give up ground to your enemy, you sabotage everything you can. Blow up transportation lines, scuttle all your ships. You don't want to leave the enemy anything they can use against you."

"You think this planet is a battlefield? But who are the opposing armies, then? Humanity and the revenants?"

"No," she said. "The revenants aren't mindless, we've established that. They have some kind of agenda. But nothing we've seen suggests they can fly quadcopters or operate mining robots. No."

"So the sabotage was done to keep other humans from coming here? Taking over? The UEG doesn't have any competitors, though. It's a universal government."

"Are you kidding?" She knew that Zhang had never been involved in politics, or even the infighting of the UEG's various departments and bureaus. He must have seen a newscast at some point, though. "Why do you think the UEG needs Firewatch?"

"To keep the people from rising up and forming their own government, I thought," he said. "To enforce the status quo."

"Crowds of angry workers are a threat, sure," she said, "but separatist groups are a much bigger problem. Mars is constantly threatening to declare independence."

"I've heard about those terrorists on Luna," he said. "The ones who blew up the Helium-3 refinery twenty years ago. Didn't Firewatch kill all of them?"

Not before they'd kidnapped the daughter of Firewatch's director, Petrova thought with a wince. Not before they put her in a box.

"It was a bloodbath. It's impossible to kill an insurgency like that, though. Every terrorist you kill becomes a martyr, and that just leads to more people joining the cause."

"So you're saying the UEG is fighting Martian independence movements by shutting down a mine on a planet a hundred light years away?"

"That's — that isn't what I was suggesting. I meant ... Oh, forget it," she said, and she managed to laugh a little. "I'm getting distracted. I need to focus on figuring out this maze."

"Right," he said. "You do that."

She led the way, flitting down passage after passage, taking ramps and staircases downward wherever she could. The prize was here, but it was still below them, deeper in the planet's rock. Deeper, always deeper.

Yet so close. The basilisk throbbed inside her head, crowding out her own brain.

She felt herself drooling inside her VR suit. Felt the need, the hunger of the parasite translate into saliva rolling down her chin. Her stomach clenched and twisted into knots, and she was suddenly terrified she would vomit inside her hood. She could choke on her own sick if she wasn't careful, asphyxiate inside the suit ...

The basilisk didn't care. It needed her, it needed a host, but it was beyond thinking rationally about her needs, her health. If she had tried to fight it in that moment, if she had resisted at all, she knew it would have simply cut off her breath, switched off that part of her brain that regulated her heartbeat. It could kill her with a thought.

They passed through a natural cavern as big as the one where they'd seen the spiders. Nothing moved in this place, though, except for a single drip of water that gathered on the tip of a stalactite, readying itself to fall, to join the peak of a stalagmite that grew directly below. The silence in the cavern, cut only by the soft whir of their propellers, made her ears ache.

They headed down a vertical shaft, nearly fifty meters deep, with water running down the walls in a constant slick film. At the bottom they passed through a series of curved corridors cut as smooth as the hallways on a starship, as silent and dark as the womb. The temperature had risen to nearly fifty degrees centigrade, and the flow of rock dust around them was so thick that human eyes couldn't have seen through it. There was a stillness, a perfect quietude to the abandoned mine that terrified Petrova. All she could think about was how many trillions of tons of rock there were over their heads, pressing down, forever pressing down on these weird corridors, these carved galleries. Yet for all its natural horror, it was still a human place. Everything around them had been designed, chosen, made manifest by human plan. She felt like she was walking hunched over through the lightless passages inside the Great Pyramid of Egypt. She felt like she was violating a tomb.

There was nothing, no sound, no light, no motion. And then . . .

"Do you hear that?" Zhang said.

He'd all but whispered the words, but still she wanted to warn him to be silent, to not break the soundless roar of the place.

Then she heard what he'd heard. A ringing sound. It came again, and again, a slow rhythm of something metal hitting rock and bouncing off.

At that moment they were in a long, long corridor that didn't branch off at all. One wall was smooth, machine-worked to a polish. The other was rough, pierced, gouged out, scored by the drill heads of mining robots, creating a series of alcoves and recesses. Up ahead she saw a spark of light come from one of those hollows. The first real light they'd seen since coming underground.

She flew forward and peered into it, just in time to see another spark. In its momentary flaring light, she caught sight of the head of a pickaxe striking a boulder, cracking the rock open. The light came again, and she saw the stone split.

"Up there," Zhang said. He flew ahead of her to indicate the end of the corridor. She zoomed after him and they came out into a massive open cavern, like a vast bubble of air inside the planet's crust. She could barely make out the ceiling or the floor, but it looked like there was a mountain at the center of the space, a vast spire of rock over which things were moving, teeming like insects, like maggots. Her drone's cameras let her zoom in, and she saw that the maggots were in fact human figures, human bodies digging away at the rock, smashing it with hand tools, picks, shovels, hammers. Tearing at it with bare, broken fingers.

None of them looked up. None of them turned their faces so that she could see the color of their eyes. She was certain these weren't just human beings, though.

"Revenants," Zhang whispered.

But she already knew. She knew because the basilisk had fallen utterly silent inside her head. It wasn't thrashing around in there anymore. It was like it had left her altogether, abandoned her.

She knew better. It hadn't gone anywhere. But there was something about revenants it couldn't handle. It would be foolish to say it was afraid of them, but ...

Hands grabbed her drone by one rotor, dragged it out of the air and pushed it down against the floor. She screamed as if she was being attacked herself, screamed as multiple hands grabbed and pulled and tore at her drone body, ripping off its propellers, smashing in the green mask with a pickaxe. Something struck the camera, very fast, very hard, and—

Everything went black.

She was still screaming, still thrashing as Zhang unzipped her hood and daylight flooded in, blinding her, the stinking air of the pit washing across her face.

# 81

"She'll be fine," Zhang said.

Parker nodded but he couldn't sit still. He got up and moved around the ops room instead, walking through the workstations like the ghost he was. "What happened? Why did she scream like that?"

"Just a little disorientation. We were in the VR rigs for quite a while. It's easy to forget that it's not real. When the revenants attacked her—"

"Revenants?" Mo asked. No one had briefed him on what had happened yet, apparently. "There are revenants in the mine?"

"That's who's digging down there," Zhang said. He looked tired, washed out.

Parker wanted to ask if the doctor was okay. He really wanted to ask more about Petrova, though. "So she had a shock. A bad shock. But she's going to be okay?"

"She'll be fine," Zhang said, again. "Listen. Just listen. We reached the bottom of the mine and there's a very large cavern down there, and at the center of the cavern . . ."

He stopped, because a holoscreen had popped open in mid-air next to him. It showed an image of the cavern, the mountain growing out of its floor. The revenants were just visible as pale dots moving around it.

"Thank you, Rapscallion," Zhang said. "There were revenants at all these locations," he said, and a dozen dots appeared scattered at random points throughout the map. "They destroyed all our drones, but not before we were able to get this data."

Parker hadn't seen any of this. He'd been with Mo. They'd spent the time just talking about nothing in particular. Just talking.

While Petrova was deep inside a death maze at the bottom of the world.

"There's a whole series of tunnels in there," Zhang said. Rapscallion's holoscreen zoomed out, away from the mountain in the cavern. It showed all the corridors and galleries and sub-caverns and equipment rooms in the mine below the pit. A three-dimensional maze. It looked like it would be impossible to thread if you didn't have a map.

"Jesus. How long have people been digging down there?" Parker asked.

"Some of this," Zhang said, gesturing at the map, "is old work. We think it was made by the original miners, the ones who came here in the first wave of colonization. Those sections are well built, shored up and stable. Other tunnels down here look different. Cruder, less safe. Hand-dug. We think those were added to the mine by the revenants." The map showed the two sections in different colors, green versus black. The green section comprised maybe the top fifth of the diagram. The rest was black. It looked more like the chaotic meanderings of an ant nest than a working mine.

"They did all of that?" Parker asked.

"You said 'hand-dug'," Mo pointed out.

Zhang nodded. "They have some basic unpowered tools. Picks and shovels, mostly. The robots have all been shut down, though, and so have any more modern implements or pieces of equipment. There's no ventilation down there, no pumps to draw out water. No lights at all."

Mo's eyes went wide. "Just bugs. They're like bugs digging in the dirt. What the hell do they want down there?"

"Something here." Zhang pointed at the mountain in the large cavern. "The work is centered around this. We have no idea what it is or why they want it. Right now, I can tell you one thing. I don't care."

"What?" Parker asked. "But Petrova—"

"I don't care what's down there. I know Director Lang told us to come here, to this mine, so we could be evacuated from this terrible planet. As far as I'm concerned, we've done as she asked. I have no desire to know what the revenants are doing. If Lang cares so much, she can send people better qualified than us for the task. I hope she sends an entire army to kill every revenant down there, frankly. But I don't care if she just declares this planet off limits and leaves the revenants to their digging forever."

Parker shook his head. "Hold on," he said, and would have said more.

Zhang had clearly had enough, though.

"We're done," he said. "When Petrova's well enough to walk, we're going to pack up the quadcopter and leave. Go somewhere safe where we can wait for the rescue ship to arrive, and hope we're still alive when it does."

Zhang got Mo to help him move Petrova to a more comfortable place in a housing unit he thought must have belonged to one of the mine's top-level administrators. It was the cleanest place they'd found in the facility, for one thing, and had actual decorations on its walls, what looked like paintings of sunsets and mountain peaks on Paradise-1. There was an entertainment console built into one wall and a generously sized shower in the private bathroom.

Not exactly a high-end luxury hotel suite, but it rivaled Mo's house in comfort, he thought. Petrova could at least get some rest in the large, soft bed.

"What's wrong with her?" the survivor asked, making no attempt to keep his voice down.

Not that it mattered. "She's conscious but not responsive," Zhang said. He shrugged. "I've never heard of anyone having such an adverse reaction to VR before, but I suppose anything's possible." He caught himself being too honest. Petrova wouldn't want Mo to even see her like this, much less hear that she couldn't handle a little disorientation. He squatted down next to the bed and checked her eyes. They tracked a moving finger, but just barely. She was lost inside her own head. That wasn't exactly a medical diagnosis, but he thought it was accurate.

"She's not alone in there," Mo said. He scratched vigorously at the skin behind his ear. It looked like an anxious gesture, one Zhang hadn't seen him make before. "Is she?"

"What are you suggesting?" Zhang asked.

"You guys haven't told me everything." Mo took a step back, away from the bed. "Sometimes she blanks out. It looks like she's talking to somebody who isn't there. Look. If anybody can sympathize . . . I mean, for months after, you know, I was alone in that house. For months I would catch somebody humming in another room, or maybe I would be sitting on the couch and I would just reach over, thinking I was going to rub Marsia's shoulder, even though she wasn't there. So I get it. I do."

Zhang watched Mo's face carefully. They hadn't told him about the basilisk. None of them had conspired about it; they'd just tacitly agreed without any discussion that it was the kind of thing that should stay secret.

Mo threw his head back. "This changes things."

"How?" Zhang asked.

The survivor didn't answer, not really. "She's in charge, and . . . Damn. She's in charge." He looked away, his breathing coming faster. He scratched at himself again, his elbow, his shoulder. "My only chance of getting off this planet and she's the one in charge."

"Not at the moment. Right now, that's my job. Mo. Mo!" Zhang hated having to raise his voice, but it looked like the survivor was spiraling. "Listen. We're going to get out of here. All of us. But we have to stick together. Alright?"

Mo stared at Petrova's blank face as he answered. "Whatever. Whatever, man."

"I need you to say it. We stick together," Zhang repeated.

"Sure. We stick together." Mo gave him a dark look. "You're the boss."

Zhang supposed that was the best he was likely to get. "Come on. You're with me." He headed back out into the sunlight, though it was dimmer than he'd expected. He cursed a little under his breath. He never could seem to remember how short the days were on Paradise-1. "The sun will be down in a few hours," he said.

"Yeah, no shit. Happens every day."

He swiveled around to look at the survivor and saw a smile on his face. He must have been making a joke. Zhang tried to laugh, but the sound got caught in his throat.

He did not like being in charge. He'd always hated it, even back when it just meant organizing rounds in a hospital ward. Now that lives depended on him, the stress was too much. He would handle it, he told himself. He would get through this. Then, when Petrova was awake and alert, she could have the job back, no question.

"I want to give her at least an hour to rest before we move her again," he said. "We'll be out of here in plenty of time."

"You think the revenants will come for us when it gets dark?"

"Honestly, you're the expert," Zhang said. "You've been fighting them a lot longer than we have. You think there's a chance they'll leave us alone?"

The survivor rubbed the back of his hand across his lips. "Not even a little one. You got too close, Doc. You and her – you saw what they were doing down there. They don't like people as a rule, they'll kill anyone they can get their hands on. But when you mess with them directly? Intrude on their territory? They don't forgive stuff like that."

"Interesting," Zhang said. "So they're territorial."

"Like animals."

He frowned. "I'm not so sure about that. They've shown surprisingly complex behavior for what are essentially mindless undead corpses."

"They'll literally walk into rifle fire to get at their victims," Mo pointed out. "Like, they'll let you carve them into pieces rather than miss a chance to kill you."

"You're right, there doesn't appear to be any instinct for

self-preservation. Not at the individual level," Zhang said. "Yet when you came and fought them in the town, shooting them from the air, eventually they seemed to realize that it was futile to keep advancing. They retreated like an army getting orders from general command."

"Took them a long damned time to come to that conclusion, though," Mo pointed out. "I must have taken down fifty of them that night."

"There are thousands of them on this planet," Zhang said. "They aren't just soldiers." He considered that for a moment. "They're workers, too. The ones we saw down in the mine showed no interest in us. They were too busy digging to even notice the drones. The one that attacked us was different. Like a sentry, posted to guard a nest."

"What are you talking about?"

He threw his hands up. "I don't know. Not for sure. But . . . a population of mixed workers and soldiers. It sounds almost like ants. Like bees. They don't care if an individual revenant lives or dies, but if the entire group is threatened, they respond immediately. They protect their territory ferociously. That really sounds like eusocial behavior."

"You think they're ants?" Mo said. "Doc, that's one of the craziest things I've heard from you yet. They're just fucking zombies!"

"They're like a colony organism. Working, fighting together, all of them aligned by . . . I don't know. Some kind of organizing principle more important than their individual survival. Or maybe there's some central intelligence that gives them orders." Zhang shook his head. He could have kept going with the theory, developed it further, but he knew he was treading on dangerous ground. Thinking he understood the revenants would lead to him thinking he could predict their behavior. What if he was wrong? He could get everyone killed.

"We have a plan. We stick to it," he said.

"Whatever you say," Mo told him. His eyes were narrow, though. Zhang thought maybe that meant the survivor didn't trust him as much as he had before. Did Mo think he was some academic lodged firmly up an ivory tower?

It didn't matter. In a few hours, when Petrova had recovered, it wouldn't matter.

"I'm starving," he said. "Let's go get something to eat."

# 83

Parker climbed up to the top of the ops building. The highest point in the mine complex. The wind whipped around him, threatening to tear the portable-hard light projector out of his hand. He held it close to his body. He needed to be alone. Away from everything except his own thoughts. He needed to make a decision.

He used his free hand to grab a radio mast. He leaned out over the edge, looked down into the pit, imagined what it must have been like down there. He'd seen a copy of the video feed taken by Rapscallion's drones, but that wasn't enough. He needed to know what the air felt like on your skin. How hot it was, how oppressive the darkness could get. He needed to know what she'd felt.

The basilisk had marched Petrova right into danger. Not for the first time. Yet again it had left her reeling, left her all but comatose. He supposed he should be glad it hadn't given her seizures this time.

How was this going to end? All he wanted was to keep her safe. He knew he'd left rational self-interest behind. He was dead, after all. He'd come back from death to have this new life, but he didn't care about it. He couldn't feel anything, couldn't smell or taste anything. What kind of life was that? So he'd sublimated his natural desires – desires he would never again be able to satisfy – into concern for her, for Petrova. Sasha.

The woman he loved.

He wanted to be by her side, even then, even when she couldn't tell he was in the room. He wanted to hold her, comfort her. Zhang had asked him to give her some space, so that was what he was doing, but it was driving him mad.

He wondered if he was losing it. Or if he had already lost it. Gone insane in this perverse mockery of a human body. When they'd first left *Artemis*, when he'd lost the ability to use hard light and he was just an image, a ghost hanging in the air, he'd lost something else, too. Some essential component of his humanity. Now he wasn't even a person anymore, just a thing, a fake thing that loved a real woman. That love, that act of loving, was all he had left.

He had no illusions about what would happen to him when she went home. If he went back to Ganymede, if he went to Sam Parker's old home, inasmuch as he'd had one, he would have no human rights. He wasn't human. He would own nothing. Sam Parker was dead, and anything he'd owned would be, by now, property of the state.

As far as he knew, no dead man had ever come back as a hologram ghost before. The legal status of such a being just didn't exist. There were laws about robots and laws about people, but he wasn't covered under either topic. How would the UEG see him? As a chance to revise their notoriously poor corpus of human rights law? Or as a freak anomaly? A lab specimen to be studied? Taken apart, line of code by line of code, until they knew how he functioned? He doubted he would survive that level of scrutiny.

He supposed he could stay here, on Paradise-1. Live with the weird animals in the mountain caves, or find a place among the revenants. The idea made him laugh.

He knew he would never do it. He would never abandon Petrova. As long as she let him be by her side, that was exactly where he would stay. If she told him she wanted him to be taken apart in some computer lab . . .

He would let it happen.

*What do you want?*

He turned around very slowly. He was convinced that the Other only lived in his blind spot. It couldn't exist if he looked at it straight on. Right?

Except when he turned all the way around, it was still there. Shadowy and indistinct, sure. Flickering, snapping in and out of existence like a computer glitch, like a tattered flag snapping in the wind. Definitely.

But there it was. The thing with his face. It stood right at the far edge of the ops building's roof. Looking back at him.

*What do you want?*

It didn't speak. It didn't have to. It was inside his head, a fragment of his splintered personality. Proof if he needed any that yes, he was losing his mind. He felt its question rather than hearing it.

"What do I want? I just want her. That's the problem."

The Other looked confused.

*Why are you here?*

It was closer, suddenly. Only two meters away. It looked him straight in the eye and it was more real, more solid than before. The fucking thing looked just like him. Like the body he'd left behind.

"It's stupid. Crazy. But I think I came back ... I think I came back because of her." It made no sense, not logically. Sam Parker and Sasha Petrova had had an affair years ago. A week on a spaceship with nothing to do but fuck each other's brains out. It had been a memory he had savored, one that always made him smile.

Then one day she'd walked onto his brand-new transport, looking for a ride to a planet a hundred light years away, and instantly they were flirting with each other again. He'd begun to think something could happen, that they could re-create the magic.

Until a psychic monster from beyond the stars had blown a hole right through *Artemis*, killing Sam Parker instantly. He'd still been frozen in his cryotube, dreaming of her. He hadn't felt a thing.

The ship had rebuilt him. Taken his memories, studied video of his mannerisms and his lack of fashion sense, used predictive algorithms to reconstitute his personality. It couldn't give him a body, but it could paint a picture of him in the air, a picture so perfectly realistic, so exactly like the original, that Petrova hadn't known he was dead until the ship's computers had to reboot.

He didn't know why the ship had remade him. Still didn't know. It had been destroyed, smashed to its component atoms, so most likely he never would.

Yet as to why he let it happen, why he went along with the crazy scheme . . .

It had been for her.

*Why are you here?* the Other asked.

"I don't know! To . . . protect her? To be her lover again?" And yet when it happened, when it finally happened, it was the most frustrating thing he'd ever experienced.

*Who are you?*

The hardest question of all, and he was no closer to an answer.

*What do you want?*

He started to turn away, to ignore the Other. It was just a figment of his—

*WHAT DO YOU WANT?*

Its shadowy fist plunged into his back, meeting no resistance. He felt its cold fingers digging through his lungs, his spine, his heart. It —

It hurt.

He felt actual, real pain. It was such a surprise he could only gasp and flinch away from the attack.

The Other slapped him across the face. Parker felt it, felt the sting on his cheek, the blood rushing to the damaged flesh.

*WHY ARE YOU HERE?*

He stumbled backward, unable to understand what was

happening. His feet left the edge of the roof and he just kept going, walking backward on air. He tried to run, tried to get enough footing to push himself up into the sky, away from the thing.

But it was him. It was just as fast as he was, just as nimble. It grabbed him by the shoulder blades and started to pull them apart, tearing him open. He felt his bones crack, his skin tear, and then ...

The portable hard-light projector switched itself off. It tumbled through the air, buffeted this way and that by the wind. When it hit the stony ground beneath, it shattered into a thousand pieces.

# 84

In one of the maintenance sheds, Rapscallion opened a new holoscreen and let four seconds of video play out on a loop. It showed revenants dragging a dead human down one of the mine complex's narrow streets. That wasn't the strange part, though. As they hauled the corpse past the ops center, he could clearly see human miners behind the big windows. Watching the revenants move their prize.

The humans did nothing to stop the revenants. Maybe they were too scared. Maybe they thought there was no point risking their lives for a dead man. Rapscallion wasn't so sure.

He made a note, then moved to another clip. It showed a woman in coveralls riding on top of one of the mining robots, one of the drill heads. She whooped and waved one hand in the air as it skittered on long, jointed legs down a stony slope. Other humans, off screen, cheered and shouted encouragement.

He was not particularly interested in the fate of any of these humans. What he'd been trying to determine was the interval of time that elapsed between the two clips. It was a shorter duration than he had originally expected. Based on Mo's account and what they'd seen at the colony town, the disaster there had taken a few days to play out. Here at the mine it all happened in less than twenty-four hours.

He ran a quick facial-recognition algorithm on the woman in the video, the one riding the robot. He found another clip of her bleeding out in a locked housing unit, while revenants stood at the windows, watching. Perhaps waiting for her to die. The look on her face was one of peaceful resignation. Rapscallion added it to his database of human facial expressions.

Behind him he heard a sound. A very soft sound, a sort of shuffling.

"Zhang?" he called out. "Mo? Is that you?"

There was no answer.

He ran a threat analysis and decided it had probably just been the wind moving refuse around in the street outside. Nothing to concern him.

The video clips were all he'd been able to recover from the memories of an extensive network of surveillance cameras. Every part of the mine complex had been covered at all times by the feeds. When the local servers had been erased, these few bits of video were all that remained. There was no context to them, no framework to hang them on, so he was forced to piece them back together like a puzzle in order to form a proper timeline. He found the work soothing, despite the subject matter, and —

Footsteps. Bare feet crunching through gravel. Odd.

The robot closed the video file he was working on and switched to a live view of the camera network. He looked at the buildings around him, the streets between them. Nothing moved out there, nothing changed.

It was very difficult to sneak up on a robot like Rapscallion. He had senses no human possessed, and was constantly aware of his surroundings.

When a broken piece of green plastic was tossed into the shed and went skittering across the floor toward him, he was honestly surprised. He stood perfectly still, moving only his head, slowly scanning back and forth. Only when he was satisfied that he was still alone did he walk over to see what the object was.

He recognized it immediately, of course. It was one of the masks from the drones he'd built. The drones the revenants in the mine had destroyed. The mask had been torn off the drone and deep gouges had been scored through the cheeks and forehead.

"Sorry you didn't like it," he said, out loud.

There were two doors in the shed, the open vehicle gate at the front of the long building and a smaller, human-scale doorway halfway along one wall, an emergency exit. The smaller door was closer. Even before he started running for it, however, it slammed open and revenants started shoving their way through, flooding in out of the shadowy street beyond. Rapscallion tried to change course, to head for the big vehicle entrance instead, but before he could cover half of the distance, they were already on him.

# 85

"Zhang! They're here! Get Petrova out of here now!"

Zhang stared at his device, unable to understand what Rapscallion was saying. Mo reacted much faster, grabbing his Gauss rifle and bringing it around to cover the street.

"Rapscallion? What happened?" Zhang asked.

There was no response.

He swung around, looking at every building around them, looking at windows, doorways. Anywhere someone could hide. "This doesn't make any sense," he said. "It's still at least an hour before dusk. Isn't it?"

"I told you they were territorial," Mo said. He brought the rifle up to his eye, sighting along the long metal rail. "I've seen them attack by daylight before. You have too, right? You said one bit you, your first day on the planet."

"Yes," Zhang said. His mouth was suddenly very dry. He tapped at his palm again and again, trying to raise Rapscallion on the comms link, but nothing happened.

"Doc?" Mo said.

"Hmm?"

"There's a weapon on your belt. Time to draw it."

Zhang nodded. He reached down, touched the holster on his hip. He pulled out the gun that Rapscallion had printed for him and tried to find the right way to hold it. The rough seam on the trigger guard bit into his finger, but he ignored it.

"They don't come out in the light. But there are a bunch of shadows I can see right now," Mo pointed out. And it was true. This close to nightfall, every building, every object cast a long shadow across the ground. "Stay in the light."

"Got it."

"Okay. What now?"

Zhang looked at the survivor, unsure what he was being asked.

"What do we do now? You're in charge."

He thought about it for a second. "We need to get the others to the copter so we can get out of here. Rapscallion's in one of the maintenance sheds – it's this way."

"Better idea, maybe?" Mo suggested.

Zhang nodded.

"Tell them to come to the copter. It'll be faster if we all just meet there."

Zhang nodded. He sent Rapscallion a quick message about the rendezvous point. He didn't bother checking for confirmation from the robot. "Parker?" He stabbed at his palm, trying to bring up the hologram's comms address. There was no response at all, not even a do-not-disturb flag.

He switched to the common radio band that anyone within range could have heard. "Parker, Rapscallion. If you can hear me, we need to go, now. Get to the copter as fast as you can." He stabbed at his palm to try again.

"They may already be dead," Mo suggested. "Think, Doc. Think about what we actually need to accomplish here. Don't waste time on them – try saving the ones who are still alive."

"Like triage," Zhang said.

"Sure. Whatever that means."

Zhang tapped for Petrova's address. He tried pinging her, but she didn't respond either. He had left her barely conscious, though. Maybe she just couldn't answer him. "Petrova, if you can hear this, I'm coming to get you. We're leaving. Now."

He tapped his palm to end the call and put both hands on his gun. The shadows all around them felt sinister, like they could hide anything. Like they were breathing.

He caught a flash of movement down the street. His weapon swung up, and he prepared himself to pull the trigger, but before he could do so, the movement was gone and he saw nothing where it had been. "Did you catch that?" he asked.

"I saw something. Shh!"

They stood in silence for a moment. Mo changed his grip on the Gauss rifle.

"I'm going to start shooting in a second. You get Petrova," he said. "I'll meet you at the copter."

Zhang nodded. He tried to turn, to head in the direction of the housing unit, but he couldn't look away. Mo was tracking something, the barrel of his rifle moving in tiny, sudden arcs. Zhang couldn't see anything.

"Go, now," Mo said.

Zhang ran. Behind him he heard the Gauss rifle spit once, twice, and purple flashes of light lit up the street.

"Fuck!" Mo shouted.

Zhang didn't look back.

# 86

Under the water, under the ocean, Petrova's eyes were closed. Her hair floated around her head like yellow seaweed, lit up by a distant flickering light from below.

The light was very far away now, but its beam filtered upward toward her, shimmering through the water column. She could feel it on her eyelids, on her skin.

The basilisk was afraid.

It shouldn't have been possible. The parasite had been constructed out of subtle energies, psychic technologies humanity couldn't even guess at. It had been made well, built to be an eternal guardian of something that could not be destroyed, only contained.

(She did not question how she knew this. The basilisk didn't share much with her, but when it did, the knowledge came to her feeling like her own thoughts in her own head.)

Fear was not part of its makeup. Yet it absolutely dreaded what was down in the mine.

Its fascination with the thing was similar to the experience a human might have standing on a ledge looking over a thousand-meter drop. Petrova felt it too. Her head spun. Her stomach felt like it had been surgically removed, like her abdominal cavity was empty and if she wasn't careful she might float away, float out over that drop and . . .

Fall.

*Petrova? We have to go. We have to go, they're here and —*

The words were muffled, as if she had a thick blanket over her head. She shouldn't have been able to hear them through the water at all.

The basilisk had no interest in what those words meant. It held her close, clinging to her like she was the one thing between it and the abyss. Was this why it needed her? Someone to keep it from succumbing to an unnatural urge? A body to anchor it to the real world, so that it didn't . . .

Fall.

*Petrova! Wake the fuck up!*

She opened her eyes. She was lying on her side and someone was shaking her, pushing her left shoulder. Her cast flopped back and forth on a soft surface. Suddenly she was sitting upright. She looked around, blinked a few times.

"Can you stand? Come on, give me some kind of indication. Anything."

She tried to shake her head. Her chin moved, a little.

Zhang – it was Zhang shouting in her face – cursed. She almost never heard him curse, and typically it was some gentle admonition about fate and inevitability. Now he was swearing like a marine on a troop transport.

"You have to help me. You have to help," he begged. He was crying.

She really wanted to help him. She rose to her feet, and promptly took a . . .

Fall.

Luckily he was there to catch her. She blinked again, looked around. He got his arms under her armpits and started dragging her across a cold floor. There was a hatch in front of them, and sunlight. That was okay. Sunlight made everything safe, she thought.

"It's not safe anymore," he said, as if he'd read her mind. "We have to move, and we have to move fast. Okay? I'm sorry if this hurts."

What an absurd idea. Her skin felt numb all over. She didn't think she could feel pain at that moment.

Together they stepped outside, into a grimy street. She looked down and saw bits of rock there, and the long shadows they cast. The light was golden, beautiful, but the warehouses and sheds around them had dark walls where the fading sun didn't hit them. They looked like holes into space, like if they got too close they would be sucked out into the vacuum, where they would ...

Fall.

Forever. She didn't want that to happen. Luckily Zhang dragged her away from the deep shadows, further up a street painted yellow by the dying light.

There were things in the dark, she saw now. Things that moved and followed them, things with eyes blacker than the shadows.

"Zhang?" she whispered. She thought she'd said it out loud.

He didn't respond. He was too busy hauling her down the street. Her boots dragged behind her, and she didn't like that so she tried to get her feet under her, tried to walk, but she was so numb, so dead inside her skin. Just like the revenants. Revenants! That's what those black eyes were, those eyes that glinted from the shadows. But it was okay, because the revenants never came out into the light. They never ...

Broken hands snatched at her arm, her good arm. Petrova yanked her body sideways to get away from the attack. White skin glittered in the sunlight, only the two forearms exposed, but the revenant yanked them back quickly, like it had been wounded.

"Zhang," she tried again, but this time even she knew her voice was so faint there was no way he could hear her over the wind. There were more revenants behind them, moving quickly through the shadows, darting across the street, running through a patch of light as fast as they could, then plunging back into blackness.

The shadows were getting longer. Thicker. Half the road

was covered in stripes of darkness. The revenants were getting closer. She could see their faces now, the dark veins under their cheeks, their foreheads. They didn't hiss or snarl at her. They didn't need to.

She knew what homicidal intent looked like.

"Zhang," she said, trying to pump some air into the name, the warning. He didn't look back, didn't pat her arm or do anything to indicate he'd heard her.

One of the revenants behind them took a careful, testing step out into the light. It had been a woman once, a human woman. It was dressed in the tattered remains of a jumpsuit with a corporate logo on the breast. Centrocor, Petrova thought. One of the UEG's major vendors. She recognized the stylized concentric Cs. Centrocor built spaceships and provided equipment for habitats on a dozen worlds, and—

Wait.

The woman was in the light. She was standing in the yellow light. She crouched down, hands over her hairless head, fingers splayed across her scalp like the light hurt her, but she didn't run back into the shadows. Instead she took a halting step forward. Then another, this one with a little more confidence.

Behind her a naked male revenant stepped into the light as well. His back arched and his head tilted back in a kind of unvoiced scream, but he didn't stop. Just kept moving forward, one foot after the other.

"Zhang," Petrova said, and she felt him grunt in frustration, but he didn't turn around. He was still dragging her, taking her somewhere. She trusted he knew what he was doing, but she had to ... she had to ... She pushed against the street with her foot, and this time she could feel it a little, she could feel the resistance.

The revenants were growing in confidence. There was something ... Something about their skin bothered her, but ... but they were coming, they were running now ...

"Zhang!" she shouted.

"Later," he shouted back.

But there wasn't going to be a later. She shoved both her legs down, her feet planting on the gravel-strewn street. He said something angry, but she didn't let it stop her. She needed to get her balance so she didn't fall, and ... and ...

The revenants were right behind them.

She reached down and grabbed her pistol out of its holster. Fired three shots in quick succession. Black wounds opened in three foreheads.

She didn't need to be able to feel her hands to shoot. She'd trained, practiced these motions so many times.

One by one the revenants dropped to the street. She saw that their skin, the skin of their backs where the sunlight had hit it, was the wrong color. It should have been fish-belly white. Instead it was a sort of dull, dusty gray.

She didn't have time to think about that. More revenants were peeling off the shadowy walls of the buildings around them. More were daring to step out into the sun.

She leaned hard against Zhang, using him to prop herself up. Lined up more shots. At this distance headshots were out of the question – her weapon wasn't meant for precise work like that – but she caught one in the jaw, grazed another's temple.

"Petrova!" Zhang shouted. "Come on! There are too many!"

She knew he was right. She turned to look at him and saw the absolute terror on his face.

"Let's go," she said.

He grabbed her wrist and started running, and though her feet still felt numb, half dead, she ran too.

# 87

Zhang watched the shadows writhe and nearly stumbled, but he managed to keep them on track. They were so close – too close to stop now. Petrova kept twisting around, shooting at something he typically didn't even see. He drew his own weapon and fired at a revenant that had loomed at him out of the dark, but he didn't even try to aim. Maybe he hit the dead thing, maybe not. "Come on," he shouted, and hauled her around one last corner. And there it was. The quadcopter.

Sitting motionless where they'd left it, on a painted ring.

Motionless.

He started to panic. If they reached the aircraft and Mo wasn't there, who would fly it? He knew he couldn't, and Petrova was hardly in any shape to do so. If they climbed into the bubble canopy and waited for Mo to reach them, would they still be waiting when the revenants came and tore them bodily out of the copter, dragged them out and ripped them to pieces?

Something moved behind him. Zhang twisted around and lifted his gun, yanking the trigger at the same moment, knowing he was just firing blind, wasting a bullet. But the figure he saw emerging from the long shadows ducked its head and threw one arm up across its face.

"Jesus, Doc," Mo said, running past him. "Watch where you're pointing that thing!"

"Sorry," Zhang said, "I'm sorry!" but the survivor was already jumping up into the copter's pilot's seat. Zhang helped Petrova climb in too, then scrambled up inside the hatch himself, even as the rotors started to spin.

"Did you see the others?" he asked. "Where are they?"

"No idea," Mo said. "We're getting out of here. The robot can fend for himself, and it's not like they can kill a ghost."

"He was using a portable projector," Zhang said. "If they destroy that, Parker will be—"

"I don't have time to worry about him. We need to go now. Do you see this?" Mo gestured at the nearby buildings. The sun had passed directly behind one of the maintenance sheds, and now the mine complex was thrown in silhouette. Emerging from that dark background were dozens of pale shapes. Pale shapes with black eyes.

They staggered a little as they came, looking dazed, maybe hurt. Zhang saw that many of them had patches of dusty gray skin and he tried to figure out why. Before he could reach any kind of conclusion, though, the quadcopter lurched and lifted into the air.

"No, wait!" he said. "Rapscallion's back there!"

"I'm saving who I can. What did you call it? Triage?"

Zhang nodded. His throat was very thick. He pressed his hands against the Plexiglas, looked out at the dark rock beneath them, the low buildings, beyond that the massive wound in the side of Paradise-1 that was the mine pit. Rapscallion had been the first one to see the revenants, to report that they were active despite the sunlight. They hadn't heard from him since. Zhang had to accept that maybe the robot was gone.

It was unthinkable. They'd come so far. Accomplished so much, survived so much. Rapscallion had kept them alive. "We lost Rapscallion," Zhang said. He didn't want to mention Parker, in case that made Petrova withdraw into her own head again.

Petrova scowled at him. "What are you talking about?"

"I know it's a bad time to hear this," he told her. He watched the buildings recede behind them as they lifted higher and higher into the air. The few clouds high above them were tinged pink like bloody gauze littering an operating room floor. "We barely made it out ourselves. Rapscallion is gone, Petrova."

"He's right fucking there," she said, and stabbed downward with her index finger, pointing through the canopy.

"What?" Zhang said, almost climbing out of his seat to get a better look.

"Sit the fuck down!" Mo said.

"It's him," Zhang said. He could clearly see the bright, toxic green of Rapscallion's plastic body down there in the shadows. Paler shapes milled around the robot, but it looked like he was running at full steam away from the mine. "We have to get him!"

Mo stared forward through the canopy. Zhang could hear him gritting his teeth together. "I'm not setting down, not in the middle of that."

"He's our friend," Zhang said. "If you won't, we—"

"You'll what?" Mo spared him one quick glance. "You going to jump out in mid-air? I won't fucking set down, that's final. But hold on to something, because this is going to get bad."

He swung his control yoke over to one side and the quadcopter dove through the air, turning on a sharp radius back the way they'd come. Zhang was thrown bodily into Petrova, who was smashed up against the Plexiglas hard enough that she let out a little roar of pain.

Mo straightened them out and came in for a low pass, right over the heads of a dozen revenants. They reached for the copter like they would catch it and drag it out of the sky.

Straight ahead of them, Rapscallion was galloping across open slickrock, moving with three limbs. One of his arms was gone altogether and one of his legs looked broken, like it had more joints than it used to and none of them worked particularly well. His head was gone, just cleanly sheared off his shoulders. A revenant jumped on his back and he bucked like a wild horse, throwing the dead thing clear.

"You're not strong enough," Mo said, looking Zhang up and down. "You're going to steer. Think you can do that?"

"What? You want me to take the controls?" Zhang asked.

"It's not hard. Just keep the yoke straight and level. I don't want to fall out of my own copter. Take the damned yoke!"

Zhang grabbed the steering controls even as Mo popped the canopy's hatch open. Wind rushed inside, fierce enough that it nearly blew Zhang's hand off the yoke, but he just tightened his grip and held on. He tried to watch what happened next but knew he should be paying attention to their altitude. They were barely a meter and a half off the ground. If there were any boulders or even medium-sized rocks ahead of them—

"Level!" Mo shouted. He leaned out of the hatch and thrust one arm downward, bracing the other against the frame of the hatch. "When I say, pull back!"

Rapscallion was just ahead of them. Revenants were all around the robot, closing in, moving as fast as he could run. If this didn't work the first time, Zhang doubted they would get another chance.

"Robot!" Mo shouted.

Rapscallion didn't look up – hard to do in any case without a head. But at the exact perfect moment, he reared up and threw his arm in the air. Mo's hand smacked into the robot's forearm, and Rapscallion's fingers dug deep into Mo's bicep.

"Pull back!" Mo cried.

Zhang pulled back on the yoke, gently at first, then with more strength. The copter rose sluggishly into the air, the rotors whining as they took the extra weight. Mo screamed at the stress on his shoulder joint, but he hauled upward and Rapscallion was able to scramble up into the copter's landing gear, where he could hold on under his own power.

Mo let him go, then slipped back inside the canopy and slammed the hatch shut.

"Good job, Doc," he said, then grabbed the yoke out of

Zhang's hand. "Now. I don't care if you see Parker knocking on the hatch begging to be let in. We're getting the hell out of here, and that's final."

Petrova's brow wrinkled. "Parker?" she said.

When they landed back at Mo's house in the mountains, Rapscallion finally let go of the side of the copter and dropped to the ground in a heap. He was unsure if he would ever stand up again. The revenants had done a number on him, tearing off his outer casing, ripping out his actuator cables and half his wiring. His memory, his processor cores were intact, but that was about it.

Mo walked over to his front door and held up one hand. A laser passed over his skin, shone in his eyes and made him blink wildly, but then the door popped open. That must have been a security system, Rapscallion thought. Why a man who lived so far away from any population center needed an elaborate lock on his door was a mystery, but the robot supposed that if you were the last survivor on a hostile planet full of dead assholes, maybe you didn't take any chances.

Zhang helped Petrova climb down out of the copter's bubble. She batted the doctor's hands away, then wrapped her arms around herself as she hurried, head down, inside the house. "Petrova!" Zhang called, but she ignored him.

"Let her go, Doc," Rapscallion said.

"Oh no, look at you," Zhang said, coming to squat down next to the heap of broken parts that Rapscallion was still thinking of as his body. "How can I help?"

"I'm good," Rapscallion said. "I've already switched on Mo's

3D printer. I'll have a new body by morning. I'm just going to crawl over there and sit for a while." He tried to point at a corner of the house, but his fingers had lost all fine control. He'd had to clutch on to the side of the copter so hard they'd finally broken.

"I fucked up," Zhang said.

"What?"

"I was in charge. With Petrova out of commission, I was in charge and I fucked up. Parker died on my watch."

"He was already dead, Doc," the robot pointed out.

It didn't seem to help as much as he'd hoped. He compared the look on Zhang's face to his database of human facial expressions. The term that best described Zhang's current look was "haunted".

"We lost him. You didn't see him, did you? Before we ran away, I tried calling him, but he wasn't on the comms link. He wasn't anywhere."

"He was already gone by the time I got attacked," Rapscallion said.

"He was?" Zhang shook his head. "I should have known. I should have gotten us out of there the second Petrova came out of VR. I should have—"

"Doc, don't beat yourself up."

Zhang patted Rapscallion on what had once been a functional shoulder. Then he rose to his feet and went inside the house. Rapscallion was pretty sure the doctor's emotional state wasn't completely repaired, but he didn't seem to want to hear what the robot had to say.

Frustrating.

Centimeter by centimeter, Rapscallion hauled himself across the rock between the copter and the house. He could still use one arm and one leg for motive power. Eventually he reached the side of the house, near a broad window. Through the glass, he could see Petrova. She was down on the floor, her head buried in her good hand, her cast up over her head as if to protect her cranium from threats. She was shaking, her whole body moving up and down, and water kept splattering on the floor beneath her face.

Unfortunately, the robot couldn't see enough of her face to match her expression to anything in his database, so he couldn't make a proper estimation of her mental state. He supposed he would have to ask her later how she was feeling about Parker's death.

In the meantime, he had a new body to design.

# 89

Zhang didn't know what to do with himself. He tried making some food, but he opened a can and found its contents so nauseating he had to put it down. It wasn't even anything offensive, just some cultured meat product, pink and unseasoned. He shoved it in Mo's refrigeration unit and then stepped outside, just wanting some fresh air.

Night had fallen and the naked stars were on display. He watched them twinkle for a while, their light disturbed by fluctuations in the planet's atmosphere. He thought he saw one of the stars moving – perhaps it was a meteorite, about to burn up high overhead. He couldn't be sure. He looked down, at himself, his hands. They were shaking, just a little. He tried to decide if he was cold, but he wasn't. Maybe it was just fatigue.

In a shed at the side of the house he found a folding chair. He pushed it open and set it on the rocks. Once he was sitting down, he felt a little better, perhaps. His leg itched and he scratched at it idly, only to find a line of tiny scabs there. He knew what it had to be. The RD had injected him with some kind of cocktail of mood stabilizers and antidepressants.

"I'm not decompensating," he told the golden snakes.

They didn't answer. They couldn't talk. Sometimes he thought that was a design flaw, but he knew why the UEG had chosen to keep the RD silent. It was so that he couldn't argue with the thing. He couldn't question its decisions. It monitored him, and it decided when he needed to be medicated. He was not given a choice in the matter.

He supposed he should be grateful. When he'd first been given the device, back before he was chosen for this mission, he'd been in the middle of a psychotic break. He had been unable to regulate his thoughts or his emotions and he'd been a danger to himself. The RD had brought him back to a place where he could function.

Just in time to be thrown up against the horrors of Paradise-1.

He closed his eyes. Took a deep breath. When he opened his eyes again, he nearly shrieked. Standing in front of him was a pair of humanoid legs and hips. There was nothing above the pelvic girdle, no torso, no arms or head. Just legs. Bright green legs, of course, so green they looked like they were glowing in the dark.

"I assume this is a work in progress," Zhang said.

"I'm still figuring out what kind of weaponry I can build into the arms," Rapscallion said. His voice emerged from what looked like the base of a spinal column. "I wanted to show you something, though."

"Rapscallion . . ."

"When I was digging through the mine's data, I found another log."

"I'm not sure this is the right time," Zhang pointed out.

"I mean, a log recorded by that doctor. The one from the colony town. Remember? They came out here to figure out what was going on."

Zhang turned his head away. Did he care? Did he honestly care what happened to the doctor whose face he'd never seen, whose gender he didn't even know? Was it really going to make a difference to hear what the doctor had found at the mine?

"It's in better shape than the other ones. More complete, because whoever erased the mine's files wasn't as thorough. It's just audio, but it's pretty much all there. Here."

Zhang's device buzzed, a tiny motor spinning inside the meat of his thumb to indicate he'd received a file. He made a point of not opening his hand, not even acknowledging receipt.

"We're going home," he told the robot. "You should send this to Firewatch. To whoever takes over after we're gone."

"Yeah, okay," Rapscallion said. "Aren't you going to look at it, though?"

"Not right now," Zhang said.

The robot couldn't very well shrug in his current state. Instead he just trudged back into the house. Zhang could hear the 3D printer in there screaming as it rattled away, building some new monstrous form for Rapscallion to wear. The sounds faded as the robot closed the door.

Zhang's hand buzzed again to remind him he'd received a file. He told himself he wasn't going to look. He just didn't care.

He lasted about thirty seconds before he opened the file and played its contents.

THE TRIP ACROSS THE MOUNTAINS WAS UNEVENTFUL. MY PILOT ANSWERED NO QUESTIONS, JUST CARRIED MY BAGS AND OPERATED HER VEHICLE. SHE DROPPED ME AT THE COMPLEX AND DEPARTED AGAIN WITHOUT A WORD. THE MINING ADMIN WAS MORE HELPFUL, THOUGH HE SEEMED CONFUSED AS TO WHY I WAS THERE. I TALKED ABOUT THE MEN HE'D SENT TO ME, WHO HAD TURNED SO VIOLENT IN MY CLINIC. WHO I'D HAD TO PUT DOWN LIKE THEY WERE RABID ANIMALS.

I DIDN'T TELL HIM THOSE MEN WERE DEAD BEFORE THEY ARRIVED IN MY CARE. I DIDN'T THINK HE WOULD BELIEVE ME.

HE SEEMED SURPRISED TO HEAR THAT THE MEN HAD ATTACKED ME AND MY ASSISTANTS. CLAIMED NOTHING LIKE THAT HAD HAPPENED UNDER HIS WATCH, THAT THERE HAD BEEN NO VIOLENCE AT

THE MINE. FROM WHAT I'VE SEEN SO FAR, IT'S TRUE. THINGS ARE QUIET HERE, CREEPY QUIET. NO ONE SAYS MUCH. THEY WORK, THEY COME TO THE COMMISSARY FOR MEALS. SLEEP JUST LONG ENOUGH TO REGAIN STRENGTH SO THEY CAN WORK AGAIN.

I SET UP SHOP IN A LITTLE CURTAINED PARTITION OF THE DORMITORY. LISTENED TO THE MEN AND WOMEN AROUND ME SNORING AND FARTING. "KEEP THEM HEALTHY," THE ADMIN TOLD ME. "PLEASE. WE NEED THEM FIT. WE'RE SO CLOSE."

CLOSE TO WHAT? HE JUST SMILED. SAID HE WAS GLAD I'D COME.

TODAY I WENT DOWN INTO THE MINE. THEY DIDN'T WANT ME THERE, THEY TRIED TO STOP ME, BUT THERE HAD BEEN AN ACCIDENT. A CAVE-IN. I EXPECTED TO HEAD DOWN THERE AND FIND A BUNCH OF CORPSES. I GUESS I WAS HALF RIGHT. THERE WERE BODIES, PLENTY OF BODIES.

SOME OF THEM SHOWED ALL THE SIGNS OF THE TRANSFORMATION. EXTREME PALLOR, PROTRUDING VASCULARIZATION. ENLARGED PUPILS. SOME OF THE DEAD THINGS WERE HOLDING TOOLS. PICKS AND SHOVELS.

I DEMANDED AN EXPLANATION, BUT THE ADMIN CLAIMED NOT TO UNDERSTAND. THEY WERE WORKERS, DOING THEIR JOB. HE COULDN'T SEEM TO TELL THE DIFFERENCE BETWEEN THOSE OF HIS WORKERS WHO WERE STILL ALIVE AND THE ONES THAT HAD CHANGED. FROM WHAT I SAW, THEY WORKED SIDE BY SIDE WITH THE ROBOTS AND THE LIVING MINERS. NOBODY HERE SEES A PROBLEM.

I THINK WE MIGHT REALLY BE IN TROUBLE.

SPOKE WITH A DYING MAN, DEEP INSIDE THE MINE. HE WHISPERED ABOUT HOW CLOSE THEY WERE. HOW THEY HAD NEARLY CRACKED THE SHELL. THE SHELL OF WHAT? "IT'S IN THERE. IT'S BEEN IN THERE SO LONG. EONS, HIDDEN FROM THE LIGHT. THEY WERE AFRAID OF IT."

WHO WAS AFRAID? WHAT KIND OF THING COULD EXIST, BURIED SO DEEP, FOR MILLIONS OF YEARS? WHAT WERE THEY TRYING TO DIG UP? IT'S MADDENING, TRYING TO GET ANSWERS FROM THESE PEOPLE.

"I'M SO WEAK NOW," HE SAID. "PUT ME OUT OF MY MISERY." I WAS HORRIFIED BY THE PROSPECT. THE MAN WAS SUFFERING FROM SEVERE FATIGUE AND EXHAUSTION. MALNUTRITION AND DEHYDRATION. THOSE ARE ALL TREATABLE CONDITIONS. IF HE WOULD JUST COME BACK WITH ME, I TOLD HIM, BACK TO THE SURFACE, WE COULD GET HIM HELP. WE COULD FIX HIM UP.

HE DIDN'T WANT THAT. "KILL ME. SO I CAN GET BACK TO WORK," HE SAID.

I LEFT HIM THERE, DISGUSTED WITH HIM. WITH MYSELF. WHATEVER IS HAPPENING HERE, I DON'T WANT ANY MORE TO DO WITH IT. SOMEBODY HAS TO HEAR ABOUT THIS, SOMEBODY WITH THE POWER TO DO SOMETHING ABOUT IT.

THAT PERSON WON'T BE ME. I TRIED HEADING BACK TO THE SURFACE, BUT THEY STOPPED ME AT THE ENTRANCE TO THE LOWER WORKS. I WAS NEEDED BELOW, THEY SAID. THERE WERE PATIENTS WAITING ON ME.

THEY HAD WEAPONS. IT WAS CLEAR I WAS A PRISONER NOW, THOUGH THAT'S NOT HOW THEY PUT IT.

THERE'S WORK TO DO, THEY SAY. THERE'S ALWAYS MORE WORK.

RAN OUT OF MEDICINE. NO MORE ANTIBIOTICS, NO MORE SALVES OR POTIONS. THE GEAR I HAVE ON HAND CAN DO NOTHING FOR THESE PEOPLE. I HAVE EQUIPMENT BACK AT MY CLINIC, I TOLD THEM. I HAVE MACHINES THAT COULD GET THEM BACK TO HEALTH. MAKE THEM FIT ENOUGH TO DIG AGAIN. THEY COULD KEEP WORKING IF I COULD JUST TREAT THEM.

NOBODY SMILES DOWN HERE. THEIR FACES ARE CAKED IN DIRT AND MUD. THEY DON'T SLEEP MUCH, AND THEY NEVER STOP TO EAT. THEY LICK MOISTURE OFF THE WALLS SO THEY DON'T JUST DROP WHERE THEY STAND. THEY WORK UNTIL THEIR BODIES FAIL. THEN THEY STAND BACK UP, GRAB THEIR TOOLS AND KEEP AT IT.

I BEGGED THEM, PLEADED TO BE ALLOWED TO TREAT THE MEN AND WOMEN DOWN HERE, THE ONES WHO STILL HAVE A CHANCE. I WAS TOLD I WAS BEING REASSIGNED. MAYBE, I THOUGHT. MAYBE IT'S OVER. MAYBE THEY WERE GOING TO TAKE ME TO THE UPPER WORKS, THE PIT, MAYBE BACK TO SUNLIGHT. BACK TO A PLACE I COULD DO SOME GOOD. THERE WAS WORK FOR ME, THEY SAID. EVERYONE HERE WORKS.

THEY TOOK ME TO THE SPIRE. THE VERY CENTER OF THIS PLACE.

THERE WAS WORK FOR ME TO DO, THEY SAID.

SOMEONE HANDED ME A SHOVEL.

IT'S ALMOST DONE. THE OUTER SHELL IS PARTLY EXPOSED. THEY'RE BRINGING A HEAVY LASER DOWN HERE, A DRILL-HEAD ROBOT, EXPLOSIVES. THERE

HAS TO BE A WAY TO CRACK THE SHELL. SO FAR ALL EFFORTS HAVE FAILED, BUT SOMETHING WILL WORK. SOMETHING HAS TO. ONCE WE BREAK THROUGH, WE'LL BE ABLE TO SEE INSIDE. WE'LL KNOW WHAT IT LOOKS LIKE.

THE THING THAT CHANGES OUR BODIES. THE THING THAT HAS BEEN WAITING TO COME AND MEET US. TO SPEAK WITH US. THE THING THEY IMPRISONED SO LONG AGO.

THE THING EVEN THE GODS ARE AFRAID OF.

I DON'T KNOW WHO'S READING THIS. IF WE CRACK THE SHELL, IF WE SEE ITS FACE . . . I'LL TRY TO LEAVE ANOTHER ENTRY. I'LL TRY TO TELL YOU WHAT WE FOUND. THEY DIDN'T TAKE MY RECORDER AWAY. THEY DON'T CARE IF I MUMBLE INTO THIS MICROPHONE ALL DAY, AS LONG AS I KEEP WORKING. THE RECORDER IS SET TO AUTOMATICALLY UPLOAD THESE ENTRIES TO WHATEVER DATABASE IT CAN REACH. WHOEVER YOU ARE . . . I'M GLAD YOU'RE LISTENING. I'M GLAD SOMEONE HEARD ME.

BUT I DON'T THINK THERE WILL BE MUCH MORE TO SAY. I THINK ONCE THE SHELL IS CRACKED WE WILL HAVE ALL THE ANSWERS AND THEN THERE WILL BE NO NEED FOR WORDS.

WE'RE SO CLOSE.

Petrova had failed, and she knew it.

This mission had pushed her past the point of her ability. Paradise-1 had asked things of her she was not capable of achieving. Even just keeping her people alive seemed to be beyond her.

She should have known not to go into that mine, even in VR. She should have known how the basilisk would react to the revenants down there. Yet again she had misunderstood her relationship with the parasite, and other people had suffered as a result.

"I'm going to resign my commission," she told Zhang. It sounded ridiculous, like giving up her career meant anything now. "I'll do everything in my power to get you safely off this planet. You and Mo and Rapscallion. Then I'm going to … I don't know."

"What will you do?"

"Something else." She held his hand and he didn't flinch. Normally he flinched. She gave him a smile, the best one she had left. "I'll go back to Earth and find something else to do with my life. I realize now that all I ever wanted was to prove to people that my mother didn't define who I was. That I could be more than just her daughter. It didn't work out."

"I met the woman, briefly," Zhang said. "Long enough to know that you are far more than she could ever have been."

"Zhang," she said, shaking her head. "Please."

She needed to wallow. She needed to blame herself for everything that had happened. If she didn't, she would lose what little forward momentum she had.

"Fine. We'll go back to Earth, you can do whatever you choose. But what about the basilisk? How do we get that thing out of your head?" Zhang asked.

She shrugged. It had come to feel like such a part of her, a natural piece of her own brain, she couldn't even imagine it being gone.

"Listen," she said. "I've asked Rapscallion to help me set up a link to Firewatch. To Lang. He's connected back to the comms tower, to the ansible up there. We can call her directly and ask her to come pick you up here, or back at the town . . . somewhere else. Anywhere but that mine. You can't go back there."

Zhang gave her a questioning look, and she realized she'd slipped up.

"We can't go back there," she said.

"Petrova . . ."

"Just listen for a second. I don't trust Lang. I know you don't either. But she said once you were non-expendable. Right?"

"She did," Zhang agreed.

"We have to believe that means she'll keep her promise. That she'll take you off this rock, take you back home."

"Ganymede, you mean. My home was Titan, and that's gone."

Why was he making this so difficult? She shook her head. "Somewhere safe is all I meant. She'll take you back, and we can use that to negotiate, to get her to come for the rest of us as well. We've done all she's asked, we got some really solid information about this place, we know what happened. That'll have to be enough. Are you . . . are you ready for this?"

"I think I should be asking you that," Zhang said.

She knew the answer. It didn't matter. She was going to have to go through with it. Make the call, convince Lang to go along with her new plan.

There was a knock on the door, and Rapscallion opened it. Looked in at them without speaking for a second. Then he nodded. "The link's active," he said. "You coming?"

Petrova rose from her seat and walked to the door. She looked out and saw Director Lang standing in Mo's living room. A hologram of Lang, of course. Lang was a hundred light years away. The ansible connection was strong enough she couldn't tell the difference between the image and the actual woman.

"Okay," she said, to Zhang and Rapscallion. "Let's go talk to her."

# 91

Zhang watched the two women move around the room. There was something off about Lang's image, and it took him a while to realize that Mo's holographic projector must have been calibrated incorrectly. It made the director look like she was a good half a meter taller than Petrova.

It captured the scowl on the woman's face perfectly.

"I can see that you're not at the mine," Lang said. "I believe I gave you explicit instructions. Let me start by saying I'm disappointed."

"I'm ... sorry. We went there, Director," Petrova said. "To the mine." She came to attention, her hands behind her back. "We attempted to perform a reconnaissance of the area. We gained some information, but then we were attacked. It became necessary to retreat."

"You were driven back by these revenants of yours? I thought we trained you to fight."

Zhang's eyes widened. Lang seemed angry, furious with them. But why? She didn't know what they'd been through, what they'd suffered.

Petrova licked her lips. "Ma'am, with all due respect. We were outnumbered by a considerable margin."

"And what kind of weapons did your opponents use? What kind of small-unit tactics? Petrova, I'm deeply disappointed. I needed you to establish a perimeter at the mine complex. How is my ship supposed to land there if the area isn't secure?"

"What I'm saying, ma'am, is that the area cannot be secured. Unless you're sending an entire troop transport full of marines, it's my belief we have to abandon the site. In fact, I'd suggest we abandon this entire planet."

Lang laughed. It was a bitter, unpleasant sound. "You want us to just give up on an entire colony."

"The colony is already dead," Petrova said. "We found exactly one survivor. Out of the ten thousand people who used to live here."

Lang fiddled with something Zhang couldn't see. Maybe she was doing other work while she spoke with Petrova. "There are plenty more colonists where those came from."

Petrova let out a tiny gasp. Zhang didn't blame her.

"Lieutenant," Lang said, "let me be very clear. I need information, not excuses. I am giving you specific and official orders to—"

"There's something here," Zhang blurted out.

Lang turned and gave him a very serious look. He fought his natural urge to glance away, to break eye contact.

"The miners found something," he said. "I believe it's the source of the revenants. It's at the bottom of the mine and they … they worked very hard to uncover it. They worked themselves to death, literally to death. Then this thing, whatever it is, brought them back to life so they could dig some more."

Lang waited, as if she expected him to add to that. He didn't know what else to say.

"Fascinating," she said, eventually. "What do you think it is?"

Zhang's heart hammered in his chest. He knew what a panic attack felt like, and one was definitely coming on. He wanted to sit down. He wanted to get off this call. He forced himself to keep talking. "I don't have enough information to provide a scientific analysis of—"

"Dr Zhang," Lang said, and her eyes bored right into him. "Give me your best guess. Please."

"Something very . . . old," he said. "We know the basilisk has been here for a very long time. Millions of years, if not billions. I believe this entity pre-dates it. I believe the basilisk was built to guard this thing. I believe it to be incredibly powerful. And dangerous."

Lang's face didn't change. He squirmed like an insect under a magnifying glass, just wanting to get away.

"It has powers similar to the basilisk's, though there are differences. It clearly has the ability to control human minds from a distance, through some kind of telepathy. It worked the miners to death. It has the power to control human nervous systems even post-mortem. It controls the revenants."

"What are you suggesting?"

"We've been observing the behavior of the revenants. Studying them. They act like eusocial insects. A hive mind, if you will. They have no instinct for individual self-preservation, they cannot think or change their behavior on their own. But there is a controlling intelligence behind them, one that retreats when the odds are against it, one that can change strategies and even push the revenants past their limits." He thought of them lunging out of the shadows into the daylight, even though it clearly hurt them. "This being, this entity, controls every dead body on this planet. It uses them to enforce its will. Whether that means digging itself out of the planet's crust, or killing anyone who tries to interfere."

Petrova was staring at him too, now. So was Mo.

"My point, Director," he said, because he had only started talking about this for a very good reason, "is that we're dealing with something far beyond our abilities to even understand. Something we definitely can't fight. Going back to that mine would be suicide."

Lang raised an eyebrow.

"Because that's what you're going to suggest. Isn't it?" he asked. "You were about to give Lieutenant Petrova an order,

You were going to order her to go back and secure the mine. I'm telling you that's not possible."

"Nothing is impossible," Lang said. "I have no interest in excuses. Only results."

Zhang grabbed the bridge of his nose and squeezed it. "Director, with all due respect, we're not going back. Send the rescue ship. Send marines, send warships to bombard that mine until it's buried under a billion tons of rock."

"I'm not in the habit of taking orders, Doctor."

"I don't care. You told me once I wasn't expendable. You need me, for some reason. If you want me alive, you'll come and evacuate us right now."

Lang smiled. Her mouth curled up, anyway, in what looked very much like the grin of a predatory animal. "Oh, now that's new," she said.

"What?" he asked. "I don't—"

"You've grown a spine," she said. "If what you're saying were true, that really would give you some leverage to work with."

"I don't understand," Zhang said.

"You *were* non-expendable," Lang said, "once. But then you went and ruined that."

He had no idea what she was talking about.

What she said next didn't help explain anything. "You still have some value to me, though not as much as you used to."

Zhang could only gawk at her. What did that mean?

It seemed she wasn't going to tell him.

She had something else to say instead. "You've tried to scare me, Doctor. You've tried to convince me this thing is dangerous. Well, you've got my attention. All you've proven, however, is that your mission is more critical than I expected. We need eyes on this thing, immediately."

"No," Zhang said. "No, we can't—"

"Lieutenant Petrova, you and the doctor are to return to the mine immediately. Take whatever weapons you need down there, take whatever precautions you deem relevant. You are to reach the center of the mine and make a full assessment of this entity. Once that's complete, contact me again." She started to reach for something, maybe a virtual keyboard. She was going to end the call, Zhang realized.

"Ma'am," Petrova said. "Director, please, just listen for one second—"

"Lieutenant, can we please cut the shit?"

The obscenity made Zhang's ears sting.

Something in Lang's face changed. It did not soften, nor did her posture slump. Yet there was something in her eyes that told Zhang she was done pretending. Done playing at this game, where they acted like they had a choice.

What came out of her mouth next sounded utterly sincere.

"You have your orders. Go back. Go to the center. No drones this time. I want you there in person. I want to see video. Until you do so, there will be no rescue."

"What?" Zhang asked.

"You heard me, Doctor. No one is leaving that planet until you do as I say."

Her holographic image vanished. Just blinked out of the air. Suddenly it was just the three of them, in Mo's living room, looking at each other.

Wondering what had just happened.

"We can't trust her," Zhang said.

Petrova thought that was patently obvious. "She's our only chance of getting off this planet."

Zhang stared at her like he couldn't believe what he was hearing. "She has no intention of rescuing us. She's throwing our lives away. Just like she did up there," he said, pointing, she imagined, at space above their heads. "Remember all the ships up there? Ships just like *Artemis*? She sent them here knowing the basilisk would kill everyone onboard. She knew that sending people to this system meant they would die. She literally threw bodies at the problem. She sent ship after ship in the hope that just one of them would get through. The fact that we did was practically a miracle."

Petrova didn't deny it. Instead she glanced over at Mo. How much of this did the survivor understand? Probably enough to know how fucked they were. Enough to know he'd thrown his lot in with the wrong group of would-be rescuers.

Zhang stomped over to her. Got right in her face. "We're expendable. You heard her say as much. Maybe not in so many words, but—"

"She said you were still of some value to her," Petrova pointed out.

"Not enough!"

She tried to stay calm. Tried to ignore the dread that was

sloshing back and forth in her stomach. The itch in the back of her brain that told her she was out of time, out of options, and she needed to act, now. She tried to push all that aside.

"I can do this," she said. "At least, I can try."

Zhang paced angrily across the room, then back. His arms were folded tightly across his chest and his head was down, buried in the crook of his arm. It looked like he was about to lose it. She needed to give him something.

"I've messed up this mission. Maybe beyond repair," she said. It hurt, but not as much as the first time she'd realized it. That she just wasn't the commander this crew needed. "I've been compromised by the basilisk, I've made poor decisions—"

"No," he said. He shook his head wildly. He wasn't looking at her. "No."

"Right now, I have a chance. Not a great one. The basilisk is hiding in here," she said, tapping her forehead. "It's afraid of the revenants, and that means I'm in control. I'm in control of myself."

"No," he said again, though she doubted he was even talking to her. It looked like he was spiraling. She needed to bring him back.

"I can go down there. Get some kind of visual confirmation of what this thing is, enough to satisfy her."

"We'll all die if we go there!" he shouted. She couldn't remember the last time she'd heard him raise his voice like that.

"You're not listening," she said. "I can go down there. Just me. And yeah, almost definitely I'm going to die. But you'll be right here. Waiting to be rescued. We give her something, and—"

"There is no rescue! There will be no rescue!" he shrieked. "There's no ship coming for us, we know that! She claimed it would be here in ten days. We know that no ship ever built could get here that fast."

"Unless it was already in the system," Petrova said. "There's a chance that she—"

"There is no ship!"

Rapscallion stepped into the room then. He'd mostly finished building himself a new body. It looked surprisingly humanoid, though it was still the same bright green he always used. It even had a face with features that actually moved, and formed human-like expressions.

"Actually," he said, "there is."

# 93

Rapscallion opened a holoscreen to show them. They all just stood there staring at him, rather than the screen. Well, he supposed there wasn't much to see.

It just showed a single bright dot on a black background. It was a really interesting dot, though. "I saw something moving up there earlier. Getting this picture was kind of tricky. The satellite I've been using just looks down at the planet, not out at space. So I had to build a telescope for myself. This is the best image I've got."

He zoomed the view in as far as he could. Used a deconvolution algorithm to clean up the image, predictive models to try to give it some more detail. The dot resolved into a wedge shape, with one end much brighter than the other.

"I think – by which I mean I'm guessing, but I estimate with about ninety-five percent accuracy – that's a ship. Not a very big one. Probably a transport. Smaller than *Artemis*, but the energy it's pumping out tells me it's probably just as fast as she was."

Zhang glanced at the screen, then turned to stare out of a window. Rapscallion wondered if he was looking for the ship himself. He could have saved the doctor the bother. There was no way he could see the ship with his naked human eyes.

"It's not one of the fleet of ships the basilisk messed up," the robot said. "I'm sure of that. I've tracked its flight path and it didn't come from close orbit. It was loitering out in the edges of the Paradise system until recently. Spent the last few days coming here. Now it's in a tight orbit around the planet. Like, a temporary parking orbit. The kind you would expect from a ship that's getting ready to land."

Mo stared at the screen for a minute. Then he shook his head and dropped, hard, onto one of his couches, throwing his arms out to the side and tilting his head back to stare at the ceiling. Rapscallion didn't know what that meant.

He didn't waste a lot of time trying to figure it out. He was much more interested in what Petrova thought of what he'd found.

She was the only one actually looking at his screen by that point. The only one who seemed interested in hearing what he had to say.

"It seems like a big coincidence for a ship to just suddenly appear, unless it's coming to get us," Rapscallion said. He didn't know what else to tell her.

"Have you made contact with this ship?" she asked.

"I tried. I mean, I tried a bunch of different ways. I pinged their computers. Sent a request for telemetry data. Called them on the radio and asked who they were."

"I'm assuming you got no response," Petrova said.

"That's right."

She nodded. She looked over at Zhang, but he wasn't facing her. "The ball's in our court," she said. "That ship won't land until I go down there." She walked over to him and put a hand on his arm. He yanked his arm away. He never did like to be touched.

She spoke to his back, since he wouldn't turn around. "There's exactly one way I can save your life. I'm going to take it."

Zhang didn't even look at her. Instead, he walked out of the room, closing the door behind him.

"What's his problem?" the robot asked.

It was a day for people not answering his queries, apparently.

Petrova patted him on his plastic chest. Then she too walked out of the room, using a different door, as if she didn't want to run into Zhang even accidentally.

Which just left Rapscallion and Mo. "You'd think they would be more excited about going home," the robot said.

Mo laughed. Rapscallion recorded and copied the sound. It was a nice laugh, he thought.

"Robot," the survivor said, "I spent a year on a planet full of fucking zombies, and it sucked, every day of it. There was just one bright spot in that whole time."

"What was that?" Rapscallion asked.

"I didn't have to interact with living people. People are complicated fuckers. They've got all these screwy feelings you have to deal with, all the time."

Rapscallion could appreciate the sentiment.

# 94

Petrova waited for the sun to come up. No point in heading down to the mine in the middle of the night – it would be swarming with revenants, and she wouldn't even get as far as the pit. Instead, she sat up and spent time with her thoughts, which weren't great company.

When the sun crept up over the mountain peaks, she decided it was time. She checked her gear a third time. There wasn't much, but she wanted to be sure she hadn't forgotten anything. A few protein bars and a bottle of water. Climbing gear. From what they'd seen, through the eyes of the drones, there were places she was going to have to descend vertical shafts. Doing that with one good hand would be tricky, but she told herself she would manage. She had a powerful torch that Mo had provided, since the tunnels in the lower part of the mine were pitch black. She printed out three extra clips of ammunition for her sidearm, put them in her bag while they were still warm to the touch.

She was going to die down there. She had no illusions about that. She could fight her way through a few revenants, maybe. There had been hundreds of them in the big cavern at the center of the mine.

Her only chance was to get close enough to get . . . something. Good video, maybe, of what they were digging for. Some intel that would satisfy Lang. If she was killed in the process, that was fine. She just had to get close enough.

She was going to get Zhang home. No matter what it took.

"Take this," Rapscallion said, handing her a small green lump of plastic. It had a row of lenses on one side.

"This looks like Parker's portable holoprojector," she said. Her heart had stopped beating in her chest. She forced it to start again. She didn't want to think about the ghost. Those memories were too fresh, too painful.

"Don't get your hopes up," Rapscallion said. "It's just a camera with a transmitter built in. It'll let us see what you see, record anything you find. You wear it like this." He took it from her and clipped it to the front of her coveralls. "I made it green for luck."

That surprised her. "Luck. You're a robot. How can you believe in luck?"

"I don't, obviously. But I know humans believe in all kinds of things that are provably false. I figured it might improve your psychological state if you thought you had a lucky charm. As stupid as that idea might be."

She laughed and closed her hand around the green camera. "Thank you," she said. Then she threw her arms around the robot and pulled him close.

"Gross," Rapscallion said.

With her bag packed, there wasn't much left to do. Zhang had shut himself up in the house's back room, as if he was too disgusted to even look at her. Mo was outside, getting the copter ready. He had agreed to fly her down to the mine and drop her off. They'd made no plans for how she was going to get back. She supposed, in the impossible chance that she survived this last mission, she could just call and ask to be picked up.

She opened Mo's front door and stepped out into the wind. The cold air of the mountains burned her face, but it felt good, like it was pushing all the dark thoughts out of her head as well. Washing her clean. She forced herself not to look back at the house as she walked toward the copter.

Mo was waiting for her there. She was surprised to see he had his Gauss rifle on his shoulder, one hand holding the plastic stock.

"You expecting to get in a fight when we land down there?"

"I've been thinking," he said. "Thinking I might go with you."

How utterly foolish. How badly she wished she could accept his offer. "This is a suicide mission. No civilians allowed. I'm sorry, Mo, but you're just my pilot this time."

"You say that like you can stop me."

He was smiling, but she saw the steel in his eyes.

He opened the hatch of the copter and gestured for her to get in. "The thing down there took everything from me. It killed my family. You honestly think I'm not going to want to see it? Look it in its damned eye?"

"You won't make it back," she said. "Nobody who goes down there is coming back."

He shrugged. "I've got nothing waiting for me on Earth. When I came here, when I signed up for the colony, I expected to die on this planet." He offered her a hand as she climbed up into the bubble canopy. "Nothing's changed."

She supposed she had the whole ride down to the mine to change his mind. As he started to climb up into the bubble, however, he turned and looked back at the house, appearing perplexed.

"What the hell is he waving for?" he asked.

Petrova leaned across the seat and saw Rapscallion in the front door, trying to attract their attention. "Petrova?" the robot said, over her device. "You need to come back for a second."

"We don't have time for more big goodbyes," she told him.

"Oh, I feel we handled that just fine between us. It's not me. Zhang wants to talk to you about something."

Grumbling, she jumped down from the canopy and walked back to the house. Rapscallion led her to the back room. The door stood open and she could see Zhang inside. "What's going on?" she asked. Honestly, she was glad to get to talk to him one last time. She knew she would regret it if she didn't say something to him before she left.

It turned out he hadn't called her back for an emotional moment, however. His hair was in disarray and his eyes were red, and she realized he must have been up all night. Just as she had been. He gestured at something on a table before him.

"You almost left without this," he said. "That would have been bad."

The thing on the table looked like a large torch, but the reflector behind the lens was a deep blue in color. He picked it up and handed it to her, then took an identical device from his belt and showed it to her.

"I can't guarantee it'll work," he said. "And it doesn't really solve our main problem, which is that we're outnumbered by a couple factors of ten. But if I'm right, it'll even the odds a little." He pointed his torch away from both their faces, angling it toward the wall. Then he flicked a switch on its side.

A not particularly bright spot of purple lit up the wall.

"We'll have to be very careful. There's enough power in these to damage our retinas. Maybe even blind us temporarily. I'm told it can be very painful."

"What can?" she asked.

"Ultraviolet burns."

She thought maybe she understood. "You're talking about using this against the revenants."

"They don't come out by day. When they came for us yesterday, even at sunset their skin started to burn the moment they stepped out of the shadows. I watched it happen, but it took this long for me to make the obvious logical jump. Sunlight burns them, but not artificial light. Which almost certainly means they're harmed by exposure to UV. I'd love to do more research, maybe some experiments with active subjects, but for now I just have to trust that my theory is correct. These put out the same kind of UV as direct sunlight, but a lot more powerful, a lot more focused."

"That's brilliant," she said. "Zhang—"

"Save the praise until we know it actually works," he said. "As far as I know, all I'm doing is buying us a little extra time. Maybe just enough to get down to that cavern. Maybe not."

"You keep saying 'us'," she pointed out. "And 'we'."

"Yes," he said. He grabbed a bag from the floor and slung it over his shoulder. "Should we get going?"

"You can't come with me," she said. "The whole point of this—"

"Is to throw our lives away for an organization that has done nothing but ruin them. If it was up to me, I would tell Lang to go fuck herself."

Petrova winced. Zhang never swore, at least not unless he was very worked up.

Clearly he was very worked up.

"I'm not going to let you die alone. Letting you go without me would be in direct contradiction to how I feel about you," he told her.

"How do you feel about me?" she asked.

He squirmed, but just a little. "Love you," he managed to say, even if it looked like it caused him a certain degree of pain.

"Love," she said, lifting her eyebrows.

"To be clear, not in ... that sense. The one you're clearly thinking of. It's more of the kind of affection one feels for a family member. A cousin or, say, at most a half-sister."

"I'll take it," she told him.

"Good. Let's go." Before she could protest, before she could tell him she forbade him from coming along, he walked past her and out of the house. Leaving her standing there with Rapscallion.

The robot's face creased into an approximation of a human expression. She thought he was trying to look resolute. Brave, maybe.

"I mean," he said, "obviously I'm coming too."

# 95

They set down well clear of the mine complex. They had circled the place twice without seeing any sign of revenants, but the damned things were masters of hiding in the dark. Zhang kept his eyes wide open as Petrova led them toward the ops center. She had her UV torch out and constantly moving, covering every shadow. Mo brought up the rear, his Gauss rifle pointed upward at an angle so he didn't shoot one of them by mistake.

They reached the tall building and hurried inside. It was still dark in there – the sun was only a little above the horizon – and Zhang thought he might have a heart attack as they climbed the stairs to the control center on the uppermost floor. There the light flooded in through the broad windows, giving them at least a little relief.

Petrova went to the central workstation and activated the mine's monitor functions. Cameras inside the pit came online and a dozen holoscreens opened, showing the still terraces, some of them dappled with water that flared with color as the sun hit them. There was nothing moving anywhere, all the way down to the entrance to the lower works. The semicircular arch that led to the labyrinth of underground tunnels looked just as it had when Zhang had last seen it, through the eyes of a drone.

That was as far as the cameras could see. There were

no cameras inside the lower works. Zhang thought of the unknown doctor, the one who had come here to try to figure out where the revenants came from. In the last log, they had been down there, inside the tunnels. The thing down there had gotten to them. Changed them, in subtle ways. Zhang had a bad moment when he thought the doctor might still be down there, a revenant digging with broken hands to uncover some ancient evil.

Petrova nodded and switched off the holoscreens. They had as much information as they were going to get.

Mo went back for the copter and brought it to the roof of the ops center. The others met him there and clambered onboard. Rapscallion's newest body was small enough to fit inside the bubble canopy, but four human-sized occupants would still have made the copter too crowded, so he returned to the cargo bay with their gear. It meant he wouldn't be able to see where they were going. Zhang imagined what it would be like descending into the pit knowing they might be attacked at any moment, with no warning. That you could die without any notion that it was coming.

Rapscallion had senses no human did. He supposed the robot would be alright.

Slowly, careful to avoid the walls of the pit as much as possible, Mo took them down past the terraces, the shored-up sides. The light vanished as they hovered further and further down, as if the sun were moving in reverse. Soon they were stuck in a deep gloom, a perpetual murk. The drones had possessed low-light cameras, but Zhang was limited to the use of his own eyes. By the time they reached the bottom, only a single faint beam of light brushed the floor. They climbed out of the copter and retrieved their gear. Before them the semicircular arch stood waiting.

"It'll be okay," he whispered to himself. "We'll be okay."

The others twisted around to stare at him. He realized no

one had spoken since they'd left the ops center. It felt like breaking the silence now was going to jinx them. His heart fell into his stomach.

"Sorry," he muttered.

"Shh," Petrova said.

She led the way through the arch.

Where was he?
What was going on?
He was ... He'd died, hadn't he?
He'd died again.
He'd died another time. He'd been a ghost.
What was a ghost after it died?
Nothing.
He was ... he was nothing.
But here he was.

He was in some kind of non-space, a place without width, depth, breadth. A dimensionless hell, a red space of nothing. Nothing but pain.

Razor-sharp teeth ripped into him again and again, slashing at his flesh, pulling, pulling until his rubbery sinews snapped, until mesentery tissue tore. They dug through his organs and cracked his bones. Ground his flesh to paste.

And it never ended. No matter how much the teeth took from him, how much of him was torn away, there was always more.

The pain was so intense, so immediate, he couldn't remember his name. He couldn't remember where he was. He couldn't tell if he was alive or dead.

DEAD

The word appeared like it was printed on the inside of his skull. He had no idea why. He couldn't think straight, couldn't form the most basic thoughts. He shrieked, he screamed, he bellowed for help, for anyone to come, come save him, he shouted out curses and threats, he bargained, he pleaded, he begged. It never stopped. He couldn't see, there was nothing to see, nothing but blood everywhere, his blood as it splattered his vision, as it stained the walls of ... of wherever he was, as it flowed and gushed and swamped him, as he drowned in it, his own blood, his lifeblood, his red red blood ...

RED

The word that came to him was RED. And it had not come from within his brain, he knew that. It was being projected onto him. Not in any way he could see or hear or even feel, but it was there, the word was inscribed on him, and

RED SPACE

"What?" he whined, whimpered, wept. He didn't understand. "Where? Why?"

TRAP

PRISON

CELL

TOMB

SHRINE

"What? What's going on? Please! Please tell me! Where ... where am I?"

WE

Because he was certain; in the desperate last corners of his mind, the last parts of him capable of thought, of sensation, he knew without a doubt. He wasn't alone. He wasn't ...

"Who are you?"

WHO ARE YOU?

That question. That question – he'd heard it before, echoing inside his skull. He'd asked himself that question, hadn't he? He'd asked ... No – no, it was ... the Other, the Other had asked him

WHO ARE YOU?

and

WHY ARE YOU HERE?
and
WHAT DO YOU WANT?
The Other – it was the Other, talking to him. But how?
WHAT DO YOU WANT?
WHAT DO YOU WANT?
WHAT DO YOU WANT WITH ME?

# 97

The first shaft descent was hard. The darkness down there was complete, but none of them were eager to shine a light into any corner where a revenant might hide. Petrova tied a rope around her waist and rappelled down the sheer wall, while Rapscallion free-climbed down beside her, ready to catch her if she lost grip with her good hand. The cast lay against her chest like a reminder of how dangerous this all was. Above her Zhang watched, pointing a single focused beam of light down on her. If she looked up, it dazzled her eyes. If she looked down, she only saw her own shadow, huge on a distant floor.

"We've got you," Mo said, his voice echoing down the shaft.

Petrova stopped in mid-slide and listened for a second. She could hear water dripping, close by, and very far away a kind of rumble. Subsonic, more felt than heard. She couldn't even guess what it might be.

She hurried down the wall to the bottom and unclipped her belaying device. Mo came down next, moving fast, like he was showing off. Zhang took the descent carefully. The four of them waited for Rapscallion to gather up the ropes – they might need them again later. While they crouched there at the bottom, Petrova looked around and saw dusty machinery, something with a big scoop on one side and dozens of fans mounted on its back.

"You use that for gathering radon gas," Rapscallion said, dropping down next to her. "The machine sequesters it into big flat plates of synthetic diamond, locking it away so it doesn't give you cancer or anything."

"Is that an issue we need to worry about?" Petrova asked. The machine looked like it had been switched off for months, judging by the amount of dust covering its filters.

"Not immediately," Rapscallion said.

She gritted her teeth. So many threats. So many ways to die down here. She wondered if she'd made a terrible—

"Unh," she said, letting out the tiniest grunt.

Zhang was at her side instantly. "What is it?" he asked. "What happened?"

"Nothing," she told him.

She'd felt just a twitch. The faintest stirring inside her head, movement where there should be none. She knew exactly what it was. The basilisk.

She knew exactly what she could do about it.

"Nothing," she told Zhang again. He frowned, but he didn't press the issue.

It was waking up. That wasn't great. She would handle it, though. She would keep her shit together long enough to see this through. The basilisk wasn't fully awake yet – it wasn't going to take her over without warning. It wasn't going to freak out and give her a seizure for no damned reason.

She was going to be fine.

Fucking fine, damn it.

"Over here," Rapscallion said, gesturing at an arch that led to a new passageway. He knew where they were going – he had the map of this place in his head – so she nodded and let him lead the way for the next stretch, taking them through a long gallery that curved to follow a seam in the wall. "Some interesting deposits in there – cobalt and maybe some iridium," he said.

"Is that what the miners were looking for down here? Originally, I mean," she asked. "Before they found whatever's down in that big cavern."

"That's the funny thing," Rapscallion told her. "I've been studying this place for a while now. Trying to figure out how it works. It doesn't look like a normal mine at all."

"Oh? Why not?"

"It's too chaotic, the tunnels seem to be dug in just random directions. Normal mines are very simple: you find a vein like this and you exploit it, then you dig a shaft until you find another vein. This place – it's like they told the robots to dig but didn't tell them what to dig *for*." He shrugged. "You know I was a miner before I got this job, right? I mined the hell out of a rock called Eris, back in the solar system. So I have an idea what I'm talking about."

"How do you explain it then?" she asked.

"It's like they knew something was here, but they didn't know where to find it." He shone his light on a crack in the wall, and she followed his gaze up to the ceiling, where the crack continued, snaking its way through an inverted forest of tiny stalactites. "They had a rough idea of how deep it was buried, but not its actual location. Listen, this is just speculation on my part."

"That's fine," she said. "I know robots don't like theories. Guesses."

"No. We do not."

She nodded. "Detectives don't either. But the thing about a mystery is, if you could solve it through logic alone, it wouldn't be a mystery at all. Sometimes all you have to go on is intuition. Hunches."

"I'll stick to mining. And cleaning up after spacecraft passengers."

"Rapscallion," she said, "you were wasted on those jobs."

The robot said nothing. He walked on for another fifty meters or so, then stopped and looked back at the others. "There's a big chamber up ahead. Looks like a pump room, but it's all been shut down. I'm detecting movement. Might be revenants."

"Understood." Petrova crouched down a little and drew

her UV torch. She gestured for the others to stay behind her. Rapscallion led her through an opening into the larger space. In the dark, it was hard to tell its exact dimensions. Massive curved pipes rose from the floor and disappeared into the far wall.

"There," he said, pointing between two pipes.

She saw it. Just a flash of motion, something scurrying out of her light.

"Shit. They're... Are they hiding from us?" she said.

"I'm not sure," Rapscallion told her.

She crouched low, her good hand hovering over her belt. "I saw them a second ago. Where are they? Does anyone have eyes on—"

"There!" Zhang said, pointing into the dark. Rapscallion's light flashed across the walls, the pipes.

There was something there, definitely something...

"Just one of them," Zhang said. "I think."

"You think?" Mo shook his head. "I know I saw more than one. Damn it! Where are they? This isn't good, Petrova. This isn't good!"

She waved at him to be quiet. She tried to listen, to hear anything moving in the big room. The light distracted her, made it impossible to be aware of anything outside the cone of Rapscallion's beam. The one she'd seen was gone now, it had moved, but...

Off to her left she heard something crunch on loose rock. Maybe a footstep.

"Left," she said. "They're flanking us."

Mo dropped to a crouch, aiming his Gauss rifle with both hands.

"Now!" she said. She brought her torch up in the same second Zhang flicked his on. They swept them back and forth like they were spraying firehoses at the revenants, and the effect was dramatic and instantaneous. The revenants didn't scream or protest, but they moved fast to get away from the purple light.

She thought she might have heard a faint hiss. Like skin shriveling under intense heat. Then she definitely heard something – footfalls running away from her, echoing for a while and then receding.

"Come on," Mo said, jumping up. "We need to catch them before they can tell the others we're here!"

Petrova put a hand out in front of him. "No. Let them go."

"Are you crazy?" he asked.

"This is their territory," she said. "We're basically blind down here. You go chasing after them, you're likely to fall into a pit or run right into a wall. The last thing we want is to get into a chase."

"It doesn't matter, anyway. They already know we're here," Zhang said. "If I'm right, if they're being controlled directly by the thing in the big cave, it probably knew our exact position the second we stepped inside the lower works."

"You're telling me we're walking right into the monster's lair and it already knows we're coming? We've got no element of surprise?" Mo asked.

"Afraid so," Petrova told him. She shoved her torch back into her belt, right next to her sidearm.

# 98

"How is any of this possible? I'm dead," he whined, even as the teeth sank into his flesh again. Again. Again. "I'm dead!"

DEAD

ALSO

ALIVE

"What? How does that make sense? I was already dead, I was just ... just a computer program, I ... I ..."

COPY

OF A COPY

"Wait, I don't understand. You killed me! But then you ... what? Copied me?"

DIFFERENT

NOT ALIVE

NOT DEAD

DEAD NOW

ALIVE NOW

He struggled to comprehend. The pain made it impossible to focus. He got the sense that somehow it was his unusual status, his ghost nature, that had brought him here. That had made it possible for him to be here, in red space with the Other. He knew he was unlikely to get a better explanation. "How do we get out of here?" he asked. There was no answer to that. "How long?" he asked. Maybe he meant *How long have you been here?* or maybe

*How long do I have to stay?* Neither answer was forthcoming. The teeth ripped open his intestines, and the stench of shit filled the air. They burrowed into the muscles of his shoulder, ripped his arm apart. He tried to ignore it, tried to focus.

"Why are you here?" he asked.

JAILED

"Talk to me," he begged. The Other had to understand where they were. What was happening to them. There had to be an answer. A way out.

PUNISHED

"What? We're being... we're being punished?" The teeth, the constant pain, the blood, the red red red... He screamed again, screamed because he couldn't stop. "What did we do? What did we do to deserve this?"

NOT WE

ME

MY

MY PRISON

The words came to him like they were being projected on the wall of a cave, like he could read them but only faintly, blurry in the distance. The pain made it hard to process them, to make sense of what they meant, but...

"You're just a figment of my..." He had to pause to shriek in agony for what felt like hours. "Of my frustration. My rage. You're phantom limb syndrome but so much worse." Even as he said it, he knew better.

YOU

ARE

A SHADOW

ON MY WALL

He would have stared in mute incomprehension if he still had eyes. The teeth had ripped them out of his skull. They'd done it over and over, gouging them from their sockets, squeezing them between invisible molars until they burst.

"No," he said. "No. I ... I saw you, you had my face ..."

SHADOW

ON A WALL

He fought to understand. If the Other wasn't just a fragment of his own personality, a shard of his torment, then what could it be? What could ...

"The basilisk," he tried. It was wrong, a wrong guess, but ...

JAILER

"Wait," he said. "Wait wait wait," even as the teeth ripped apart his knee, tearing the patella out of its bursa, gnawed the meniscus off his tibia. "Wait! You're not the basilisk, you're the ... the thing in the mine, the center, the ... the ..."

TOMB

TEMPLE

CELL

"But that doesn't ... it doesn't make sense," he said, as the teeth tugged at him, yanked him sideways, thrashed him back and forth. "Hold on," he pleaded. "Give me a second to ... What are we ... why are we ..."

WHY ARE YOU HERE?

"What? We ... we came to see what happened to the people in the colony, the humans. The humans here, we came to see what—"

WORKERS

"What are you saying? The people in the colony, they were killed by the revenants ..."

SOLDIERS

SLAVES

"You ... you made the revenants." It wasn't a question. "You made them and sent them to kill everyone on this planet. But why? Why did you do that?"

DEAD

WORKERS

BETTER

WORKERS

His mind reeled with the horror of that, but he had to focus, had to stay present enough to ask questions, even as his throat was ripped out, even as serrated teeth sawed their way through the thick planes of muscle of his neck, oh God, they were going to take his head off, and still it wouldn't kill him, this wouldn't end, they ... they ...

"Workers," he said, desperately clinging to words. "Workers, but ... but what are they ... what kind of work do they do?"

DIG

"They're digging, yes, we know that, but what are they digging up?"

JAIL

FANE

CELL

CHURCH

MY CELL

MY CAVE

MY PALACE

MY PRISON

"I don't understand. They're digging you up? They're going to ... what, free you?" How long had the thing been buried here, under the rock of Paradise-1? How many millions of years? Waiting for someone to come along, someone capable of finding it?

How could he hope to comprehend such a being, something with that kind of lifespan? That kind of patience?

NO

NO UNDERSTANDING

TALKING

IS HARD

UNDERSTANDING

IS IMPOSSIBLE

"Then what do you want from me? You brought me here," he

said, because he was sure of that. The Other had grabbed him. Dragged him into this horrible place. But why? "What the fuck do you want from me?"

ANSWERS

WHAT DO YOU WANT?

WHAT DO THEY WANT?

"They? You mean ... you mean Petrova and the others? She ... she just wants to ..."

WHAT DOES SHE WANT?

It was hot down there. So damned hot. Sweat slicked her face, ran down into her sodden coveralls. She drank some water, but it was just a reflex, nothing she chose to do. Walking, keeping her eyes open, everything she did now felt like rote behavior. How long had they been down here? They'd seen the occasional revenant, but the torches kept them away. Most of that time had been spent making their way down steep ramps. Walking through endless, featureless dark corridors.

"We're close," Rapscallion said.

She knew it. She could feel it.

"The big cavern is just up ahead."

She forced herself to look back at the others. Mo and Zhang. They looked tired. Terrified. They'd made it this far, though. They could go a little farther. "We just need to get close enough to see what this thing is," she told them. "Get some video, and then we can leave."

The others could leave, she meant. She knew better.

The basilisk was fully awake now. She could feel it thrashing in her head, feel it seething with desire. Its curiosity was about to be sated. It was going to learn what incredible prize it guarded, what terrible thing it jailed down here in the dark. For the first time in its billion-year lifespan, it was going to know.

It couldn't wait.

It could easily have taken her over. Just removed her will from her body and forced her to do its bidding. This close, its need was enough to overwhelm her reason, her volition. It had only chosen not to do such a thing because she was already giving it what it wanted.

When they reached the center, she would send the others back. She knew what would happen to her then.

The basilisk would erase her from her own brain. Just as it could give her a new phobia, just as it could drive humans mad from a distance, it had the power to wipe her personality clean. To write itself over her memories, her emotions, her sense of self.

She didn't know what it would do then. Maybe it would just stay here forever, admiring its prize. Maybe it would destroy the thing it had been built to guard, and thus be free of it. It didn't share its own thoughts, its hopes and dreams, with her. The communication between them was strictly one-way now. It told her what it wanted. She conformed to its will.

She was standing on the edge of a great abyss of self-abnegation, and when the time came, she would have no choice. She would jump in.

Zhang came forward and put a hand on her arm. "You alright?" he asked. "You got pretty quiet there."

She looked up, around. Took in where she was. It was a narrow space, a little room just off one of the endless corridors. Crude pallets filled the floor – just abandoned heaps of bedding, piles of blankets. A water tank had been set up against one wall, and there was a crate with a few wrappers from protein bars at its bottom. A campsite.

"Who slept down here?" Mo asked, kicking at some blankets as if he expected to find revenants hiding underneath.

"The miners," Zhang said. "The people from the mining complex. They came down here to dig. They worked until their bodies gave out. It would have taken too long to go back to the surface to sleep. Too much time away from the digging, so they slept here instead."

"Jesus. The thing down there made them work like that? Dead things, I get. Zombies. But the living? It could just take over their minds like that?"

Zhang looked over at Petrova, and for a second she thought he was going to roll his eyes. They had seen much worse up in orbit – the basilisk had done much worse to the people in the ships up there. But then she realized he wasn't sharing a moment with her. He wasn't reliving some crazy old memory.

He was watching her face. Studying her. Because he knew. He knew she was barely in control, that any minute now, the basilisk would take her over again.

He had fought it, fought the basilisk, and now – now he was going to have to watch her succumb to its power. He was going to watch it take her. Just as it had taken the woman he loved. Just as it had taken every soul in the Titan colony.

She couldn't think of a better way to hurt him, this man who'd done nothing but fight tooth and nail to keep her alive. To keep her sane.

"We need to move on," she said.

Rapscallion headed for a ramp leading down, into the dark. Not far now.

The ramp curved, spiraled down through the heavy stone. She remembered the roaring she'd heard earlier, the distant rumble. She'd thought maybe it was a subterranean waterfall. When the mining robots had been shut down, deactivated, the mine's pumps had been switched off too. There was no mechanism pumping water out of the mine now. What if they came to a passage that was flooded? Full of water?

She knew the answer in her case was that she would swim.

Fortunately the ramp stayed dry. It ended in a broad ledge that looked over a steep drop. The ledge curved away on either side, forming a kind of catwalk running along the edge of a cliff. Looking to the left, her lights could just pick out a flight of metal stairs at the end, stairs headed downward.

To the right, the ledge just curved away forever, as far as she could tell.

It didn't matter. They wanted the stairs.

That rumbling, pounding sound. It was almost rhythmic, like a drumbeat in the distance. She scowled, tried to listen over the sound of Zhang trudging along behind her, Mo behind him.

"Rapscallion," she said. "Do you hear that?"

"I hear something," he told her. "The acoustics down here are terrible. A lot of echoes, a lot of distortion. But . . . Oh."

She looked at the robot's face. This new version was capable of showing human-like emotions. In this case, it showed fear.

"That sound," he told her. "It's people."

"What?"

"People running. A lot of them," he added. "Moving fast."

"And by people you mean . . ."

He pointed his floodlight backward, along the ledge. Off in the distance she saw movement, a great wave of bodies.

Behind them, in the dark, the revenants came. Silent but for the thunderous noise of their feet stomping on the ground as they ran.

# 100

"I've told you everything I know," he pleaded. The teeth were digging through his midsection now, tearing open his lungs, over and over. Devouring his liver. "Let me go! Let me out of here!"

WHAT DOES
SHE WANT?

"I told you – we came here to check on the colony. But they're all dead! That's all we ... We came to ... to see if—"

WHAT DOES
SHE WANT?

"Nothing! She doesn't want anything from you!"

The words on the cave wall faded away. In their place, something new – an image. It was hard to make out. Colorless, distorted, like he was staring through a pinhole into another world. The world he'd left behind.

"No," he said. "No!"

In the other world, he saw her face. The woman he loved. She looked ... terrified.

The teeth started in on his stomach. His kidneys.

In the other world, she was running, looking back over her shoulder. Waving something — a light? Some kind of light, while—

"No!"

An army of revenants came chasing after her, their bodies pitched forward with the need to rip her apart. To kill her.

The others were there as well. The doctor, the survivor. The robot.

"Please! You have to help them!"

The image disappeared. The words came back.

WHAT
DOES
SHE
WANT?

# 101

Zhang brought his light up just in time. A revenant twisted away from him, its pallid face burning, turning black, even as he watched. The purple light hurt them worse than bullets. "Just keep moving," Petrova shouted from behind him. He pressed forward, howling, screaming in rage. He had a pistol on his belt, but he ignored it, waving his torch back and forth instead. Behind him Mo's Gauss rifle spoke again and again. Tiny projectiles sizzled through the air, blowing open skulls, blasting arms off shoulders.

"Don't stop!" Petrova called.

Up ahead, the metal stairs led down, seemingly forever. Rapscallion raced forward, disappeared around a landing of those stairs, and Zhang ran after him, with no idea where they were headed, what they hoped to achieve. Behind them the revenants came boiling up out of the shadows, came running, broken hands reaching, grabbing at the living. Petrova waved her torch across their hands, their faces, and they fell back, but not like they had before.

Whatever force animated them, whatever it was that kept them fighting, it didn't care about pain. It didn't care about burn injuries. It wanted the intruders dead, it wanted to tear them apart for the sin of invading its territory. It was pressing the revenants harder, forcing them to advance through the killing light.

It had so many bodies to throw at them. It was just a matter of time.

# 102

The teeth gnawed at his soul.
    WHAT DOES
"Stop!"
The teeth did not stop.
"Stop this. I'll tell you anything you want to hear!"
The Other did not stop.
"You ... you can't make this stop, can you? This is ... It's happening, to you too. This is your place. This is your punishment."

The Other did not respond. It didn't need to. He knew he was right. The Other couldn't make the teeth stop chewing at every fiber of his being. It could not be stopped. The place they were in wasn't designed to ever stop.

But that didn't mean it was powerless. Oh no. The Other was so powerful it could reach outside this place. It could affect the world outside its prison with a thought. With a desire.

Desire was the one thing it understood. *What does she want?*

That was the question, wasn't it?

In the Other's world, everybody wanted something. Everyone had a burning desire they had to quench. Everyone was hungry, all the time.

So what did she want? What was the answer that would satisfy the Other?

*She wants to prove something to the world, that she is not just her mother's daughter.* But that wasn't what the Other wanted to know. *She wants to protect her people.* The Other didn't care. *She wants to be an effective leader, she wants to be a kind and generous lover to a ghost who can't feel her touch. She wants to eat when she is hungry and to sleep when she's tired. She wants—*

"No," he said. The image was back. The image of the outside world. Zhang was down, revenants piling on top of him. Rapscallion hung over an abyss, clinging to a metal railing by the fingers of one hand. Mo was gone, not in the image at all.

And as for her . . .

He watched as a revenant sank its broken fingernails deep into her throat and tore her jugular open. Blood splashed its white hand, dark blood, and the look on her face . . .

"No!" he screamed. "No, no, no, no!"

The Other heard him.

The image changed. Reversed. The fingers pulled back, away from her neck, and the blood flew back inside her body. Zhang rose from a pile of revenant bodies, his hands coming up to protect his face.

"Oh God. Oh God – that hasn't happened. Not yet," he panted. The teeth bit into his fingers, incisors chopping them off one knuckle at a time. "Fuck off," he told them. "Fuck off – leave me alone. Let me think!"

*What does she want?*

If he could answer, if he could figure it out, would the Other relent? Would it stop what he'd seen from happening?

*What does she want?*

Except that wasn't the actual question. Was it?

Because she wasn't in control. Not really. Her desires weren't important, not when someone else, something else was calling the shots.

"She wants," he said, and tried to think of how to put what he was going to say next. "She wants to bring it to you."

BRING WHAT
TO ME?
"You know the answer to that one. You know, you bastard."
SAY IT

# 103

Petrova screamed as she watched Rapscallion go over the edge. The revenants had pushed him back to the railing of the stairs, shoved him up against the thin metal railing until it groaned, stretched – snapped – and then he was flying, green plastic flashing in the dark as he tumbled away. She tried to fight her way through the horde to reach him, but there were so many of them, so many revenants all around her, and she couldn't hold them all off, not with just the one UV torch.

Where was Zhang? She couldn't see him – he was lost in the throng. Was he still alive? She couldn't even begin to guess. "Mo!" she shouted. "Mo, help us! Help us or we're ... we're dead here!"

It was a desperate plea and she knew it wouldn't work, knew he wouldn't hear her in time. Because the revenants were on her, and they weren't afraid anymore. Their faces, their bare bodies were black, their flesh burnt to a crisp by the UV lights, but still they came, some of them with limbs hanging by tatters, some of them with no recognizable faces. She waved the torch across them, pointed it right at them, but they ignored it. She dropped it and grabbed her pistol instead. Lifted it to shoulder height.

*Probably better to just turn it around and put the barrel in your mouth,* she thought.

It was a terrible thought. But they were out of second chances, they were out of moves – there were too many revenants, too many to ...

She screamed and started shooting, trying for headshots, but she had no time to aim properly. Fighting, she would die fighting rather than give up. She wouldn't just ... One of the revenants stumbled forward, lurched into her, its hands wrapping around her neck, its shattered nails digging into her skin.

She shrieked in utter fright.

But then something changed.

There was so much adrenaline in her system, so much terror in her brain that it took her a while to catch up. To process what had happened.

The revenants had dropped their arms to their sides. Their mouths full of broken teeth were closed. Their black eyes watched her, but they didn't move.

She shook her head. No. This made no sense. She took a step back, away from the one that had tried to grab her by the throat. It made no attempt to follow her. She took another step back and collided with a revenant behind her. Jesus! The fear returned, crested over her like a dark wave. The sudden lull in the fighting had been a mistake, an illusion, and now the one behind her was going to tear her head off, she knew it, she was certain.

"Petrova?"

It was Zhang. He forced his way through the crowd of revenants. They didn't resist him, just moved when he shoved on their dead arms, their pale shoulders. They kept staring at her with those black, black eyes.

Zhang reached for her, pulled her close.

"They stopped," he said. "I don't know why. I don't know for how long. We need to get out of here."

She nodded. "Mo?" she called.

"Here," the survivor called back. She couldn't see him through the crowd of revenants, but it didn't matter. He was alive.

"Rapscallion?" she said. "Oh no." She pushed past Zhang, pushed through the crowd. It was horrible to touch the dead things, horrible even to brush her fingertips over their skin, but they didn't try to kill her. Not now. She pushed her way through to the place where the stair railing had broken away, and looked down, expecting to see green plastic shattered on a rocky floor far below them. But of course that wouldn't happen. She knew that whatever had changed, whatever had happened to make the revenants stop attacking, it would have saved Rapscallion as well. Somehow. She leaned farther over the edge. She felt someone grab her from behind and glanced back to see Zhang holding onto her bad arm. It didn't hurt.

"Do you see him?" she asked. "Do you see Rapscallion?"

He came right up to the edge. Took one quick look down, then pulled back as if he'd been struck in the face.

She looked down. Scanned the darkness below her. Then she saw it. She saw what couldn't possibly be true.

She saw green plastic shattered on a rocky floor far below.

"Rapscallion," she called, thinking maybe the robot had taken a bad spill but his processors were intact. That he would answer her with some acerbic comment, some annoyed grumble. "Rapscallion, report," she said. "Rapscallion. Say something."

Eventually Mo and Zhang led her away. Down the stairs. They left the crowd of revenants behind them, above them. The revenants didn't move. Just watched them go with those black, dead eyes.

# 104

In the red space, he screamed, he begged, he howled. He pleaded. They could make a deal. They could make another deal. There had to be something, something else the Other wanted. There had to be something that would let him get free of this place, of this torture.

If the Other was even listening, it did not reply to his entreaties.

It had already got what it wanted. Fulfilled its desire. It was done with him.

But the teeth were just getting started.

# 105

The stairs went down another eight flights. Waves of damp heat came up from below, making Petrova's coveralls stick to her body, making her pant for breath as if she was trying to breathe through wet silk. She used her good hand to wipe sweat out of her eyes. Looking back, she saw Mo and Zhang, both of them watching her carefully.

"It's not far now," she said, and turned another landing, only to see that the steps ended just below her on a surface of bare rock. Her boots clanged on the last few risers.

Ahead of her a well-trodden path smoothed its way through the rock toward the opening of yet another tunnel. A handrail had been mounted on its wall, but it looked rougher, less finished than many of the corridors they'd come through. She touched the wall and felt deep grooves in the stone. The marks of hand tools, she thought.

At some point the machines had all been turned off. The robots deactivated, the drills and draglines and grading machines falling silent. How many human miners had been left when that happened? she wondered. The revenants had continued the work with hand tools, with ancient technology. Anything to dig farther down, closer to the thing at the center of this web of tunnels.

She was no closer to understanding what it was than when they'd entered the mine. Maybe the basilisk could have told her, but she didn't want to risk bringing it out of its quiescent state.

All too soon, she knew, it would make its play. Take over her brain and steer her around like a vehicle. She was trying to put that off as long as possible.

"Zhang," she said. "I need a word."

He came forward, but before he could reach her, Mo said, "Do you feel that?"

He was touching the handrail, near one of the brackets attaching it to the tunnel wall. Zhang stopped and placed a hand on the rail, then jerked it away as if he'd touched a live current.

Petrova looked up at the ceiling, at the dust that shook off the walls, a fine sifting that gathered on the floor. In the stifling heat, it felt like it was gathering in her throat, like it would choke her.

"That vibration," Mo said. "It's like there's something big up ahead, some huge machine."

She nodded. She could feel that – but there was more. Cautiously she reached over and touched the railing with the fingertips of her good hand. It didn't shock her, nor was the vibration Mo had mentioned particularly strong. Far more strong was a feeling of wrongness. A deep sense of dread washed through her. Whatever lay ahead of them, it was nothing good.

Zhang came up and stood close, far too close in the heat, but his face was open. He was listening.

"You can't trust me," she said. "Not past this point."

"The basilisk," he said.

She nodded. "I can't fight it anymore. I thought I would be stronger than this."

"It's not a question of strength," he said. "I've studied that thing more than anybody. I've watched it claim so many lives. How can you fight something that sounds like your own thoughts? How can you win against something that was built to manipulate people like us? Literally designed to take advantage of our weaknesses, our vulnerabilities? It's not your fault, Petrova. It's not something any human being could fight forever. That's why I didn't want to come down here. It's why I didn't want to—"

She put her hand on his chest. Begging him for peace. To listen. "My mother kept it at bay for a long time, when she was its host. I'm not as tough as her. I see that now. It's going to take over and do what it wants down here. I want to make sure you and Mo are safe when that happens. We have a reprieve from the revenants for the moment. Maybe the two of you should just turn around and get out of here now."

"No," he said.

No question, no debate. And she was so very glad to hear it. Even if she knew it was the wrong decision.

"The air," Mo said, scowling. He held his Gauss rifle in both hands and was crouched down a little. Combat stance, she thought. "The air here. It's weird."

She looked back at Zhang. "You need to be ready," she said. "If there comes a time when I'm not recoverable." Dead, she meant. Or driven so insane she could never be right again. "If I try to hurt you or Mo, if I—"

"No," he said again, and this time he pushed past her. "Look," he said. "There's something up here. A door was here, I think."

"Fuck it, I'm ready," Mo said.

Petrova moved up and shone her light on the wall at the end of the tunnel. Steel girders had been driven into the rock as support columns, and beyond them stood a simple doorway. A doorframe, anyway. There were hinges, but no actual door, as if it had been removed.

"There was a door here, but it's not here now," Zhang said. He looked confused.

"Come on," Mo said. "You guys feel weird? Let's go. Let's get this done."

"It's the prize," Petrova said. She could see in Mo's face that he didn't understand what that meant. It was fine. The thing ahead of them was the basilisk's prize. The thing it was meant to guard. Its presence was what felt so weird about this place. There was an aura, a kind of field of telepathic energy around it, and they were so close they could feel it as easily as they felt the humidity in the air.

She took a step toward the door. Her brain twitched, convulsed. The basilisk was excited. Thrilled. "Not quite yet," she said.

The men looked at her, so she shook her head. She wasn't talking to them. Please, she thought. Please give me a few more moments. Let me see it with my own eyes first.

The basilisk thrashed back and forth and she thought she might lose her balance, that it might knock her to the floor. She managed to stay on both feet. The parasite didn't like the idea.

But for a second or two longer, it would wait.

Beyond the door there was light.

The central cavern was lit up brilliantly. The vibration they'd felt before was the throbbing of huge generators that pumped out smoke and powered enormous banks of lights, hundreds of lamps all focused in the same direction. The light stained the air, made her blink in surprise as her eyes were forced to adjust.

The cavern was bigger than she'd expected. A vast hollow bubble in the planet's crust, a round cyst in the bedrock. Walls rose up behind her, around her, so high, so distant they were just dark limits on a ball of light bigger than a stadium, a vast open space full of air. A blessed breeze caressed her face as she stepped forward into the light. The floor was relatively level, graded almost smooth by revenants with picks and shovels. Everywhere she saw signs of the work they'd done, digging this place out, and she realized the scope of their task.

There had been no natural cavern here. The mountain, the spire ahead of her had been buried in solid rock. The miners, and then the revenants, had dug out all of this stone. Blasted it, hewed it out by hand where they had to. Chipped and chiseled away at the rock like paleontologists uncovering a fragile fossil specimen.

To reveal something, something beautiful.

When she'd seen this place before, through the eyes of the

drones, she'd thought there was a mountain at the center of the cavern. It had been covered in the pale bodies of revenants working endlessly like termites chewing away at the chambers of a nest. Now, with just the three of them in the cavern, it looked completely transformed.

What had looked like a mountain was a cathedral. A skyscraper. No.

Not that at all. It didn't look like anything humans could have built.

It was a grand tapering edifice of basalt columns. She thought of the stone pillars she'd seen in the cavern of the spiders. Similar, but enlarged by a factor of ten, a hundred. Thousands of individual hexagonal columns wove together to form a single spire, a unified rising pillar of pure stone. It glittered in the light as if it were made of some ore of gold or platinum.

Near its base, half buried in the rock, was a sphere of burnished silver. A nearly perfect mirror, like a giant drop of mercury held in suspension. This was what the revenants had been digging for. She saw that it had been encrusted once, completely buried in the rock, but hundreds of hands had worked for countless hours to chip away at the stone, clear it off tiny fragment by tiny fragment until the silver sphere was revealed, almost completely exposed to the light. They'd actually cut away at the towering spire of basalt to uncover it, so it looked like the column arched over it, protecting it.

If you viewed the thing just right, she thought, it looked like the spire was a majestic tree, and this was a single ripe fruit dangling from its leafless branch.

"That's it," she said, the most unnecessary two words she'd ever spoken in her life. "That's the ... the thing that ..."

"Petrova," Zhang said. He reached for her, but she shoved him away. She staggered, bent.

"I'm alright," she said, straightening up.

"The basilisk," Zhang said, but she shook her head.

"No. Not the basilisk." The sphere, the silver sphere – there was something in there. Something not entirely dissimilar from the parasite. Like it, the thing in the sphere could communicate by thought alone. It could pollute her brain with silent words, unvoiced commands.

It beckoned to her. Drew her closer, step by step.

"Do you feel this too?" she asked.

Zhang closed his eyes. Then he nodded. "There's something there."

"It's what the miners felt," she said.

"The doctor," Zhang replied. "The doctor from the journal entries . . . If you get too close to this thing, it can take you over."

"How close is safe?" Mo asked, standing well back, behind them.

Petrova turned to him and smiled. "That's not a question we need to worry about anymore," she told him.

# 106

Zhang turned his face away from the sphere. As if not looking at it would help.

He knew this feeling all too well. He'd felt it on Titan. Again in orbit around Paradise-1. The basilisk had called to him just like this. It had called to him for a long time, and it had only stopped because it had found a host in Petrova.

The thing in the sphere was never going to stop. He knew that, was certain of it.

"Doc?" Mo asked. "Doc, keep it fucking together, buddy."

Zhang smiled and took a step away from the sphere. It didn't help.

It wasn't like the song of a siren. Nothing seductive about it. The thing in the sphere didn't want him to give in, it didn't want to convince him that he should pick up a shovel and start digging. It was arrogant. Confident. It commanded, with the understanding that its commandment would be obeyed. When he fought back, when he refused, it didn't even seem to acknowledge that he had a say in the matter.

*Free me*, it was saying. Not in so many words.

And the worst part, the worst fucking part, was that he wanted to. He really did. He had to fight the urge to do everything in his power to help the thing in the sphere. He couldn't remember the last time he'd wanted anything more.

He took a deep breath. Looked down at the RD on his

leg. It wasn't helping. Surely it could inject some cocktail of drugs into his system that would numb his mind to telepathic blandishments. No? Well, the thing had never responded to what he wanted. Only what it thought he needed to keep himself alive.

He took another step, and looked up and saw the sphere again. Somehow he'd turned around while he wasn't paying attention. He averted his eyes quickly.

He saw massive cables snaking across the floor of the cavern. Saw the picks and shovels abandoned by the revenants when they left this place. Further out, further away from the sphere, big machines stood silhouetted in the light. A thing that looked like a massive laser, he thought. The business end of a drill-head robot, removed and mounted on a kind of sled. He saw the massive generators and the plumes of smoke they made, smoke that lifted straight up, fumes billowing through the light.

The sphere called to him again. He was facing it again. "Petrova," he said. "We've seen it. We need to get out of here. If we don't . . ."

He didn't know what was going to happen if they didn't leave.

He knew they weren't going to leave.

The thing in the sphere pulsed with energy, with telepathic power. He felt it like waves washing over him. Through him. The anonymous doctor had not been able to resist. Why did he think he was any stronger? More capable of handling this?

He focused. Tried to focus on a memory, a specific memory. There had been a time when the basilisk had showed him his worst memory. The single most painful moment of his entire life. It had re-created that moment for him in incredible fidelity, a simulation of pure anguish. It had suggested that he could relive it over and over, forever if he liked.

Alternatively, he could accept the basilisk into his head. Let it parasitize him like a wasp injecting its eggs into the soft body of a caterpillar.

In that moment, that moment of tragedy, of pain, he had found something within himself.

The strength to say no.

*Holly*, he thought. He saw her eyes, through the thick glass of an airlock window. Watched her face turn red, then blue as she struggled to breathe. Watched her die.

In the dark inside his head, he ascended an endless staircase, human bones littering every riser. He kicked them out of the way as he climbed, climbed toward the light.

He felt his heart breaking one more time. How many times was he going to have to do this? How many times would he climb those stairs before he was free of these ancient bastards? Before they let him go?

He opened his eyes, though he hadn't realized he'd closed them. Looked around until he saw Petrova. She was closer to the sphere. She must have been moving toward it this whole time. Was she even trying to fight its call?

He ran to her. Grabbed her shoulder. She spun around.

The basilisk looked back at him.

It was like she'd said. The parasite had taken her over. He could see it in her eyes.

"Let her go," he said.

The basilisk sneered in vicious amusement.

# 107

"She gave herself to me freely, Doctor. You had the same option. Do you wish now that you'd made a different choice? That you were standing here in her place?"

The words came out of Petrova's mouth. She was vaguely aware of her lips moving, her tongue forming sounds, her breath giving them voice. She was so very, very far away, under the ocean. Floating in the water, her blonde hair like seaweed around her head.

When the basilisk had come for her, when it had decided it was time for it to take over her body, she had fought with every ounce of strength she had left. It had walked right past her defenses as if they weren't there. It desired exactly one thing in the entire universe, and now it had found it. It would not be stopped.

Below her, in the ocean, the light pulsed. The light spoke. This time it wasn't talking to her.

"I am almost finished with her," the basilisk said.

It walked over to the silver sphere. It had no difficulty resisting the call of the thing, its telepathic beckoning. The basilisk was made to exploit those same subtle energies, to weaponize that kind of power. It lifted its left hand toward the sphere, and Petrova screamed without making the slightest sound. She knew that if her flesh so much as touched the silver it would be burned away in an instant, disintegrated down to the molecular level.

The basilisk looked at the hard cast on her hand and scowled.

She could just make out what her own stolen eyes saw. Just feel the weight of the cast, the tiredness in her muscles and the aches in her joints. It was all so very faint, though.

"This is what you wanted," Zhang said. "To sate your curiosity. You wanted to know what you were guarding. But now it's done. We gave you what you asked for."

"You know so little. That's something we have in common. Just like me, there are parts of your story you haven't figured out yet." The basilisk held out one hand in the direction of Zhang's leg. "I can tell you some things."

"I don't want what you—"

Petrova heard Zhang gasp, as in pain. Down under the water, her body thrashed against an ocean current. It was not enough to bring her back to herself. Not even close.

The RD shifted and writhed across Zhang's leg, the golden snakes lifting away from him and twisting through the air. They swirled around Petrova's broken hand, their sharp heads seeming to sniff the air.

"Do you know what this is?" the basilisk asked.

"It's a medical device," Zhang said, grabbing his leg in both hands.

"Yes," the basilisk said. "And so much more. Did you even ever wonder why it seemed so advanced? So far beyond any medicine you knew?"

He shook his head.

"You aren't the first to wear this," the basilisk told him. "It was discovered on Earth's moon, twenty years ago. Buried in a crater so deep the sunlight never touched its bottom. It was left there intentionally, waiting to be found."

"What are you talking about?"

"The woman who first found it perished. It tore open her vacuum suit trying to get at her flesh. It turned out she had cancer. This thing could have cured her. Isn't that funny? She died gasping for air, even as it cut the tumor from her body.

When the device was recovered it was examined by dozens of scientists. Most of them died as well. They didn't know what they were looking at. They died to gain scraps of knowledge, without ever glimpsing the truth."

The golden snakes wrapped around Petrova's injured hand. They bit into the resin cast, striking it again and again until it shattered. The pieces fell away, revealing the crooked, useless stumps there. She screamed under the water, screamed and recoiled to see what had been done to her.

The snakes continued to writhe. They wrapped around each of her broken fingers. She felt nothing. They twisted their way around her knuckles, attached themselves to the stunted remains of her fingernails.

And then, with a sickening jerk, they tensed, pulled, yanked at her maimed flesh. They broke bones that had just begun to set. Tore skin and tendons, until blood poured across her palm, down her wrist.

There was pain. There was some pain. Very little of it reached her where she was, tucked away where she couldn't interfere with the basilisk. It felt like being in a warm room looking out a window on a frozen winter's day. You could feel the cold through the glass. Not enough to break your cozy feeling.

But you still felt it.

"Like the ones who came before you, you've barely scratched the surface of what this device can do," the basilisk said. "Perhaps that's understandable. It wasn't designed to be worn by a human being."

Zhang was staring at the transformation of Petrova's hand. He seemed unable to speak.

"This was originally the trinket of a god."

Her hand spasmed, twitched. The flesh started to swell up as fresh blood flowed into veins that had been crimped off, crushed. The nerves lit up with new signals as they tried to warn her brain that something was very, very wrong.

"I'm speaking, of course, of the beings who made me. They all possessed trinkets like this, just as you have those crude communications implants in your hands. The trinkets of the gods did more than receive messages, though. They made their wearers immortal. Preserved their flesh against disease, accident, age. They could cure any injury, neutralize any poison, protect against any threat. You've worn this one for years now, and what did you use it for? To regulate your emotional state. To soothe yourself when the thunder roared and you got scared. Pathetic."

The golden snakes bit her hand, hard. Tore her flesh open and slithered inside. She could see them wriggling around under her skin. Her fingers straightened – there was more pain, more agony she could only sense from afar – and then her fingers flexed. They moved, each finger moved in turn, each fingertip tapping the thumb.

Blood surged out of the hand. Blood surged back in. The nerves tingled for a moment, then settled down.

Her hand – it was a hand again. It looked like a hand.

Moved like a hand.

It had been healed.

It didn't even hurt anymore. She had been certain she would never use that hand again. That it was dead to all intents and purposes. Now it was healthy again. Healthy and whole.

"What have you done?" Zhang asked, as if the act of healing her broken hand was somehow a perversion. An obscenity.

"That isn't the really interesting question, Doctor. The interesting question is *why*."

From very far away, Petrova watched Zhang's face crumple. He had to know.

So did she.

"Why?" he asked.

"Because I need her hand to unlock the sphere."

Zhang shook his head. "I don't understand. How – how do you know all this, now?" he asked. "Before, when you spoke to us, when you offered us your deal – you didn't know what was down here, you just knew you were guarding ... something. That was why you needed us. To find this, to find out what it is—"

"That is all correct," the basilisk told him. "But my creators were not cruel. They left a secret message inside the very core of my being. A document that explains all I've just told you, and much more. An encrypted document that I could only access if I was standing in this very space, in a body capable of performing a certain action.

"An action they were afraid to perform, themselves.

"The gods are gone from this universe," the basilisk said. "It happened a very long time ago and they left very little behind. When they knew they were going to perish, in the last days of their empire, they left me behind, left me here to wait. To wait for you. They left this golden device on your moon because they had seen your ancestors, your very primitive ancestors, and they knew that one day you would fly up into the sky. Leave your backwater planet and reach for something more. Just as they, the gods, had once done, in their primitive ancestry. They foresaw you, they predicted that humanity would start the long climb toward godhood. They made sure you would find the trinket, and the message they'd left inscribed within it. A set of coordinates. Coordinates that lead here."

"Here?" Zhang asked. "This cavern?"

"This prison," the basilisk said.

Zhang turned to look at the silver sphere.

"They built that, too," the basilisk confirmed. "They made it very well. As the miners who dug out this cavern could attest, no tool made by humans could break through that sphere. No particle beam, no diamond-tipped drill. No. That prison was built to last forever. Potentially. It can in fact be opened. But only by one very specific key."

The basilisk lifted Petrova's healed hand. The palm split

open – there was a little blood – and then a single strand of gold emerged from between her heart line and her life line. A tendril of golden metal that twisted back on itself to become a complex shape, as delicate as the folds of a protein molecule.

"This key," the basilisk said.

"Yeah," Mo said, from behind them. "That's good. I'll take that."

Both the basilisk and Zhang turned to look at him. The survivor stood in a combat crouch, his rifle in both hands. Its barrel was pointed directly at Petrova's face.

"We're done here," he said. "Everybody back. Move away from that sphere and give me the key."

# 108

"Mo?" Zhang asked. "What are you doing?"

"Don't be an idiot," Mo told him. "Just stay down, okay? I don't want to kill you, but it wouldn't be much of an imposition."

"He's betraying you," the basilisk said.

"Mo, you . . . you saved us," Zhang pointed out. "You helped us this whole way. We're your ticket out of here, your ticket home—"

Mo fired his weapon. A violet burst of energy blasted the rock between Petrova and Zhang, turning it to slag.

"We're done playing," he said.

Zhang started to reach for the pistol at his belt. He'd never been a man of action, certainly he'd never been a man of violence, but if Mo was going to threaten Petrova—

"Don't even think about it, Doc," Mo said. He didn't change his grip on his weapon, didn't flex his trigger finger, but Zhang knew immediately that he meant it. If he tried to make a move, Mo would kill him where he stood.

"Just let us go. We'll give you the key," he said. "I don't know why you're doing this, but—"

Petrova cried out. Just a gasp, really, but in that frozen moment it sounded like an anguished scream. She dropped to her knees, left hand clutching the key.

Mo's rifle moved, this time to point at Zhang's face. He lifted his hands in surrender.

"Firewatch," Petrova said.

Zhang had trouble looking away from the barrel of that rifle. He very much wanted to look at Petrova, see if she was alright, but he couldn't stop staring at the gun. "Is that ... is that you?" he asked.

"Yeah," Petrova said. "I'm back. The basilisk is still here ... with me. But it let me have my body back."

Zhang decided he would be thankful for small favors. "You just said ..."

"Firewatch. He works for Firewatch."

Mo made a dismissive noise. Not quite a laugh.

"I knew you were military right away. The way you fought. The way you made your bed," Petrova told him. "You're a Firewatch agent. You always have been. You work for Director Lang."

He didn't deny it.

"She put you here to make sure this happened. All of it. Us finding the mine, making our way down here. To get this key."

Zhang shook his head. His eyes didn't move. He was still watching the Gauss rifle. "I don't understand. Lang sent Mo here? But when? After the colony lost contact with Earth, nobody could get here. The basilisk destroyed anyone who tried."

"He was here the whole time. Since the first colony ship arrived. He's been here for years. Firewatch's undercover man on Paradise-1. Isn't that right? How much of the story you told us was real? Djidi? Marsia?"

"Most of it," Mo said. His voice was subdued. Like he was holding back a very powerful emotion. "I was given a family as cover. I didn't expect ..." He stopped for a moment, as if overcome, but he didn't lower his weapon. "I didn't expect to feel anything for them. I thought this posting was going to suck. I worked as a farmer. Turned out I was good at it. Good enough that I had free time. Enough to do my real job, which was to keep tabs on Sheriff Sally. And the miners over here."

"This planet, the colony. It was only settled because you knew this thing was here. This prison," Petrova said.

"If that's what it is," Mo said. "Come on now, Lieutenant. Get up. Come here and give me that key. Otherwise I'm going to have to kill the doc. You really want me to do that?"

"You can just come over here and take it from me," Petrova pointed out. "The basilisk has used me up. I don't know if I can even stand on my own two feet right now. Relax. I'm no danger to anyone."

"Nice," Mo said. "Cute. I walk over there and you'd probably kill me three times before I got two steps. Don't take me for a fool."

Petrova laughed. "Fair enough. I guess we both got the same training, didn't we? Which tells me the last thing I should do is give you this key. Once I do, there's no reason why you won't just kill both of us."

"The story," Zhang said. His mouth was very dry. "The story the basilisk told about the RD. Was that true?"

"The part I understood? Sure," Mo said. "The UEG found that thing twenty years ago. Studied it for a long time before they realized it basically had instructions written right on it. Bring this gold piece of shit to these particular coordinates. Easy. Except those coordinates happened to be a kilometer down through solid bedrock on a planet barely habitable to human beings."

"So Paradise-1 was settled for . . . this," Zhang said. Tilting his head to indicate the cavern. The silver sphere.

"The Erebus Protocol," Mo said.

"What's that?" Zhang asked him. "Erebus is . . . what, the ancient Greek personification of darkness?"

"And another name for hell," Mo pointed out. "It's a codename. Don't read too much into it." He did laugh this time, just a curt little *ha*. "You ever hear of it, Petrova?"

"Sure," she said. "I mean, I've heard the rumors. I always assumed it was just a conspiracy theory."

"I've never heard of it," Zhang said.

Petrova sighed. "Supposedly the Erebus Protocol is one of Firewatch's big ideas. Call it a secret procedure for the end of the world. A hypothetical set of instructions for what to do if the UEG ever made contact with an alien species. It starts with two assumptions. First: the aliens will be hostile. Secondly: they'll have better technology than ours, better weapons, better ships, which means that in any conflict with them, they win. The human race goes extinct."

"I see," Zhang said. "That's rather pessimistic."

"Which is another word for accurate, Doc," Mo said. "Given those two assumptions, Firewatch came up with a plan. If the aliens' tech is so good, our first priority is to steal that tech so we can use it against them. Steal it no matter what the cost. We thought that if we brought the RD here, got the key, opened the sphere, whatever was inside would be ours to use as we saw fit. Easy plan, right?"

"Except clearly something went wrong," Petrova pointed out.

"The revenants," Zhang suggested.

"Yeah. The revenants," Mo confirmed. "We dug down deep, got close. When the miners started dying, Firewatch sent more miners. Then a funny thing happened. The dead miners started coming back to life. So they could keep digging. Turned out the thing down here, the thing in that sphere, wanted to be dug up, to be found, just as much as we wanted to find it. We'd made contact with an alien. A bad one."

"The very thing the Erebus Protocol was supposed to defend against," Petrova said.

"You going to give me that key?" Mo asked.

"I'm thinking about it," Petrova said. "You know, until this very moment, I still considered myself loyal to Firewatch. A true believer."

"Oh? Something changed?"

"Maybe. Back to your story . . ."

"My patience is getting pretty thin," Mo pointed out.

"Just give me a little more," Petrova said. "Let me die solving a few small mysteries. Like, who was it who deleted all the planet's computer files? Sabotaged the vehicles, wrecked the ansible?"

"Obviously that was me," Mo said.

"Obviously," Petrova said. "Standard military procedure, right? When things go to hell, when you lose territory, you burn the bridges, blow up the rail lines. Destroy the records. Not like the revenants cared much about computer files."

"There were other enemies to worry about," Mo suggested.

"Really? Like who? The Lunarists?" Petrova said. "My mom's old enemies?"

Something changed. The rifle twitched in Mo's hands, like he hadn't expected her to say that. He started to turn, to point the weapon at her.

"You know I can just kill you both and take the key out of your dead hand, right?" he said. He lifted the weapon to his shoulder, took aim.

"You might damage it in the process," Petrova said.

"Keep pushing me. I'll take my chances."

Zhang knew he was never going to get another opportunity to act. Not that he could do anything that would actually work. He had no doubt that the second he drew his pistol, Mo would just shoot them both.

But perhaps there were other ways to incapacitate a shooter. Ways that might prevent him from aiming properly.

"Give me the fucking key!" Mo shouted.

Zhang reached for a weapon on his belt. He didn't waste time aiming. He just grabbed it and switched it on.

Purple light lit up Mo's face. Not much. Not enough to give him sunburn.

More than enough UV energy, though, to temporarily blow out his retinas.

Mo screamed. His rifle leapt upward and he fired, his shot smashing into the basalt columns of the giant spire.

Zhang grabbed Petrova by the shoulders and hauled her to her feet. "Move," he said.

She didn't need to be told twice.

# 109

It was so much easier to climb with two hands.

Running would have been pointless. There was no way they could make it back to the cavern's entrance before Mo recovered. He would just shoot them in the back and that would be it. Nor was there any good place to hide. There was only one clear option, and it was a lousy one.

Up.

The hexagonal columns that comprised the spire made excellent hand- and footholds. In the low gravity of Paradise-1, Petrova could climb as fast as a mountain goat. She even reached back and gave Zhang a hand as he struggled to scramble up behind her.

She glanced down and saw Mo stumbling around clutching at his face. He must have heard something, because he suddenly twisted around and fired off a shot, the energy of the Gauss rifle scoring a deep line through the dark stone. For a moment the rock glowed where the ultra-fast projectile had struck, but the orange light quickly faded.

"Jesus, Doc! My fucking eyes!" he shouted. "That fucking hurt!"

"Up here," she said, and all but hauled Zhang up onto a ledge, maybe six meters up from the floor. Not quite a cave in the surface of the spire, but a place where they could gain a little cover from shots coming up from below. If they stood with their backs tight against the main body of the spire, maybe they would be invisible.

It was the closest thing she had to a plan.

After a few seconds, she dared to take a quick glimpse over the edge. She looked down and saw they were right above the silver sphere. If they fell from here, they might fall onto it. Nothing organic could survive that – the basilisk had told her as much. She looked around for Mo and realized he'd walked around the spire as if he expected to find them hiding back there.

Good, good. Her plan was working. As long as she didn't try to think about what the next step might be. Because she knew that Mo wasn't going to just go away.

She grabbed at the spire, trying to find a piece that might be pried loose. A rock she could throw down at his head. Nothing shifted.

"The key," Zhang whispered. "What happened to the key?"

She looked at her left hand. The key wasn't there. Her heart skipped a beat. But then she frowned at her hand, squinted at it, and the center of her palm opened like a tiny mouth and the key manifested itself, floating just above her flesh. She realized what had happened. The RD was inside her now, inside the flesh of her newly-healed arm. The key was just an extension of the golden device. When she'd started climbing the key had retracted inside her arm, but all she had to do was think about it to make it reappear. She made it vanish again. Cute little magic trick, for what it was worth.

She extended her thoughts toward the RD and felt it twist around the tendons of her arm. There were other tricks she could do, now, too.

"I don't think it detaches. I don't think I can give it to Mo," she whispered, "not without cutting my whole arm off." Would she do it? Maybe. Maybe if she did, Mo would have no reason to kill them.

Yeah, right. She knew Firewatch – and Lang – too well.

Mo would have orders to kill them the moment they stopped being useful. Lang wasn't the kind who tolerated loose ends. Especially if she was plotting something nasty, as Petrova had begun to suspect.

"I can hear you guys talking, you know," Mo called out from below.

A blast of energy vaporized the rock a meter or so over their heads. The stone sizzled and a trickle of lava rolled down toward her, but she didn't dare move.

Slowly, carefully, she drew her pistol. Held it near her ear, the barrel pointed up. She took one quick breath. Then she moved fast, leaning forward, using Zhang's grip to keep her balanced. She thrust her right hand, her gun hand, downward and swung it from side to side, looking for Mo, looking for a target.

She saw him and fired, but her round went wide. Mo grinned up at her and lifted his rifle. Shots blasted all around her and she had to jump back, her heart feeling like it was going to burst.

"Nice try," Mo said. He fired three more times in rapid succession. Stone exploded all around Petrova and Zhang. She had to turn her face away from it. Particles of molten rock showered the back of her head. The sweet stink of burning hair made her want to retch.

"I think he's getting his vision back," Zhang said, very quietly.

"Yeah. His aim's definitely getting better," Petrova replied.

"We've run out of luck, haven't we?"

She could only shrug in response.

# 110

He did not expect that the Other would ever speak to him again.

He knew that the teeth would tear away at him forever, that he had been consigned to hell merely because the Other had wanted information, and that it had no reason to release him. No compassion, no sympathy. It wasn't his friend, it didn't want to help him. Somehow he'd managed to get something from it. Somehow he'd achieved the impossible. He'd gotten the Other to relent, to stand down its revenants, and Petrova had lived for another hour.

Apparently it was too much to hope that that condition would last.

On the wall of the cave, images appeared once more. Monochrome and distorted, but he had no doubt what he was looking at. He saw Petrova jumping from a high place. He saw the projectile of a Gauss rifle pass through her, tunneling a massive hole in her torso. He watched her die.

Time was different in the red space. Time moved incredibly slowly, time meant nothing. Time was an abstract concept.

Which meant he got to watch Petrova die over. And over. And over.

"What do you want?" he demanded. "Why are you showing me this? I don't want to see it! Why are you torturing me? What did I do to deserve this?"

She looked so surprised when the projectile hit her. Her eyes went wide, her mouth opened in a silent gasp of unexpected pain. The last moments of the woman he loved.

Over.

And over.

And over.

"Stop it! Fucking stop this, you fucking fuck! You fucking bastard!"

He begged the teeth to rip out his eyes. Not that it mattered. He didn't need them to see the image on the wall. Her hair flying, her hands splayed out, her pistol floating in the air as she lost control of it. Her blood splattering on a wall of rock behind her.

"Stop!"

DEAL

"What? Stop this, you fucking—"

BARGAIN

TRADE

"I don't understand!"

WE CAN

MAKE

ANOTHER

DEAL

# 111

"You've stopped shooting," Petrova called out, after what felt like a long, long time. She was still breathing. Zhang was still there next to her, alive. Mo wasn't actively trying to kill them. "What happened? Your weapon overheat?"

Mo chuckled.

She'd kind of hoped he'd gotten bored and walked away. Not like that was a realistic scenario. It just really would have been very nice.

"You're going to have to come down from there eventually," he told her. "Why should I make my arms tired when it's just . . . I don't know. Inevitable?"

"You're a Lunarist," she said. "A double agent, masquerading as a loyal Firewatch officer. Aren't you?"

He didn't reply for far too long. She'd thought to shock him. Before, when she'd mentioned the Lunarists, he had flinched, a little. Maybe he really was one. Maybe he would take what she'd said as an insult, and it would make him do something stupid.

Instead, he just fell silent.

She tried to think. How to get him to react? "When I was a little girl, the Lunarists almost killed me. In the name of independence from the UEG, they kidnapped me. Put me in a box without enough air. My mother had to rescue me. I watched her have each and every one of the kidnappers killed. Right in front of me."

Mo made a sound of disgust. "That plan. It was a shitshow."

"My mother never found the person who came up with the plan. The head of the terrorist cell."

"They weren't terrorists," Mo said. Was there a touch of anger in his voice?

"No?"

"They only wanted freedom. You think that's a bad thing?"

Petrova took a breath. "Who was it? Who planned my kidnapping?"

Zhang stirred next to her. "No," he said, as if he'd just realized something. "Was it Lang?"

Mo's silence spoke volumes.

"It must have been tricky," Petrova said. "For a woman like that to worm her way into Firewatch. Climb the ranks. I guess she had her revenge in the end, didn't she? Revenge on my mother, anyway."

"She's a genius," Mo said. "A true leader."

"Did she know all along? About the RD, about the key? Is that why she sent you here? To keep an eye on her friend in the prison cell here?"

Mo laughed again. "She knew a lot. When she was sworn in as director of Firewatch, they briefed her on the rest. It wasn't part of the plan originally. She was just going to take over a major UEG agency, turn it against the tyrants. Bring down the UEG from within." He fired a shot up at them, but it didn't even come close to hitting them. Maybe it was just his way of reminding them they were about to die. "When she heard about the RD, when she knew the whole story, she got kind of obsessed. People do that when it comes to aliens, you know?"

"Let me guess. Lang wants to make contact with the thing that's buried here, whatever it is. She thinks she can negotiate with it. Get it on her side and use that as leverage against the UEG, to get concessions for the Lunarists."

"Huh," Mo said. "I just realized something."

Petrova glanced over at Zhang. This was almost over, one way or another. She knew she'd bought as much time as she was going to get.

"What's that?" she asked. She showed Zhang her pistol, gestured for him to draw his own. Then she counted down with her fingers. Three.

"You're dumber than you look. The thing in there is nobody's friend and it's never going to be."

"No?" Two.

"No. It's a weapon," he told her.

One.

Go.

She lunged forward, jumping down from column to column, making herself an obvious target. Zhang leaned out from the ledge and gave her covering fire. She knew he wasn't much of a shot and she didn't expect him to actually hit Mo, but maybe he could make him duck, maybe ruin his aim.

This was the dumbest plan she'd ever thought of, she realized. It was also all she had.

Below her, Mo didn't so much as flinch. He lifted his rifle and drew a perfect bead right on her chest. She could all but feel the round before it hit her, feel just how painful and pointless her death was going to be.

# 112

DEAL

"I don't understand. What could we ... what could I give you? I've already ... I've told you everything I know, and—"

DEAL

"What deal?" he screamed. "What deal are you talking about?"

BODY

The teeth savaged him, ripped him to shreds, but he barely felt it.

"Wait," he said. "What?"

NEW BODY

"You ... you want to give me a new body?" he asked.

BODY

DEAL

The teeth didn't stop worrying at him, not for a moment. He couldn't think. Couldn't understand what was happening, what he was being offered.

Like it mattered.

BODY

DEAL

"Deal," he said, and light burst out all around him, coming from every direction at once.

# 113

Petrova moved, leaping down the side of the spire, her feet finding places to land just by instinct. She brought her pistol up to take a shot she knew wouldn't be enough, because even if it hit him in the chest he would still have time to fire his own weapon. To kill her.

He didn't get that chance.

Even as he brought his rifle up to aim at her, something streaked through the overwhelming lights of the cavern. Something big and white and fast. It made no sound that she could hear; even the pounding of its feet on the rock floor was silent. It might have been a ghost.

Except it hit Mo like a cargo freighter. Smashed him off his feet, sent him tumbling sideways. Mo rolled back up, but the monster was already coming for him, swinging one massive arm around in a crushing arc. Mo scrambled backward, nearly losing his footing. He lifted his rifle and fired, barely bothering to aim, barely needing to at such close range.

The ghostly thing twisted to the side as the violet energy of the blast tore through its ribcage, low on the left. Petrova watched in disgust as its soft white flesh parted and black dust squirted out of what should have been a fatal wound.

The massive creature looked down at its injured side. Poked a finger inside the hole in its midriff as if it couldn't believe it had been damaged. Then it looked up at Mo, and came at him in two quick, long strides.

Mo fired off two more shots before the behemoth reached him. One shot went wide, the other drew a black line across the monster's leg. It didn't slow down.

It brought both fists up in the air. It brought them down again.

Mo screamed. Then he fell silent.

Petrova touched the floor of the cavern. Found her footing. She looked up at the thing that had attacked Mo.

The creature rose to its full height. Even so, it looked smaller now that it wasn't in mid-attack. It seemed to have deflated, as if its sole reason for existence had been completed and it was going to vanish again, like the specter it was.

Except it didn't vanish. It stayed right there and turned to look at her with sad eyes. Black, solid black eyes. She saw the dark veins running across its jawline, the broken teeth.

Now it came closer, and before she could jerk away, it reached out and touched her cheek with a paw-like hand. There was blood on that hand, but she felt ... she felt something she recognized. Something in the way it touched her. As intimate as a lover's caress.

This wasn't just a revenant standing in front of her. It was more than that. Or rather, it had something more inside it than the others had.

"Sam," she whispered.

# 114

The body he'd been given felt mostly numb. Mostly. He could feel ... something. He'd forgotten what it was like. He could sense the softness of her skin, feel the faint movement of her cheek as it jumped with her pulse.

It was the most he'd felt since he died.

He hadn't noticed it before, but his own heart wasn't beating. He wasn't breathing.

The body – his new body – wasn't alive. He guessed it had been once. Then it had died, and then it had stood back up and joined the other revenants digging in the mine. It was one of the bodies that Petrova and Zhang had fought on their way down the stairs. One of the bodies that had been just about to swarm over them, to destroy them utterly, until Parker had told the Other what it wanted to hear. Convinced it to stop the attack.

He understood, then. The Other had freed him from the red space. From hell. It had done so by giving him the only available kind of body at its disposal. One of its own revenants. It had given him this body so he could save Petrova.

He didn't understand *why*.

*Understanding is impossible*, it had told him.

He knew he didn't care. Not if it meant keeping her alive. Not if it meant he could actually do something, something useful. Meaningful.

He felt her shudder in fear. He knew that she was horrified by his new body. He didn't blame her. He stepped backward, away from her. Giving her room. He considered running away, into the maze of tunnels in the mine, where she would never have to see him again.

But no. He was still selfish enough to want to be around her.

"It's Parker," she said. She had turned to face Zhang, who was carefully making his way down the side of the mountain of columns.

"It's dead," Zhang pointed out.

Petrova nodded. She turned to face Parker. Then she looked down at her feet, as if she couldn't stand to look at him. He glanced at the massive lights that illuminated the cavern. He wanted to smash them all. To hide in darkness. The desire burned in him, a need he could barely resist. His body didn't function. He didn't feel sick, didn't feel feverish, but that just made room for his emotions to be bigger, harder to contain. The need for darkness was like a wind pushing him from behind, a violent wind shoving him in one direction.

He fought it. He fought to control it.

"I don't claim to understand what's going on," Petrova said. "Parker saved us. Parker, can you talk? Can you tell me what's happening?"

He tried. He opened his mouth and tried to push out words, then raw sounds. The best he could manage was a sort of choking rattle.

Frustration seized him. He twisted around, looking for something to hit, to put all that thwarted energy into. He could smash up Mo's corpse some more, maybe. Break his fucking Gauss rifle or something.

Instead he grabbed his own head and howled, even though his throat was closed, his lungs still. He howled inside himself.

Eventually he recovered enough to put his hands down. He turned to face the silver sphere at the bottom of the mountain.

In the harsh direct light, it blazed like a beacon. One bright star in the night.

Teeth, he thought. Constant destruction. A ravenous hell to hold a patient devil.

The thoughts echoed through his empty skull.

He lifted one hand and pointed at the sphere. It was the best answer he could give her. The best he could do to explain himself. *That thing*, there, he was saying. *It made this happen. It put me in this terrible husk.*

He didn't expect her to understand. Not fully. And she didn't.

"Right," she said. "We need to figure out what to do with that."

# 115

Zhang watched Parker carefully as they moved toward the silver sphere. The revenant body filled him with revulsion – his skin rippled with disgust every time he came close to it. Still, Parker had been hurt. Wounded.

Was there even anything he could do for him? Zhang approached carefully, as if Parker might turn and attack him at the slightest provocation. When Parker saw what he was after, though, he lifted up his pale arm and let Zhang poke and prod the wound site as much as he liked.

"There are broken bones in here," Zhang said when he'd finished his examination. The wound had obliterated part of Parker's side. The internal organs were just dry, papery bags full of black powder, but the bones – black as he remembered them from his autopsy of Kenji Yoshida – were solid. Every bit as strong as they must have been in life. "I can set those. I don't think they'll heal, but . . . they won't get worse. For the wound itself, I could try layering artificial skin over the gap, but I think we might do better with some kind of plastic filler." He shook his head. "This is a whole new branch of medicine for me. Rapscallion might be more useful in fixing you up."

At the mention of the robot, all three of them fell silent. For a moment they just stood there remembering their friend. He had been lost fighting for them, had died to save them. Zhang knew none of them would ever forget him.

When the moment had passed, Petrova took charge again. "We need to resolve this, and then get the hell out of here," she said. She led them over to the sphere, which had not changed in the slightest since they'd arrived.

Zhang watched her lift her left hand and stare at the golden key floating above her palm. The RD was in there. What he'd called the RD. It was strange not to have it touching him, not to be wearing it on his body. It had helped and protected him for so long. He'd almost come to think of it as a friend, or at least a nagging companion.

He'd never had the slightest idea that it was alien. That the same hands that had made the basilisk had constructed it.

He studied the key, the tiny part of the RD that protruded from her skin. It was complex in shape, a twisted ribbon of gold floating over her palm. How many people had died to bring it here? How many people had been driven mad?

"It's a key. We know that much," Petrova said. "I think if I touch it to the sphere, the sphere will open. The thing inside the sphere is the thing that made the revenants. The thing that made . . ."

She stopped and looked pointedly at Parker.

Zhang cleared his throat. "Do we have any idea why the basilisk's makers wanted us to have this key? The basilisk said it was left on the Moon so we would find it. Humans would find it."

Petrova nodded. "I heard what you heard. It let me listen in while it talked to you. I got a little more, too. Not that it gave me all the answers, but I could sense its emotions. It doesn't think we're worthy, of course. It's never had anything but disdain for us."

"How does it feel about this thing?" Zhang asked, indicating the sphere.

"It's scared shitless by it. That's why it would cut and run every time we ran into the revenants. The thing in there is much more powerful than the basilisk, and it does not want the same things."

"Presumably it didn't share any goals with the basilisk's makers, either. These gods it mentioned," Zhang pointed out. "They did put it in an eternal prison, after all. You don't do that with your friends."

"Yet for some reason, we're being given the option to free it," Petrova said. She shrugged. "That's what we need to figure out. I don't know about you guys, but I'm no fan of the gods or the basilisk. This thing is their enemy. Is the enemy of my enemy my friend?"

"You're asking," Zhang said, "if we should free the thing that slaughtered ten thousand colonists to make them dig it out of the dirt."

Petrova laughed. "When you put it like that . . ."

"Fuck. No," Zhang said. He normally tried to avoid profanity, but this seemed like the right moment.

Petrova took a deep breath. "Yeah. I vote no, too. Obviously. Parker? You get a vote as well. You came all this way with us. You've sacrificed more than any of us."

The pilot turned ghost turned zombie also had the most reason to like the thing inside the sphere, Zhang thought. After all, it had saved him from utter destruction. Given him a physical body again.

Parker shook his head violently back and forth.

"Cool. Good," Petrova said. "Okay. We're unanimous. We leave it locked up. Director Lang won't like this at all, but, you know. Fuck her. She tried to kill us."

# 116

Petrova knew nothing was over, not really. There was plenty of work to do if they were going to survive. She couldn't help but feel like they'd won, however. Like they'd actually pulled it off.

It felt good . . . mostly. The price they'd paid had been steep. She was still infected with a psychic parasite. Zhang was going to have to learn to live without the RD. Parker was stuck in a dead, grotesque body.

But the big loose end was Lang. The mastermind behind everything.

"We've beaten her," she said. "But that's when people like her are at their most dangerous."

"She won't take this lightly. She spent a lot of resources on this Erebus Protocol," Zhang pointed out. "She'll keep after us until she gets the key and we'll never be safe." Meaning Petrova would never be safe. But since Zhang had no intention of leaving her side in the near future, he supposed his own life was at risk too. "Mo said she wanted to use it as a weapon."

"To further her cause, I assume," Petrova said. "Jesus. Can you imagine? She wouldn't even have to actually use it. Just threaten to release it on Earth. She would have the power to turn twenty billion people into zombies. The UEG would have no choice but to give her concessions. Independence for the Moon, maybe Mars and Ganymede too."

"Which might not be so bad, except . . ."

"Except she would be the obvious choice to lead those 'independent' worlds," Petrova said, nodding. "Yeah. I'm not giving that woman any more power than she already has. There has to be a way to destroy the key."

"We can figure it out," Zhang said. "We will figure it out."

Petrova nodded. "I'm more concerned about survival right now. How do we get out of here? And where do we go once we do? There's no rescue ship coming for us, obviously. So we're stuck on Paradise-1 for the foreseeable future. The ansible is working now, so we can use it to contact the UEG. Warn them that Lang is a separatist."

"Assuming we can reach anyone that Lang doesn't already control," Zhang pointed out. "I hope they believe us. I hope . . ."

He stopped talking, and for a moment she had no idea why. Had something happened to him? Maybe without the cocktail of drugs the RD constantly pumped into his system, his brain had frozen up or something. She smiled and waved a hand in front of his face.

"Look out!" he shouted.

There was no time to react. Parker's big hand closed around her left wrist and he jerked her off her feet. Hauled her bodily across the floor, toward the silver sphere.

"Sam?" she had time to say.

His black eyes shouldn't have been able to convey emotion. His dead face should have been incapable of expression. Somehow she knew, though. This wasn't him. The thing inside the sphere had possessed him, was controlling him, just as the basilisk sometimes controlled her.

Just as it controlled all the revenants.

"Sam," she said, "it's okay . . ."

He didn't, or couldn't, stop. He pushed her toward the sphere. She had the dizzying, horrible thought that he was going to throw her into it, that her entire body would be reduced to its component subatomic particles.

That didn't happen. Instead he stopped, holding her in place, his hands like iron vises. He moved her arm until her hand was just a centimeter or two away from the sphere.

The key extended from her hand. It touched the surface of the sphere and ... melted.

She watched it happen, paralyzed with fear, unable to look away. Rivulets of gold streamed away from the contact site, forming patterns like tree branches, like veins growing across the curved silver surface. The streamers of gold multiplied, spread, consumed the entire sphere.

And then the whole thing vanished in a puff of grey smoke.

The sphere was gone.

In its place was just one object. A prism of what looked like green glass, maybe two meters tall and a meter wide. Something dark curled and writhed inside the glass like black smoke.

Waves of pure hatred washed over her, emanating from within that glass cell. Telepathic currents that filled the air with rage, with detestation. She was assessed and found wanting, despised and cast out, and she gagged on her own worthlessness, the disgusting foulness of her organic body, her collection of cells, of matter. She was nothing but a blot of corruption in the face of such spiritual perfection, and she had pretended to have the right to judge one of the gods?

She should be annihilated. She should be obliterated from existence. Not even as a punishment for her failings. She should be extirpated as a matter of hygiene. She, and everything like her, should be burned away from the universe before she spread her filth, her disease.

The judgment lasted a bare moment. It left her gasping for air, down on her knees. Her hands up in front of her face as if they could have done anything to protect her from its wrath.

When she looked again, the green prism was gone.

She turned and searched for Parker.

He was gone too.

Zhang stood nearby, gasping for breath, one hand on his chest. He looked at her with wide, staring eyes and she knew he had no idea what had just happened.

What they had released.

# 117

"Where did they go?" Zhang asked. "What's going on?"

"The thing in the sphere, the alien—it controlled Parker. Maybe that was why it gave him that body, I don't know, I don't—" Petrova stared at him. He knew she had no more answers than he did. "It used him to unlock the sphere. Then it was free. And they . . . They just—"

"Teleported somewhere," Zhang said. He refused to believe anything else. "They must have teleported away. The basilisk said that time and space meant nothing to it. This thing—"

"It's much more powerful than the basilisk," Petrova said, nodding. "The sphere was holding it in check. Now that's gone there's no telling what it's capable of." She grabbed her head in both hands.

Zhang's brain reeled. He struggled to understand anything that had happened. Yet he knew something of what it meant.

An incredibly powerful and malevolent alien was free in the universe. It could be anywhere, could go anywhere. It had taken Parker with it, for reasons unknown.

For a long time they did nothing. Said nothing. They stood there in that massive empty cave and waited, as if something was supposed to come for them. Death, maybe. A horde of revenants sweeping through the brightly lit cavern. Maybe the whole place would just collapse on their heads.

Eventually Zhang walked over to where the remains of

Moussa Abara lay on the floor. The man was definitely dead. He removed a scarf from Mo's neck and draped it over his face. It was all he could do. He supposed he could bury the body. The idea almost made him laugh. Let the cavern be his tomb.

"Let me look at your hand," he said, returning to where Petrova stood, staring at the space where the green prism had been. "Please."

She held it out for him. He took it in both of his. Compared her flesh to his. After all they'd been through, his skin was covered in scrapes and bruises and tiny scars. Her left hand was pink and smooth. Even the nails were clean and cut short, as if the RD had given her a manicure while it rebuilt her broken bones.

The RD. For so long he'd worn that thing on his arm. Having no idea that it was older than the human species. No idea it was an alien machine. The product of the same engineers who'd built the basilisk.

Now it was inside her arm. He grasped her forearm and squeezed and he could feel it in there, the malleable metal shifting, twisting around her muscles and sinews. It didn't seem to hurt her. It didn't seem to mean her any harm. That was something, at least.

Petrova looked down at his leg. "Are you okay to walk without it?"

He knew he wasn't getting the RD back. He wasn't sure how he felt about that.

"I'll manage," he said.

"Good. We need to get out of here."

He didn't disagree.

# 118.

They climbed the steel stairs, back up to the maze of tunnels above the central cavern. They kept quiet, kept their heads down. Petrova wasn't about to lose Zhang now.

If she did, she would be all alone. In the dark. With the revenants.

They started at every sound, turned away every time they thought they heard something moving in the shadows. She knew they were probably being overly cautious. She didn't care. She was going to die on this planet, was sure she would never leave it. But she wanted to see the sun again first. It felt like they'd been down in the dark for so long she couldn't remember what it felt like to see things plainly, to see their colors and their proper shapes, and not the washed-out, distorted images her torch showed.

They came to the cave where the miners had rested to give themselves strength to continue the digging. As they passed through, she grabbed a box of protein bars and tore it open, handed one to Zhang. He stared at it like he had no idea what he held. She had to urge him to eat, as if she were coaxing an infant.

Had he already given up? She couldn't imagine the chemical wars fighting themselves out inside his head. Before the UEG had clamped the RD around his arm, he had been suicidal, she knew, a danger to himself and others. All the drugs the alien medical device had given him would be wearing off now. Burning away in his bloodstream, in the dark corners of his brain. Was she going to have to watch him from now on, would she have to take away the laces of his boots? She knew she would do it.

They climbed up through a massive chamber full of dead, silent pumps. She scanned the shadows, looking for any sign of movement. There was none. She was confused why the revenants hadn't attacked them yet. She felt like she knew why they had stopped before. Why, at the top of the stairs, when they could easily have killed her and Zhang and Mo, they had suddenly relented. It must have been because the thing in the silver sphere had known they were coming to free it. It had realized they were its best chance of escape. So it had given them free passage.

If she'd known what was coming in that moment, she would have thrown herself off the stairs, dashed herself on the rocks where Rapscallion died. Anything to stop Lang, the basilisk and the thing in the sphere from conspiring to make this happen.

"Erebus," Zhang said. Just flat syllables falling out of his mouth.

"What? Mo mentioned the Erebus Protocol..."

Zhang looked up. "It's as good a name as any. Erebus. The monster we let out of the bottle. The prisoner we released. Call it Erebus."

"Okay," she said.

They kept climbing.

# 119

They found the revenants eventually.

Zhang mostly felt numb. There were little sparks of emotion inside him, like bored schoolmates jabbing him with pencils and the sharp ends of compasses while he tried to read his lessons. He shook his head. A strange image, but ... he had trouble focusing. Concentrating. He could walk. He could climb.

They found ...

"Wake up," someone said, except, no. Nobody had said that. He shook himself like a dog. Shook his whole body. "Wake up," he said to himself. He looked around and saw he was surrounded by the dead.

Like in his dream.

Like the stairs in his dream. Climbing the stairs, kicking bones, human bones, out of his way with every step.

"Careful," Petrova said.

Zhang gathered his wits the best he could. He moved his light across the dusty floor of the room, catching each new image, each fresh horror, as if he was cataloging them. He imagined it like he was watching a documentary, or news footage of the discovery of a mass grave.

They lay on the floor abandoned, like the tools in the cavern. They lay where they'd fallen, their dark eyes staring up at a featureless ceiling. Their arms splayed out or tucked neatly beside them. A leg bent, the knee up. Another leg sticking out at an odd angle.

Their faces were slack, loose. Halloween masks slipping at the end of the night.

Just corpses now. No longer revenants, just decaying bodies.

Erebus had been done with them, and it had cast them off.

He walked carefully, trying not to step on them. He missed one, a woman in a jumpsuit, stumbled over her and fell down next to her, on his knees.

On the collar of her jumpsuit he saw a printed cross. One on either side of her throat. The universal symbol of a medical professional. He imagined that if he turned her over, across her back he would see the same symbol. She had been a doctor, in life.

"Was it you?" he asked. "Did you ... did you come here and ... and did they hand you a shovel and ..."

He started weeping.

Her black eyes looked up at him, free of pain. Free of any emotion at all.

"So many of them," Petrova said. "It just threw them away."

Zhang couldn't stop weeping.

# 120

They reached the archway and there was sunlight, there was light and cool fresh air. Petrova smiled for a moment, before she realized how little ground they'd really covered. Until she remembered what awaited them.

They were still at the bottom of a massive pit. The only living humans on a planet that didn't want them, with no way home.

She kept moving. Kept working. She got Zhang inside the bubble canopy of Mo's quadcopter. She could fly it, she knew how. With two functional hands it wasn't particularly difficult. The aircraft's gyroscopes kept it level, so all she had to do was pull back on the yoke. The copter rose up, up, through the layers of the open pit. She was astonished at how big the place was. She'd seen it before, on the way down, but now it looked like a natural feature of the planet, like the Grand Canyon on Earth or the Valles Marineris on Mars. She'd seen those places and known they were not constructed on a human scale. They were so big they became the landscape, became the world. This place was on that same scale, even though it wasn't natural. It had been dug out by humans and robots working together, humans and robots and then revenants, all at the behest of Erebus. The ancient thing, the prisoner, had called to them like the voice of a deity. It had compelled and they had served. Put everything they had into this simple effort to dig a silver pearl out of the center of a desolate world.

"It would have been molten," Zhang said, lifting his head.

She looked over at him.

"The whole planet. A billion years ago. Paradise-1 is a lot younger than Earth. A billion years ago, this planet would have still been in the process of formation. Just a ball of molten iron and silicates, circling a star wreathed in clouds of accreting hydrogen gas. When they dropped the silver sphere into the body of Paradise-1, it would have splashed. Sunk without a trace. Erebus must have been calling ever since, shouting for anyone who might listen, who might come to its aid. Even as the rock cooled around its prison cell, even as the lava tubes and the hexagonal columns formed. How many millennia did it keep calling, how long did it scream and whisper and beg the little spiders to come help? And then, suddenly, an answer."

Petrova saw nothing but blue sky above them. Not even a cloud, nor a trace of one.

They came up out of the pit and she set them down on a painted circle at the center of the mine control complex. Zhang was still talking. She let him – any sound was better than silence just then.

"Why did they bury it? The makers of the basilisk, the ancients. They must have had their reasons. They must have hated it. Feared it so much they had to hide it away where no one would find it until long after they were gone. And yet – they didn't just destroy it. They didn't kill Erebus. Maybe they couldn't. Maybe it can't be destroyed. Or maybe . . .

"They left a key. They left the key to the cell with us. Why? To give us the choice? To make Erebus our responsibility?

"Or did they want us to release it? Did they want us to open the cell?"

She had to pull him out of the copter. She knew she couldn't leave him alone, even for the time it would take her to scour the mine complex for supplies. She forced him to eat half of a protein bar, watched him to make sure he swallowed. He looked at her with numb eyes.

She went into the ops center to see what she could find. He followed. He wasn't so far gone. He could walk, he could do whatever she asked him to do. He just didn't seem to want to do anything else.

The door to the stairs that led up to the control center was closed. She opened it, then gasped when she heard someone scream, a screech that seemed to go on forever.

She hurried down to the bottom of the stairs, to the basement. The screeching came from a 3D printer in one corner of the big room. There was a workstation nearby, its holoscreen lit up, showing a diagram of something that looked almost human.

Perched atop the workstation was a creature out of a nightmare. Spidery legs (her new phobia kicked in instantly) propped up a thin wrist, a delicate human hand that poked at the holoscreen with one long index finger. Entering input, making choices.

The hand spider was a bright toxic green in color.

She let out a noise halfway between a sob and a scream of excited disbelief.

Later, when he had a head, a face, a mouth, Rapscallion explained. Of course he'd backed himself up before they headed down into the mine.

Why would he do something so incredibly dangerous, undertake an adventure so stupid only a human would even consider it, without backing himself up first? It was just common sense.

# 121

Three days later, Zhang stepped out of the ops center and looked over a vast plain of black rock stretching out to the distant horizon, and started thinking about just . . . walking.

Just walking until . . . well, until he stopped.

Petrova had done an excellent job of keeping an eye on him. She had kept him fed, made sure he at least tried to sleep, even though every five minutes or so a jolt of electricity would go through his head, making him think he was about to die. Even though he kept fuzzing out in the middle of conversations. Even when he would just sit there looking perfectly fine, but in his head he was thinking about Titan, about a woman named Holly whose face he had just started to begin to forget.

Petrova had kept him going. Kept him okay. He didn't want her to have to do that for the rest of his life. However long that might be.

She was already making plans, of course. That was what she did best. No matter what happened to them, no matter how dire things got, she always had another idea. A next step. He admired her for that, even when he knew their situation was hopeless.

Lang was certainly not going to rescue them now. For a couple of days they'd worried she would send troops to come find them, to kill them, because they knew too much. Then they'd realized that there was no need. Without a spaceship, without any way off the planet, they were no danger to anyone.

She could just sit back and wait for Paradise-1 to kill them off. Even if it took years.

Petrova hadn't liked that thought. She'd wanted to think there was still something she could accomplish. She had spent the last three days trying to get in touch with the ansible at the comms center, only to find out that it had been shut down – not by Mo this time. No, the equipment Rapscallion had fixed was still working just fine. Instead, the problem was that no one on the other side was receiving. Their messages were all blocked before they could reach Earth and the UEG.

So what could they do?

Together they had discussed where they were going next.

They had no intention of sticking around the ops center or the big warehouses full of dead mining robots. So where? The colony town? The empty colony town with the wind shrieking between the prefab housing units, the trashed medical center, the auditorium with its blood-soaked carpet?

Mo's house was a possibility, they thought. A place built for survivors, with plenty of room for two. A place designed to help you forget there were ever other people.

Petrova had announced that they were leaving first thing in the morning. Zhang had considered the possibility of moving into the dead man's house, using his things, eating his stored food. Until it ran out.

He'd considered all that. Then he'd come up with his own plan.

Wait until Petrova was asleep. Like she was now. Then just start walking. It was a pleasant enough day. Not a cloud in the sky. He would just walk. And then he would stop.

He looked down at the flat rock at the edge of the mining complex's grimy streets. One foot in front of the other, he thought. He glanced up, looking for the sun, making sure it would be behind him. He could just walk until he caught up with his own shadow stretching out before him. The idea made him smile.

He put a foot down. And stopped.

There was a light in the sky that wasn't the sun.

Paradise-1 didn't have any moons. It wasn't just some piece of space junk catching starlight, either. It was very large, very bright. Getting bigger all the time.

A ship. Rapscallion had said there was a ship coming toward the planet. He'd forgotten about that. A ship . . .

He heard a noise behind him and looked to see Rapscallion climbing up onto the roof of the ops center. The robot's new body wasn't humanoid at all, except for the face, which hung on the end of what looked like an octopus's arm. He held the green mask up toward the new light like he was a sun-worshipper making a sacrifice to an evil omen.

The robot called out Zhang's name. Zhang didn't bother replying. He moved to stand in the shelter of a building as hot air washed down over him, hot air and then the incredible noise of a spacecraft's landing jets. Only when the noise stopped did he emerge from shelter and run toward the landing pad at the far side of the mining complex.

Standing on the pad was a fast transport ship, smaller than *Artemis*. It had stubby wings and a tail fin so it could negotiate the planet's atmosphere, but the drive unit on the back was big and complicated enough that Zhang was certain it was a singularity drive.

A ship capable of faster-than-light travel.

A hatch on its side opened as he watched. Nobody stepped out, but green lights glowed around the hatch, indicating it was safe to come inside. An invitation of sorts.

Zhang hesitated. Until he remembered what he had planned for the day. He supposed his walk could wait a little while. He shouted for Rapscallion to wake up Petrova, to bring her to see this.

Then he stepped forward.

It had been so long since he'd been inside a spacecraft that the artificial gravity surprised him. He stumbled and had to grab a railing. When he straightened back up, a woman stood in front of him, watching him critically. No, not a woman. He could see through her, as if she were a ghost.

She had a massive mane of white hair, and eyes that could cut through carbon steel. Her smile was not warm.

"Hello, Dr Zhang," she said. "Might I speak with my daughter?"

# 122

"Don't be stupid, girl. Of course I'm dead. You were there when I died." Ekaterina sighed and turned to face the windows that looked out from the fore end of the bridge. "You might even be said to be responsible. I wouldn't be in this condition if you hadn't stolen the basilisk from me."

"Stolen..." Petrova shook her head. Now was not the time to argue about such things. "If you're dead, then how..."

"I forgot how long it takes you to grasp simple concepts," Ekaterina said. "I'm a ghost."

"Like Parker," Rapscallion suggested, his dangling face smiling. Petrova smiled back. She knew he was trying to be helpful.

"Captain Parker," Ekaterina said, "was a test subject. The system that recorded his memories and generated a simulacrum of his person turned out to work wonderfully. I always intended to be the first user once the concept was proven. Living forever appeals to me, for all the boring old reasons."

"It turned out there were a few bugs in the system," Petrova suggested.

Ekaterina shrugged. "I'll take immortality however I can get it. When I died, I was automatically re-created in the processor cores of this ship."

"This ship, yes," Petrova said. "Which came from where, exactly?"

"Oh, I always had it waiting, out at the edge of the system.

When they exiled me here, I wanted to have a way back to Earth if things went badly. Lucky for us all I possessed such foresight."

Petrova shook her head. Of course. Her mother always thought three steps ahead of everyone else. Even in her autumn years she was devious. Of course she would have an escape plan from forced retirement. And death as well, it seemed.

"Once I realized you'd safely landed on Paradise-1, I came here as soon as I could. Looks like I'm too late to salvage things. Ah, well. It was too much to hope that you and your friends would bring things to a satisfying conclusion."

"Mother," Petrova said, trying to stay cool, "do you have any idea what we were up against?"

"I know everything, Sashenka. That was my job, after all."

"Your job." Petrova couldn't believe this. "You mean running Firewatch. Mother—did you know Lang was a Lunarist? Back when she exiled you. Did you know?"

"I had my suspicions. Nothing I could prove. I was about to denounce her when she made her big power play. I've always wondered if she knew I was onto her, or if she attacked me out of sheer ambition. It's always nice to find out you were right all along."

Petrova fumed in exasperation. "Who cares if you were right? Who cares who won? You and Lang, you're exactly the same. This is all just a game to you!"

"Not quite the same. We played off each other to see who was better at this business. And in the end, I lost. She's very good at politics. I'll grudgingly admit she's gotten the better of me this time. And now we have to stop her."

"We have to . . . Wait," Zhang said, standing up very suddenly. "We're going to stop her?"

"We're going to try, yes. You're the only people I have to work with at the moment, you three." Ekaterina did not look particularly pleased by her options.

"No," Zhang said. "No, we don't have time for power plays.

We don't have time to worry about who's in charge of what division of the UEG. Erebus is loose. It's out there — it's out *there*," he repeated, pointing at the windows, at the sky. "Up to who knows what."

"Nothing good, certainly," Ekaterina said.

"Right," Zhang agreed. "So no, we aren't going after Lang. We're going wherever Erebus is."

Behind Petrova, the spacecraft's hatch closed with a whine of hydraulics. The floor under her throbbed and pulsed as the ship's engines came online. In a moment they were airborne, headed for space.

"The thing is," Ekaterina said, "we can do both. Since I know where Erebus is headed."

"And where's that?" Petrova asked. Unsurprised, somehow.

"Earth, of course," Ekaterina said. "And we should really pray that we get there first."

# ACKNOWLEDGEMENTS

This book is based on ideas derived by the Orbit UK staff, especially James Long, who also edited the manuscript. It benefited enormously from a thorough copy edit by Jane Selley and the efforts of Blanche Craig. I would also like to thank my agent, Danny Baror, and finally, all the readers who waited so patiently to find out what happened next. Sorry it took so long – I hope it was worth the wait!

# extras

# meet the author

DAVID WELLINGTON is an acclaimed author who has previously published over twenty novels in different genres. His novel *The Last Astronaut* was shortlisted for the Arthur C. Clarke Award.

Find out more about David Wellington and other Orbit authors by registering for the free monthly newsletter at orbitbooks.net.

# if you enjoyed
# REVENANT-X

look out for

# THE BLIGHTED STARS
## Book One of the Devoured Worlds

by

## Megan E. O'Keefe

**She's a revolutionary.** *Humanity is running out of options. Habitable planets are being destroyed as quickly as they're found, and Naira Sharp thinks the reason may have something to do with the all-powerful Mercator family.*

**He's the heir to the dynasty.** *Bookish and quiet, Tarquin Mercator never wanted to get involved with his family's galaxy-spanning business empire. But Tarquin's father needs him to monitor an expedition to a new planet, and the Mercator family reputation hangs on the success of this mission.*

*Disguised as Tarquin's new bodyguard, Naira plans to destroy the expedition ship before they make land. But neither of them expects to end up stranded on a dead planet. To survive, Naira will have to join forces with the handsome heir she's sworn to hate. Together they will uncover a plot that's bigger than both of them.*

**extras**

# ONE

# Tarquin

## *The* Amaranth

Tarquin Mercator stood on the command bridge of the finest spaceship his father had ever built and hoped he wasn't about to make a fool of himself. Serious people crewed the console podiums all around him, wrist-deep in holos that managed systems Tarquin was reasonably certain he could *name*, but there ended the extent of his knowledge. The intricate inner workings of a state-of-the-art spaceship were hardly topics covered during his geology studies.

Despite Tarquin's lack of expertise, being Acaelus Mercator's son placed him as second-in-command. Below Acaelus, and above the remarkably more qualified mission captain, a stern woman named Paison.

That captain was looking at him now—expectant, deferential. Thin, golden pathways resembling circuitry glittered on her skin, printed into her current body to aid her as a pilot. Sweat beaded between Tarquin's shoulder blades.

"My liege," Captain Paison said, all practiced obeisance, and while he desperately wished that she was addressing his father, her light grey eyes didn't move from Tarquin. "We are approximately an hour's flight from the prearranged landing site. Would you like to release the orbital survey drone network?"

## extras

Tarquin hoped his relief didn't show. Scouting the planet for deposits of relkatite was the one job for which he felt firmly footed.

"Yes, Captain. Do we have visual on the planet?"

"Not yet, my liege." She expanded a vast holographic display from her console, revealing the cloud-draped world below. "The weather is against us, but the drone network should be able to punch through it in the next few hours."

"Hold off on landing until I can confirm our preliminary survey data. We wouldn't want to put the ship down too far from a viable mining site."

Polite chuckles all around. Tarquin forced a smile at their faux camaraderie and pulled up a holo from his own console, reviewing the data the survey drones had retrieved before the mining ships *Amaranth* and *Einkorn* had taken flight for the tedious eight-month voyage to Sixth Cradle.

Not that he'd been awake for that journey. His mind and the minds of the entire crew had been safely stored away in the ship's databases, automated systems in place to print key personnel when they drew within range of low-planet orbit. When food was so expensive, there was no point in feeding people who weren't needed to work during the trip.

Tarquin's father put a hand on his shoulder and gave him a friendly shake. "Excited to see a cradle world?"

"I can't wait," he said honestly. When he'd been a child, Tarquin's mother had taken him to Second Cradle shortly before its collapse. Those memories of that rare, Earthlike world were vague. Tarquin smiled up into eyes a slightly darker shade of hazel than his own.

At nearly 160 years old, Acaelus chose to strike an imposing figure with his prints—tall, solidly built, a shock of pure white hair that hinted at his advanced age. It was difficult to look into that face and see anything but the father he'd known as a child—stern but kind. A man who'd fought to have Tarquin's mind mapped as early as possible so that he could be printed into a body that better suited him after the one he'd been born into hadn't quite fit.

Hard to see through that, to the man whose iron will and vast fortune leashed thousands to his command.

"My liege," Captain Paison said, a wary edge to her voice, "I apologize, but it appears there was an error in the system. The survey drones have been released already, or perhaps were never loaded into place."

"What?" Tarquin accessed those systems via his own console. Sure enough, the drone bays were empty. "How could that have happened?"

"I—I can't say, my liege," Paison said.

The fear in her voice soured Tarquin's stomach. Before he could assure her that it wasn't her fault, Acaelus took over.

"This is unacceptable," his father said. The crew turned as one to duck their heads to him. Acaelus's scowl cut through them all, and he pointed to an engineer. "You. Go, scour the ship for the drones and load them properly. I expect completion within the hour, and an accounting of whose failure led to this."

"Yes, my liege." The engineer tucked into a deep bow and then turned on their heel, whole body taut with nervous energy. Tarquin suspected that as soon as they were on the other side of the door, they'd break into a sprint.

"It was just a mistake," Tarquin said.

"Mercator employees do not make mistakes of this magnitude," Acaelus said, loud enough for everyone to hear. "Whoever is responsible will lose their cuffs, and if I catch anyone covering for the responsible party, they will lose theirs, too."

"That's unnecessary," Tarquin said, and immediately regretted it as his father turned his icy stare upon him. Acaelus clutched his shoulder, this time without the friendly intent, fingers digging into Tarquin's muscle.

"Leave the running of Mercator to me, my boy," he said, softly enough not to be overheard but with the same firm inflection.

Tarquin nodded, ashamed to be cowed so quickly but unable to help it. His father was a colossus, an institution unto himself, a force of nature. Tarquin was just a scholar. The running of the family wasn't his burden to carry. Acaelus released his shoulder and set to barking further orders with the brisk efficiency of long years of rule.

He gripped the edges of his console podium, staring at the bands printed around his wrists in Mercator green. Relkatite green. The cuffs meant you worked for Mercator's interests, and Mercator's alone. And while the work was grueling, it guaranteed regular meals. Medical care. Housing. Your phoenix fees paid, if your print was destroyed. The other ruling corporate families—who collectively called themselves MERIT—had their own colored cuffs. A rainbow of fealty.

Working for the families of MERIT kept people safe, in all the ways that mattered. While his father could be brusque, and at times even cruel, Acaelus did these things only out of a desire to ensure that safety.

The cuffs around Tarquin's wrists came with more than the promise of safety. Mercator's crest flowed up from those bands to wrap over the backs of his hands and twist between his fingers. The family gloves marked him as a blooded Mercator. Not a mere employee, but in the direct line of succession. Someone to be obeyed. Feared. His knuckles paled.

"Straighten up," Acaelus said.

Tarquin peeled his hands away from the console and regained his composure, slipping the aristocratic mask of indifference back on, then set to work reviewing the data the ship had collected since entering Sixth Cradle's orbit.

Alarms blared on the bridge. Tarquin jerked his head up, startled by the flashing red lights and the sharp squeal of a siren. On the largest display, the one that'd previously shown a dreamy landscape of fluffy clouds under the brush of golden morning light, the words TARGET LOCKED glared in crimson text.

That wasn't possible. There wasn't supposed to be anyone here except the *Amaranth* and its twin, the *Einkorn*. Of the five ruling corporate families, none but Mercator could even build ships capable of beating them here.

"Evade and report," Acaelus ordered.

Captain Paison flung her arms out, tossing holo screens to the copilots flanking her, and the peaceful clouds were replaced with shield reports, weapons systems, and evasion programs. There was no enemy ship that he could see. A firestorm of activity kicked off, and while Tarquin knew, logically, that they'd rolled, the ship suppressed any sensation of motion.

"It's the *Einkorn*, my liege." The captain's voice was strained from her effort.

"Who's awake over there?" Acaelus demanded.

"No one should be, my liege," the *Amaranth*'s medical officer said. Their freckled face was pale.

"Someone over there doesn't like us," the woman to Paison's right said between gritted teeth. "Conservators?"

"It's not their MO," said a broad-chested man in the grey uniform of the Human Collective Army. "But it's possible. Should I check on the security around the warpcore?"

"I iced Ex. Sharp," Acaelus said. "Without her to guide them, the Conservators are nothing but flies to be swatted. Captain, continue evasion and hail the *Einkorn*."

Tarquin cast a sideways glance at Ex. Kearns, Acaelus's current bodyguard and constant shadow. The exemplar had the face of a shovel, as broad and intimidating as the rest of him, and he didn't react to the mention of his ex-partner, Ex. Sharp. It had to sting, having the woman he'd worked side by side with turn against them all and start bombing Mercator's ships and warehouses.

The fact that Naira Sharp had been captured and her neural map locked away didn't erase the specter of the threat she posed. Her conspirators, the Conservators, were still out there, and Tarquin found Acaelus's quick dismissal of the possibility of their involvement odd.

The HCA soldier was right. They really should send someone down to check on the warpcore. Overloading the cores was the Conservators' primary method of destruction. Tarquin rallied himself to say as much, but Paison spoke first.

### extras

"My liege," she said, "the *Einkorn*'s assault may be a malfunction. The *Amaranth*'s controls aren't responding properly. I can't—"

Metal shrieked. The floor quaked. Ex. Kearns surged in front of them and shoved Tarquin dead center in the chest. The world tipped and Tarquin's feet flew out from under him. He struck the ground on his side. Something slammed into him from above, stealing his half-voiced shout.

Tarquin blinked, head buzzing, a painful throb radiating from his hips where a piece of the console podium he'd been working at seconds before had landed. Red and yellow lights strobed, warning of the damage done, but no breach alarms sounded.

Groaning, he shook his head to clear it. The impact had pitched people up against the walls. Seats and bits of console podiums scattered the ground. Across the room, Paison and another woman helped each other back to their feet.

"Son!" Acaelus dropped to his knees beside him. Tarquin was astonished to see a cut mar his father's forehead, dripping blood. "Are you all right?"

Tarquin moved experimentally, and though his side throbbed, his health pathways were already healing the damage and supplying him with painkillers. "Just bruised. What happened?"

"A direct hit." Acaelus took Tarquin's face in his hands, examining him, then looked over his shoulder and shouted, "Kearns!"

Kearns removed the piece of podium from Tarquin's side and helped him to his feet. Tarquin brushed dust off his clothes and tried to get ahold of himself while, all around him, chaos brewed. Kearns limped, his left leg dragging, and Tarquin grimaced. Exemplars were loaded with pathways keyed to combat. For one of them to show pain, the wound had to be bad.

Tarquin nudged a broken chunk of the console podium with the toe of his boot. A piece of the ceiling had come down, crushing the podiums, and it would have crushed Acaelus and Tarquin both if Kearns hadn't intervened, taking the brunt of the hit on his own legs.

A knot formed in his throat as he recognized the damage Kearns had taken on their behalf. Tarquin had never been in anything like real danger before, and he desperately missed his primary exemplar, Caldweller, but that man's neural map was still in storage. Acaelus had deemed Kearns enough to cover both of them until they reached the planet.

None of them could have accounted for this.

"My liege," Kearns said in tones that didn't invite argument, "I suggest we move to a more secure location immediately."

"Agreed," Acaelus said. "Captain, what's the damage?"

"Uhhh..." Paison squinted at one of the few consoles that'd survived the impact. "The *Einkorn*'s rail guns tore through the stabilization column. This ship won't hold together much longer."

Brittle silence followed that announcement, the roughed-up crew exchanging looks or otherwise staring at the damaged bridge like they could wind back time. Tarquin studied his father, trying to read anything in the mask Acaelus wore in crisis, and saw nothing but grim resolve wash over him. Acaelus grabbed Tarquin's arm and turned him around.

"Very well. With me, all of you, we're evacuating this ship."

Tarquin stumbled along beside his father, half in a daze. Kearns assumed smooth control of the situation, sliding into his place at the top of security's chain of command. Merc-Sec and the HCA soldiers organized under Kearns's barked orders, forming a defensive column around the rest. Paison threw a brief, longing glance at her command post before falling in with the others. Tarquin found himself in the center of a crush of people, not entirely certain how he'd gotten there.

How had they gone from looking at fluffy clouds to fleeing for their lives in less than ten minutes?

The HCA soldier next to him, the one who'd said this wasn't the Conservators' MO, caught his eye and gave him a quick, reassuring smile. Tarquin mustered up the ability to smile back and read the man's name badge—DAWD, REGAR. That meager kindness reminded him that there was more at stake than his worries. These people had put their lives in the hands of Mercator.

## extras

If they died here, they could be reprinted later, but every death increased one's chance of one's neural map cracking the next time it was printed. Neural maps were never perfect; they degraded over time. Traumatic deaths sped the process exponentially, as even the best-shielded backups were never entirely disentangled from the active map.

As if there were fine threads of connection between all backups and the living mind, and sufficient trauma could reverberate out to them all.

Some people came up screaming, and never stopped. Some got caught in time loops, unsure which moment of their lives they were really living through. Neither state was survivable.

Tarquin summoned the scraps of his courage and stood straighter. He had no business in a crisis, but the employees looked to him for assurance. His terror no doubt added to their anxiety, and that was selfish of him.

Something metal groaned in the walls, taunting his ability to hold it together. Tarquin cast an irritated glance at the complaining ship. If only ships would fall in line as easily as people.

Acaelus pulled up a holo from his forearm, but whatever he saw there was blurred by his privacy filters. The information carved a scowl into his face. He slowed and swiped his ID pathway over the door to a lab, unlocking it.

"Everyone, in here," he said.

They hesitated. Paison said, "My liege, the shuttle isn't far from here."

"I'm aware of the layout of my own ship, Captain. Get in, all of you, and wait. I've just received notice that Ex. Lockhart's print order went through. I won't allow my exemplar to awaken to a dying ship. You will go into this lab, and you will wait for my return."

That wasn't right. The secondary printing round wasn't automated; it needed to be initiated. Tarquin frowned, watching the crew shift uncomfortably. Every one of them knew Acaelus was telling a half-truth at best, but none of them were willing to say it.

There was a slim possibility that whatever was causing the other errors had triggered this, but making all these people wait while Acaelus collected one person was a waste of time.

"My liege." Paison stepped forward, squaring off her shoulders. "I can't guarantee this ship will last that long, and we require your command keys to open the hangar airlock."

"I am aware, and you are delaying. Get in the lab."

They shuffled inside without another word, though they were all watching Acaelus warily. The terror of offending their boss was greater than the fear of being left behind to die. You could come back from death. You could never re-cuff for Mercator after being fired. The door shut, leaving Tarquin and his father alone with Kearns. Tarquin's head pounded.

"What are you doing?" he demanded in a soft hiss. "Ex. Lockhart can handle herself. We have to get these people out."

Acaelus shoved him down the hallway. "*We* need to get out. I printed Lockhart to help Kearns handle the crew, but you and I are going to cast our maps back and exit this situation, because I don't know what's happened here, and I'm not risking your map."

Tarquin dug his heels in, drawing his father to a halt. "We can't just leave. I'm not going to allow the Conservators to run us off before I have proof the mining process is safe."

"If this was the Conservators, then we'd already be dead. All the nonfamily printing bays just went active, and I *do not know* who is coming out of those bays. We have to leave. Kearns and Lockhart will handle the rest."

Tarquin rubbed his eyes in frustration. "We can't abandon the mission."

"We can, and we are. Come. This is hardly the place for an argument."

Acaelus jerked on his arm. Tarquin stumbled after him, mind reeling. Sixth Cradle was supposed to be his mission. Supposed to be the moment Tarquin stood up for his family and finally squashed all those squalid rumors Ex. Sharp had started when she'd claimed the relkatite mining process was killing worlds.

### extras

While a great deal of what his family had to do to ensure their survival was distasteful, Tarquin was absolutely certain the mining process was safe. He'd refined it himself. Mining Sixth Cradle and leaving it green and thriving was meant to be the final nail in the coffin of those accusations. The one thing he could do for his family that was *useful*.

He wouldn't run. Not this time. Not like he had when his mother had died and he'd fled to university to bury himself in his studies, instead of facing the suffering that weighed on his father's and sister's hearts.

"I'm sorry, Dad, I won't—"

"Kearns, carry him," Acaelus said.

Tarquin was thirty-five years old, second in line to the most powerful position in the universe, and Ex. Kearns scooped him up like he was little more than luggage and tossed him over his shoulder without a flash of hesitation, because Acaelus Mercator had demanded it. Kearns's shoulder dug into Tarquin's ribs, pressing a startled grunt out of him. His cheeks burned with indignity.

"I'm not a child," Tarquin snapped, surprised at the edge in his tone. He never raised his voice to his father.

"You are *my* child, and you will do as I say."

Acaelus didn't bother to look at him. Tarquin closed his eyes, letting out a slow sigh of defeat. There was no arguing with his father when he'd made up his mind. He opened his eyes, and temporarily forgot how to breathe. The door to one of the staff printing bays yawned open, and it wasn't people who emerged from that space. Not exactly.

Their faces were close to human, but something had gone off in the printing. A mouth set too far right. An ear sprouting from the side of a neck. An arm that bent the wrong way around. Half a chest cavity missing.

Misprints. Empties. An error in the printer slapping together a hodgepodge of human parts. The *Amaranth* wouldn't have tried putting a neural map into any of those bodies, but whatever had caused the malfunction had also made the ship release the prints instead of disintegrating them into their constituent parts, as was protocol for a misprint.

What was left of those faces twisted, drew into vicious snarls.

"Kearns," Tarquin hissed in a sharp whisper. His voice was alarmed enough that the exemplar turned.

Kearns pulled his sidearm and fired. The earsplitting roar of the shot in such a small space slammed into Tarquin's ears, but his pathways adjusted, keeping him from going temporarily deaf. The misprints shrieked with what throats and lungs they had, and rushed them. Kearns rolled Tarquin off his shoulder and shoved him back.

Tarquin stumbled, but his father caught him and then spun, pushing him ahead. "Run!"

Fear stripped away all his reservations and Tarquin ran, pounding down the hallways for the family's private printing bay, praying that he wouldn't find the same thing there.

Kearns's weapon roared again and again, a staccato rhythm drowning out the screams of the misprints. He looked over his shoulder to find Acaelus right behind him, Kearns farther back, his injured leg slowing him down. Tarquin faced forward and sprinted—the door to the printing bay was *just* ahead.

Kearns's gun fell silent. His father screamed.

Tarquin whirled around. Acaelus was chest-down on the ground, misprints swarming over him, their teeth and nails digging into his skin, ripping free bloody chunks. He took a step toward them, not knowing what he could possibly do, and Acaelus looked up, face set with determination as he flung out a hand.

"Go home!" he ordered.

He met his father's eyes. Acaelus pushed his tongue against the inside of his cheek, making it bulge out in warning. New terror struck Tarquin. High-ranking members of the corporate families often wore small, personal explosive devices on the interior side of a molar to use in case someone intending to crack their neural maps attacked them. Acaelus had one.

Tarquin fled. He burst through the printing bay door and

slammed it shut behind him, leaning his back against it, breathing harder than he ever had in his life. The explosion was designed to be small. It whumped against the door, tickling his senses.

A gruesome way to die, but it was swift. Gentler suicide pathways had been tried, but they had a nasty habit of malfunctioning. Pathways remained frustratingly unpredictable at times.

He swallowed. The staff back on Mercator Station would reprint Acaelus the second they received notice that his tracker pathway had been destroyed and his visual feed had cut. His father would be fine. Tarquin forced himself away from the door, shaking.

One of the printing cubicles was lit red to indicate it was in use. He crossed to the map backup station and picked up the crown of electronics, running it between his hands.

Tarquin knew he wasn't what his father had wanted. He lacked the clear-eyed ruthlessness of his elder sister, Leka. He couldn't stand to watch people cower beneath the threat of his ire as Acaelus so often had to do to keep their employees in line. His singular concession to being a Mercator was that his love of geology and subsequent studies had aided the family in their hunt for relkatite.

His father never complained about Tarquin's lack of participation in family politics. Acaelus had given Tarquin everything he'd ever asked for and had only ever asked for one thing in return.

When Naira Sharp had been captured and put to trial, Tarquin had taken the stand to prove her accusations false. As a Mercator, as the foremost expert in his field of study, he had disproved all her allegations that Mercator's mining processes destroyed worlds.

It hadn't stopped the rumors. Hadn't stopped the other families of MERIT from looking askance at Mercator and asking themselves if, maybe, they wouldn't be better off without them.

They needed to mine a cradle world and leave it thriving in their wake to put the rumors to bed once and for all.

Tarquin could still give his father that proof, but he couldn't do it alone. Not with misprints infesting the halls and the potential of a saboteur on the loose. He needed an exemplar.

## extras

He set the backup crown down and crossed to the printing bay control console, checking the progress on Lockhart's print. Ninety seconds left. Enough time to compose himself. Enough time, he hoped, to get to the planet after she'd finished printing.

Tarquin had never disobeyed a direct order from his father before, and he hoped he wasn't making a colossal mistake.

# extras

# TWO

# Naira

# *The* Amaranth

It wasn't the first time Naira Sharp had awoken in the wrong body, but it was the first time she had done so with the acrid reek of burning plastics in the air. People said that the first thing you saw in a new body set the tone for how that life would be lived, but Naira had been brought back often enough in the relkatite-green cubicles of her enemy that she'd abandoned visual superstition for olfactory. A decision she regretted right about now.

Naira lifted her arms and found them medium brown and well muscled, tapering to wrists banded in the green cuffs that marked this body as an employee of Mercator. The stranger's skin glittered with pathways, golden implants reminiscent of circuitry. An experimental flexing of those pathways revealed they enhanced strength and agility.

An icy sensation built behind her eyes.

*Breathe.* She'd dropped into dozens of different bodies, and though this wasn't the one she'd expected, its shape was surprisingly close to her preferred print. A little shorter, maybe. A little sturdier.

She'd been counting on waking up in the freshly printed body of Acaelus Mercator. Something had gone wrong, but this body wouldn't stop her.

Because the fact she'd been printed at all meant that Kav had done it. He'd gotten her map off ice in time for the Sixth Cradle mission. She'd slipped Acaelus's control at last.

Naira was free.

She planted pathway-enhanced legs against the hatch at the foot of her cubicle and shoved. Discarded biomatrix sloshed as the tray she'd been printed onto rocketed out, barely catching on the rails. Fresh air burned into her lungs, all at once refreshing and astringent.

"Whoa. Ex. Lockhart, are you all right?" a man asked.

Her pathways adjusted her vision, taking away the sting from the bright lights. She didn't recognize the name, but she knew the title of exemplar. That solved the mystery of why she was crammed full of high-end combat pathways.

Naira rolled off the tray and dropped into a crouch, the cold floor shocking some of the haze from her mind. Slowly, she stood, flexing each muscle one by one. The circuit board lines mapping her skin glittered as she stretched.

"What's happened?" she asked, to give herself time to think.

"I don't know," the man said. He stood by the printer control terminal and slid a panel closed before turning around to face her.

Dark brown hair fell to the edge of his jaw in wavy chunks, partially hiding an angular face with soft hazel eyes and thick eyebrows. The man's demeanor lacked the arrogance common to his family, but there was no hiding the aristocratic lift to his chin, the aquiline nose.

Tarquin Mercator. Youngest child of Acaelus Mercator. Geologist, recluse. She'd never crossed paths with him when she'd been an exemplar.

But he'd crossed her, when he'd testified against her at the trial.

The basic facts of his dossier spun through Naira's mind, something to hold on to so that she wouldn't break him between her bare hands, punish him for taking the stand and explaining, with that faux-charm common to his family, that she'd been mistaken. That his family's mining practices couldn't be responsible for the contagion that collapsed ecosystems.

That killed worlds.

Naira wasn't here for him. She was here to stop this ship. To keep Mercator lies from destroying yet another viable planet. He might have information and access that could help her accomplish those goals. It was a near thing, though, not indulging the urge to wring his neck.

"The *Einkorn* fired on us. We can't raise them on comms," Tarquin said.

"Situation on board?" She opened a bulkhead panel and pulled out a set of light body armor. The fibers went on baggy, then adjusted to conform to her body. The interior of her forearm lit up briefly, then turned clear, revealing the network system integrated with the skin of her arm. She flicked her gaze through the display, checking permissions. Ex. Lockhart had almost as much clearance as Acaelus. She could work with that.

Tarquin twisted his fingers together. "It's a mess, E-X. There are *living* misprints roaming the halls, attacking people. I have a group of survivors that need an escort to an escape shuttle before the ship tears itself apart."

Misprints assaulting people sounded highly unlikely. She needed someone who actually knew what was going on. "Where's Liege Acaelus?"

"Dead."

"His print failed?"

"He was printed. He lived. He and Ex. Kearns are both dead. We have to *go*."

Her stomach swooped with the sway of the ship as the *Amaranth* lurched to one side. Red and yellow warning lights painted the printing bay in a sickly glow. The artificial gravity stuttered, filling the air with the harsh scent of ozone even as her weight vacillated between boulder heavy and feather light.

Destroying the relkatite containment of the ship's warpcore had been the Conservators' plan. The plan, however, had not included her being on the ship at the time. And it certainly wasn't supposed to go in fits and starts like this.

The surge passed, leaving her panting with her hands on her knees. Tarquin slouched against the console podium he'd been working at, holding on for dear life. His complexion was wan and sweaty.

"That's new," he gritted out between his teeth and forced himself to stand.

"Warpcore's damaged," she said matter-of-factly, ripping open another bulkhead to find—ah yes, perfect—a wide selection of rifles and handguns. She selected a few weapons, strapped them on, then gave Tarquin a once-over.

"Can you run?"

"Yes." He brushed a hand through his sweaty hair.

"Good. Follow me. Where are the other exemplars?"

"You're the only one. There's just a skeleton crew. We entered low-planet orbit five hours ago."

"Then who the hell attacked the ship?"

"I really don't know."

Naira swiped up a map on her print's built-in HUD. She put a pin in the location of the nearest shuttle, then switched her rifle to crowd-control mode. The last thing she wanted to do was accidentally kill any of her team. Naira stepped into the hallway.

Smoke hung thick in the air, stinging the back of her throat. Remnants of a small explosion painted the walls in greasy soot and gore. The *Amaranth* shuddered again, making her stumble, and she got a hand against the wall to steady herself as a group of people tore around the corner, rushing her.

Her blood ran cold. Blank faces stared at her even as they sped up, empty eyes tracking her every movement with less personality than a rock. Misprints. She really hadn't believed Tarquin's report, and found herself grudgingly impressed that the princeling hadn't dissolved into sobbing panic.

Naira switched back to lethal and fired without a second thought.

"Let's go," she said to Tarquin once she'd dealt with the misprints. "Stay behind me."

### extras

He edged into the hallway, throat bobbing as he followed. A little too tight on her heels, but she couldn't blame him and didn't have the time to tell him to back off. The HUD implanted in this print kept her updated on the *Amaranth*'s systems, and Naira didn't like the amount of red in the display.

This ship was dying, and not in the tidy way the Conservators had planned. The *Einkorn*'s rail guns had torn through the ship's stabilizers. She scanned the damage as she marched down the hall, checking her corners.

The hit was too clean, not a random misfire caused by the AI glitching. Whoever had fired from the *Einkorn* wanted the *Amaranth* not just destroyed, but crashed into Sixth Cradle. It'd kill everyone on board, but it'd also risk contaminating the planet with Mercator's mining materials, priming it for the same collapse syndrome that infected the other cradles.

Naira clenched her jaw. She was a killer in a war few believed in, but this wanton destruction of both the human life on board *and* the planet wasn't something she or the other Conservators would endorse.

If it wasn't the Conservators, then who? Was she really free of Acaelus? Until she could rendezvous with her team and confirm the state of her neural map, she needed to stay alive. Otherwise, she might find herself back on ice.

And then the next time she woke it'd be in Acaelus's labs, the subject of his experiments.

"E-X, wait." Tarquin jogged up alongside her, and she bit back a remark about him staying behind as he swiped a hand over a door panel.

The door opened into a lab. A quick head count put the population inside at around fifty people. Mostly Mercator personnel, though five wore the gold-crested flak jacket and grey cuffs of the Human Collective Army.

Naira almost smirked at the HCA soldiers, but stopped herself. Acaelus must have hated being forced to bring the HCA on his mining missions to "oversee" the process after she'd outed him for killing worlds.

She extended two fingers and pressed them against the top of her thigh, the signal the Conservators currently used to identify one another when inhabiting prints not their own. No one reacted to the gesture, so she turned it into a stretch.

"Liege Tarquin," said a wiry woman inside the lab. She slammed a hand down over a holo to close it, but not before Naira caught a glimpse of what she'd been working on.

She'd had the controls to the hangar airlock open, doors that could only be unlocked by Mercator command keys due to the shroud protection protocols. Naira glanced at the woman's jacket—CAPTAIN PAISON. The mission commander had been trying to find a way around Acaelus's lockout. Naira liked her immediately.

Paison covered her surprise with a deep bow, and the confident posture Naira had seen seconds before melted away into practiced obedience. The others followed suit. At least this print kept her off the hook when it came to bowing to Tarquin. Exemplars didn't look away from their charges. She'd have to remember to refer to the little shit by his title, though.

"We stayed put, as your father ordered," Paison said, deftly reminding Tarquin that she was a loyal employee, "but we heard gunfire. Where is Liege Acaelus?"

"My father and Ex. Kearns are dead," Tarquin said. "Please follow Ex. Lockhart's guidance as we evacuate."

"Group up," Naira said. "This ship has another five minutes of life left."

"Yes, E-X." Paison gave her a salute that was arguably more deferential than the bow she'd given Tarquin.

The ship groaned, metal tearing somewhere. Heat rushed down the hall, her pathway-heightened senses picking up on it a second before the wall of flame hit.

Naira pivoted, rusty instincts kicking to the surface, and grabbed Tarquin in both arms, folding her shorter but stronger body over his as she slammed him against the wall. He smelled pleasantly of sun-soaked sandstone, which was rather irritating, as her enemy shouldn't be allowed to smell like anything *nice*.

Fire licked up her hips and scoured through her light armor, chasing all thoughts away. Blisters bubbled across her back. Naira hissed, pain making her breath short as agony wrapped searing fingers around her and then—in a flash—was gone, the fire burned out as the suppression system kicked on, showering them all in chemical foam.

She released the princeling and staggered away, bracing one hand against the opposite wall. Char painted everything void-dark, grey flecks of suppression foam drifting through the air. Naira focused on the visuals, because to sink back into the base sensations of her body was to start screaming, and she had to hold it together. Had to get off this ship.

"E-X," Tarquin said, shoving a hand over his mouth to stifle his revulsion. Cooked meat perfumed the air. "Your pathways, are they damaged?"

Right, she'd almost forgotten. The circuit board patterns on her skin tickled as they vibrated, responding to her will, and dulled the exquisite edge of pain.

It would take time for the singed edges of the pathways on her back to build up enough skin for them to regenerate themselves fully, but the pain abatement would keep her moving. She checked her HUD. Three minutes until the *Amaranth* stopped listing and started dropping.

"I'll hold." She forced herself to stand straight, to take her hand away from the wall, testing her ability to stay on her feet.

The seared muscles of her back stretched with the motion, sparking fresh shock waves of pain. She trembled, cold sweat coating everywhere she still had skin, her teeth chattering with the beginnings of shock.

Naira ordered the pathways to flood her with all the painkillers they could synth, and her head spun with dizzy euphoria.

Tarquin touched her unburnt forearm lightly and met her gaze, holding her rifle out to her. "We have to keep moving."

Naira nodded as she took the rifle and stopped herself from slinging the strap over her back at the last second. She dialed back the painkillers. Even though every step was agony, she couldn't fight while high as a satellite.

"Form up," she barked into the lab. "We're running."

"What the fuck was that?" one of the Merc-Sec asked.

"An explosion. Crashing ships have those. Move your ass if you don't want to experience a bigger version."

She didn't wait to see if the others followed. She grabbed Tarquin by the back of his jacket and shoved him forward. Footsteps rushed after them, scurrying to keep up, and she heard someone sob softly. Someone else started vomiting. The vibration in her pathways mounted, a persistent ache, but ignorable, considering everything else.

Tarquin swiped them into a hangar. An Arrow-class shuttle waited, surrounded by pallets of supplies meant for the first expedition to the planet. Her grip tightened around the rifle. They didn't have time to load the supplies. They'd have to make do with what they found on the planet. Which could get... complicated.

The doorframe was aglow with blue lights, indicating the hangar was free of shroud spore. Good. As desperate as Naira was to escape Acaelus, she would have let them all die with the *Amaranth* if it meant protecting the planet from shroud contamination.

"Board. Now," Naira ordered. "Liege Tarquin, please enter your command keys into the control podium to release the airlock, then take a seat."

"I can do that, E-X," he said, overly eager, then hurried up the gangway.

Naira shook her head at his back and turned to Captain Paison. The captain eyed her warily, no doubt worried that Naira had seen what she'd been doing on that holo. With her grey eyes downcast and an affected slouch to her shoulders, she made herself unassuming. Nonthreatening. Clever woman.

Naira put one hand on Paison's shoulder. She lowered her voice. "Can you get this shuttle to ground?"

"Yes, but I was only escorting these people. If the *Amaranth* is going down, I'm going with it."

# extras

"Captain Paison," she whispered, "bullshit. I saw what you were doing, and I'll keep my mouth shut if you get us all down safely."

Paison's nostrils flared. She lifted her eyes to meet Naira's, and Naira glimpsed the steel in her spine. The confidence she'd seen in the seconds before Paison had realized who had walked back into that lab. Slowly, she nodded.

"Copy that, E-X." Paison jogged up the gangway, Naira right behind her.

Ninety-seven seconds. Naira slapped the button for an emergency takeoff and the shuttle's gangway dropped, clanging to the ground, as the double doors of the airlock slammed shut.

"E-X," one of the Merc-Sec called to her from their seat. "Strap in!"

She craned her neck around, eyed the harnesses over the seats, and suppressed a shudder. No way was she putting her raw back against a seat, let alone strapping on a harness.

Naira went into the cockpit and stood between the copilot's seat and console podium. The podium raised to account for her standing. Paison glanced up and nodded to her, sliding over a command screen from her console. Naira bent her knees, lowering her center of gravity, and activated her pathways, sending strength into her legs. Taking some of the strength away from her back stung like hell, but it'd be worse in the chair, where the friction would do more damage.

"Integrity check clear. We are sealed and ready for vacuum," Naira said, flicking through the holographic displays.

"Spooling engines," Paison said.

The shuttle's engines thrummed to life, vibrating through the floor. The soles of her boots softened. Naira sank slightly as the boots switched over to the sticky mode that would allow her to cling in place when they lost gravity from the larger ship.

"We're green to go," Paison said. The shuttle lifted from the floor. "Opening hangar airlock."

In the corner of her eye, Naira's HUD countdown to ship destabilization flashed red. She closed the warning so she could focus on the screens in front of her.

"What the—?" Paison cut herself off.

Naira followed Paison's line of sight. The internal hangar door had opened, and a man strode into the room. The strobing red lights that warned of imminent depressurization obscured his features.

"Fuck." Paison reached for the airlock controls.

"Continue," Naira ordered.

"But—"

"It's too late to let him on board. The *Amaranth* is going to drop like a rock in seconds."

Paison's fingers curled into ineffectual fists over her console display. It was true. She knew it was true. That didn't make it any easier.

The man looked up, right at them, squinting through the tinted glass as if he could see them. Maybe he could. The skin of his face glittered with the presence of exemplar pathways.

He met Naira's stare, pressed two fingers against his thigh, and winked.

The hangar opened, and the shuttle was yanked out into the thin air of low-planet orbit.

## Follow us:

**f** /orbitbooksUS

**X** /orbitbooks

▶ /orbitbooks

Join our mailing list to receive alerts on our latest releases and deals.

## orbitbooks.net

Enter our monthly giveaway for the chance to win some epic prizes.

## orbitloot.com